George R. Parkin

Edward Thring, Headmaster of Uppingham School

Life, Diary and Letters. Vol. II

George R. Parkin

Edward Thring, Headmaster of Uppingham School
Life, Diary and Letters. Vol. II

ISBN/EAN: 9783337017101

Printed in Europe, USA, Canada, Australia, Japan

Cover: Foto ©Raphael Reischuk / pixelio.de

More available books at **www.hansebooks.com**

EDWARD THRING

HEADMASTER OF UPPINGHAM SCHOOL

LIFE

DIARY AND LETTERS

BY

GEORGE R. PARKIN, C.M.G.

M.A. HON. LL.D. UNIVERSITY OF NEW BRUNSWICK
PRINCIPAL OF UPPER CANADA COLLEGE

London

MACMILLAN AND CO., Limited

NEW YORK: THE MACMILLAN COMPANY

1898

CONTENTS

CHAPTER I

THE VALLEY OF THE SHADOW OF DEATH

1875

WE have now seen how, through more than twenty years of patient, unflinching endeavour, Edward Thring had striven to realise in actual outward fact the conception of what a great public school ought to be as he had outlined it in the days of his earlier teaching enthusiasm. During these years the equipment of boarding-houses, chapel, schoolroom, hospital, and workshops ; of gardens, cricket fields, fives courts, and gymnasium, with many other minor appliances, had grown up around him, and into these the school fitted somewhat as the living organism fits into the curves and convolutions of a delicately complicated shell— the one so adapted to the other that the outer structure seems essential to the inner life.

With the limits of numbers which he had fixed long since reached and easily maintained, Uppingham seemed to have gained a secure place in public regard. Passages in his diary at this time show that even his exacting judgment was beginning to be satisfied ; that in structure and working power the school seemed to him something near what he had so long toiled for, and about which he had dreamed. But from any pleasing feeling of content or security there was to be a rough awakening. The structure had been planned with the object of nourishing strong and true life ; now the strength and truth of the life developed was to be tested by rude separation from the structure. He had held that the " Almighty wall " was everything in moulding the moral and intellectual life of a school. He was now to prove that important as structure was it was nothing to the inhabiting spirit ; that it is not walls which make or secure a city, but the men who dwell within them ; that though machinery has to be relied on to give efficiency to the ordinary routine of work, there may come extraordinary moments when life asserts its power to perform all the functions of the highest existence and exertion without the aid, or even in defiance, of machinery. Thring used to say that to train a man to the highest capacity for teaching, and then put him into an unequipped and unfurnished schoolroom, was like preparing a person to be the captain of a great ocean steamship, and expect him, with a canal boat or lighter, to bring his goods and passengers with speed and safety to the other side of the Atlantic. As an ordinary working rule this view is true, and cannot be too strictly insisted upon, yet we know that the genius and courage of the old navigators enabled them to accomplish very great things with very poor ships, and Thring was to prove that he at least could violate his own theory with splendid results. He was to become known as the " mobilising Head Master."

Until 1875 Uppingham had been fairly fortunate in escaping what must always be the schoolmaster's most serious risk in grouping numbers of boys together —infectious or epidemic illness.

An elevated situation gave the place a naturally bracing and healthy atmosphere; what were apparently sufficient precautions had been taken in house-building to secure sanitation; a hospital had been built at large expense to provide for the isolation of infectious cases; and for twenty-two years the arrangements had proved sufficient, with vigilant care, to ward off serious danger.   But the school had been built up in a remote and unprogressive country town, whose tax-payers dreaded the heavy expenses of the sanitary engineer. The system of town drainage was very imperfect; the water-supply inadequate; in many cases when building schoolhouses cesspools had to supply the place of sewers; later it was found that connection with the town system of drainage was the most dangerous of all, since the sewers were unflushed.   Long immunity had begotten carelessness among the townspeople, and even among the masters themselves, and the place was ripe for a disaster—a disaster which from the circumstances of the case could not but fall with crushing weight upon the school.

In earlier years slight outbreaks of scarlet or typhoid fever had occurred in the town at intervals, sufficient to make the masters anxious, and leading them to bring what pressure they could upon those responsible for the sanitary condition of the town.   During the early part of 1875 there are several suggestive entries in the diary.

February 5th.—Much illness in the town—scarlet fever. This is anxious work.   I fear we shall not escape.   Most certainly in former days this perpetual fear of epidemics was not on schools as it now is. . . .

February 7th.—There is much scarlet fever in the town. This does not lighten matters. . . .

February 8th.—We have sent in a memorial to the Guardians requesting them to have the water analysed with a view to getting a proper supply for the town.

February 9th.—I saw the sanitary inspector this morning, and hope to get a step forward. The masters all signed the memorial to the Guardians on the subject.

February 13th.—Scarlet fever very bad in the town, which makes it anxious work. We can scarcely hope to escape, but yet I will hope. God can keep us free. In spite of this and all the scheme worry, etc., I feel so full of life and spirits that I hardly know myself. God has given me back some of the old elastic work power. I can do ten times as much as I have been able to do for years, and I feel cheery in proportion. . . .

February 28th.—Received an anonymous letter yesterday denouncing the filthy state of the town, and in a half-sneering, half-real way telling me to look to it, as no one else would. But I don't see how it can be done. The law helps us very little, and like most weak laws is a better instrument of oppression than of help. The Rector is more jealous of power, though unwilling to do anything, than any one I ever met, and . . . the other local authority is equally jealous of power, and represents the cheap business view. I fear nothing can be done, busy too as we are, and not united, and not rich. Altogether it is a bad job.

The Guardians seem to have taken no action on the memorial of the masters, and, lulled by the freedom of the school from illness during the winter and spring terms, the masters themselves did not realise the imminence of the danger. Not till the school was again at work after the summer holiday did the blow fall. On what Thring afterwards speaks of as "that fatal fourth of October," he makes this note in his diary :—

Two or three cases of low fever in the school. This begins to make me anxious.

The anxiety soon deepens.

October 6th.—A complete change of weather, which I hope may sweep away the strange wave of low fever that has swept over us.   It is cold and fine and bracing now.

October 7th.—Much care.   Two of the boys at Woodfield very ill, one dangerously so; little Nash.   Then we have two mothers and a father down here; very natural, but at the same time not likely to mend matters, as the sick boys are not kept so quiet as they should be.   Then David's baby is very ill and will scarcely recover.   All this presses heavily and makes one nervous about one's own children too, for that is one of the penalties of being a schoolmaster, that one's own family is so much more exposed to any epidemic than under ordinary circumstances.   However, this will pass as other things have passed, and God is God.

October 8th.—The cloud still heavy, though there is now some hope, but little David, Mullins, and Nash are all in a very critical state, and Hastings at the Lower School. . . . Altogether it is very trying.   The bell tolled this morning, and I was in great fear, but a man had died in the Union.   I very much fear we shall not quite escape death, but no new cases have fallen.

October 10th (Sunday).—A trying day, though the rest from work and the chapel is always a blessing.   Little Mullins only just kept alive to-day, though all hope is not gone.   The other is better, but poor Mullins has had three fresh cases since yesterday morning, and the pressure is very heavy.   I had a very nice talk with Mr. and Mrs. Nash to-day; they were both kind and sensible.   I trust their boy will live. This is a heavy time.   How soon the sky can be overclouded. "Thou didst turn Thy face from me and I was troubled."   It is hard to prosper and not be a fool; harder still perhaps to *feel* that trouble works blessing, however much one may know it is so.   I do know it, but I am like a naughty child some-times in feeling.   Just as if other people were not tried, or any good could come without training, or I myself had not been blessed again and again by these merciful lessons.

Panic had now begun among a section of the parents; some were telegraphing that their children should be sent home ; others advising that the school should be broken up ; while the majority awaited with apparently complete trust the judgment of the masters upon the situation. How to deal with the natural fears of the more timid parents, how to act justly by the fearless, how to prevent the panic from extending to the boys, were, as they always will be in such cases, anxious questions. At first Thring's feelings were all for presenting a firm front to the danger. To many parents, he reasoned, the return of their children was a grave inconvenience and expense ; the appliances for combating disease had proved sufficient in the past, and would probably prove so now ; to break up the school involved the risk of spreading infection far and wide through the country ; it was poor training in manliness to permit boys to run away at the first hint of peril. He spoke vigorously to the boys about what he called "this cowardly panic," pointing out that the greater safety lay in courage. The report was that he described as "deserters" those who asked their parents to remove them. The statement is probably true, and is certainly characteristic. Its wisdom will be judged differently by minds of differing temper. Thring had the soldier spirit himself, and would fain give it to his boys. Meanwhile, he and his colleagues were beginning to realise that they were dealing with something more than an ordinary or temporary outbreak.

October 11*th.*—Mullins, before I went into school, suggested having Dr. Haviland over to inspect, and I sanctioned it. After dinner a telegram from Mr. Jacob saying that six Liverpool parents had just been closeted with him, and would not be satisfied unless a sanitary authority was called in. Sent answer to say we had already decided on it. . . . Wrote to get Dr. Haviland to come and inspect. . . .

In this letter to Dr. Haviland, Thring says :—

It is very important to us to correct any evil if it exists, and to be above suspicion if it does not.   I should be greatly obliged if you could come over without delay, and test and examine the drain system of all these houses and their water-supply, as well as the schoolhouses generally, and anything likely to be of use in putting things on the best footing.   If you cannot come yourself, perhaps you would kindly telegraph to me, as it is no use to us to have the inspection of any man whose name will not carry respect and conviction, not only in this immediate neighbourhood, but also in other parts of England amongst the parents of the boys, in the great towns especially. . . .

October 12*th.*—At my lowest point to-day.   I trust now refreshed.   This morning a long letter from Dr. Grimsdale at Liverpool, speaking in the name of many parents in a kind spirit, but also in an imperious one.   Then I had scarcely finished breakfast when two mothers came in to get an arrangement made at Woodfield (the hospital); then the masters' meeting; then in school an interview with Bell about Woodfield arrangements.   To Fairfield, saw Cobb, saw Mrs. Grigg, met Christian coming back, who said Nash was supposed to be dying.   Mullins had already told me there was no hope of his little boy; wrote part of another letter, went to dinner, lay down, but was sent for by poor Mullins.   I found him quite perplexed about his house, overdone both in body and mind, expecting his little boy to die every minute. I did what I could, decided his questions for him, and had a little sympathetic talk.   Then I came away and went out with Gracie for an hour.   On my return I knelt down and prayed more thoroughly—more from the bottom of my heart than perhaps I ever remember.   I felt moved to pray for little Mullins and the school, and I got up from my knees with a perfect feeling of answered prayer, and of my prayer being granted.   I believe the little boy will be spared us and this plague cease, but I know that God is working and has made Himself felt in my heart, and is with us, and that all will be well.   So I feel since then another man. . . . Yet I have such a feeling of God being near that the whole of this great trial is for the present changed, and I pray to be kept strong in spirit through what is yet to come.   Amen.

9.50.—My class gone.   A message is in that little David is much better, little Cecil Mullins a decided improvement, and Nash not hopeless.   God has heard me and comforted me exceedingly.   But indeed, alive or dead, I had in my soul that feeling of being able to pray straight up to God, and of being answered that nothing could shake.   I feel that God heard and granted my prayer.

October 13*th.*—A weary day of telegrams, letters, parents, and masters.   Little Nash very ill still.   Heard of the Sanitary Board here, and that they have telegraphed for Dr. Haviland to come and make a thorough inspection.   Saw poor Hodgkinson, who is driven out of his wits by the calamity and fuss ; I fear very much that he will not stand it. . . . At four saw our sanitary inspector.   Was not a little amused to hear from him that he had known nothing of any fever in the town till to-day at the Board.   So I may be excused for having known nothing. . . .

I am most thankful, too, that as yet none have died, and I trust God has given me their lives.   But as for me, I am getting quite indignant at the way we are badgered, and the reckless, not to say insolent, manner in which the people set on us.   If schools are to be treated in this kind of way it is a bad look-out for the parents.   They will make the schools something they little expect or desire.   I am equally weary and indignant.   It reminds me of old days.   I am tied to a post, and must abide the onset.

October 14*th.*—A very wet day, and a very weary one. Numbers of letters this morning, not bad though.   An excellent one from Mr. Jacob, which made me think more of him than ever.   Before ten Earle came in with a most astounding lie coming through Dr. Grimsdale, which at present is quite inexplicable, viz. that Dr. Cayser had told him he had heard from Mr. Bell that there had been thirty-nine cases in the school.   Bell denies ever having written to Cayser, ever having given any estimate to any one, and, moreover, stated that, reckoning doubtful cases, fourteen was the utmost number in the ,Upper School from first to last. . . .

This led me to make a short statement to the masters on my

principles in these matters. That under no conceivable circumstances should I break up the school; that it was a great injustice and wrong to many forcing them to have their boys home; that, in the first instance, when a house was at all got hold of by illness, I should have parents written to to be told the fact, but strongly dissuade the removal of the boys; then if it spread I should make the removal optional, and if it got very bad should throw the responsibility of keeping them here on the parents. That we should always stay so long as there were any boys here to teach and keep them. I said we were not in a big barrack with one common establishment, but each with his own house and separate arrangements, which renders it quite unnecessary to break up the school. I also told them I should not permit the school to be overhauled by any but a competent and true authority. Had another telegram from Liverpool as to whether Haviland was here. When will it end? I really fear it will send poor Hodgkinson into his grave, just recovering as he is from such an illness. I myself am very tired and done up. It is as bad as old days, although I am not so thin-skinned. Still, what with one's human feelings about the invalids, and one's human feelings about possible misfortune, which makes one dread every knock at the door, and one's human strength which this great strain tries sorely, it goes hard with one. I mourn over the state and prospects of schools, my experience in these years is so disastrous. All one's feelings of joy in doing one's best, and the happy sense of unselfish working and pouring out of liberal free life on one's work is so utterly destroyed and nothing left behind but a sense of bitterness at being kicked by fools always, and the deep low down feeling that God will judge, not man, and that one is a fool to care about man. But it is not a right condition of things, this weakness of schools which makes even a strong school a prey to an apothecary and his following, and I don't see much hope of things bettering, indeed the contrary. I am thankful to say that this weary day, though it has not brought much cheer in the matter of our invalids, has yet passed without worse. O God! protect and keep us. " Give me not over for a prey unto their teeth." And spare my boys, O Lord! Spare them, for Jesus Christ's sake. Amen.

October 15*th.*—God has taken little Cecil Mullins. I misinterpreted somewhat His will, but not the gracious answer to my prayer in the spirit He gave me. And the revival even for a time shows me God's will more clearly, and was a great boon both to me and, I think, his father, who was worn out and overwrought. . . . A kind letter from Mrs. Spence this morning, wishing to help me in allaying the panic at Liverpool. I took occasion to tell her I could not give way to it, and had rather lose Liverpool to the school altogether than be exposed to such mistrust. . . . Haviland is here, and there was a sanitary meeting, and Barnard Smith has given instructions that the very fullest investigation is to take place into the town and school-houses' drainage, water, etc. That is good. . . . Eighty telegrams came in and out yesterday, and as many to-day.

October 16*th.*—Saw Mr. P., who was very nice, and put me up to an improvement about the hospital cooking, and also brought under my notice the wine. I have accordingly sent up some of my own. Then I came home and walked in the garden, as I did not feel very well. I had already written some letters. After dinner at 3 P.M. I attended little Cecil's funeral. At 4 P.M. went to hear Haviland's private report to us. He had not much to say, but he pronounced that "it was quite safe for the school to go on." . . .

I confess that my blood rather boiled when I heard this man deliver an *ex cathedra* judgment, as if all he had said was gospel on a question where there was so much to be considered. But such is English ignorance. It was very nearly gospel to us, and had he decided otherwise, I don't know what I could have done. It was strange, too, to hear . . . fussing about the lies that had been told and following them up. I have learnt to think that about the surest test whether a fellow past thirty is a fool or not is whether he vapours about truth, and expects always that a case must be cleared by jaw, and wants to clear lies, and cannot sit quiet under a little painting, but talks big of justice and of following up the impalpable.

October 17*th.*—Little Richardson at Hodgkinson's died to-day. A heavy blow, poor Hodgkinson is quite beside himself through sorrow, anxiety, illness, and work. I trust he may not himself be killed. The other patient is going on fairly well.

But I need scarcely say my heart is heavy enough still, though less so than it was. I feel more faithful. . . . I walked out with Skrine after chapel, and on the Stockerton Road, when we were about a mile out, heard the bell toll. How it did go to one's heart, but it was for an old woman in the town. . . . I hope we have seen the worst. But I will try not to faint and be faithless. Good will come as it always has done. Good must come when all we long for is good, since " All things work together for good to them who love God."

October 18*th*.—Hodgkinson came in to me. He, poor fellow, bears up wonderfully. He told me there was on Saturday a sort of small indignation meeting of parents at the "Falcon." On a friendly parent of one of the boys going into the room, he was saluted with the question, "Whether he was come to take his boy out of the hands of these murderers?" Nice for poor old Hodgkinson, whose whole life has been bound up in the house and boys; nice for me too, for I am murderer No. 1. Encouraging, but let that pass.

I have sent up two stone jars of water to be analysed by Savory and Moore on my private account—one from Fairfield, one from our well here, and shall probably send another sample to-morrow.

October 21*st*.—I went out of second school early because Haviland was here, and have inspected the whole house and drains with him, and am now master of it. I am glad to say there is little to be altered, and that not of much consequence. He also passed both my wells officially as perfectly pure. That is very good; we shall see what Savory and Moore say. . . .

October 22*nd*.—A cool telegram from Haviland curtly saying "that all boys in infected houses must go home." . . . I sent it to Mullins and Hodgkinson, but have declined to act about Campbell, till I know what is meant by infected houses, and what authority there is for such an order. But this is pretty fair for a country official to our sanitary officer, who very properly brought it to me. . . .

October 23*rd*.—I can hardly help laughing, harassed as I am, when I think what a downfall my china jar of vanity has had these last three weeks. I thought I had done something,

and that Liverpool thought so too, and lo! Liverpool and no
small portion of my world have set upon me this last three
weeks, as if I had brought their children into danger by my
proceedings and possessed neither sense nor honesty.   It is a
comical upset.   Alas! there is little laughing here. . . . Got
a letter from Mr. Birley to-day.   He and Mr. Jacob think my
statement too dictatorial.   They, however, imagined it was
meant as a circular.   I have written to Mr. Birley to say that,
as a private document, I do not feel inclined to abate its tone
of authority, as recent legislation, while it has strengthened
the headmaster within the school, has broken down the school
authority outside, and I do not mean to play the part of servant to the public and bow to the *Times*.   I was able to send
Mr. Birley a letter from a man of business in Liverpool who
said he thought it admirable. . . .

How utterly I feel the baseless character of my old dreams
that true work would live here because the foundation was
true.   I now see it was only a worshipping of nets in a subtle
form.   Nothing will live unless the presence of God makes it.
Even now I see how full of weakness and corruption and
death the place is; how a breath would upset the life in the
place; how easily in a year or two these walls might be turned
into something—Oh! how different from what I meant them;
how utterly the outer world takes the mean trade view of them;
how greatly the inner world does too.

A statement to parents of the principles by which
he would be guided in dealing with the outbreak now
became necessary, and it is worth giving in full.

The question has been raised as to what ought to be done
when illness breaks out in the school.

The answer in our case is simple.

The school consists of eleven different boarding-houses;
each complete in itself, and in the majority of cases standing
by itself.

The school is not a barrack, in which all live together
under the same conditions, using the same diet, and inter-
mingled always.

Therefore, it is not my intention under any conceivable circumstances of illness to break up the school by a public act.

It is a great injustice and wrong to many parents to send their boys home with the possibility of introducing illness into the family.

If the disorder is infectious, it is not right to scatter possible bearers of infection all over the kingdom.

It is not right to put parents to the inconvenience of their children being sent home when they ought to be at school, or to saddle them with this additional expense.

It is not good to teach the young to run away from illness. It is likely to make them far more susceptible to infection, and liable to catch disease in after-life, as fear is no slight cause of ill-health.

On the other hand, due account must be taken of the parents' views with regard to their children.

These considerations lead directly to the following conclusions :—

First, When illness makes its appearance in only one or two cases, and is not spreading, the discipline and good of the school require that no boy should be allowed to leave the school.

Second, If the illness threatens to be somewhat more troublesome, and does not remain stationary, then parents should be dissuaded from removing their boys, unless in special instances, but be allowed to do so.

Third, If the illness seems to have fastened on a particular house, the parents of all boys in that house must be written to, and the option given them of taking their sons home.

Fourth, If the illness is really serious in any house, the parents leaving their boys in that house must do it on their own responsibility, though we shall always be ready to keep them.

These four gradations mark the course of treatment that will be pursued in this school. We shall not in any instance leave our posts. As long as any boys remain to be taught, we shall remain to take care of them.

But, indeed, scattered as we are in so many different houses, each a centre in itself, nothing is likely to occur to overthrow the experience I have now had in the worst years of epidemics.

It is, however, true that a large school is exceptionally liable to infection, from the fact that upwards of 300 boys come into it from all parts of the world, and often from unhealthy districts. But this is our misfortune. The healthy discipline and conditions of a good school are very favourable to general health.

As a point of school order, I would mention that no boy will be permitted to go home, unless the case is very special, on the bare receipt of a telegram by us. We must first be sure on what grounds the telegram is sent, and I shall not give permission unless satisfied on this point.

These general principles, and the rules arising from them, which I have stated, will, I hope, be sufficient for all ordinary cases.

Sunday, 24th.—I feel myself again to-night for the first time. I preached a sermon on gospel character this afternoon, which has done me great good, if it has done no one else. God put a new spirit into my heart, and the baseness of all this panic and turmoil and implied views of sickness and death has come into me, as if scales had fallen from my eyes. I pray God my heart may keep strong. "Let not your heart be troubled, neither let it be afraid." Amen.

October 27th.—A letter from Childs this morning proposing to come as sanitary officer to the school. I hope we may manage it. I have been much struck by our helplessness before these Jacks-in-office during this row. . . .

October 28th.—This morning brought the analysis of water from London, flatly condemnatory of the well pronounced by the sanitary authority perfectly pure. This, together with the refusal to give any information about what ought to be done, convinced me that these proceedings are useless to us and noxious, and that London authorities must be called in ; so, after all, as so many boys are gone, and all nearly will go under these circumstances, I shall be obliged to break up the school. I have conferred with Mr. Birley and Jacob and they agree. So to-morrow after the meeting I shall have the notice printed. Alas !

October 29th.—A most bitter disappointment. The trustees, with all this great school handed over to them, have simply refused to get a sanitary engineer down to set the school right, and have appointed a sub-committee to urge the sanitary authorities here (whom we mistrust and despise), and to see about appointing the day of reopening the school. In other words, they have grasped at all meddling power and officious grinding us down, and shirked doing anything whatever. . . . It is the old thing over again, alas! I do feel most down-hearted about it. We break up on Tuesday till Christmas, at all events. So far, I believe, it will save me an illness. That is something. But it is hard, very hard, to keep down the bitter, sour feeling which this day has once again curdled within one. God help us, and bring good out of it. . . .

November 1st.—The last evening, alas! of our maimed school-time. It is strange, though, the childish relief I feel at not having to get up for school to-morrow. A true and real relief, however, is the lifting off that fearful weight of the possibility of fresh fever. For the first time for many days I have drawn something like free breath. Mr. Jacob and Birley left this morning. They have been invaluable ; a great strength and comfort. . . . We hope to get Dr. Ogle down to inspect our houses carefully, and the working Liverpool man to set us to rights. . . .

November 2nd.—At 9.45 a full masters' meeting. Two important things which are noteworthy were brought out strongly. In answer to a question from Rowe I was enabled to declare emphatically before every master and with no dissentient voice raised, "That no master in a society like ours was an individual ; that however attacked as a master he had no right to send any letter or document to the newspapers without consulting me ; that it was positively illegal to do so, and not to be permitted for a moment." The second was that I was able once more before all of them, Hodgkinson included, to state decisively that whilst there was liberty of judgment so long as Bell did not pronounce on an illness, which might either be dealt with by the individual master, or he might come to me ; that there was no liberty of judgment the moment the doctor had decided a boy to be really ill, but that it was law admitting of no choice that the parent must be told at once. . . .

November 3rd.—Wrote to Jacob and Birley, but could give them no information excepting that we were going to be condemned by the Sanitary Committee and made a scapegoat of. And sure enough they have been and done it. I got to-night such a document, the most wonderful bit of Jack-in-officism I ever knew. Considering the Sanitary Board and town generally have steadily resisted all improvement as far as possible these twenty years, and jobbed everything they were obliged to do, and in this very instance have ignored fever in the town for the last six months, they have had the audacity to attach serious blame to our houses for having had fever; no reasons given, no hearing of the case. It is astonishing. Altogether it is the most insulting thing I ever knew. It is truly laughable, but it is noxious too, as they mean to send it to every parent whose boy has been ill. . . . They think nothing can touch them. The inspector calmly told Guy that if we applied to the London Board they would only send down the complaint to him, and he had better save himself the trouble. I shall have some difficulty in keeping the masters reasonably quiet under the insult. But the worst is, Childs cannot get us masters any help from the London Board for ourselves, and we are quite at sea. Altogether this is a time of humiliation and sackcloth.

November 4th.—It is a curious turn of the wheel which has made the criminals judges, and set the men who have systematically opposed improvement, and in this very instance fatally neglected their duty about the fever, to pass sentence on us. It is noteworthy in these enlightened days. . . .

November 5th.—A remarkable day, and my courage has quite risen, and I feel cheery once more. This morning brought me the petition to the Central Board of Health from Mr. Jacob, and I convened a meeting of masters at twelve, and proceeded to write it out. Skrine helped me. When the *Times* came in we found a most venomous notice of Uppingham in the paper, evidently from headquarters here. . . .

Meeting of masters at twelve. . . . I had the *Times'* notice read, and observed it was just as well to face the facts at once. We must either have an inquiry and be absolved by the

central authority, or we might go.   Ruin or not was the simple question before us, and I for one meant to try and win.
. . . So we have on this day at the same moment received the greatest proof of the venomous feeling in some quarters against us, and been able to throw the die boldly for victory. . . .

I said I had made up my mind that I never would appeal to the newspapers or acknowledge them as a tribunal ; that I was the servant of the public, but held óffice where God had placed me, and should not render account to the news-papers. . . .

I wrote to Henry to put in a word for me if possible.   At all events we have now done our best, and are fairly pitted against these tyrants and their falsehoods.   This cheers me. The attack in the *Times*, too, rouses one.   It is far easier than the moving about, as it were, in prisoned air, powerless to resist and unable even to see one's enemy.   This is better far.

The following is the petition in which Thring and his masters challenged the closest inquiry on the part of the central authority in London into the condition of school and town :—

To the Right Honourable G. Sclater Booth,

President to the Local Government Board.

November 5th, 1875.

Sir—Owing to an outbreak of enteric fever in some of the schoolhouses and in the town, and also in consideration of the unsatisfactory state of the water-supplies, the trustees of the school determined at the last meeting to break it up—and the boys have all been sent home.

We are large ratepayers and responsible for the health of upwards of 600 persons, and we approve this action, although it is to us in a pecuniary point of view of most serious import. We are prepared to do everything required of us to contribute to sanitary improvement, but we should like to feel assured that our outlay will not be valueless—that the main sewer of the town was large enough and deep enough, and that it was not necessary, as discovered by the Local Board in July last, to close a further number of wells.

The trustees of the school have invoked the assistance of the local sanitary authorities; looking, however, to the excitement caused amongst the parents of boys, it has been intimated to us very decidedly that confidence can only be restored by the central authorities ordering a strict and searching inquiry into the causes which have led to this outbreak, and by their applying a remedy.

We would therefore pray you to send down two of the most experienced medical and engineering inspectors of the Board to make a searching inquiry, and at the same time to give directions as to what they consider necessary to be done to our schoolhouses, as well as, by the Local Board of the district, to the town. We enclose a communication made to us by the trustees we elected to represent us on the Trust, and we have the honour to subscribe ourselves, etc.

To Sir Henry Thring.

November 5th, 1875.

If you can get to Sclater Booth and the Central Board, it is simply *all in all to me.*

My case lies in a nutshell. You know well I have given everything to trying to make schools better and improve boy life. Most of our arrangements here are very good, and if it rested with us the few things wanting could be set in order without difficulty. But it does not rest with us. *The town is in fault.*

During all these years at intervals we have been trying to get improvements set on foot, and these efforts have been resisted and resented bitterly by those who are now supreme authorities over us. Unless we can get the central authority turned on, it is pretty well ruin for a time, for my time, that is, to the school. The Local Board from its former tactics *cannot* act with vigour enough, and if it could do so, the row and panic amongst our parents is so great, that it would not help us much after the lies and exaggerations that have been set going, unless we are able to state that the highest authority has overhauled and settled everything. I enclose a copy of our petition signed by every master present, and sent up in pursuance of the directions given us by our two trustees.

The town is trying to make the school its scapegoat, for the double purpose of hiding past mismanagement and preventing present outlay and exposure. This is the whole matter. It would not signify to me at all that they were hostile if they acted. They might fill the newspapers with fictions if they drained the town properly. But their present show of movement cannot be trusted; all we are sure of is that we shall get the worst they can give us. We are having water-works set on foot at last—that is, one of my own (old) boys is starting a company, not the town. We have friends in the town, but at present they are squashed; as Lord A. Churchill said of Oxford, "Uppingham may forget but cannot forgive," that it exists mainly by the school. All we want is a thorough overhauling and impartial justice. They may abuse and lie as much as they like, or condemn us justly, in their opinion, only don't let us be sacrificed through the shortcomings of our local Dogberries. You government men have no conception of local tyranny.

To Dr. Jex Blake.

November 6th, 1875.—I prize your telegram and letter exceedingly. It is very cheering and pleasant to me in these heavy days to have a little sunlight let in. . . . We are trying tooth and nail to get out of the local sanitary clutches and call in the Central Board. It is a strange turn of the wheel that has made the judges criminals, for that is the real state of the case here. I have been striving for years to get improvements set going, and now have fallen into the hands of the men who resisted them, and a jolly time at this moment they have of it. However, we shall see. I assure you, your kindness cheers me more than my words can express.

To Sir Henry Thring.

November 8th, 1875.

I am much cheered by your letter. It has been a hard time. You fellows don't know what it is to be the prey of local tyranny. We want two things. *Power* to do the right thing, which *can only* come from the Central Board. And the authority which can declare that we have done the right thing, which can only come from the Central Board.

I don't care who criticises, or how they sift my government and actions here, provided the man is competent.

I want nothing but fair play and no favour. Nor do my masters; they are honest, and hard-working, and ready to do anything that is judged right.

To Rev. Godfrey Thring.

November 8th, 1875.—I appealed to the sanitary authority within a week of the first case reported to me in the upper school. The lower school is not under me in the same way as the upper. Don't believe the papers; they are full of lies and misrepresentations. The local authorities are very interested in throwing the blame on the school. I have no time to explain.

Thanks for your offer of room. I hope to be down south before Christmas, but we have made arrangements for the rest of the family.

If I can get the Central Board to take the matter up, all will be right. But don't either believe or mind the papers,— practice makes perfect; the Jackson row years ago has made me quite indifferent to newspaper abuse. As to the work here, that is in God's hands. The life of it will live, if not here, elsewhere. And as to myself, I shall not flinch, nor will my belongings. I had sooner, as far as my private feelings go, be kicked out of here to-morrow and begin life again than remain headmaster. But that is not the question. I only mention this to let you know that I am neither in a funk, nor cast down. I shall stand by my guns, and if knocked over, will begin again.

I don't mean by begin again, try headmastership. The workhouse is open before that.

November 9th.—I had a letter from Henry this morning telling me he had called at once at the Central Board, and that Government would do everything it could. I was able to read this to the masters, and to tell them that young Adderley was very friendly and had borne strong evidence against the sanitary authorities here. I telegraphed to Manchester and Liverpool, and later in the day heard from Liverpool that they had received notice from headquarters to the same effect. This is cheering.

November 11*th.*—The plot thickens. No official notice, however, of our appeal as yet. . . . All the papers and notices for the water-works in order. Gave the order for boring to-day at a cost not to exceed £100. Engaged Mr. . Tarbotton, a Nottingham engineer, at Mr. Jacob's request, to conduct our business. The papers still full of me. I marvel how little I care for it. But I hope the worst is past. If the answer to the appeal comes to-morrow it will put a stop to all this. . . .

November 16*th.*—How much is past since I last wrote. On Friday I got positive news of the appeal coming off. . . . Then I got a circular printed about the coming inquiry. Next morning I got the official answer, and a letter from Rawlinson, the engineer who was to come. The telegrams crossed and re-crossed about it, and as to whether I should go to town or not. At last I determined to go. . . . I found my people all right, and saw Henry next day. He gave me some good instructions for my guidance with Rawlinson, and what was more comforting still, the most absolute assurance that whatever Government could do would be done for us in this matter. On Monday I came back, having been put in another world by this day's absence—lifted clear out of the old rut, and set with a stronger, clearer faith, on higher ground.

During the next few days the Government engineer visited the town, inspected it in company with the engineers appointed by the school and by the local Sanitary Board, and expressed the most decided opinion that the town authorities should deal with the work at once. "If the work was not done, and done quickly," he said, "they would send down their own engineers and men, and charge it to the parish. There is this whip to resort to, though we should be very unwilling to use it."

This decisive interference of Government brightened up the gloomy outlook.

"Thus ended," the diary goes on to say, "a great day for me. The local tyranny is shut up now for a time, and in a great degree for ever. They never again will dare to indulge in dreams of complete security. . . . Altogether I feel a great cloud rolled away and rolling away, and begin to see light and breathe freely. How wonderful it is how God has sent me the right men at the right time to deliver me. I am filled with astonishment and thankfulness. It is very wonderful."

November 26th.—The late trouble already seems more like a nightmare than a reality; at least the reality of it now seems so small beside the greater reality that one has "lifted up one's eyes" and seen that it becomes by comparison unreal. I thank God for my life and work. . . . I could not help being really amused at a leading article in a daily paper which I found awaiting me on my return, in which I am described as a "bigoted, old-fashioned hater of pure air and water." So much for the public and their way of going on.

November 27th.—What a life this is—this perpetual warfare and danger on every side! It seems strange, in the midst of our boasted nineteenth century, that such tyranny should go on and no remedy exist but calling in the supreme power. What a satire on our Government and its imperfections.

The dangers of the outbreak were infinitely increased by the conflict which henceforth went on between the school and the local sanitary authorities. The latter were exceedingly irritated by the appeal which Thring, in justifiable distrust of them, had made to the Central Board in London, and no effort was spared to throw the whole blame for neglect in the past upon the school alone.

During the month of December, under the direction of Government and other engineers, all the school buildings were thoroughly dealt with, and were certified by the highest authority to be in perfect sanitary condition. Having thus done their best, without regard to expense, Thring and his masters were naturally anxious to reopen school.

Having no reserve of foundation or other public funds to fall back upon, the long discontinuance of work placed the severest strain upon their private resources, and hence upon the very life of the school.. But the influence of the Sanitary Board made itself felt in the governing body, and permission to reopen was with difficulty obtained. The story proceeds in the diary :—

January 18th, 1876.—Trustees' meeting. What a curious chapter, if I had time to write it, the events of the last two months would be, with all the danger, all the meanness, all the moving to and fro, the hanging about Government offices, the reports from Uppingham of more evil and more lies, the delay that was ruin, the dead weight of tyranny that under the guise of law was destruction, the activity of Mr. Birley and Jacob, the kindness and help of the Government, the sulkiness and resistance of the locals,—all make a jumble of work and trial most strange and dreamlike. To-day, in spite of my bringing down on Saturday not only Rawlinson's report but a Government authorisation based on it for calling together the school, Mr. Jacob and Birley had great difficulty in getting it done. And they sat playing with men's lives— talking blandly of waiting for Haviland's and Field's report. Had they done so, I should have sent in my resignation this very day. For carrying on the school under the local authorities would have been impossible. As it is, to-day marks an epoch. The first great campaign in this war marks a victory, though what will yet be the end God knows, for much is yet to come. Rawlinson's report is all we can wish, so is Tarbotton's. The first has gone to every parent ; the second is going. The water-works on the hill are going on well ; the new well in Fairfield is getting forward. All has been done by us that mortal man can do, but to this hour nothing has been done by the town, not even the ventilation of the sewer ordered by Rawlinson. It is a strange outburst of evil. I did not think till to-day that the phalanx was so strong, but it appears that great sulkiness prevails in the county at the local authority being overridden. And I feel that this place is not going to be more wise or more kind than heretofore. I do cry to God to judge my cause against these evil men with their smooth words, and their pretences of doing right, and the law which they abuse. We did not succeed in getting the Trustees to fix earlier than the 28th, but we did succeed in forcing them not to wait for the report. . . . To think, too, of the weeks of care and work necessary to get even thus far. But God has made it. He has willed to humble us and crush us and bring us low, and blessed be His will. For I feel infinitely freer, less selfish, more manly, for this great shaking, and though the anxiety and risk of next term must be very great . . . and we hardly know what is coming, and all is distorted like a nightmare, nevertheless, I have never felt at the beginning of the half-year less a coward than now, or so little moved by the petty vexations and thorns. The Government were wonderfully good to me.

The hostility of the local authorities culminated in a report of the medical officer of health for the district to his Board. This document was an arraignment not only of the sanitary condition of the schoolhouses, but of the structure and management of the school, and even of the motives by which the masters were actuated in dealing with the outbreak of fever. Had this report been generally accepted as an accurate and unbiassed statement of the facts, Uppingham must have been ruined. The best answer to it lay in the unshaken confidence of parents in the management of the school. Within ten days after this extremely hostile report had been issued under the sanction of the Sanitary Board the whole school, with the exception of about a dozen boys, had returned, while the number of new entries was nearly as large as usual. Meanwhile, the local authorities, vigorous in denouncing the defects of the schoolhouses, displayed an almost incredible apathy in dealing with the purification of the town. Their hostility and neglect were not to be finally overcome for many weary months, till several deaths from fever, including that of the chairman of the Sanitary Board itself, had disclosed the true nature of the situation, and till the school had been well-nigh wrecked by a new outbreak of fever.

To Sir Henry Thring.

January 19th, 1876.

I think you ought to know my views on school matters, and in a quiet way understand the probabilities, and the kind of line I take.

Yes, we have had a squeak for it, a much greater squeak than you are aware of. Yesterday the Trustees met in solemn conclave as of old, and in spite of the Government warrant, in spite of all the expense we have been at, in spite of delay in any case being very like ruin, Mr. Birley and Jacob had great difficulty in carrying a resolution that the school should reassemble next week. Well, this means of course intense danger for the coming term. They meant to wait still for the report of Messrs. Haviland and Field; it will go in to Whitehall. So there is plenty of scope for danger ahead, the more so, as up to this hour the town has positively done nothing during these three months, nothing since five years ago the wells were condemned. They have neither flushed the sewers, disinfected them or the houses, provided water, or even yet ventilated the sewers, which Rawlinson expressly ordered, and they promised should be done. There is danger enough in the air, without doubt. You are quite right too about the sensitiveness of a school. When the school was weaker fifteen or sixteen years ago the least mismanagement in any house was followed at once by a falling off in entries.

This was often the first indication I had of a master's short-comings. So delicate a barometer is a school. The lies about the flogging case cost me at least a thousand pounds, and cost the school as much again. We heard of them for many years. This affair will last my time as it is. If we have fever again, however slightly, it may crumple us up finally for this generation. And as the town does nothing, and will continue its policy of a masterly inactivity as long as it dares, I don't feel very confident on this head so far of the state of things. Now for my judgment. No vexation, pain, or humiliation that is merely personal will make me alter my work. But the moment anything is done that permanently lowers or affects the work of education prejudicially I go. Don't be afraid; I shan't come on the parish, neither do I mean to act in haste. This is the deliberate policy of a lifetime, held to during all these twenty-two years in which I have met with humiliation, hindrances, and kicks to a degree you have no idea of, and, I venture to say, have never dreamt of as possible. I bore it all, I can bear it again. But the Endowed Schools Bill, with its Trustees and popular meddling, is making school life in an honourable, frank, free way more and more impossible, and whenever, if it so happens, my work here as a leader in education is hindered seriously, I go. Yesterday, if the Trustees had put the school under the local people by waiting for their report, in spite of the Government action, I should have sent in my resignation immediately. I can assure you solemnly, I have given no cause of offence by word or deed to the local men. I have simply been silent and worked. The proof that I have not, is this, in spite of the deadly wrongs done me by the old governors, which for years involved possible ruin, I never quarrelled with them, and yesterday one of the most active on my side, next to Birley and Jacob, was one of the old governors who has been a governor the whole of my time, is a leader amongst them, and in earlier days always led against my views and work. . . .

The position I take up is simple. It is this.

For twenty-two years I have worked solely for the good of boys and true education. I might have made a fortune twice, and had much greater glory, but at the expense of true work, and I did not. I do not say this to boast, but to show calmly that I know what I am about, that I have counted the cost, and am not acting on impulse, or hastily, but on the settled deliberate convictions of a life. The work of schools is very complicated, anxious, and exacting, requiring knowledge, management, life-power to an unusual degree. It cannot be done if it is liable to have ignorant outsiders deciding on questions of life and death, and interfering constantly. I do not mean that men will not be found to undertake the work, but there will be a steady downward drag and lowering of the kind of work and the kind of men. There is a steady downward drag going on now. It would be ludicrous, if it was not so important, to see my Trustees, an exceptionally good set, sitting in solemn conclave playing with other men's lives. . . . Yet there they are totally ignorant of the business of school, also passing judgment on us and our work and our fortunes, and prescribing, as yesterday, business matter on which our all hinges. As far as this is only personally humiliating, as I said before, I have borne it and shall continue to bear it, but the moment the life of school work is in question, and anything is done here which really affects the broad interests of education in the country, I shall overthrow it, or resign. No power on earth shall compel me to stay in this place an hour beyond the time that the true work I have lived for continues to be true work. I do not think the contingency likely to arise, for, though a school is very sensitive, it is also very powerful; and though hundreds, perhaps thousands, will be cooled off from us by this affair, very many are roused in defence, and much sympathy and fellow-feeling for us exists. I hear plenty both of good and evil from the thousand sources of information which are always setting {into the schoolhouse as a centre. I hope you will not mistake anything I have said for momentary excitement or impulse; you are hearing the things which have been the backbone of my working life, the calm deliberate utterance of my soberest thoughts. As long as the life-power of the work goes on I go on. I feel really confident that we shall come through this and get out at the other side safe and sound, but I am not frightened at the chances even should they stump me up, and I am not going to act on hasty extempore *data*, but on long and well-digested views. I can assure you, I have given no cause of offence to the men who are acting against me by intemperate words or deeds. I feel no anger and would gladly act with them now, but nothing less than my slavery, I fear, will be oil to them. That cannot be.

Sunday, January 23rd.—What a great thing it is, our having got our reports out first. Whatever happens, I see God's hand most plainly in this permitted outburst of evil power. It is so utterly irrational that it is clear we are meant to be sifted and the sifting is meant. Many things also fit in and persuade me that God is guiding it all, so I am less troubled than I should be, though so much present cares, so much certain loss in my poverty-stricken finances, so much deadly danger for the coming term, and so much malice round about one, are all heavy and full of fear. Yet, I am sure it is God's work we are doing, sure that the end now or hereafter is to be good and blessed, sure that the present has very much of spiritual power and grace, making the cross endurable. "Though I am sometimes afraid, yet put I my trust in Him."

January 24th.—Private copies of the indictment of the school going about. The masters very troubled, and there is plenty of reason, for it is, I hear, as was to be expected, clever and scurrilous to the last degree. Certainly there is much darkness. But as we have often said in old days, "If this thing is of God, it will stand; if not, let it go." It is some years now since I felt any sense of possible ruin to the prosperity of the school. All the troubles have been the internal ones that threatened the inner life. This, however, aims at smashing up the outer fabric and destroying us as a school, and I feel accordingly something of the old days over again, with the shadowy spectres of outward rumours and outward coldness and falling off gathering up and closing all our horizon. . . . These are life realities—these bitter attacks of unprovoked evil. How strange it seems to live the Psalms in this way!

Tuesday, 25th.—The report not out for sale yet. The well at Fairfield bricked to-day; that is a right good thing. To-night the Davids spent the evening with us, and we had "Meet" in the hall, and afterwards the children danced,

David sitting on a table playing to them.   It was so pretty to see G. dancing; she did it so well.   I don't know how it is, but dancing always sets me in a dreamy sort of pensiveness. When I was young, even to look on at a dance filled me with a quiet sense of human life and its passing grace; and now I am old, the young days come back, and the ghosts of dances long ago sweep through my brain in quiet soothing thought- fulness, mixed with a sweet feeling of beauty and flowerlike grace, a delicate vision as of something not real yet not phantom, the strangest visible poem of youth and hope and beauty floating between eye and mind, I know not now. To-night in this hard, careworn home of ours the little idyll of half an hour was charming as a bit of a lost world—a glimpse of another less stormy existence.   It moved me out of myself.

Wednesday, 26th.—I cannot help my heart feeling heavy.   I wonder during how many years of my life *bed* has been the one haven and longed-for forgetfulness of care.   Ilminster three years, then a long interval in which it only occasionally was better than waking, then a short period of knowledge-hunting joy, when one would gladly have got rid of it, and then since coming here almost an unbroken period in which, on the whole, the one human solace has been the rest and the for- getting.   I do not mean that I have not had much, very much, that I am grateful for, of mere human pleasantness, but that, on the whole, the cares of the day have outweighed the joys and made one glad of bed as an escape.   So it is now.   All this turmoil, and soon added to it the hard routine of school work, overshadowed by the dread of fever and under- fretted by the troubles with masters, either from their short- comings or their self-assertion.   Truly, bed is a wonderful haven, and I do thank God for having given me through so many years *sleep*.   "He giveth His beloved sleep"; may it not be in this lower sense as well as in the higher?   I would fain think so; at least, I know His gift of sleep has been nothing less than a gift of life to me. . . .

January 27th.—My God, my God, look upon me this last night of the long break with the danger and the work in front of us!   How hard it is to carry on such a complicated thing as this school in these hard days.   Yet I have been cheery and not oppressed to-day. . . . I have heard from London that the report is going about there. Beale has seen it and is very disgusted. Jacob and Birley also have seen it. I hear the Bishop of Peterborough says the Trustees must notice it. This is a fresh danger. . . . Altogether 'tis a dreary prospect. But I never felt less afraid, though much tormented. Have been conferring with Bagshawe about school work. . . . How pleasant it would be if school work was one's only care!

January 28th.—Most of the boys back. It seems very natural. Pray God keep us this term. Masters' meeting this morning. Had to speak to them strongly about tittle-tattle on questions affecting the common body, when the individual tongue carries a certain authority as belonging to the body. . . .

January 29th.—Quite pleasant the boys being back, and with active work some of the fears go. There is less time to think of them. I am not afraid either when brought face to face with the thing. It is the expecting you know not what that is so trying. As far as I can find out, counting those who were ill and left, and those who have been withdrawn because of the fever, there are twelve—six of each set.

I have read the report to-day. It illustrates what I have so often pointed out—the impossibility of getting at the truth in a complicated matter. It is simply impossible to answer it, as every virtual lie always is. You can perhaps outflank it, or make an adverse judgment be passed, but as for putting out the actual truth, that is impossible; it is too subtle. . . .

I was almost amused when I read it, at the ease with which I was made out a liar and a scoundrel. . . . It marvellously opens a man's eyes when he has once or twice seen himself pictured in the " devil's looking-glass "; he gets a sounder idea of man's praise and blame, the latter especially. I may yet go down to posterity as the great flogger, and " bigoted old hater of pure air and water," and senseless, unfeeling tyrant over boys which these fellows paint me.

Sunday, January 30th.—I think sometimes of the ship on the sea and the useless rowing, and Jesus away, as I brood over this strange visitation and its wild senseless clamour, " the sea and the waves roaring," and the fine fresh enthusiasm which in old days made me *feel* Jesus with me dulled and blunted by many an hour of buffeting and many weary days. And I trust that Jesus is now coming to us too, and that we shall find a great calm, and be at our haven where we would be.   I know how good this all is, but my heart is tired and I am growing old.

January 31*st.*—There are thirty new boys at once, and 305 on the school-books, so we have not suffered an appreciable check.

February 4*th.*—When shall I ever get to any quiet intellectual work and my proper business of teaching and training boys, instead of defending the school and myself against evil men? It seems very strange, and is not encouraging after all the money one has spent and given up, and all the life in all ways that one has poured out, how that one should be fiercely attacked for illiberality and self-seeking at the expense of the boys.   Well, God knows—He will bring good out of it all. But at present I cannot see how anything but discouragement to true work and a low debtor and creditor trade in school is to come out of it.   I see, though, the devoted feeling that the old boys and many parents have for the school.   And I *am* sure that good is to come out of these evil days, though I cannot see how.   For one thing, I do see that the greater the crucifixion the greater the salvation, and I do see that the crucifixion means the death of all human trusts and hopes and stays, and divine life coming out of the rocky tomb.   So be it here, my King and my God.   Lord Christ, Thou knowest. . . .

February 6*th.*—The first week over, such a blessing, and Time, the healer, moving slowly on, carrying us, please God, out of immediate danger by degrees.   It is a great relief, the having begun, and not simply waiting and waiting for another stage of trial.   The being *in it* is so much less trying than the waiting for it.   Moreover, when a thing is begun it can come to an end. . . .

February 7*th.*—Had a great refreshment of spirit to-day. Professor Wanklyn has written a letter to the *Sanitary Record*, in which the calumnies first appeared, and signed it with his name, exposing thoroughly their false spirit.   In fact, the report is smashed as an authority by such a letter, and it will probably bring out more. It looks like the beginning of the end. But in any case it alters our whole position, and enables us at once to value by this independent witness the whole report. I am greatly cheered by it. The whole thing shrinks down to its proper spiteful level when touched by a word of independent truth.

But great as had been the trials through which the school had gone, greater were yet to come. Barely three weeks of the new term had passed when a fresh outbreak of fever changed the whole aspect of affairs, and brought the school to the very brink of ruin.

February 20th.—This morning I have entered once again the Valley of the Shadow of Death, and the dark creeping blackness is coming over us again. Cobb came in before chapel to tell me he was almost sure he had a case of typhoid in his house. Poor fellow! he quite broke down as he told me; and, indeed, the thought is deadly enough, and all day I have moved in a dream of fear in the pleasant sunshine. But I have not heard yet the final decision. It is likely enough, I fear, as the town has done nothing, neither flushed the drains nor disinfected them, and in fact really done nothing except the ventilators they were compelled to put in, and these were not put in till the school was here. . . . Cobb has just been in to say it is so. T. in his house has typhoid, and I have given him a notice for Hawthorn to print to send out to every parent to-morrow night, and all his boys will be sent off to-morrow; the Valley of the Shadow of Death is round us again. "God's hand is heavy upon us day and night."

February 21st.—Sent Bagshawe to try and get the sewer flushed. The town is feebly moving under this fresh pressure. . . . All Cobb's boys sent home, and much fear that there is a case in Haslam's house. Sent a notice to every parent in the school of the fact of the case of typhoid. I expect an exodus rather this week, but we must face the worst. If the town incubus was off us we could get on. But unless it can be hauled off our shoulders we perish. It is hard to lie under the feet of such men.

February 22nd.—A beautiful spring day with showers and sun. Not so many boys gone home as I expected as yet. But it is quite possible that we may be left here pretty well alone. If Waugh in Haslam's has the fever, I expect we shall be. This morning we had to consider the question of going to a meeting of the Sanitary Board to-morrow, to which we had been partially invited. I pointed out the impossibility of meeting on any common ground until the report had been formally disclaimed in public, but that it was necessary to meet every advance as well as we could ; that, in fact, it was a game of tactics. We finally agreed unanimously to send Bagshawe and Christian as our representatives with instructions to lay before them the flushing and disinfecting of sewers regularly ; the disinfecting and care of houses where fever had been or was ; and the supply of water to people drinking poisoned wells—to stick to this ; to enter into no discussion ; and if occasion arose, to disclaim all responsibility and all coalition unless the report was first publicly disowned, but to express readiness to help in every possible way. For the first time to-day the sewers have been flushed. The sewer in the school lane has been examined and found foul enough to account for any fever. The rector was hauled to see it, and has heard some plain truths too, I understand. In the meantime we perish. The tradesmen are beginning to be anxious, as well they may. . . .

February 23rd.—Got up this morning quite prepared for any amount of boys going home and letters to match. My own letters, with one exception, all full of sympathy and confidence. One from Mr. Jacob telling me that the Liverpool parents, through their town clerk, are going to send in a memorial to Mr. Sclater Booth to get the town ordered to do its duty, and that there is a strong feeling of sympathy and confidence there. Haslam's case pretty well decided to be not typhoid. Bagshawe and Christian delivered their embassy, and the Board was maundering away and seemed frightened at the gathering storm. They told the Board in conclusion that, while we were ready to give every help as individuals, we could have no common action with them till the report was withdrawn. They drew out of Barnard Smith that he had presented it to Mr. Lambert in person. . . . Tarbotton here to-day, satisfied with all our work in the houses; indignant with the town; will represent it to Mr. Rawlinson, and probably Mr. Lambert on Saturday. Owen well satisfied with the houses on the whole. So we have both the medical and engineer department agreed. All the masters have had nothing but kind letters. There has been a wonderful steadiness in our parents this time. No boy has been sent home to-day.

February 27*th.*—Yesterday morning a letter from the Central Board inquiring into the typhoid, in consequence of the Liverpool movement, and Rayner's letter to them, which I received a copy of from Mr. Jacob, requesting them to do the work here.

February 28*th.*—An eventful day. Barring an hour at dinner-time I worked from 9 to 5.15, and so got off the answer to the Central Board by to-night's post. This is the last death-grapple with the town in its worst features. They would have it, and now the whole truth of their culpable supineness is brought out after they have emptied their quiver, and prevented themselves from taking up another line. I could have wished it had been otherwise, but there is no help for it. It is a simple matter of the school continuing to exist. Mr. Birley and Jacob helped me, suggested and approved, and I consulted them on the main line to be taken. So, though I wrote it nearly all myself, and sent it in my name, it has their *imprimatur* on it. It is a good piece of work. I had no idea what a fatal case could be marshalled against them. . . . No fresh case of fever, I am thankful to say. Every day's respite gives hope. Even if another attack does come it will not empty the school with a rush as might well have happened last week, and we have now, too, a great power moving, and the confidence and support shown by the parents last week is wonderfully encouraging. . . . I cannot but marvel how always at the right moment we receive help, and strange enemies and attacks are met by stranger and more powerful friends always. And men would tell us God is far off, and that there are no miracles. Fools! there are no eyes.

Ash Wednesday.—Truly a day of sackcloth and ashes, yet with sunshine. This morning in much dread about D., who is still reported doubtful, but also poor Mullins came up to me in Fairfield to tell me that Paley says he thinks little Turner in his house has typhoid.   So to-morrow he is to come again, and if it is so, the school will slip away like a wreath of snow.

March 2nd.—The blow has fallen.   Turner, a little boy in Mullins's house, decided to have typhoid.   The house goes home to-morrow.   In the face of the malignant and watchful enmity we encountered last half-year, nothing else can be done.   I am postponing till to-morrow the notice to all the parents, because we expect to be obliged to add D. in Christian's house, and one notice is better than two. . . . Altogether the clouds gather round very heavy, and there seems small hope, yet I cannot help seeing that if we are to be delivered from these wicked, dull-hearted men who oppress us, it can only be by a great external power being called in, and that, methinks, is what God is doing.   But like the Israelites in the wilderness, I am still inclined to murmur at the new difficulty, however often I have been delivered before. This is however very deadly, and unless speedy help does come the school is ruined for years, and I and mine.   Well— the wilderness does not look inviting at this moment.   Paley ascribes these cases to the state of the town.   I called him in partly to relieve Bell of a responsibility he ought not to be called on to bear, partly to stop the mouths of W. and his crew.   How like a dream it all is! or, if the chief actors on both sides were set in position, a picture.

To T. H. Birley.

March 3rd, 1876.

One thing I feel quite sure of, that this is the beginning of the end.   Unless prompt measures are taken in London the school is done for.   In spite of the great feeling shown, it is not possible that the beliefs of those who believe best will stand these repeated shocks on a different tack, and one of dim and uncertain fear.   Neither can the masters, who are, as a body, needy men, hold out long against the strain of no income and large establishments.   The Chancellor's letters furnish us with an admirable barometer of what to expect from the powers that be in this place.   I fully think we shall be pulled through ; but I know that this dead corpse of the locality must be hauled off us quickly, or we perish.   There is no foundation to fall back on for a while, not even a friendly and energetic neighbourhood.   People will be very resigned to Providence till the thing is done, then those who have lost money will mourn over their purses ; that is about all.

But no ordinary measures could stem the torrent which now threatened to overwhelm the school.   It "rained telegrams" from anxious parents.   Another week of inaction, Thring often said afterwards, would have settled the fate of Uppingham.   A new school might in years to come be built up there, but the school that then was, its boys and its masters, would have been scattered without hope of reunion.   Before return could be made possible the boys would have found new schools ; the masters, for the most part men with families, with their property tied up in the school-houses, and dependent on the incomes derived from them, would have been forced to seek new posts. Immediate and practically irretrievable ruin stared Uppingham in the face.   Schools had suffered from epidemics before, but from nothing like this.   Rugby had once been broken up for some weeks, and the masters had taken groups of boys to keep up a portion of .the teaching work at various points in the Lake district.   But Uppingham could not be treated piece-meal in this way ; the tutorial and house system made it impossible ; the school from its very organisation had to be dealt with as a unit if dealt with effectively.

Migration began to be talked of among some of the masters.   Thring, battling with local stupidity and enmity, caught at the suggestion.   If his men were willing to follow him in a great enterprise, he was prepared to lead.

To Sir Henry Thring.

March 4th, 1876.

Believe me, I am no alarmist, nor am I in a state of excitement.   But things are in quite as critical a state as I told you.

Winchester with its foundation and ancient renown could be torpid for fifty years and recover.   Marlborough with its busy squadrons of shareholders could also wait till they had worked things round.   But Uppingham has no foundation and no shareholders, and instead of the latter a neighbourhood that will very resignedly accept the will of Providence when they ruin the school by doing nothing.   We cannot hold the school together much longer; I doubt whether Tuesday next will see us with a third of the boys left here.   They are melting away.   The town will practically do nothing—that is, it will think itself immensely energetic if in the next six months it is preparing the preliminaries for beginning.   But this is ruin.

We are thinking if we are deserted by the boys next week of migrating to the Lakes and getting all our classes together there till the summer, just to keep the school connection going. You see the last six months have been wasted.   Our putting things right has not been sufficient.   Lost time is at this moment absolute destruction to the school.   Really things have come to that pass that I have little to suggest.   Time is so important.   The quickest thing that will put matters in ordinary routine decently is the best; there is no flushing of the sewers going on now even.   Next, the quickest way of getting the town set in order finally.   My own conviction also is somewhat decided that a medical officer should be sent, at all events before the matter ends, to thoroughly investigate what has really taken place, and get to the bottom of this quagmire of deceit if possible.   I will ask Mr. Jacob of Liverpool to communicate with you, if he has anything; he is Mr. Birley's colleague as school trustee, a very able, practical man, and strongly backed at Liverpool.

March 5th.—On Tuesday morning Haslam came up to me at prayer time and suggested that Dr. Beale should be sent for, and that he would gladly pay his share of the fee. This exactly jumped with my own idea, and I telegraphed for him. He came at night, having missed his train, so I was obliged to send out the circular of Mullins's case before the case at Christian's could be decided. He saw both, and told me they were anxious cases, though he thought both would get over it, and I got two reports from him—one on Christian's case, and one on general treatment—and sent them out last night. He left in the middle of the day.

The migration idea has been started, and I have encouraged it so far as to say that I should seriously entertain the idea of taking the school to the Lakes if we could not hold it here.

I have written to Jacob and Birley at once, offering to go to Manchester and meet them, and told them that nothing remains but to take our Easter holiday at once and go to the Lakes or somewhere, and reassemble the school for the summer there. So I trust this dreary drama will be played out, and the town authorities left to beat the air. . . . In spite of all the difficulty ahead, the feeling of cutting short this dreadful state of deadness and spite here is as the feeling of a prison thrown open, and a walking out into free air. How wonderful God's ways with us are! I am filled with wonder.

Action was now a question not merely of days, but of hours. Thring felt that it would be useless in a crisis requiring such rapid decision to wait for the opinion of his uncertain governors. Upon his Liverpool and Manchester men he knew he could rely for resolute action, and them alone he decided to consult.

To T. H. BIRLEY.

March 5th.

Campbell has just come to me with a letter from one of his parents whose boy has gone home, to say he has typhoid —came home with it.

It seems to be absolutely impossible to hold the school

together.   I have proposed to Mr. Jacob to meet him at your
house to-morrow.   He or you or both will wire me.   The
only plan left, it appears to me, is to take our Easter holiday
in town, to send out to-morrow or next day a circular to all
our parents asking them if they will send their boys to us in
three weeks' time at the Lakes or elsewhere, and to migrate
till the summer whilst things are being set right here.

March 7th.—Back from Manchester. . . . We decided to
break up the school on Tuesday next, and reassemble, probably in Wales, as a place which seems especially appropriate
offered itself, and a great hotel-keeper there has come into Mr.
Birley to-day eager to get us.   When I got near Uppingham
I met Rawnsley and Skrine, the former very eager to stop the
school breaking up.   No doubt it is a grievous thing.   However, I showed them it was impossible to stop.   Then when
we got here, there was a desire to delay and shilly-shally from
one or two, and finally —— made a strong set for the hill
houses remaining, backed by ——   This I am determined shall
not be. . . . However, on the whole, there is an absolute
unanimity on migration.   The rector has put his foot into
it, having prevented a meeting of governors being called by
saying there was no need, and he has already been using
threats against us for our action.   However, we shall see.
I wrote to Mr. Johnson (the patron) on Monday morning.
I shall write again to-morrow, and I am acting with the two
school trustees.   Let them do their worst.   We shall achieve
a great deliverance for schools from local tyranny and governing bodies.   Their only power of action is to dismiss me,
and that would not take effect, if they were fools enough
to try it, without a struggle.   But, indeed, this stroke is
simple destruction to the rector.   It is a grievous necessity,
but it is a necessity, and must be worked out to the end. . . .
God help me in all this turmoil and battle.

To the Same.

March 8th.

A medical inspector comes down to-morrow from the Local
Government Board.   I don't know who.   I have just had a
telegram from my brother. . . . I fear Field in my house has

the fever, though it is not quite certain yet.   I have been able
to do nothing about Borth to-day, but all looks well.   I hear
there is a cricket ground there. . . . The rector was senten-
tious and threatening to one of the masters last night.   "The
Trustees would stop it all."   He might just as well try to stop
a train with his finger.   All the masters are unanimous.
Legal or illegal, the only thing left is to do it in the best way.
Most assuredly neither boys nor masters remain here to be
doctored.   Change of air is the only possible prescription.
In great haste.

The support of the Trustees elected by the masters
was backed up by that of the hereditary patron, Mr.
Johnson, who wrote to express his entire approval of
what had been proposed.   In reply Thring says :—

To A. C. JOHNSON.

March 8th.

Circumstances were so critical that I went into Manchester
on Monday to meet Mr. Birley and Jacob, as the only trustee
power that in a combined way was accessible to me.

Your letter this morning thoroughly takes in the gravity of
the case, and I am very grateful for the interest and sympathy
you show, and for the support you give me under these unprecedented circumstances.

I found on reaching Manchester that the question, if I may
say so, had become a matter not of days even, but of hours.
The editor of one of the papers had been applied to by many
parents to find private tutors and schools for the boys at
Uppingham, but had told Mr. Birley he would wait the result
of our meeting at his house before taking any step.   After
much anxious deliberation we decided that we had no choice,
that unless immediate steps were taken, there would simply be
no school left to take any steps about, and I came back to
announce that the school will break up for its Easter holidays on
Tuesday next, and that we shall reassemble in three weeks' time
from that date in some healthy locality away from Uppingham.
Most probably Borth, near Aberystwith, will be the place, but

we must look carefully before settling. It will be impossible to come back after this second move until all things here are completely set right, and declared to be so by Government authority.

It is very sad. But this plan will certainly keep the school together, and it will be as easy to stay a year as six months, if necessary. Were there no other reason, neither I nor the masters could endure the deadly strain of these trying days and not break down in health.

We can take the day boys with us, if necessary; they are not numerous, and the Trustees would no doubt pay their actual board and lodging out of the tuition fees, which would be no great sum.

Pray accept in my own name, and that of all the masters, our most hearty thanks for your encouragement and support.

Once the decision was made vigorous action was taken. Masters had already been detailed to visit various parts of the country, and inquiries had been made in many directions. Meanwhile, notice had been sent to parents that the school would reassemble in three weeks at some place as yet unknown, but which would at least be healthy. It soon appeared that Borth, near Aberystwith, in North Wales, gave the best promise as a temporary home for the school. There followed a fortnight of what Thring afterwards described as "a fierce race for life."

CHAPTER II

UPPINGHAM BY THE SEA

To pull up by the roots a school "as old as an old oak tree" and transplant it to the seaside 200 miles away ; to find some roof-tree to shelter for an indefinite length of time each of the 300 boys and the 30 masters of the school with their families ; and to do this under the pressure of grave doubts as to whether parents would lend their support, with very insufficient means, and in the short space of an extemporised Easter holiday, was, in truth, an enterprise without precedent in English school life.

It might in after-days become tinged with the soft colours of romance and furnish material for poetry, but at the moment it meant indeed "a fierce race for life." But the spirit of Thring and his masters rose to the occasion. The diary and correspondence once more become our best guide in following the course of events :—

March 8th. — A little news from Borth—the hotel will accommodate 200. Considerably relieved by a letter from Earle honourably caving in and saying he will do whatever is judged best willingly. Much pleased by Bagshawe coming to me in the gardens and in the frankest manner saying he quite agreed with my view and would do whatever I wanted in whatever way. Christian, Haslam, and Bagshawe came to ask me what they had better do for raising the immediate sum necessary. I recommended them if the bank here would not go on in the usual way to write to Mr. Jacob or Birley and lay their case before them : first, if the Trustees would do anything ; next, if they would themselves do anything. In the afternoon a telegram from Henry to say that the Local Government Board will send down a medical inspector to-morrow. I don't know who, but it is a move, and will supersede the local authority. But in very truth the relief of not being tied, Mezentius-like, to this dead corpse of the town any more is in itself an inexpressible relief, if it was possible yet from stress of work to realise it.

March 9th.—At last the great wheel is, I think, fairly moved. Our migration has put an end to all temporising, and given the Local Government Board an excuse for moving. Altogether there is a real stir. I had an opportunity this morning of referring to the perfect unanimity of masters, and the hope that no half and half talk would encourage Trustees to set up their backs on the hope of internal dissension. . . . The fearful strain and race against time a little relaxed to-day. A tendency towards headache all the week ; possibly a far-off touch of the dreaded foe.

Skrine came to me yesterday to say that money would be wanted, and to put his salary into my hands. I accepted it if there was any expenditure incurred of a public character, *e.g.* cricket fields, etc. But it is very good. How much of good I have to be thankful for !

March 11th.—The first battle of the new campaign fought to-day, and on the whole won. The Trustees have sanctioned the break-up of the school, but on ——'s dictation would not put on record any expression with reference to the migration ; in his own words, " They knew nothing of the school till it came back again." He spoke of the chapel and buildings as burdens to the Trust, and endeavoured, whilst taking over some £14,000 worth of property from our hands, to saddle us with the burden of any occasional deficit on the small outlying debts. . . . Then he brought forward the day boys and of the necessity of having a master here. I simply said I should not leave any one of my staff, but if necessary a man might be got to do it, but that they could come with us, and the Trustees could pay a fair proportion of their board and lodging. Then he threatened that the Trustees would have to cut down the masters' salaries. I quietly pointed out to Mr. Finch, who was sitting next to me, that the scheme appointed that the tuition fees must first go to paying the masters.

March 12th.—A quiet day at last. Holy Communion, a very good sermon from Christian in the afternoon. When shall I spend a Sunday again as headmaster in this place? I had a feeling as I stood in chapel to-day, never—never; but then I looked up at Maurice's statue and Anstey's carvings, and the memorial to Green and others whom I loved, and whose lives were living lives here, and then it came back to me again that much was left, and that even this place, with its deadly blight of dull, dead hearts worse than the typhoid, might breathe new life and remain a light. . . . One thing I feel more than I ever have felt, that a great shaping power is round about me, guiding, and ruling, and making, and moulding this fierce crucible work and fiery rush of evil and danger, and friendship, and help all round about one, and that some strange birth of strange good and marvellous divine purpose is to come out of it all. To-morrow I start for Liverpool, and on Tuesday for Borth and other places in North Wales. Borth seems likely to suit from a letter of Cobb's this morning.

To Dr. Jex Blake (Headmaster of Rugby).

March 13th, 1876.

A thousand thanks. It seems to me clear that you should take our boys if they offer. All you can do to help me is to say that in three weeks' time we mean to have established the school elsewhere, probably near Aberystwith, until it is safe to return to Uppingham. I go to-morrow to see places; we have one in view—Borth—which seems very suitable—others also.

But at all events we settle somewhere so long as Uppingham continues unclean. . . . Nothing has been done yet by the town, not even the sewer flushed. . . .

To T. H. Birley.

March 16th.

All is settled, thanks to Mr. Jacob. We came down through Wales on Tuesday, receiving Cobb on our way and his reports, and reached Borth on Wednesday. The hotel is really excellent, and we have secured the whole of it, with accommodation in it for myself, family, and 160 boys. Then we have taken the adjoining row of lodging-houses, and in fact entered into possession of the whole place. The hotel contracts to do us for £1. a head, we sending in all boy beds and bedding, and finding servants for the boys, he boarding and lodging the latter free. Altogether I feel we are as we could be. The sea is beautiful, so is the view on the hillside at the back, and there is *plenty of space.* Then Aberystwith at our back secures us against any downfall in ways and means of getting on. You may suppose it has been no small matter getting all our agreements in shape. The water and drainage are exceptionally good. So now we have only to work hard this next fortnight and get all things ready, and then may a blessing rest on Uppingham by the Sea.

March 18th.—Started on Monday with Skrine for Liverpool, picked up Cobb at Chester on Tuesday and came on to Llandrindod, which Mr. Jacob had been told to look at. Slept there, went to Borth on Wednesday, when we met Haslam and Bagshawe, and made a bargain to take the hotel and all the lodging-houses we could lay hands on. We were much pleased with Borth, if we can but pack into it. Mr. Mytton, the lessee of the hotel, is very honest and kindly, and I hope all will be well. On Thursday evening went on to Aberystwith; parted with Cobb, Haslam, and Mr. Jacob on Friday morning; then took lodgings for three weeks for my family, came with Skrine to Shrewsbury, where he stayed, and home that night. A brief summary of an important week. Some of the travelling and our evenings were really very pleasant, and anxious and busy as it has been, it was refreshing to be out of this poisonous air and its meanness and malice, or perhaps ignorance and ill-nature.

March 19th.—This morning got news to my great relief

that the best lodging-house at Borth, the one I most feared about, is to be had.   This greatly eases matters.   I feel so grateful at the deliverance from the town and the having time once more at our disposal.   It is like an escape out of prison. Things may be hard at Borth ; there must be much difficulty, but it is the hardness of liberty, not the close deadly grip of a prison.

March 26*th.*—At Aberystwith, with a delightful sense of freedom. . . . Sir Pryse Pryse has given us an excellent cricket ground at a nominal rent, and is kindness itself.   Mr. Skrine has made a donation of £25 to our extra expenses for amusements and boy comforts, and if there was nothing else, the sense of being away from Uppingham is in itself a delight —out of prison.   It is very curious, the strong inward feeling I have that I shall never go back there again but work else- where.   It may be nothing, but it is here.   Perhaps the true fulfilment of the feeling is rather to be found in the widening of the life-power than in the mere change of places.   To- morrow morning begins real hard work, but liberty.   Thank God !   How happy it is to be Christ's servant !

March 27*th.*—A day of hard but most cheery work, every- body so kind and helpful—such a contrast to Uppingham.   I have really enjoyed my day, although I was kept at it in- cessantly from 8 A.M. till 6.   I found to my great satisfaction when I got to Borth all the sanitary improvements going on briskly under the engineer of the Cambrian Railway. . . . I inspected all the houses, went home, made plans assigning them, came out again to see whether I had them right, and finally settled everything, getting all the boys and most of the masters in place.   Then I went out and secured three more small houses, and now I feel myself fairly level with the numbers and on a good basis. . . .

March 29*th.*—Such a day's work yesterday. . . . The un- packing and confusion was very great. . . . Marie and Sarah and I worked hard.   Sarah put beds together, and I carried mattresses with the men, and we got all our beds put up.   To-day we have had all the rooms washed and are ready for the boys, barring making the beds.   Things are clearing to-day.   I got to my great delight house-room for sixty or seventy boys' study work.   It was great fun bargaining with some of the old Welsh women. One old lady, to Cobb's great delight, shook me affectionately by the shoulders. How we laughed; they are very pleasant and primitive some of them. I feel now so free. Uppingham and all its abominations, . . . gone for a time, albeit danger and difficulty and toil are before me.

To Sir Henry Thring.

March 31st, 1876.

I see my way here and have got through the heavy work. Things are falling into place better than I dared hope. Every one helps us, and I feel such a sense of freedom and liberty in work, now for a time Uppingham and its abominations are left behind. We shall do well, I hope. The place pleases all of us; a fine sea, and most lovely views.

You never saw such a scene as last Monday and Tuesday: eighteen trucks of bedding and furniture unloaded and to be set in order again. We get 150 boys, myself, and family, a master, and two matrons into the great hotel. The passage on the ground floor is fitted up with a narrow table for dining and will seat 140. Then we have twenty-two lodging-houses of various kinds occupied by us and our belongings. We move in nearly 400 strong—such a colony starting at a moment's notice means no little stir. I arranged where everybody was to go last Monday after having worked the thing out carefully. I could almost write an inventory of Borth lodging-houses, rooms, and prices from memory.

We shall be ready all right on Tuesday next, as far as I can foresee. But you would be amused if you saw our human hive settling down.

April 6th.—How much has passed since Sunday and what a whirl it all is. On Tuesday the first batch of boys came in, and a proper tussle it was to get the confusion settled; upwards of 100 boys and their luggage let loose on us without any practice to meet it.

April 7th.—The first happy day I have spent for many months. This morning I got a letter from Captain Withington at Liverpool, who has sent back his boy, saying that he

and Mrs. Withington agreed that now was the time to show
that they cared for the school and appreciated our great effort,
and that he proposed writing to every parent to subscribe
towards the expenses—the subscription to be limited to £5.
This is immensely cheering, both as one more sign that our
work is blessed, and also as giving us the sinews of war in
our new circumstances.   Thank God for His goodness in this !
Then to-day I finished off assigning a place of work to every
boy in the hotel, and was able to do it really very fairly well.
This is an intense relief—the having cleared out the chaos into
reasonable working shape for every boy.

April 8th.—A fine day again.   Such a blessing that the
boys just at this time get pleasant impressions, and that we can
let them out of doors during the crush of the first settling.
. . . The end of the first week here.   It is marvellous ; all
things are working well, and really we shall, by God's blessing, spend a happy and good working time here.

How strange life is !   How little one knows what is best !
Life is best, the living the day manfully, truly, and humbly.
Not what we plan but how we live.   Not what we aim at
doing, but how we do what we have to do—that is God's
life.

The misfortunes of the school and the bold step of
removing it to the sea-coast had attracted much public
attention.   The editor of the *Times* asked Thring to
send him some account of the removal and settlement
of the school in its new home.   This account was sent
off during the first week of the stay at Borth.   Some
of its paragraphs give vivid pictures of the migration.

There is a comical side to most disasters, and the sudden
uprooting of the school at Uppingham has been no exception
to the rule.   The contented owners of houses over-night
practically found themselves, like Aladdin, staring into vacancy
in the morning.   The houses were there, indeed, as usual—
that was the jest—but as far as living in them went, they had
vanished.   Four hundred people were turned loose, with just
three weeks given them to hunt for a place to settle in, to

find it, and to settle in it when found. So the school was adrift, sent out its pioneers, explored, discovered its haven, and then straightway found itself, with a curious sense of relief, the temporary master of a goods train running through to Borth in Cardiganshire. Not that hearts were not heavy for the past and present troubles, heavy with anxious fear of the work and the risk of the experiment. Sorrow, too, there was in the last looks at the homes that had to be left. Gardens and flowers and fields were seen through a haze of parting and wistful regrets. Nevertheless, there was a freshness in the new opening; a quickening sense of freedom and escape in the possibility of being able to work once more in peace.

So Uppingham was left, and faces were set towards Borth. At Borth, of course, every one was on the *qui vive* about the strange colony that was coming in so suddenly in this rolling lump. Very kind and very willing was the reception given by the little village to the school pioneers; and right well they worked. Workers, indeed, were wanted, for, if any one wishes for a new experience, let him try the unloading and rearranging eighteen railway trucks, and the distribution of their contents among twelve or fourteen houses in a fierce match against time. This was all done and finished off between Tuesday, 28th March, and Tuesday, 4th April. The great hotel was arranged to receive 150 boys, the head-master, and his family, an assistant-master, and two matrons. A row of lodging-houses flanking the hotel take another 150 boys, and most of the masters; long narrow tables are run down the hotel passage on the ground floor, the large coffee-rooms and the billiard-room below are treated in the same way, and 350 people—boys, masters, and masters' families—dine at one time by this extemporised arrangement. Twenty-seven lodging-houses in all, and a large public hall, have been secured for school use. A room, 83 feet by 20 feet, is being put up of rough shingle behind the hotel, in order to hold the whole school when needed. The stables are turned into the school carpentry, the large coach-house shed into a gymnasium; a lavatory, with thirty basins, is being roughly put up; and altogether the school has shaken into place and got its working machinery in most unexpectedly good order. A beach, 4 miles long, with splendid sands, stretches away in front of the hotel, with plenty of pebbles, and the sea to throw them into.   An aquarium will be started this week.   An octopus, most liberal of its sepia, has been already caught.   The beach is closed on the south by the hills, on the north by the river Dovey and the hills beyond it.   These hills seem to form an amphitheatre behind, round a broad stretch of peat which lies between them and the sea.   The views are lovely, and the place is suggestive of shells and aquariums and sea-birds in front, and of botany and rambles in the rear, while Aberystwith, with a railway running to it, forms a good base of operations for the colony to shop in and fall back on. Cricket goes on on the sand in a bay, and an excellent field, unfortunately 4 miles off, but on the railway, has been secured for half-holiday practice and matches.   Sir Pryse Pryse, of Goderdden, may simply be said to have made a present of it to the school for the time.   Indeed, everybody, high and low alike, has given ready help and welcome.   The Bishop of St. David's, who owns some land near the hotel, has allowed the school to have what they want for cricket there, if practicable ; so Uppingham by the Sea can do something besides throwing stones into the water.   One short week saw this all done.   It was like shaking the alphabet in a bag, and bringing out the letters into words and sentences, such was the sense of absolute confusion turned into intelligent shape.

On Tuesday, 4th April, a new phase began, and a week of stiff preparation was succeeded by a week of experiment. About half-past six in the evening a long train was seen winding along the flat, and as it drew near to the station, which was crowded with masters and spectators, it might be supposed to turn into a gigantic poultry train, so thick were the heads thrust out of the coops all along.   Soon it ran up and outpoured the garrulous mass, and Babel began.   However, they were soon, in true poultry fashion, hurried into the long table and tea, then turned out on the beach ; while the still more difficult task of reducing trunks, hampers, book-boxes, and everything conceivable, which heaped the station platform, into something like order began.   This went on till night fell at last on weary masters and curious boys in their new berths. Much the same scenes, only in more orderly fashion, ensued next evening; by which time the whole school, some 290 odd, had arrived. But the arrangements were now not all strange, and the kitchen stood the shock of war with unexpected success; no mean thing for hungry boys. Then came the billeting them off for work. Various cottages receive some eighty or ninety, as a substitute for the studies they have at Uppingham. The class-room accommodation is surprisingly good. The new room, however, is not yet up. This will relieve pressure, especially in rainy weather.

There are many of the old resources at Borth, but, whatsoever pastime may flourish or languish transplanted to this strange soil, there are two sources of enjoyment unfailing here, unknown to the school in its Midland home — the mountains and the sea. The boys wander out from the hotel doors, swarming like bees round a bee-hive, down to the broad reach of shingle and sand. Tea is over, and all the school is flocking to enjoy the sunset and watch the rising tide. They are doing what boys always do on the sea-shore —dodging the waves, hurling pebbles at them as they come in, burrowing in the sand for shells, cracking stones in the vain hope of finding jewels inside, or poring over the wooden reefs that rise so strangely from the sand, as the tide is not yet up—the long buried fragments, so says the legend, of the lost Lowland Hundred. Those clear colours in the west where the sun sets in the sea, the rippling light beneath the clouds, the scattered groups of figures moving in the twilight somewhat darkly, with a pleasant freshness of boyhood all round, form a scene not easily forgotten. The dusky headlands stand out to seaward, with a white gleaming of broken waves at their feet; and landward shadowy mountains beyond the purple still catch a little glory from the sun. The low talk of pensive strollers, the rattle of pebbles, the laughter of those who chase each other in merry vein, all mixed with the roar of the sea, and perchance some strains of music from the choir at practice thrown in, give sights and sounds that may make the school, if not unfaithful to Uppingham it has left, yet more than half-reconciled to the new land.

New, indeed, and strange enough it all is. The whole scene and circumstances, both in and out of doors, have to be readapted to the old familiar work in unfamiliar ways. A partial shaking down has been accomplished; and, as if to make the first week truly represent the old school life, the last foot-ball match of the season, a broken-off fragment of the Uppingham left behind, was played out on the Saturday half-holiday; and the champion cup of the year awarded to the winners. So the jerseys, white or red, met in their mimic war in the new land. Thus ended the first week, and its evening closed on a quiet scene of school routine; as if doubt, and risk, and turmoil, and confusion, and fear, weary head, and weary hand, had not been known in the place. The wrestling match against time was over, and happy dreams came down on Uppingham by the Sea.

To G. R. Parkin.

BORTH, *April 20th*, 1876.

I got your welcome letter this week just after our exodus and its great rush of work and danger. 'Tis a strange world. Uppingham has fairly turned us out of house and home, and here we are, having had just three weeks to colonise in. . . .

I send you my article in the *Times* as the easiest way of telling you the main facts of the migration. . . . But it tells nothing of all the knocking about to try and get things right in the first instance. It tells nothing of all the delays and antagonism, nothing of our anxious experiment to try and maintain our ground independently of the town before the second outbreak of fever. Nothing also of the deadly doubts and fears when it was on us again, and of the dire need there was to fly elsewhere, or else no school would have been left in another week to deal with. As it is, all the boys followed us, and the parents have stuck to us with wonderful steadiness, and are now going to subscribe to pay part of the expense. But it is a fearful time, and success only means great pain and risk and loss not ending in utter overthrow and destruction. As for me, I should have resigned long ago if it was not for the cause I have at heart and the men who are engaged in it with me. I begin to doubt what the end of it all is to be, in England at all events. This crush and haphazard scramble, this incessant work, and high demands and low pay and low estimate of the workers. This putting them under mere amateurs of lower calibre than the men put under them.   It all seems to me a sort of witches' caldron, out of which no good brew, nothing holy and just and true can come.   This place is wonderfully adapted for our purpose, and though there are great difficulties we shall, I think, pull through and save the life of the school.   Yet it is gall and wormwood to me to have to think of going back to Uppingham.   Is success in this great strait only to end in that?   But I will not be faithless. Uppingham itself may be a very altered Uppingham by the time we return, its moral sewage much drawn off and in its proper place as well as its physical sewage, or there may be a wise purpose to come out elsewhere in consequence.   I quite agree with you in your dread of Government, but there is a worse evil still—"inferior local authority" set over you.   If you must put the *life* into leading strings, and the living acting power is not to be trusted to do its own work, at least put the leading strings in the hand of the highest, and do not have a low neighbour, *always on the spot*, get his dead hand on your heart.   *Keep free* if possible.   Resist everything but the right of the Government to see that good *average* work is done. Otherwise all improvement, all deviation from routine, all new teaching method, and new ways of training become impossible.

As to America, I do not see how a country which puts itself up for sale every four years can fail to be a mass of corruption.   The wit of man never devised anything more effectual in the way of certain ruin.   I am sure the *glitter* of power ought never to be made a prize for the ambitious ; or in other words, that a king in some shape or name is a necessity for liberty.   Our responsible Prime Minister, who resigns as soon as he cannot carry out his policy, is another necessity.

I am so full of care and work at present that I hardly know what to do.   An examination going on is the reason I have time to write at all.   A scarlet fever case declared to-day is another bit of trial, but it is astonishing how much can be borne as soon as the mind is made up to work and bear, and how a great trouble quite swallows up a little one.   It is a real truth in life that eels get used to the skinning, and take with much calmness events that in their earlier hours of ease would have driven them wild. . . .

The history of the Uppingham sojourn at Borth has been written by the skilful hand of one who took an active part in the migration, and who had a poet's eye for the picturesque aspects of the situation. To this record the interested reader may be referred for detailed and graphic descriptions of the life of the school in its temporary home.[1]

While Thring himself exulted in the new sense of freedom which he felt in being away from Uppingham, and was keenly alive to the romantic features of his great enterprise, he still found that he had on his hands a task of almost crushing weight.

Masters and boys alike were to be inspired with the campaigning spirit; the routine of school life had to be worked out under the greatest difficulties, so far as school machinery was concerned; questions of finance were knotty and perplexing. All these things and many more had to be dealt with, while he received scant sympathy, to say the least, from some of his trustees at Uppingham.

An old pupil who knew the circumstances well compared, not inaptly, Thring's position at Borth with that of Hannibal in Italy, the pusillanimous government at home giving him quite as much trouble as the difficulties immediately around him on a foreign soil.

Numerous letters among his correspondence at this time show with what deep interest his great venture was being watched, and especially by fellow-teachers.

A Rugby master writes :—

I have been intensely interested in all that I have heard about the carrying of the school to Borth, which, I think, is as wonderful and encouraging an event as has happened in the

[1] *Uppingham-by-the-Sea : a Narrative of the Year at Borth,* by J. H. S. Macmillan and Co.

history of any school. It seems to me that any master in any school, thinking of it, might feel that no difficulties ought to make one despair. And I take the liberty of writing now both to assure you of my personal sympathy and to thank you and your colleagues, if you will let me, for a splendid and inspiring example.

The headmaster of Wellington (afterwards Archbishop Benson) says :—

I cannot help writing you a line to tell you what sympathy I have felt for you in the sad renewal of your trouble at Uppingham, and what admiration at the pluck, if you will forgive the word, of your move off to Borth. It is quite Roman, and quite of a piece with the recent history of Uppingham. I hope it may be quite as successful as it deserves, and live by and by in the annals of Uppingham as a successful as well as gallant stroke.

Many troubles within and without added to the anxieties of this trying time.

May 11th.—I have learnt that to persist in truth is a great offence. How glorified I should have been if I had raised the terms or increased the numbers of the school, allowing each master his two or three more as they asked, and ruined the life by doing it.

May 14th.—Have been rather downcast to-day, partly at having, I fear, to go to town—though not till Wednesday at all events—partly at having written the two letters to Mr. Birley and Henry, which will, I fear, involve more correspondence, and I never quite make out in my own mind whether it is personal feeling or truth which makes me put out my views. When I write I think it truth; after I have written I am downhearted. It is so hard to know what is selfish and what isn't.

May 26th.—My bank-books came in this morning—a heavy weight there. I don't quite see how my expenses should be less. But very likely I am wrong. But I have seen such strange things in my life experience, and I so fully believe that modern martyrdom is loss of money and braving that kind of disgrace in a good cause, that I am not so sure that I am wrong. I suppose the martyrs often thought in their hours of prison sadness that, whilst they were right on the whole, they might have said or done this or that better and been spared this or that torture had they done so. Even so do I. The main love for Christ and giving up wealth for His sake I am sure of, whilst some of my debts and difficulties and heart-tearings may very likely be my own selfish mismanagement. But my Father will bless the work and worker for all that. Perhaps as Abram was first brought from Ur to Haran, and then called out of Haran, and his life led on by steps, and the break did not come at once, so it may be with me. At all events, this move to Borth does make another move right away a comparatively easy task, if God wills. Powell of Bisham here. He is a comfort to me, for he believes thoroughly in the guiding of God, and in seeming disaster in a good cause not being a thing to be downcast about. Yet I am very, very troubled, and all the present is strange and dreamlike, and all the future dark and dangerous. . . .

May 28th.—We have now been half our time here; what a blessing! I shall not easily forget that morning before prayers in upper school when I stood—about a month before the typhoid — and in a sort of Christian Nebuchadnezzardom rejoiced in the school, and thought that though God could easily shake the school and destroy it I did not quite see how. Now all is floating; nothing solid any more; but the faith in good and in the ark on the waters. . . .

The Trustees were now discussing the question of recalling the school to Uppingham after the summer holidays, in the expectation that the sanitation works would by that time be carried out. Thring had little faith in the promises which had been made on this point.

June 10th.—Went over to Aberystwith yesterday and talked over our critical position with Mr. Birley. He made the excellent suggestion that I should write to Mr. Johnson and require the Trustees to affirm that the town drainage will be forward enough for the school to return on the 15th September.   This is a grand move.   First, it is a step when no step seemed possible.   Next, it relieves me of antagonism to the Trustees and puts me in seeming obedience—a great fact. Next, it compels them either to affirm that the town will be ready, in which case they are bound to see to it, or to decline the responsibility, in which case I am free to act.   This is a great immediate relief. . · . .

To T. H. Birley.

June 15th.—No doubt we shall lose boys.   But a loss at Borth is temporary, another case of fever at Uppingham final. Moreover, bear in mind that a *fiat* of the Trustees on Saturday for return, *without an affirmation of safety*, means the break-up of the present school.   If they *order*, without giving assurance of safety in their judgment, the order *will not be obeyed*.   And I think I may add a large number of the masters will stand by me in this refusal.   At all events, it is the end of the present school.   As regards losing boys, I hear of probable loss which-ever we do.   It is strange sitting here and waiting quietly for one's doom, and at such hands.

June 22nd.—S. is now convinced that we ought to stay here next term, and shall probably have to do so.   I said this should have been the masters' opinion six weeks ago, when it would have made all things easy ; that now it was impossible to move after we had entered into communication with the Trustees ; that all along I had said it was running our heads into a rat-trap, but the conduct of the masters up to a fortnight ago, in fact up to the meeting, had almost been such as to make me tell Birley and Jacob that to hold Borth with such disaffection was impossible, though easy enough in itself.   That we had lost, as I told them weeks ago, almost all the advantage we had gained by our daring move and its trials, and that all that could be done now was to avoid uncon-ditional surrender.   I told him also that I knew he thought me headstrong and impulsive, but that the bold dashes or resistance, when I made them, were the most solemn and deliberate acts of my life; that these subjects were on my mind night and day; and that I never did anything dangerous without having very carefully counted the cost, made up my mind to possible defeat, and the more dangerous the more deliberate, at all events, my action was.

June 26th.—Called on Sir Pryse Pryse on our way back. . . . Spent a very pleasant half-hour or so there, and went round his splendid gardens. He certainly is the most genial fellow I ever saw. The pleasant surroundings here of friendly people and glorious country do make much of this life with all its troubles and deadly chances at the moment often enjoyable, sometimes really delightful, and I feel healthy and strong.

The splendid campaigning of the school naturally stirred the enthusiasm of old Uppingham boys. Those at Oxford took the opportunity of the Old Boys' Annual Cricket Match to present to the masters an address expressing their feelings. To this Thring refers :—

June 30th.—After luncheon the whole school was called up, and Nettleship presented the Oxford address to the masters, and this is to be followed by a Cambridge and a London one. He made a very good speech, and I replied, and, as I felt it much, did not do badly. It is of wonderful value at this time. . . . It cheers our hearts, and gives us strength, and it enabled me to speak to the school from a point of view not otherwise possible, and was a great boon in that way. . . . How wonderfully all things are working. I feel, too, so much the beauty and freedom of this place. Here the great trials are battles to be fought in a manly way, and skill and courage are to be exercised.

At Uppingham one's life is that of Job, sitting on a dunghill and scraping boils. Truly, God is wonderful in His arrangement of human life.

July 1st.—I think things tend more and more to a final breaking away from Uppingham, though at present apparent

submission and throwing responsibility on them is the policy
to be pursued. . . . Bagshawe yesterday had a long talk with
me about this fresh case.   He was strong about abandoning
Uppingham altogether.   So it is clear that he is sound on
main points, as I thought.   I said it might come to that, and
if it did, I certainly should try to refound the school elsewhere, but that in the present state of things it was a game of
skill of which I had only part management, and that we must
follow the lines already · laid down of working through the
Trustees, and, above all things, avoid collision with them.

To the Same.

July 7th.—Major Tulloch said the state of the place "was
a scandal," and that the works must be done.   The locals
were indiscreet enough to betray their animus by only having
their own report on the table, not Rawlinson's or Tarbotton's.
Major Tulloch observed significantly on this.   Also Brown
was silly enough to demur to sending out the advertisements
for tenders on a point of form, and Mr. Wirtley did it.   The
drains luckily stank on that day their best.   Major Tulloch
said his duties took him to many queer places, but he had
never been in one so openly foul.   Sundry of the townspeople
at the meeting (it was but small) spoke pleasantly of the
school, and money statistics were advanced without contradiction to show how much the town gained by the school.   Field
expressed himself warmly for us, and the doing the work well,
and I believe him.   Major Tulloch sent me reiterated messages
through Bagshawe on no account to allow the school to
return before Christmas.   He said it would be very dangerous,
with the movement of the earth and all the work that had to
be done.

To Rev. Godfrey Thring.

BORTH, *July 11th*, 1876.

Our term ends next week, not so our troubles, though
this has been a splendid success, and the beautiful surroundings, the space, the freedom, but, above all, the welcome, have

made this time, in spite of the deadly cares outside, one of the pleasantest on the whole I have ever spent. The cares have been the other side of the hills, the immediate circle fresh and free. I have not had, as at Uppingham for so many years, to sit like Job, scraping over boils on a dunghill. It is quite certain we shall stay another term here, and a very good thing too; the climate is mild, and we shall do very well, though some of the masters have done their best to cut the ground from under us. Others, however, have behaved very well. It is wonderful how human nature repeats itself. Read the Exodus and you have a grand example of this in small; the flesh-pots of Egypt are boiling as briskly as in old days still. It is true the Trustees about a fortnight ago were silly enough, in the face of a memorial signed by all the masters, to take on themselves to order the school back without medical authority, and they have trammelled us tremendously, but the Government inspector has delivered so strong a judgment now against the school returning that they will have this week to rescind their resolution. In this hour of trial that has come on me to the full, which I have always denounced—amateur power. . . . There is no dead hand like the dead hand of outside power thrust into the heart-strings of a living work. And we are just catching it. 'Tis a dreary prospect, where success, after immense suffering and loss, means the going back to a place which after all may still be ruinous from the evil condition of its population, the apathy or worse of its leaders, and the foulness of its streets.

July 13*th.*—A meeting to-morrow morning about the water-works; but the fact is, we are all tossed backward and forward in such a way, and kept in such a state of uncertainty and dependence, that all the self-acting vigour is cut out of us. I myself, though the school's existence depends on these water-works, am quite knocked off, and feel so enslaved and tied from outside, that I have no heart for pushing forward anything of the kind.

July 14*th.*—It is wretched work waiting about all day whilst —— at Uppingham are deciding our fate; better far, however, here on the seashore than dancing attendance at Oakham as in old days. About five o'clock a telegram came in with their resolution, that they saw nothing in Uppingham to cause them to rescind their resolution, but permitted us to stay next term at Borth in consequence of the unanimous protest of the masters. It is fun seeing what a sour face they make over it, and are foolish enough to show that they make. . . .

July 20th.—So the fight is over, and the first battle won. The long day's struggle ended, and "happy dreams at last come down on Uppingham by the Sea." Yesterday was a glorious day, bright and hot, but with a good sea-breeze making it thoroughly enjoyable, and a prettier sight than Sir Pryse Pryse's great party and cricket match I never saw. I wish the scene had been photographed. Then the boys presented him with an address and testimonial, and cheered right heartily. Then we sang Uppingham songs. And finally came home after a very pleasant day. A fair ending of a stormy year. . . .

I made my usual speech to the school after the prize-giving, and told them they were living history, and that it was a stirring thing and a great to live it well, to rise equal to their day, and show that they were neither cowards nor fools. I told them their rough schoolroom typified their life: a poor and makeshift outside, but full of vigorous life— more vigorous than in nobler buildings and a more finished shape. Altogether, my heart is so full of gratitude and thankfulness that I cannot feel it. It is too much to feel. It is like an unreality—a dream. Yet much remains to be done. . . .

During the summer holiday, which Thring spent at Grasmere, preparations were being made for a winter campaign at Borth. Counsels of delay still prevailed in the Midlands, and events had justified the distrust of the masters in the local powers. The school re-assembled at Borth on 15th September—only the day before had the engineers begun their work at Uppingham. The prospect of return, even at Christmas, therefore, seemed most uncertain. The hotel and lodging-houses, intended chiefly for summer visitors, were fitted up in order to lessen as far as possible the discomforts of winter weather.

It had been urged that parents would not send their boys back to face a winter under such circumstances on the Welsh coast, but on 25th September Thring was able to record that " the entries exceed the leavings by one—a refutation of the prophets of evil."

He notes, too, the kindly welcome which the school received on its return to its seaside home. Sir Pryse Pryse, for instance, arranged that his harriers should come twice a week to hunt near Borth for the benefit of a portion of the school—a great boon to boys cut off from the manifold appliances for amusement and exercise at Uppingham.

Scarcely, however, had the school settled itself to work when there was an outbreak of scarlet fever.

October 26th.—Once more we are on the sea and the tossing begun. Three cases of scarlet fever to-day. This is very trying. I fear we are in for a severe time. What a hard life it is! However, we are doing our best, and I trust our efforts and care may be blessed to keeping down any great outbreak. But in these evil days these things press hard.

October 30th.—No fresh cases. I trust the plague is stayed, and our prayers have been granted. Not that I would pray to have anything removed that God sends, yet one can pray for help, and if that help comes in the removal of the trial, it is good. But I have learned not to wish to have trials taken away rashly. They are so full of blessing if one can but bear them. Not much trouble in the way of parents. One telegram deserves to be recorded as the right stamp of thing. Mr. Donaldson of Glasgow sent to his son, a new boy here : " Stick into your work and don't mind such a trifle. Tell Bullock that his father agrees with me." That is education. Young Donaldson is not likely to turn out a selfish coward.

While the fears of anxious parents were once more aroused the school had now compelled confidence. A letter written at this time by a parent from Borth to

Mr. Jacob in Liverpool is worth quoting, as indicating the energy with which this new danger was met. It shows, too, how little of the holiday excursion there was about the stay at Borth.

I am truly thankful to say that I found my dear boy progressing most favourably, and the other boys who have had an attack are doing as well as possible. Indeed, I cannot express to you my admiration of the foresight and preparation made in every way; houses prepared in the most admirable manner for any emergency, and accommodation as though half the school might possibly be attacked. Further, they have a number of nurses from the London hospitals, so that I feel satisfied that the boys who should get it are much better off than they could be at home.

I should not think of moving a boy, for the lads I have seen all look so well that I doubt if it will extend further.

Anxieties were great, but they were softened by the kindness of the Welsh people. The school was without a hospital, and could only rely upon the cottagers for the means of isolation.

Thring, after searching for hospital quarters, records the spirit in which his needs were supplied :—

Certainly the nice Welsh people are very nice. I have found great kindness and willing help here. So now I feel somewhat master of the immediate difficulties.

The vigorous measures taken checked the epidemic, and the work of the term went on quietly to its end.

Meanwhile the progress of things at Uppingham was being anxiously watched.

November 1st.—We hear that the drain work at Uppingham has brought out some fearful revelations, and that the Chairman has had to come and see to it, as the workmen refused, near the Workhouse, to keep on the whole day. I grieve to say there is more typhoid going on there. I suppose at last their eyes must be getting opened, but I don't know. . . . The popular feeling at Uppingham, if not stirred up, must gradually find out that we have been most patient, instead of aggressive.

November 27th.—A letter from Dr. Beale to Campbell, which will help us much, saying that of course we cannot go back if there is typhoid in Uppingham, and that the danger in any case would make it far preferable to spend another term at Borth.

November 29th.—Skrine gave me another £100 to-day as a birthday present for the school expenses, making up his whole year's income for the school.

As the Christmas holidays approached, the further news from Uppingham made it clear that no safety could yet be found in the place. A few of the governors were again bent on recalling the school, but Thring was resolute that till the work of purification was complete no such step should be taken. Were the return ordered he would resign. The services of Dr. Acland [1] of Oxford were secured, and his strongly adverse report, coming in on the very day of the final meeting of the Board for the decision of the question, convinced wavering judgments, and saved once more the fortunes of the school.

The New Year opened with a tragic proof, in the death of the Chairman of the Local Sanitary Board, of the danger still lurking in the town.

January 6th.—On New Year's Day the sad and fearful news reached us that Barnard Smith had died of typhoid fever—apoplexy the immediate cause. Poor fellow! he has fallen a victim to his own obstinacy and delusions. It brings home to us very close, " He forgives us our trespasses as we forgive.'

On 21st January the school was back again in Borth for the winter term. In refutation of the

[1] Sir Henry Acland.

prophets of disaster the new entries of pupils exceeded the leavings, and the total number was up to the standard maximum of the school. Thus it had lost nothing in numbers by its great adventure. It was found on reckoning that when they should return, one-third of the whole school would see Uppingham for the first time.

Masters and boys were now trained campaigners, and in spite of many winter discomforts the routine of work went on steadily to the end of the term.

To W. N. Lawson.

January 21st, 1877.

Though naturally very sorry that Uppingham is not ready to receive us, it is an unspeakable relief to me for the sake of the school that we spend another term here. As far as the boys are concerned, there are so many advantages here that they are great gainers, in my judgment, by the change, and by and by they will find it out, if they don't now. There are defects here which in the long run would tell unfavourably on boys who get all their training here, but as a temporary measure for boys trained elsewhere it has been a real good, even if it had not been forced on us. *We* are the main sufferers.

To Rev. A. H. Boucher.

Borth, *February 2nd,* 1877.

In spite of all prophets of evil, and such prophecies go a long way to fulfil themselves, we are two more in number than last term, and fairly settled down here again. It is indeed great expense, and worry, and loss, but then it is also deliverance from utter destruction. And Dr. Acland's decided judgment against our return was too powerful for our opponents to kick against, though they had publicly given out that we must and should return, and that if I did not choose to do so I must resign. That I most certainly should have done under the circumstances, but now that danger is past. It is curious that after so many years' work one's working life should have been on the scaffold, so to say, three or four times this last twelve months, and each time a reprieve at the eleventh hour.

Our weather compared with England generally has been very good, though the great storm on Tuesday morning did much damage by the high tide. The lower part of the village has been turned into a beach, and the water came through many of the houses; 4 miles of railway between Glandovey and Ynyslas have been broken up. It was a very fine sight seeing the sea come in like a great wild beast, twisting and swirling and foaming under the fierce wind. In the afternoon I set all the school at work down the village to help the people, and we did a great deal of good work. This was a grand thing for them to do, and I hope will tend to raise the life here, as well as to make it helpful another day.

To G. R. Parkin.

Borth, *April 10th*, 1877.

I believe I owe you a letter, and I never was more puzzled in my life what to say, or even to know with any accuracy what my real feelings are. Here I am, sitting in the room, with my VIth doing their English school paper, in the *last week* of the stay of the school at Borth. And such a confession of feeling as cannot be described ebbs and flows in my breast. Sorrow, however, predominates. Sorrow at going back to my prison at Uppingham with its bounded roads, its petty annoyances, and its ill-will, and leaving this free bright shore, these glorious hills, the hearty welcome, and the helping hands of the people here. Then there is much dread of the unpleasant business questions that are sure to crop up in our making our exit here; then there is the dread of the resettlement and all its risks at Uppingham; then there are money troubles many, and packing troubles many. On the other hand, there is the fact of our having brought this wonderful year to a successful close, and been permitted to perform a great feat, and have a great deliverance. It is marvellous when one thinks how a year ago we were turning out into the wilderness not knowing where to go, exiled in a moment, with certain destruction if we did not move, and no-where to go to if we did, and now we are bringing back a full school from our camp of refuge, far more powerful than when we set out on our pilgrimage. Many of the Trustee questions too have been settled in our favour. Yet it is wonderful how in England here a few amateurs of one's own rank and station can be set with power over the experienced workmen, as they are. I trust you colonies will succeed in preventing amateurs from being put in authority over skilled work. No court ought to have the ultimate control of any profession, or part of any profession, which has not some professional men sitting on it. You would have enjoyed some of the school excursions here exceedingly ; if for nothing else, there was a strange pleasure in seeing some 200 boys in the middle of school time, as part of their working life, getting a day's run on the mountains, and scattered over the whole of this beautiful country in various parties. Then we have had such fun collecting shells : collecting shells is as uncertain as any other hunting ; and if you could have seen little Buzz and me, you would have laughed heartily sometimes ; or one day the tide coming in, Margaret and I at a floating shell bank, making frantic dabs at the waves, and rushing in and out as far as we dared, and of course sometimes farther than we intended, to secure imaginary prey. We did get some good ones though that afternoon. The elation at discovering a good bank, and the rivalry were often most amusing. I never have had a happy year in my working time, apart from the work itself, before, and this year, when the cares and dangers were not too heavy, the working time has really had a delightful daily life. And now it is almost over, the end has come, and though there is a great sense of a work done, and a danger escaped, there is a great immediate feeling of a free time gone, and of a return to prison.

The picture you draw of your new home is very pleasant, and I think you will like, on the whole, the having the boys in your house. It is so much richer a life than the life of the teacher only : many more cares it is true, many more disappointments, and incessant daily, hourly attendance, but many more interests, and deeper, truer rewards. If you send one of your boys to Oxford, give him an introduction to us, and we will give him an occasional run, if all goes well with us, a week or two at Uppingham, or at the Lakes, or both, and make him feel he is not quite an exile. But I daresay he will have friends in England. I on my side next year shall have two boys in Harvard College, U.S. Trenholm, whom I think you saw, and Warren, Macmillan's brother-in-law, a very nice northerner, who leaves us with a first-rate character. How the meshes of the world do get interwoven now to be sure! We break up this Friday, 13th April, and begin at Uppingham on 4th May, just as you are beginning it seems.

Remember in good house-work more than anything else even, unvarying order in little things is the bulwark against evil, the silently and secretly and unobtrusively framing the system so as to give little opportunity for evil.

I gave an address to the Aberystwith students the other day, but the papers have not reported it sufficiently to send you. I hope to hunt for shells this afternoon; we have a beautiful spring day. . . .

The Easter holidays of 1877 saw the termination of the year-long exile of the school from its home. Masters and boys had won the regard of the people of Borth, and the term closed with a demonstration of their feeling which touched Thring deeply.

April 12th, 1877.—But most of all, and a greater thing than I have ever had in true life, a thing which makes one feel that any adversity may be patiently borne, the people of Borth gave us an ovation last night. They had a procession up the street, halted in front of the hotel, and all the school children formed in semicircle and sang exceedingly well, whilst the school and village stood round. Then the grown people went to our schoolroom and put Mr. Jones of Owen something in the chair—a farmer at the bottom of the village—who made a most excellent speech, really first-rate, and they all bore such testimony to the school: that they had dreaded their coming;

that they soon found their mistake; that no boy had ever done an ill action. They seemed particularly struck that they had never laughed at any one; and if the people of Uppingham did not treat us well, they were proud of us. Altogether my heart felt strong within me as I heard the witness borne to the true life. And I was particularly struck all through, that though the room was full, and in fact it was a complete village gathering, neither inside nor out was there an unseemly act in word or deed. There was complete refinement, no vulgarity, no exaggerated language, but simple, powerful, really good thinking, no speaker showing any vanity or false shame, but speaking in the most genuine way. It was very striking, and it has made me very proud, and happy, and strong within. And, indeed, I wanted strength at the thought of leaving this place and the many troubles that are still round one. . . . Just come in from dismissing the school. I made, thanks to Borth and last night, as effective a speech, I think, and one as likely to last in a living way, as I ever made in my life. And so this grand page of life is turned, and never more do we tread this shore as a school. It is a thought full of sadness to me, the having to go, full also of grateful relief at our having finished in so noble a way on the whole this eventful year of trial. I praise Thee, O God, I acknowledge Thee to be the Lord! O Lord, have mercy upon us!

April 13*th.*—The boys gone, the page turned, the chapter come to an end. How thankful I am. With so many possibilities of evil, so many cankers, so many conceivable accidents. But it has been glorious. . . . The people sang a farewell to the boys this morning. I feel as in a dream; it has been so strange, and is so strange, such a mixture of good and evil. The good, however, most living and strong, the evil shadowy fears, yet sorrow for leaving this place is no shadow. . . .

April 25*th* (Uppingham).—Home yesterday with wonderfully mixed feelings. Thankfulness to God most at a great page closed and turned; intense dislike to the place, mixed with a feeling of home and being master once more in my own house; the old constriction of stomach and feeling of dread, mixed with a sense of no longer being at the mercy of others, and subject to the racket and disturbance of hotel life. A fine day yesterday. Sundry of the Borth people came to see us off. On Monday my Uppingham by the Sea appeared in the *Times*, and so I have been able to give a public return to Borth and Wales, and Sir Pryse Pryse for all the good they have done us this past year. What a strange bit of life it is! how the goodness of those village people has been everything to us, and a light shining out in many lands! Such is a life seed.

May 3rd.—A clear week gone by, and very natural it seems. How strange, how exceeding strange habit is, and the power of habit. All things go on in their familiar track, and the mere familiarity makes them easy, yet I trust there is a great move. The town is really making a grand demonstration : arches and flags all up in the street, and they must have taken much time and care and spent much money in doing it. This calling out of feeling and drawing attention to the school, and creating an interest or deepening it, is a new start in life here internally as well as externally. It is also a signal refutation of the calumnies vented on us last year, and the whole moral atmosphere of the place will, without doubt, be changed in future. . . .

May 7th.—The reception on Saturday night was even better than on Friday, and the whole town was in a wonderful fervour of enthusiasm. Whatever deductions have to be made, a new world has come out in this week, and all the position is altered. For such demonstrations produce the feeling as they go on, and are at the same time a great public pledge forbidding retreat.

And so the year of exile at Borth passed into the fixed traditions of Uppingham School. Congratulations poured in upon the "mobilising headmaster" from many sides.

"I must send you," writes the head of another school, "a few words of heartiest congratulation on your return to Uppingham. In my judgment, your exodus was one of the bravest exploits ever performed, and you deserve to be hung all over with Victoria Crosses, and so I believe you will be in the world of immortal achievements."

" I think your move to Borth one of the pluckiest and noblest deeds I ever heard of, and I am very thankful that God has crowned it with such success," was the message from the head of an Oxford college.

The signal flags, which at Borth, on account of the stretches of noisy sea-beach along which the boys wandered in play, took the place of a bell to mark school hours, were brought back, and now, like the battle flags of a regiment, hang in the Chapel to remind Uppingham boys of this striking episode in their school's history. They are indeed mementoes of a soldierly feat. A military man wrote to Thring :—

" I have always thought that one of the most striking episodes in all school history was the great exodus of Uppingham to Borth. . . . It was one that strongly appealed to me as an old staff officer who had had to deal with the movement of troops on a large scale. I always felt that the operation was akin to a large military one, full of difficulty really, and dependent for success on the nicest organisation."

A little volume of verse, *Borth Lyrics*, embodies some of Thring's thought about this eventful year. There is in it little note of exultation at the success he had achieved. It was characteristic that his thought turned rather to self-examination.

After the return it was determined to have an annual commemoration service for the great deliverance of the school. The chaplain, Mr. Christian, together with Mr. Mullins and Mr. Skrine, had been appointed to arrange the service and select for it the lessons, psalms, etc. When they submitted their selections to the headmaster he at once said : "You must put in the 30th Psalm"; and he went on to explain that just before the fever outbreak, so strong was his conviction that what had been built up could never be shaken, he had practically applied to himself the sixth verse of that psalm : "And in my prosperity I said, I shall never be removed ; Thou, Lord, of Thy goodness, hast made my hill so strong."

Thenceforward as long as he lived, year by year, at the Commemoration Service, he recalled to boys and masters the events of the year at Borth as a proof that God had saved the school that it might do His work in the world.

"There was a day," he says in one of these commemoration sermons, "when our eyes looked on these great walls, and we doubted whether we should ever worship here again. Utter ruin had come, utter and absolute to the life here. We had to go out and, in the sight of all the world, live or die as a school. Few know, very few know, what it is, day by day, to see the giant deadly force of irresistible, invisible ruin drawing closer and closer, and to look straight in the face of overwhelming evil power. There was a day when the school here in this place had come to an end, and when, unless the great venture came out right, all the life we had stored up here was lost; and the good cause, the cause of Christ, which had been our hope here in striving to give each boy true justice in work and play, 'none favouring, none forgetting,' had perished from this hillside. You know it ended in deliverance. Lo! we are here to-day. But that great deliverance is David's second reason for his faith. Christ the Deliverer has delivered this school, and gave it safety at Borth in that dread year, even as David had been saved. Then, as soldiers in the army of the living God like him, and like him, too, holding a life saved by a special deliverance such as has never happened to any school at any time, we are bound to stand faithful and true ; to stand here on our hill, in this our chapel fortress, with the schoolroom at its side—twin fortress homes, the one of holy worship, the other of the work made holy, one great building of God's truth, though two, each upholding the other—we are bound, I say, to stand fast; we are bound to go out from here, calm and confident that none who defies the armies of the living God shall conquer. Sons of the chosen people of England, with its eight hundred years of the shield of God to look to, and with a great deliverance that has made that shield our own, we stand here to do God's will and live or die for Him. Let there be no cowards here."

And again in another sermon :—

In one week's time this present school would have been no more. By the end of one week I, who now speak to you, and others with me would have been taking their last looks of these walls, never more to set foot within them again, and all our life here would have been scattered and gone. I can never forget how the place looked to eyes dim with thoughts like these—eyes that saw all too clearly, and yet as in a vision saw what seemed passing away. You may forget, men may not believe—yea, as time goes on the story may be scorned, and the words that tell it sound fantastic and feverish and unreal. Be it so ; but let none who has not tried think he knows.

One thing is certain, whatever we felt, this school came to its end ; and even as it ended the deep waters parted, and it was saved, and it is here.

It is certain also that a great deliverance, whether of a man or of a society, is a great claim on the life that is saved.

The Israelites carried with them a grand inheritance of holiness and truth. They were saved because of it. As a nation they betrayed it.

I do claim also for this school, that the very deliverance is a grand inheritance for those who come after : a certainty that a truth, which God thought worthy of delivering, is here ; a certainty that it is entrusted with a special mission of life, with a precious germ of holy work which it is bound to carry on. That year at Borth stands alone in the history of schools.

As long as these walls rise in their strength, so long will

they plead with those who worship here : plead with those who were cast out and brought back again, with them and their descendants for ever ; plead for the price that ought to be paid, the price of the life that was given back, the truth and the purity that shall show they were worthy of deliverance, the honest, active power of the sons of a great inheritance, of sons who remember ever that a great gift is a claim for a great future, and that destruction, when it is a resurrection, is a passing from lower to higher life.

Do not betray your life. The school died and is alive again. Do not betray that life.

CHAPTER III

AFTER BORTH

1878–1881

THE year at Borth had been to Thring a period of acute anxiety, but his cares were mingled with keen enjoyment and deep satisfaction. His school machinery had stood admirably the extraordinary strain put upon it. The system established by years of painful endeavour had proved adequate to meet a great and unexpected crisis. Besides this, the year of exile had appealed to all his soldierly qualities—to those sides of his character which often made his friends regret that he had not chosen a military career. On the whole, it may be doubted if he ever passed a happier year of school life than that spent at Borth, though he had gone forth from Uppingham holding as it were his life in his hand; and though the issue of the enterprise long hung in doubtful balance. The freedom of the long line of coast in front of Borth, and of the splendid hill country behind, the bracing air of sea and mountain, the more bracing atmosphere of daring enterprise in which he moved, all gave him a health and buoyancy which he had not known for years before. So we find that it was almost with regret that he returned to the familiar but comparatively inglorious routine of life at Uppingham.

He had still much to think about. The troubles of migration did not end with the actual campaign. When Thring decided upon removal, the main body of his trustees had given but a half-hearted assent to the enterprise. Their official resolution sanctioned the breaking up of the school ; they knew nothing of it (this was the theory expressed by one of their number) till its return. Now that the school was saved and was back in its old home, the question arose whether the masters should be recouped from the funds of the Trust for the large expenses incurred at Borth. It is not easy, and it is perhaps useless to disentangle the threads of a dispute which ended in an appeal to the Charity Commissioners. The reply of the commissioners showed that they had no doubt on the question. It says : " Although the removal of the school to Borth had not the express sanction of the Trustees, yet their subsequent acquiescence in it must be assumed from the absence of any disavowal, from the part they took in the management of the school during the time of its stay at Borth, and from the fact that contributions were made by them out of the Trust funds for purposes connected with its removal.

" The expenditure therefore to which the attention of the commissioners has been called must, in their opinion, be regarded as a liability incurred in the administration of the Trust, and one therefore which may properly be met in some way out of the resources of the school."

It was some time before Thring was entirely relieved of the large financial responsibility which he had been forced to assume in order to carry through his bold policy for the salvation of the school.   It was a period of much anxiety.

February 12*th*, 1878.—It is very strange how all my life I am to be in money difficulties.   Just as I had really a breath of freedom, and was for once quite square, came the scheme and Borth, and knocked me back into debt again.   My bank book shows a deficit of some £3000, and I know not where to retrench save in Ben Place and the summer holidays. That must be given up as soon as possible.   I always think we live expensively, yet as headmaster I do not well see how to cut down any important item.   I do believe that the how to face money difficulties in a good cause is modern martyrdom. But then it is a subtle thing to judge whether one's own personal self-indulgence is not the cause of the pain, though quite certain that there would have been plenty of money if the good cause had been betrayed.

To his money difficulties was added another which touched upon what was to him the most vital of school principles.

February 16*th.*—The Trustees have had to acknowledge the Borth expenses, but have sent an answer through me in which they have, without consulting me (as the scheme enjoins), recommended taking more boys, and thrown in a pretty firebrand amongst my subordinates.   Luckily I have now some staunch friends, and the majority are not mutinous.   It will have the effect, however, once more of showing them and every one in their true colours, and of bringing out and proclaiming on the housetop the principles on which this school has been built up, which they are now trying to pull down.   How strangely different all this is from what one once pictured to one's self in case the work prospered, and we lived to see it !   How much greater the blessing has been on the spirit life, how much keener the pain, how endless !   Yet—

> Be the day weary or be the day long,
> At length it ringeth to evensong.

Against any increase in the number of boys to be taken into the houses and the school Thring vehemently protested. In a letter addressed to the Board he reviews the growth of the school, reaffirms his claim that a strict limitation of numbers is essential to true work, urges that " the Trustees should so arrange the payment of the headmaster as not to make it his interest to destroy the school by raising the numbers above this limit," that it was " also important that the assistant masters should not be advised to destroy the school by taking extra boarders," and concludes by throwing the responsibility for any such action upon the Board.

" Whatever difference there may be on this or that point, the school takes rank among the first in England. It is now in the hands of the Trustees to make or un-make. The times have been full of trouble. For five years or so before the scheme came in force, impending changes made any movement from within impossible. Thus there were five years of inaction with all their arrears of improvements to be made and expenses to be met. Then came the heavy losses and dangers of the typhoid crisis which might well have brought an older school to ruin. That is past, and my responsibility is past also.

" The task is entrusted to you of carrying on a work which, through good and evil days, has steadily advanced up to the present time." He appealed for support to the Charity Commissioners.

May 7th.—My petition has gone to the Charity Com-missioners. Jacob approved greatly of it, and said it was a capital document, and we are now sending out seventy or eighty of it in good quarters. It is a manifesto, the first time I have opened my mouth freely at all in five-and-twenty years. I am very curious to see what the men say who receive it. It will be a considerable test of the characters. How little men in power think they are being judged when they pass judgment ! It is like the gospel invitation to the great supper very often, the judges pass sentence on themselves.

On this occasion the assistant masters heartily joined Thring in protesting against any increase of numbers as an interference with the central feature of the Uppingham system. This support, given at a time ·when almost all the men had been greatly straitened by the successive disasters which had befallen the school, gave him the most unbounded satisfaction, as proving how firm a root his principles had taken.

As the true alternative to the policy which had been proposed, he now used all his influence to secure from the Charity Commissioners permission to make such an increase of school fees as would place the masters in a satisfactory financial position. This point he finally carried, thus saving his principle without unduly sacrificing the interests of his masters.

He took the first opportunity that offered to publicly recognise the stand taken by his colleagues.

July 31*st.* — (Prize - giving). . . . I said three things in my speech that I very much wished to. First, the great honour to the masters of having proclaimed the creed of not increasing numbers in the time of their sore need, that the school might be proud of it as I was. Second, that the Charity Commissioners had given us the most free constitution of all the schools under them, and acknowledged our position. Third, that I regretted Mr. Rawnsley was going to take his general and varied powers to another sphere ; that he had undertaken a well-known preparatory school in Hampshire, which we doubted not would be not less well known for many a year to come ; that as a mother country we ought to rejoice to send out colonies, and that as boy and man long connected with Uppingham none could be a better colonist than he.

Another note in his diary for this year shows how hard it was to get his methods fully recognised.

October 11th.—It was too ridiculous, however, at the end when I mentioned about numbers being destruction to a true school to hear the naïve way in which they (governors) said, with surprise, " Then you condemn several of the great schools." So entirely ignorant are they of this school and all its works. I simply told them that they knew that if I had raised the numbers, as I could have done, I should now have a large fortune, and a much greater public reputation, but that it was dishonest.   I did not mean that the men working in other schools were dishonest, there was much to make them ignorant and keep them so, but it would have been dishonest in me who knew it. . . .

It need not be said that the triumphant return of the school from Borth placed Thring in a new relation to Uppingham.   The little town had learned the value to itself of the school and its headmaster.   He took advantage of the kindlier feeling which prevailed in the place to carry out many plans which he had long entertained.   He had always felt that a great public school given up to the culture of the richer classes, and drawing together a large body of highly cultivated men and women, should make itself a centre of light and helpfulness to the community in which its work was done.

He was elected President of the Mutual Improvement Society of the town, and threw himself into its plans with characteristic energy.   Instructive or amusing lectures, classes in singing, music, and drawing, in literature, cookery, and sewing, were all planned or carried out under his direction or advice.   Cricket and tennis clubs and other means of recreation he helped to organise, in the belief, often expressed, that to give healthful recreation to those who had least of it, was one of the most Christian works to which people's attention could be turned in this busy, mechanical, and often overstrained age. Some of his letters at this period illustrate the spirit with which he entered into this exchange of friendly offices with his townspeople.

To E. F. BENNETT.

January 26th, 1880.

I shall very gladly give you any information.

I do not think the work requires any special influence.

It is based on two or three common-sense principles, and is calculated to work well under very ordinary circumstances.

First of all, though religion is the sole aim and object of it, I have nothing to do with religion in it. We have all been a deal too religious. I mean we have all been trying to get up to heaven without a staircase ; the drawing-room in our house is splendid, but it wants stairs, and the stairs have nothing whatever to do with the inside drawing-room life. Recreation is my object, combining good amusements with good interests and culture.

The name is important : "Mutual Improvement Society" is a good name. Several times members have appealed to the name to prove that they would not do a low thing, and I have appealed to them publicly to be true to it.

Now the whole backbone of such work as we are doing here consists in having a little good regular teaching on an attractive subject, the more of course the better, but if you have not got that it is no use trying to do anything of this kind. We also keep trying to employ people in good games, cricket, football, lawn tennis, chess, draughts, etc. Music and drawing are the most attractive of all subjects, music far above everything else. A good choral society learning really good music is quite enough for ordinary purposes. But then the music must be good, I mean of the highest kind ; nothing has been so successful here as oratorio music. I cannot but think any neighbourhood can furnish teachers if you do not demand too much from them. Our main work only lasts four months of the year. I mean the lectures and other classes; the only thing the year through—that is, barring sixteen weeks' holidays—is the choral class. Then you must not get bad lecturers; any well-informed gentleman can talk on his own subject well, and a man should not deliver more than one lecture a year, unless specially circumstanced, and any subject will do in good hands.

This is really all. A sound backbone of real regular teaching, united with as much good amusement as possible, and with a total and entire absence of any attempt to pull in religion.

In management, I just *manage*. We meet as equals, and have very pleasant committee meetings; I never patronise, but just discuss with them and sum up as one of themselves; above all, I have been very patient, and preferred to let them experiment to a certain extent, rather than shove a better thing on them before they were ready. I have found it very interesting and with very little vexation. . . . I assure you, if you have some attractive teaching, it is all easy; if not, you can do nothing. Lastly, the "Evening" you were at is a great power; it makes them feel their unity, and you do a great favour at a small expense.

To Rev. Edward White.

April 10th, 1880.

You will be interested, however, to hear that since Borth I have been at the head of the movement for improvement in Uppingham. . . . I am ably supported by five or six of the masters. My text is, " Good amusement for the people is the most religious work that can be done in modern England," and we are accordingly hard at it here. There was a Mutual Improvement Society already in existence, of which they made me President; it then numbered 130 members; it now numbers 400. The Rector is Vice-President, the Dissenting minister a prominent member of my committee, and a very sensible good fellow he is. At Christmas we have a gathering in the great schoolroom, when I give them tea, etc., and we have an exhibition of objects of local skill. I have got a first-rate cricket ground going for them, a good lawn tennis club; the young women of the place have two days a week allotted to them to make up their sets, the young men two, and two are open. Then we have athletics. During the winter we undertake to provide a lecture or some entertainment every Tuesday night, first-rate music being part of this. We have evening classes in drawing, arithmetic, history, reading, and two choral classes numbering together rather over 100. We have started a Horticultural Society, and have a show in July, so I think you will say something is going on. A coffee tavern also is just going to be started, and we have a little boys' cricket and football club for boys under fifteen.

I like your plan very much. Many of the attempts to get at people have failed from being "too religious"; we want powerful common-sense exposition of common truths and interesting facts of history and life, mentally, not direct religion, still less mere amusement; that must fail. Interesting teaching, in fact, is the want, and physically we want thorough good games. What a wide field for union this is. I think too such a mistake is made in giving the people parks and merely throwing open public spaces; every inch ought to be sub-let to clubs of all kinds and gardens under a committee, so as to make every one have a private interest in the ground, while the public walks would remain just as free as before.

I am very downcast about the elections, not so much because the Liberals come in, as because I look upon it as the triumph of Billingsgate, the popular reward for the most virulent and empty vituperation during these past two years that it has ever been my misfortune to listen to. That the men who stooped to such meanness should be rewarded makes me feel personally degraded as an Englishman; for such things lower a nation permanently. I admit also to thinking that there is a great principle involved in Imperialism, even what you say, looking to our Empire as a whole, protecting Englishmen and English trade, early instead of late, at a small cost, instead of at a great cost, for I have always seen in large concerns, public or private, that the most expensive thing in the world is a cry for cheapness, and putting the pennywise first.

April 14th, 1880.

Remember in music, it is the only thing which all nations, all ages, all ranks and both sexes do equally well. It is therefore sooner or later the great world bond, the secular gospel, and that is why, though . pitifully unmusical, I set such store on it. But I have been bold enough in our feast week in June to have a band playing every night on the cricket field, and dancing, and it has been thoroughly successful and decorous. You omit, perhaps only in thought as being to you impracticable, that great power "acting" and the stage. Now in the Christmas holidays you may see me dancing nearly every night, and these last two years my family have got up theatricals and given a rehearsal to many of our town neighbours, and an evening to our friends. Now if acting, or still better, "acted readings," were universal, then you have a power for good incalculable. I don't want to leave acting to the devil a bit more than dancing. Good acting is the most literary thing in the world, the most living instiller of new thought and bright brain power possible. I want my children and my boys to know and feel that nothing is unchristian but want of self-control. The philosopher says, "A dangerous beast—human nature—a kicker, a bolter, a very devil ; don't let him go out for a walk, for goodness sake."

Christ says, "A noble, a divine creature is human nature, learn to ride, put him to his speed, spur him to his noblest leaps, but ride him." . . .

And I suppose I ought to be content. But I am so weary, so overmatched, so beset with cares, so worked, so baffled and hedged in that I long sometimes for one hour of the desert or primeval forest, where one might walk and talk without a fool or a knave near to stop or prevent your steps.

We may now turn once more to the diary to follow the current of his school work and thought.

May 16*th.*—On Monday our Borth commemoration ; £35 : 18s. collected, a real collection. Skrine wrote a hymn, and David composed the music ; this was a great thing, as it gave a school life to it apart from me, and had no doubt great effect. I preached and made an historical statement, as well as a religious, and was asked to print it, which I am doing, as it is a contribution to a very remarkable time for school life. Altogether the day went off very well, and made a strong impression, I think. . . . A sad thing; a poor boy, C——, in H——'s house, has just died of typhoid fever at home, taken ill the last day of the holidays. He would have been back, only he stayed away a day for some slight hurt. Had he come back, what a scare it would have been, most ruinous. It makes one's blood run cold to think of the danger we have escaped, and . . . on what a hair our welfare hangs! But ruin or no ruin, God will bring our cause through.

June 29th.—Then I brought forward what I had meant to have made the main thing of the evening, the welding the school into a lifelong corporation, by having a school fund, every old boy belonging and subscribing not less than five shillings a year either to the general fund or to any special object he pleased; that we should have a committee with members in all parts of the world to collect and keep the thing up, and a smaller committee to administer the funds.

For several years after this Borth became his place of holiday resort.

September 27th.—The people of Borth made quite a gala day of our arrival, the whole place was dressed with flags, and a crowd was at the station with a brass band to welcome us, and play us in. And all the holidays through we found the same hearty feeling.

October 11th.—Have been reading Andersen's life. Strangely painful to me from my having had to pass through so much of the same trials myself. Especially struck by his saying that enemies scourge with whips, and friends with scorpions.

October 30th.—Yesterday morning was most important, as I laid down to the school after talking with the masters three great canons: 1st, That nonsense, or making a fool of himself in class; 2nd, Carelessness, or not thinking it worth while;

3rd, Rebellious inattention, or repeating the same fault over and over again, should be, for a boy, supremely penal, and always come down on ; and above all, that every master should insist on having the exact question answered, and never take an answer excepting to that. This is a most common master fault, and most ruinous. It is immense good having got that out.

November 4th.—Yesterday a quiet happy day, though my debt is ever on me day and night. I ought not to be so faithless. God has always shielded me, and He knows I might, humanly speaking, have been rich. I marvel at my miserable, poor, faithless heart that can believe so in the right, and be so tormented all the time by the "shadow of death."

November 10th.—Skrine preached, and took for his sermon the faith of Abraham offering Isaac, pointing out that up to that Abraham's trials had all had some admixture of earthly gain in them, but this was utter overthrow of everything excepting faith in God. Then he drew a short parallel of the boy and young man life, in which all the hardships are connected with personal gain ; but a time comes when the demand is to give up all the personal dream, and he ended with the noble sentence, "Let not the holder of the promise think he can lose it by too much obedience, knowing that God is able to raise it up even from the dead." I knew he had made his choice. And my own heart swelled, and was comforted.

As we came out of singing practice this afternoon I touched him, and said softly, "John, you have grasped the sword to-day, the conqueror's sword ; hold it fast, *ora et labora ;* and he looked very solemn and earnest, and said, "Yes, I know it," or words to that effect, and we parted. How I do feel the power of this spiritual step and bond between us ! How I do feel another onward life set living, and I am strengthened by the sympathy that there must be now that he begins to understand what it is to be true *and to be sacrificed for truth*, as well as by the feeling that the truth has found a champion to carry it on. May God and Christ accept and purify him and us.

November 12th.—This morning at the masters' meeting T—— (who is a good fellow) blurted out that "fellows were doing music when they ought to be doing mathematics." This was *apropos* to nothing, but simply a bit of the old-fashioned Spartan brutality theory *versus* true education. I said I had studied the subject for fifty years both as a matter of human nature and of experience, that a very small part of the day comparatively could be given to learning really hard subjects, and that I gave it as my judgment that the study of hard subjects was greatly helped by occupying the mind with other culture of a less serious kind.

November 19th.—A foggy day and dreary, all the morning I felt very dreary, but after dinner I chanced to see a gang working in the cricket field at levelling, and I went up and took a turn of digging for half an hour, and the exercise did me good, and the sight of the work did me good.   There were two or three masters and five or six of the town digging away heartily, and a fine lot of the field they will level too, and a very different place it will be to them after they have laid their sweat into it well and made it their own, than it ever was before ; and how much good this common work and spirit of helpfulness is !

November 28th.—Have been paying bills, and in con-sequence had my heavy debt more than usually on my mind. I marvel at my want of faith when I remember Borth, and Christ's promise which in these twenty-five years He has so often made good to me.   To-morrow my own birthday ; fifty-seven years old.   Only to think how aged I should once have thought it.   It does not feel so, though, excepting in the one fact of the horizon closing round one with the absolute certainty that the greater part of life has been lived, though what remains may very well be in value and importance the greater part. Bishop Claughton's prophecy, " Thou shalt see greater things than these " fulfilled, as it has been by Borth, may have a much greater fulfilment to come, and I have a strange conviction that it has.

December 4th.—It is a great comfort, though, how the life is advancing in the town.   And the school, I think, is on the mend in many ways.   It is astonishing to myself what a coward I feel, and how these thoughts grip my stomach, and make me feel weak as water.   Can I not remember the five loaves and the five thousand ?   Can I not remember Borth ? Can I not remember the twenty-five years of anguish and protection, which had I trusted fully would have taken all anguish away, for has it not been the "valley of the shadow" only?

December 15*th*.—Somehow I feel more and more that my work is not talk, but working and living, and that this fierce conflict always going on is God's mission for me, though it is less attractive than writing and thinking, and a less storm-tossed existence.

February 16*th*, 1879.—Holy Communion to-day. The worst attendance I ever recollect. My heart sinks to think that the school is no longer religious as it used to be ; I felt that to-day. I suppose now the upward struggle has ceased ; they are being drawn into the school *world* and will imitate the fashion-able vices. "We will be as the nations, as the families of the Gentiles, and serve wood and stone," and forget the pride in truth and trustfulness. Partly to a wave of non-religion and modern non-thought beginning with ——, I think, and certainly culminating in ——, has been passing over us. Partly also and worst by far the intermittent confirmations, with their long intervals, tell heavily against the school life.

February 23*rd*.—David came in in the afternoon and has been at me to write a series of Borth Songs. I shall try and do it. Had a very interesting talk with him about our town work. He is going to give a music master's concert, a Monday popular once a month, and see if we cannot touch the neigh-bourhood. I am quite sensible of the much greater interest that is flowing into my life from these things. I thank God for it. All comes in His good time. I think over three hundred of our parents having paid the advanced terms without a word, all those already in the school doing it voluntarily, is a greater fact, if possible, than the following us to Borth. . . .

I pray we may be kept full of life. When I think of the dictum that has gone forth, that fifteen years is as much as a headmaster can do without rusting, and find, so to say, eternity not too long for the human work of school done in our common humanity, teaching, that is, dealing with the minds and hearts, not lecturing, which is dealing with subjects with logical clear-ness ; when I think how day by day some growth seems to be, something new, and we hardly appear yet to have begun to get true principles on foot, I marvel at the fifteen years' dictum and the blindness out of which it came. God gives us hearts and work for eternity ever new in living power.

March 25th.—A new step to-night in our mutual improvement work, and a most important one. David gave an evening of chamber music to the members, and we had a first-rate and most appreciative audience. It is a very great point getting forward another thing of this kind, where we get hold of the people with an entirely higher type of refined education.

April 11th.—To-night I caught five of my house making a row in their bedroom. I struck two of them, I believe, for the first time in my life, not that I was particularly angry, but to show my contempt and indignation at what they were doing. I am rather puzzled what to do to-morrow with them, as it is a very bad discipline offence, but one of them, indeed two, are very good boys generally, and it was but a lark after all, though if the house was in good order it would not be thought a lark.

April 17th.—Every one of us, I believe, has the conviction that we have been sinking lower and lower in the scale of truth as a school. I feel it strongly. There is less of the hearty, genuine honour and unity that there once was; however, we must begin again, and try to produce it again.

June 3rd.—To-night I had all my class in for a literary talk, saving two, whom I would not allow to come, as they had so disregarded my teaching in class, and we had a most interesting conversation for an hour. It was a great success. Osborne thanked me after, and said he thought he should be able to get on a great deal better after it altogether. I look upon it as a grand invention, and feel sure it will do much. I feel very happy at having set it going, and these two days have brought much to cheer me. I prayed on Saturday morning for some spirit help, and it has come bountifully.

June 4th.—Last night I had my construing class immediately after prayers, and when I came out of that a few minutes past ten met Childs here prepared to make a strong attack on the school caps, talking of sunstroke, etc. I told him plainly I would not open the question, or hear of any change. If any boy wanted special protection he might wear a pugaree by special leave. But that I regarded the want of fixity in school life as a *very serious evil*, and I would not admit of main arrangements which had been settled after much thought being subjects of discussion. No doubt he would say we knew nothing about it, but I had a considerable amount of experience to appeal to, etc. The fact is, doctors do lay the law down in a most one-sided way. They are accustomed to deal mainly with disease, and accordingly, in my opinion, are very often very bad judges of health and the healthy. We do not seek to avoid colds by wrapping boys up in furs, but by making them strong (doctors do wrap them up a great deal too much, and cure one cold by producing two), and so it is in all matters of health, there is a certain risk to be run; the question is, which is the most risky, the undue avoiding of risk, or the striving to make all the ordinary conditions sufficient? Then he went on to a real evil and a very perplexing one—room in chapel. . . . If we turn the servants out altogether it is very evil. They have no proper place in the parish church, which is much too small. And besides they are of our body, though in these days, unhappily, with the daily change and vagabond tone of mind more in theory than in practice.

June 8th.—I felt quite happy for a little time to-day. A letter from Benjamin Kennedy very flattering about my *Elements of Grammar*, asking me a couple of questions, as he is going to publish an introduction to the *Primer*, so some seed is sown. Curiously enough Marie and I were just talking as we were getting up this morning of what might have been done had our first men had any heart really to work with us, and I had said, "Well, God has seen that it was good for me not to reap, but I am sure some seed has been sown," and at the moment this letter was lying downstairs.

June 11th.—A very bitter experience has taught me how deadly a policy is which tries to succeed by smoothing over the declared and proved traitors. It alienates in more than proportion the true-hearted, and takes all the enthusiasm out of truth, and chills back the generous warmth of strong feeling.

June 12th.—I caught a fellow to-day having his exercise done for him, and I have just sent the whole class, and as the boy who helped him was in his house, the whole house in for two hours to-day and to-morrow, and put them in for every Tuesday. This is how I mean to treat these lies, not punishing the individual more than his social circle. They shall learn that lying does not pay if no higher motive stops them.

June 14th.—A fine day. I felt very weary. There is such incessant knocking, and not least the confirmation with all its work, and all its anxiety. To-night I had in the confirmation candidates, sixty-two or sixty-three. Not so many as we ought to have, but our religious life suffers greatly by our not having a fixed annual confirmation. I am so thankful, though, at being able to speak to them and give to them a solemn warning against uncleanness of all kinds. They shall not sin blindly. On Monday I shall have in those who have been previously ·confirmed, and on Tuesday all the unconfirmed. So no boy in the school will be left in ignorance. May God keep us in these evil days. It is a sore trial. Now to bed thankful that another week is past. Yea,

> Though it blow or cold or hot,
> The work goes on and slacketh not.

June 15th.—Very wet all the morning, fortunately it held up a little before three when the confirmation was. The rector brought the bishop as usual ready robed to the chapel. I met him at the end of the schoolroom. The service was very striking. The bishop made an excellent address as usual, and the burst of singing was thrilling. Seventy-six, I find, were confirmed. I feel so thankful at having this day over. It has been a high day and holy to the school, I think. The strain is off me now, for a while now it is over.

June 16th.—Have had in all the communicants, with two or three of the elder boys who are Nonconformists, to-night, and spoke plainly to them of the deadly sin. I feel so thankful at having warned and advised them. May God bless it and pour His Holy Spirit on us.

June 17th.—They treat the money made over by me to the State on a distinct covenant as if they were supreme lords of it, and doled it out to beggars as a favour. It is very trying. There is always some meanness on. How thankful I shall be when God permits me to draw my neck out of the slave's yoke they press on one ! But His will be done. I had much rather have this, which after all is, in the main, a mere kind of streetboy annoyance on their part, than any real evil touching the inner life either òf school or family. . . . Had in all the non-confirmed to-night and warned them against impurity, and gave them some rules of life. Thank God that is done.

June 18th.—This morning in Essington's book I found a kind of sonnet to me, which gratified me very much, as it exactly took the one point in my life which has made my work tell, the never allowing any other thing, however tempting, to interfere with it.[1] . . . At twelve I had a very gratifying thing. One of the upper boys came to me and made a confession, very touching, about his having taken the first step (very slightly) towards, perhaps, harming a younger boy. I have felt exceedingly cheered by this confidence. It shows too, conclusively, that the public opinion on the question must be high, as what he confesses would not have been considered any evil elsewhere. He also asked my advice about religion when doubts came into his mind. I was able to set him at rest, but I shall have another talk with him.

June 19th.—But I see —— will spoil it if he can. He will compromise and be politic. But heart things and life things are not done by policy, but by spirit.

June 27th.—Old Boucher gave me the first money he had earned, £6, for any purpose I liked.

July 6th.—I have felt rather downhearted to-day. The natural reaction of the great work and strain lately. The fever, too, hangs over me, but I will try and be faithful. "Why are ye fearful, O ye of little faith?" I understand it now. How many miracles have I seen and how many deliverances experienced, and yet—I am fearful. To-morrow I have to go to London for a committee meeting. . . .

July 9th.—I begin to breathe freely again. The meeting was satisfactory, all there, and we were pretty unanimous on

---

[1] THE KING OF BOYS.

A scholar reared beside the Thames and Cam
Built up an Eton at his Uppingham.
Whence this success? To make all teaching real
Was, with this King of Boys, life's beau-ideal ;
So, though his bow had many strings, this one
He plied, this always. Thus his work was done,
This made him famous. All should learn from Thring
That he does well, who does his life's one thing.

R. W. ESSINGTON.

the open scholarship question, which was the main subject. Jex-Blake and Wickham gave some exceedingly strong and valuable testimony from Cheltenham and Wellington on the fact that the classical pupils beat the modern side on their own subjects. Ridding also had given up dropping Greek in the case of unpromising or backward boys as a failure. . . . Delighted at Stephenson coming to me to-day to see if we could not do anything towards a playground for the little boys in the town, offering a subscription. So I met him on .our ground at 5.15, and we selected a bit of ground, and we are going to have one shilling subscription for the first member of a family, one penny for every other, and he is going to set about at once getting the ground ready and gathering in his flock. This is very cheering.

July 10*th.*—Much shocked by hearing when I came out of second school that General Fellowes had died suddenly ; leant back in his chair and died. How well I remember him stroke of the Eton boat, the first boat-race between Eton and Westminster that I saw !

July 13*th.*—One more week over, thank God ! quietly and without harm. No fever. I can thank God, too, from the bottom of my heart of at last having given me in a great degree the spirit of being content with my day, satisfied and not restless in the daily work, not looking forward to change either from weariness or ambition. I am thankful for this advance.

July 26*th.*—A masters' meeting this morning to see to leavings and entries and break-up business. An enormous leaving—50 now, and a moderate entry, 27 or 28. If it did not pinch so much I must say I should not be sorry for this. Masters require to feel that their prosperity depends on the excellence of their work. I cannot think the work in the lower classes has been good. The wonderful want of accuracy points to very slipshod work, and I am sure things have been dropping into self-indulgent, complacent, easy-going ways.

July 27*th.* —— came in and said that everybody knew of his thefts, though I had not told them, and that his life here was wretched, and he could not stay. I told him that I should leave that to his father entirely, but it might well be the thing for a true repentance and recovery of character that he should live down the reproach here, and not leave with the stigma on him.

July 28th.—The last Sunday of a school year. A better year, as far as I can judge, than lately has been the case. A year of many trials, and many deliverances, clearing out some of the old difficulties. May God still be with us. My heart is very fearful and faithless, yet I trust less self-willed than it used to be. May God deliver us.

July 29th.—A hard day's work; taken leave of over 50 boys to-night, but I am thankful to say have not had to really reproach any one of them. Things are much better in my class than they have been for some years, and I am in good hope, though I am very tired.

Sept. 23rd.—Back from Borth after a happy time, though less diversified than usual on account of the bad weather. We had our usual friendly greetings and welcomes, and I cannot feel grateful enough for the twelve years following of happy summer holidays we have now had. To-night I will only thank God, who for twenty-six years has shielded my head, and who will still shield it. As I was coming from Seaton to-night, thinking how I had been taken to Borth and brought back in safety, the sense of God's power round about comforted me greatly in my fear for the coming term. Θεῷ δόξα.

Sept. 25th.—A pleasant day in many respects. Some very nice parents here. . . . There was much cheering testimony to the school, which strengthened my heart. I have written to Jacob to tell him I do not mean to take any notice of the examiners' report, and to give some reasons why. Not least that we stand first or second in the certificates amongst all the schools, and that our main work is highly praised. I have read over the report again. It is impertinent and omniscient. Will schools be able to stand this kind of tyranny? I fear no improvements will soon be possible. I could not in early days have borne up against it. Between trustees and examiners I know Uppingham could never have risen. I begin to fear that I shall hardly be able to keep it going. What a queer world it is!

Sept. 27th.—I held the masters' meeting, and read the

examiners' report.   There was little to say about the classical part of it, the main judgment on which, though very nastily expressed, was decidedly good, but there was a severe condemnation of the mathematics. . . . Now came the real gist of the matter.   I prefaced my judgment by saying that there were two reasons which made this a very special time to us : the first, that six or seven years of intense strain and unsettlement, first from the scheme and secondly from the fever, had just come to an end, and that it was idle to suppose that the school, either masters or boys, had gone through such a trying period without strain, which had both made weak points, and discovered them when existing ; and, secondly, that the great depression in trade made it very important to examine our ship well, and see whether it was seaworthy, and that we should as a body be able to present a sound bold front ; that I felt sure that the old principles zealously worked would save us from harm.   After this preface I proceeded to condemn in very strong terms the inaccuracy in reading, writing, and pronouncing words, which I said was so widespread as to have become a school canker, and that it had grown worse and worse, and must be put an end to. . . .

Then I proceeded to say I had a far more serious matter to speak of.   I referred to the unpunctuality of masters themselves, not, I said, occasional yielding to temptation or accident, but deliberate law-breaking and neglect of duty.   I said to explain, when Mr. —— on being spoken to by me for going to Hawthorne's after coming down at ten o'clock, justifies himself boldly by the example of the masters going to get their newspapers.   The disorder must indeed have reached far, and this was deliberate breach of law and open neglect of duty.   How too, I asked, could a man, when an exciting time of war, for instance, was on, go into school in a proper frame of mind with the newspaper, quite apart from the loss of time?   Also, I said, it had reached my knowledge that masters left their class-rooms during school hours, which was as bad, and I myself had had reason to remark on their remaining talking together after I came down from the schoolroom at the same time.   All this was received in dead silence, not a tongue wagged. . . .

[Of a master.]   He has many very eminent qualities,

and, I think, with all his faults of inexperience and want of sharpness of decision, likely, unless put in very difficult circumstances, to make a good headmaster, perhaps a very good one, ἀρχὴ ἄνδρα δείξει, as the Greek says; till tried it is impossible to say whether blemishes are blemishes or defects.

Sept. 30*th.*—And once more, for the first time for a considerable number of years, I have an upper sixth ready and willing to work in a different spirit, perhaps, than I ever have had before. The old louts are cleared out with their sulky, jackass tricks, and I am with a set who come and talk over work, and are friends. This must bear fruit. I heartily pray God to give us a little breathing time of peace and quiet work. What a strange wavering this has been in seeming "sunshine in the fair springtide"! How, too, it has seemed to be school life and school work, and will be judged as such, whereas it has not been school life or school work, but a long fight with danger and tyranny and rebellion, perils within and perils without, with school thrown in.

October 3*rd.*—Had a talk with B—— to-day about his going to Oxford. Sorry to find he has an army craze. I pointed out to him what a monotonous and unsatisfactory life it generally was, and that it was my strong desire he should be of a profession which would raise him, and not he to have to raise the profession. That, indeed, every man ought to be content to risk poverty and overthrow for his beliefs, but that it was well to consider whether the beliefs were worth the risk.

October 5*th.*—I think I always felt so, but I certainly feel now that this effort to push out of good work into government is a strange delusion. I am sure I felt it always. I can well remember my readiness to be anywhere where there was good work, without any hankerings after being head. But no man can live another man's life, and I would not prevent —— for the world from trying his luck anywhere where honest work is possible. But I pity him heartily. A letter from G——. He feels the restraint of the first start much. But this is only the law of all life. The man who won't accept the yoke of work must wear his own, which is far heavier.

October 13*th.*—Made a most stinging and telling speech this morning on the *caddishness* of irreverence. I don't think they will easily forget it. I felt it strongly, and it came out sharp and clear-cut. I could feel it did.

October 18*th*.—The resolutions of the trustees in to-day and the money paid. . . . Now if I was but out of debt there would be no great weight left on working life. How strange it all is! once the work seemed the trial and the weight, and to do the work well the great object of life. Yet for years, not the doing work well, but the being hewn and carved into a greater work one's self has been life. Not what I have done, but what has been done to me has been God's will and training. And faith in the unseen rather than the doing, even what had to be done has been the lesson.

October 22*nd*.—The fact is, bad workmen and workmen of a low type always want to put on this or that (new lessons) instead of making their own work more living.

October 23*rd*.—Saw to-day, in the *Guardian*, the death of Bishop Chapman, my first tutor at Eton, a man who will not have the credit due to him of being the only schoolmaster of his day who admitted the idea of teaching each boy into his horizon, and tried manfully and skilfully to do it under impossible circumstances.

October 24*th*.—I explained what I meant about criticism by saying I respected the fools above all things in forming a judgment, but not after. The fools were most powerful, and I quoted the story of Lord Shelburne consulting old Lord So-and-So always, because after a talk with him he knew what every fool in the country would say about his measures, also Henry's fierce injunction to me to get the misprint on the cover of my *Porson*, "which every fool understood," altered at once, saying it had rung in my head ever since. That I never did anything without having spent weeks or months, or sometimes years, in considering the questions, especially in the light of what the fools would say. . . .

Have been thinking over school finances, and have been much struck here, as is often the case, that the judges are the criminals. If the rise of terms, which was dangerous certainly, does damage the entries, the trustees will shake their wise heads and say they always thought so, but Mr. Thring against their will forced it. The truth is, that their action in the Borth crisis and since so impoverished masters, and so convinced them that there was no hope excepting what they could get hard and fast by law, that it became impossible to carry on the school without a rise, whereas a spirit of help would have rendered the rise comparatively unnecessary.

November 11th.—To-night David's musical evening for the town in the great schoolroom. A very good audience. Drake, the mason, told me the publicans are beginning to complain that the classes and entertainments are taking away their custom.

November 12th.—This morning a letter from the Commissioners on Wellington College requesting me to go on Tuesday and meet them. . . . I suppose something is gained, but I confess I feel some disgust at being sucked time after time, and then flung, like the gay young chafer, flat into a corner.

November 14th.—I wrote immediately to say I had no doubt of his sanity, and that I fully believed now, as always, messages fitted to the mind and circumstances of the individual could come from the spirit world ; indeed, after what I have seen and felt myself in my life in ways as convincing to me as if an angel spoke, perhaps more so, I should be mad not to believe and acknowledge my belief. . . .

November 22nd.—This morning I received a letter from Birmingham saying that a Professor Felmeri from Transylvania, who had been sent to England by the Hungarian Ministry to inspect and report on schools, would visit me to-day, which he has accordingly done ; a little, dark, intelligent fellow. I have had a good talk with him. I put this as a set-off to the Tuesday ὕβρις. I think this will really have some power in getting true ideas out. He is shrewd and observant, to judge by what he says of what he has seen. It is strange in the same week these two school investigations coming to me.

December 7th.—Had a meeting yesterday at Bagshawe's, and settled the schedules of the lower part of the school. May God bless this our work. I feel greatly comforted at getting some hold on the work again. The slight depression in the entries is a thing to be grateful for, as it has brought masters to their senses, and made them ready to obey. Altogether, in the six-and-twenty years I have been here I have never felt so clear, so hopeful as now.　I trust to be able to establish a St. Luke's summer before my winter comes.

December 12*th.*—Had a pamphlet sent me from Willis from Cuddesdon, addressed to the Regius Professor, advocating a celibate brotherhood for India.　Have written him, as he sent it to me, a short quiet statement of a few heads why I think brotherhoods wrong.

December 14*th.*—Preached my last sermon to-day.　Skrine and others asked me to print the two last; so I shall.　There is a statement about life and its true principle which I trust may root in the school, a picture of Alington in them, too, which may be a blessed memory to us.　My examinations have on the whole delighted me.　I have never since I have been here had such good work the whole class through, and I am cheered exceedingly.　It seems at last as if, after all my wasted toil, . . . I was going to see a little scholarship in the school and an upper VI. in earnest.　Moreover, never since I have been here, never in six-and-twenty years, have I spent the last Sunday of any term in peace like this.　I can thank God to-night, and I do thank God from a full heart, for having given me peace, even if it be for the time only, peace in my borders, no great evil in sight, no mutiny able to shake the whole fabric, no enemy from without menacing the school, but peace and hope.　Θεῷ δόξα.

January 22*nd*, 1880.—E—— was so struck with our mutual improvement work, that he has written to ask me for all I can tell him about setting such things going, which I have done. Indeed the thing is simple enough; though religion is the object, there is no religion in it at all.　That is the first thing. We have been a deal too religious, and forgotten how to live in talking about heaven.　Then there must be a backbone of attractive and real teaching.　Music is the best subject, if only one, but it must be good.　Then amusements and no patronage. . . .

For my part I am heartily glad that Johnson[1] has taken me in my most natural self—as up to fun and undonnish,

---

[1] Cyrus Johnson, the artist, who painted the portrait of Thring which hangs in the great schoolroom at Uppingham.　It is to this portrait he here refers.

rather than in the severer character which circumstances have put on me, though natural enough when the work is there. In as far as the picture influences, its influences will be better as showing the genial rather than the sterner side. Any fool can be stern, but to be really hearty is a blessed gift of God.

February 6th.—A curious illustration of the kind of thing we had to deal with came out when C——'s class appeared to construe. A boy of sixteen, not naturally stupid, made an astounding translation, in which he said, "The wild boar pursued the stag to eat him"; then, that he did not know whether it was not that the stag pursued the boar to *eat him*. I then had a chat with him, and he told me he had no idea what a wild boar was like, or what its habits were. A stag he knew, it had horns on its head. I then said, "If you had a stag, what would you feed it on?" He said, "Grass." I asked him quietly whether he was sure that a stag did not feed on flesh, and he answered, "he was not sure that a stag did not eat flesh." This is almost worse than my quadruped whale of old days. Indeed much worse, I think, for how could he have got through life so ignorant of common things? But it is another curious instance of the marvellous ignorance of the wealthy middle class. I am sure in different ways the school is full of such ignorance, and we get blamed for it. In one sense I think justly, for with all the go and movement here it is marvellous how routine and self-satisfied much of the work is.

February 8th.—Nothing strikes one as more curious than the way in which men who have been taken in over and again, on vital points, too, patch up the differences again, not from the higher ground of a great Christian charity which forgives, but does not be cheated again, but from sheer want of character, or worse still, playing with the edged tools of a supposed expediency. . . . Perhaps the reason also to a great degree is a blunting of the moral sense, which on detecting a cheat is angry at the loss or pain and not at the wrong-doing, and so when the impression of loss or pain wears off all is gone, and they are ready to be cheated again, and to repeat the process.

March 1st.—Went to Cambridge on the 28th. The vice-

provost, Austin Leigh, put me up in my old rooms. I had
not slept in the bed for thirty years, and as I woke in
the morning this seemed the dream, and Uppingham, wife,
and children all a delusion, and I lying there with all my
life before me to begin. I was strangely conscious that in
feeling there had been no change whatever in those thirty
years. I felt just as eager, fresh, and, in fact, exactly the
same. . . .

March 10*th.*—This morning I spoke to the school about the
autotypes, telling them they were not mere ornament, but had
a purpose, to get rid of the mean schoolboy idea of lessons,
and raise them to some notion of noble thought and higher
life, and that I hoped by degrees to get rid of all the mean
furniture, and of the reproach that "on every wall and stool
one sees the name of a fool." . . .

A curious instance of the tricks memory may play in a very
busy life occurred to me. Mr. Huddlestone at King's spoke
about the throwing open degrees. I said that my first literary
effort was a pamphlet on it which made a stir at the time.
He asked if it was in '48, as he had just been reading a very
able pamphlet which put Dean Peacock's arguments very well,
etc. I disclaimed all knowledge of Dean Peacock's work, and
thought my pamphlet was earlier, but said I would send it to
him when I got home. When I got home I found, to my
great surprise, that I had written two pamphlets, the second
in '48, the one he praised. I had absolutely forgotten all
about it, though when I read it I remembered it perfectly and
recognised it at once, and all the old lines of thought, and
my pet passages. But I was astonished to discover that I had
totally and entirely forgotten the existence of it till I found it
in my drawer. Certainly the ceaseless rush through a very
busy life of events and thoughts and work teaches one
strange possibilities about evidence.

March 18*th.*—It is odd how no Frenchman I ever met
can look at a question in an impersonal way. He went
off like any number of hot chestnuts. I simply told him
it was no question of right or wrong of his doing his duty
or not, or of the boys being bad or good, but of *skill*, and
that if he allowed the boys to get the better of him in
their struggles he was unskilful, just as a rider who is kicked

off is unskilful, and abusing the horse does not make him a good rider.

April 4th.—It is one of the bits of disinterested upholding of good for its own sake that I have known, and I prize it wonderfully. If those who have higher and truer views would show them, how different the world would be. Or rather, if persons would not so blur the lines between good and evil in practice, how different the world would be. This has cheered me.

April 8th.—Been appalled to-night at the amount of bills to pay. May God have mercy on me, and either take this lifelong burden off or give me more power to bear it. It grips my stomach in the old way so that I was sick again to-night, which I have not been for a long time. It is a grievous thing to be so worked and busy as to be unable to look to one's own affairs, and yet to have a very large circle of necessary expenditure.

May 6th.—A letter from Mrs. Barnard of Yatton to-day, asking leave to make selections from my Uppingham sermons in a way which makes me happy. She says she has read them to the boys and girls in the Yatton N. Schools till she almost knows them by heart, and that no words can express what they have been to her. I am so thankful. This cheers me. It weighs against the fever.

May 7th.—Mr. and Mrs. P—— brought their only son to-day, and I fear we shall have no slight handful in him, as they seem more doting than any people of sense I ever saw, and they seem people of sense. However, we can but do our best.

May 9th.—Yesterday morning met James, the Inspector of Nuisances. He said he thought he had a clue to the origin of the fever at Freer's, and he added that he thought the Local Government Board ought to order an investigation into ——'s conduct. . . . When I think how he, the last of that nest of iniquity, is now brought to justice, it is a fearful thought of judgment, and one to make one pray for an humble and contrite heart, and to pray to have all evil triumph taken away, and mercy only for me and mine, yea, for them also. It is a fearful thought, and all going on in the ordinary sunshine of the ordinary day.

May 18th.—Quite ill to-day of the bank book illness, as I determined to go for them and begin the business of inspecting them. It is a marvel to me how I can be so faithless and so weak. After all these years of peril and deliverance to be full of torment because of a sum of money, even though it be a debt which nevertheless can be paid, is to me wonderful, and yet it is. I am ill from a fact which in my heart I despise, yea, even when I think God may permit it because I am not unselfish enough and economical enough, and that my self-will is punished, still I marvel how it crushes me in spite both of reason and faith.

May 30th.—An excellent sermon from the bishop, and a very pleasant day I have spent with him. He told me a curious fact to-day as illustrative of the way life works. We were talking of the School Home Mission, and he mentioned that Eton was now going to have a missionary clergyman, as Bishop Hobhouse had put up his son to what had been done here. He mentioned the one in the Black country from London, which I understood him to say Bishop Selwyn had suggested to the clergyman in consequence of Uppingham. He said that after a time the clergyman had taken down a number of his poor parishioners to see this Black country parish, and they were intensely interested. Shortly after the zeal of the rich people cooled, and there was talk of dropping the mission ; the poor people said it should not be dropped, and they formed a club to collect waste paper, and made £50 a year by this for the mission. This again roused the rich, and then the Black country parish was so struck by the interest taken that they were roused, and have now a magnificent church and overflowing congregation where no one went anywhere in days before. So flows the tide of blessing.

June 4th.—I am obviously at one with him in thinking everything should be done to win men over and remove stumbling-blocks, only my experience proves that this is not done by allowing evil to think there are two sides to a question. Where evil is involved, there are not. No mistakes of a man striving honestly for good puts his cause on a level with men who are evil, and working from false motives. The victim on the rack does not play the calm game so well as the torturer who is racking him and watching to catch up the least outbreak of gesture or word.

June 23rd.—After twelve Schlottmann came up and gave me a lecture on my policy and behaviour, the gist of which was that I ought to be more autocratical in action and less in manner. I fear there is a great deal of truth in the last statement. I have such a hunted life, and am so worried on points on which my whole existence has been staked all these trying years, that I fear my manner is far too earnest and decisive. I am very grateful to Schlottmann, for it was the work of a real friend done in a real friend's spirit, and few would care to do so disagreeable a task.

July 2nd.—I had the opportunity of giving Hodgkinson his due. I said many that evening would be thinking of Mr. and Mrs. Hodgkinson, who for twenty-five years had done good and honourable work here, and of their approaching departure, that he left behind him memorials they all could see, which would long tell to every eye of him, but few knew that in the darkest hour the school had ever had since the new system begun, in the very darkest hour, had it not been for his faith in the principles and in his courage in running very great risks in setting up a house, the school could not have started, and that we owed the actual start at that time to him, and that every good wish would follow him wherever he now went, and that no one who cared for Uppingham ought ever to forget this.

July 20th.—This morning I gave out to the masters that I had considered the question seriously, and did not mean in future to let any boy go into a house and change it, that no house should be used in this way as a warming-pan for another unless there was private friendship to be alleged. Much harm has been done by masters keeping boys to themselves, and working for their own houses and not for the school, stopping boys coming if they could not get them into their own houses.

July 30th.—Bagshawe to-day came to me and thanked me in the most feeling way for all he had learnt under me ; he said when he spoke to me about teaching I breathed a new spirit into him, and his life here had been full of training and progress. I told him how much I valued what he said, that he cheered me amazingly, that I had poured out my very blood for years seemingly to no purpose, but that now I really felt a new life was coming into the place, and I no longer wished to go as I had done if I could have left without deserting a post which I felt was given me. This is very cheering to me. It was most touching, too, on Wednesday night to hear my upper sixth telling me, sundry of them, "how happy they had been here, *especially in my division,*" scarcely able to speak for coming tears. When I think how I slang them sometimes I feel half inclined to laugh, half to cry, at their affection, but indeed there is much affection between us. And now God keep me and mine these holidays, and increase our power of work. Amen.

September 23rd.—The money, £62, given to the Borth Path this morning without a dog barking. A new world has begun.

September 24th.—Wrote to Borth to-day to say that I had £76 from here towards the path. Heard to-day that Mr. Fryer had been spoken to, was very favourable, and spoke of a road. I have written to counsel a road if possible. . . .

I saw Powell major this evening about a case of bullying in Christian's house. It makes my blood boil when I think how well the fellows are treated here and yet to find them behaving to one another as louts and cads.

September 29th.—Some of the masters going over to-day to the Church Congress. I am not. The Congress I think an excellent thing, as unobtrusively providing by degrees the machinery of an independent church, and accustoming the clergy to move and act. But I have long determined not to go out of my own line in public, and not to be tempted to platform work or writing for the press.

September 30th.—Miss Heutschy came back to-day. I am very glad to have a good teacher, whom I can trust and speak to with the girls. We all like and respect her.

October 24th.—I have felt immensely cheered by my conference with Bagshawe last night. The fact of getting an intelligent man really to work with one at last has revealed to me what a frightful load has pressed on my life all these years of dull, heavy inability to appreciate better things on the part of the men I have had to deal with. . . . I have been thinking, too, of the dreadful state of the great schools, and in one way it nerves and encourages me all the more to believe that God will protect this home of His and not suffer His truth to fail here, and that a day must come when the attempt we are making to do true work will be a saving power in the land. O God, do Thou bless us and strengthen us to do Thy will.

November 20th.—Wrote to Gale this morning announcing his appointment. Telling him I appointed him because I honestly thought him the best man, and that he must uphold my choice by his life. That I knew the danger he could be, either a great help or a great pain, and there would be many lies told, but it would be for him to make his working life overcome all evil. I told him he would have to take the lowest class as private pupils, and that he must never consider his work ended if he could get on a stupid or backward boy by more. May God bless this choice and pour His Spirit on my son, and make him a son in spirit as well as in the flesh.

December 3rd.—Liberalism certainly is a nasty kind of slavery as times go.

December 7th.—Went for my bank book to-day, and am weighed down by the amount of debt. My publications have certainly been an additional expense, but still it is a fearful burden, and as to the expenses, so few of them pass through my hands that I don't know what to do, and my public position makes it impossible to control expenditure as a private man can. But I will trust in God. He sees it is best for me to be kept thus low, for often have I seen His hand directing my lot, and good has always come from the pain. Yet it is pain, very great pain. And how far it is my own fault or not makes it greater pain.

December 11th.—A strange feeling of rest in the midst of cares, as a man might feel lying on a moss bank in a bramble brake after having been plunging through it. There is, too, a strangely solemn feeling of blessing come on the work, of true progress, and overshadowing wings. Even if it be for a time only, I have peace in my borders, no great evil in sight, nothing able to shake the whole fabric, no enemy from without menacing the school, but peace and hope. Praise God.

Christmas Day.—It was very strange being at Eton. I had not been there for twenty-seven years since I was last there as poser. Young of Sherborne and Butler of Harrow were at the Provost's. Joynes dined there, and I sat next old Dupuis, eighty-four years of age. Durnford was at dinner also. Carter and Mrs. Carter, whom I have not seen since I was in Italy with Henry on my first travels, I believe. The whole scene was to me weird and dreamlike in that strange, weird room of old days.

January 11th, 1881.—To-night, as I was thinking over some of my sermons, owing to an observation in a letter to me, it suddenly struck me how years ago I had felt as if I should like to go out into the world as a missionary of the Holy Ghost, the Spirit of Life; well, it suddenly struck me how all these years I have been, according to my powers, such a missionary, and that God has chosen me, unknown to myself, to do it. Oh may He carry me to the end.

January 20th.—The social evening came off on Thursday, a bright night, snow on the ground, and it was wonderfully successful; 299 present. Five parishes sent in something or other to exhibit besides Uppingham. The Cottage Cookery prize was won by Mrs. Nichols, who gave us a capital dinner of soup, meat, potatoes, and bread at twopence a head. Mr. Rossiter was indefatigable in the arrangements, and we had some excellent water-colour and chalk drawings, his own oil painting for the Academy, which is very good, and our shop pictures, as well as art needlework. We gave a prize for needlework to domestic servants and to the National School girls.

January 23rd.—Mr. Rossiter has undertaken to decorate the schoolroom. This will be an immense onward step in educational power, the making the lesson-place refined and fit for true teaching, making it teach refinement and high thought instead of mean and slovenly habits.

January 25th.—I see clearly had we succeeded earlier that the whole life would have gone out of the place,—indeed, it was almost gone out of the place, I felt it to be,—and the school have become a mean commercial scramble; but now that the shadow of death has been on us all, and the great obstructions removed, I trust the resurrection time has come, and that my feelings are part of the resurrection life. May God bless and keep us, and make us true missionaries of the Holy Spirit. This morning I was greatly delighted by hearing that little Francis Harmon, who was ill last term, burst into tears at seeing his brothers coming back to school because he was not yet allowed to go. Truly to have drawn tears from a little boy's eyes because he could not come back to school is something worth having lived for, when I think what bitter tears I shed at having to go back at his age.

May 22nd.—The Comptons came up. I had a very nice talk with Compton himself. He said the masters in order would like to take some part in the service. I said I always in my second cycle asked some of them to preach, but that I would have no routine or seniority. He said he would like to take the prayers, and so would some others. I said they should do so. I had not asked them for two reasons : one that I would not put on them what they might think work ; the other, that when young I had had a notion that the service was despised by dignitaries who did not take their part, and that I was determined that no one should accuse me of despising God's service rightly or wrongly. I am so glad he has spoken.

May 24th.—This morning the great question of the room decoration. . . . It all went off capitally, no jaw. All the masters present practically gave their guarantee, and I went to Mr. Rossiter when I got out of school and gave him the commission at once. A memorable fact in the history of schools. A very memorable fact. The painting is now hung up in the schoolroom, and on Saturday I shall make my appeal to the school. Thank God.

May 26th.—This afternoon the Coffee Tavern opened. It is very nice, and has every prospect of doing well, I think, from what I hear. At all events this earnest effort throughout all England to make the life of the poor more cheery is very striking and full of hope. I let loose the idea of decorating the National schoolrooms, and making them places of eye education.

June 9th.—This morning unusually pleasant letters. One from Brind in India, very pleasant, with £6 life subscription

to the Old Boys' Society for himself and brother.   One from
Percival, Trinity, Oxford, asking me to take an evening sermon
at St. Mary's next term at the special services held for the
men. . . . Pleased at the recognition, it gives me confidence.
Then I had a most cheering letter from Mrs. Marriott, sister
of the two Gibsons who used to be here, entering her *five*
sons, speaking of the way her brothers always talked of
our work here, and her own admiration of her brothers' characters.   I do not know that I ever had a more delightful
morning's post.   I had on Tuesday a very nice letter from
the Bishop of Oxford, quite in the old friend's style.   I have
answered it in the same strain ; it will be curious if we meet
at Borth. . . .

Altogether I feel a new life.   The days no longer drag
full of fear and ever-watchful expectation of treachery and
evil.   I almost feel buoyancy.   It is another world.   I can
scarcely believe the new security and peace.   I now have
time to work and think of work instead of being hunted like
a wild beast.   Thank God.

June 17*th*.—How strange that a few country squires and
parsons with a dash of *ex officio* magnates should be set in
supreme authority over the available funds and the work of a
body of men like the staff of a great school.   And so besotted
is England that the absurdity of it seems to strike no one.

June 21*st*.—A very nice letter from a schoolmaster near
Carnforth, saying he has made my book on Education the
standard of a higher life ever since he began.   This
cheers me.

June 26*th*.—I am surprised beyond measure at the result
of the cultured family.   There he is full of thought, interest,
and true and noble views of life, not a bit priggish, holding
his own steadily but gently, asking the most intelligent
questions, and expressing the most striking opinions.   I
am fairly astonished.   I really have very seldom met so
intelligent a companion, and yet he is not strong in knowledge, and in school decidedly on the whole mild.

July 2*nd*.—I had a glorious bit of spiritual comfort that
day ; —— came in ; he had left much suspected by me and
implicated in some evil.   He is now a clergyman, and he came
to say he had often written to me, but always torn up the

letters, and now he did not know how to speak. I told him he need not speak, it was written on his face that he had risen to higher things; and after some comforting talk to both of us, when he got up to go, he stood with tears in his eyes, and said "he owed his life to me, and all he hoped for and was." Truly it is worth living for to have but one such witness. Thank God for it. . . .

Two very cheering things to-day. Tuck showed me an extract from a paper to-day containing an account of the launch of a ship by a great building firm at Middlesburgh, which has been named *The Uppingham*. Fair be her future. We don't know who is behind in the matter, but it is a bit of fame and valuable as such. Then that good fellow ——, the son of the tanner here, comes in after dinner to tell me he has just won the first class Common Law scholarship of £105 at the Middle Temple, and to consult about going to Cambridge, as he is now only twenty-three. I have asked him to dinner to-morrow night. He is just the stuff winners are made of, clear-headed, earnest, persevering, and full of work. He will be famous if he lives. So ends the week rich in all manner of encouragements.

July 3rd.—The more I think it over the more I am struck with the new world in which I now live, and the blessings that are being made visible to me. This week has been so rich in varied bits of comfort, and there is no jarring note. One moves amongst the masters so secure and at ease, and not on the watch any more for the next plot or stab. Tuck preached a good, manly sermon yesterday. He took over a strong eleven from here to play Oakham, and beat them.

July 4th.—Tylden came in with Marie as I was sitting in the shade, and began talking philosophy, and set me going. I think I have given him something to ponder for many a day. He is worth talking to. I could not help being struck to-day that for the first time since I have been at Uppingham I have been able, as it were, this term to sit down and look at the work and take in some of that new creation of happier life and power which God has permitted me and Marie to create in this school and town.

July 5th.—A meeting to-night, the rector in the chair, set going a Building Society, a grand fact. Penny Savings Banks and Building Societies, and life insurance of the poor (if Lord Carnarvon succeeds) are to save England.

July 7th.—Mr. Martineau told me to-day how greatly he had been struck by the old boys at Cambridge, their appearance and manners, which led to some interesting talk with him.

July 17th.—Have been much troubled in my heart about my debt, but God has given me a more restful spirit, and increased my feeling of faith. Sure I am that whatever mistakes I have made in practice my main plan of life and trust in Him has been right.

July 27th.—The best examination I have ever had for the work of my class as a whole; the lower half have done so well. Bishop Mitchinson here to-day, with such a nice young black son of the Bishop of Hayti. I got him to make a speech, and he delighted the school, and touched me almost to tears, by his once more in the most manly way recounting how he first came here in search of school information. After the concert he came up, and said he had a petition, that he wished to be more connected with the school than just his confirmation visits, and would I let him preach once a term to the school. I was only too glad. It is so cheering having this sense of ready help. How wonderful is the power of mere good-will! My whole life here is sunshine by this feeling of his helpful presence near. Indeed, there has been much to cheer to-day, much "testimony to the life of the school."

September 19th.—Back from Borth to-day. Scarce two hours here, and yet Borth and the holidays might be a thousand years away already, so strange is this marvellous life. It is like awaking from a dream. But which is the dream and which is the waking, God only knows. Every day more and more makes shadowy all I ever thought or knew, all I once thought I could judge. The only thing that stands fast is the pressing onward to strive to serve Christ. Though what is Christ's service, plain enough in my own case, becomes more and more doubtful to me in the case of others. These holidays, wet and uneventful as they have been, have been the most restful to me of any that I have ever passed. Our stay at the hotel answered on the whole perfectly. I finished my translation of Agamemnon to my great pleasure, though I cannot afford to publish it. I have also rewritten the first four chapters of *Life Science*, which, please God to grant me health and inspiration, in two or three years I hope may be ready for the press. Then the Bishop of Oxford, my old school friend Mackarness, with all his family, spent six weeks at Borth, and we renewed our old ties, and all of us were delighted with his family. Mrs. Mackarness is particularly pleasant and attractive. Things at Borth go on gradually. We opened the Uppingham Path which connects the shore with the hills, and I have had four seats put up, three with inscriptions to perpetuate our memory. This pleased me much, besides being a great boon both to visitors and country people.

September 28*th.*—Exceedingly pleased with my new class in construing. There was an elastic spring from end to end, a life in answering, a real thought put out from top to bottom unlike anything I have ever had. What I have always aimed at and never succeeded in getting in the least, till I began to think it impossible, but certainly I had it to-day. Oh, may it continue. The school time is a real pleasure to me.

October 5*th.*—To-day four boys, Jackson major the chief, have taken the new division of the aviary. I am much pleased with this, every new occupation of an intelligent eye-opening kind is a gain to the school, and this will make the aviary more practical.

October 14*th.*—I have lately had brought home to me in a very strong form a truth which has been in my mind many years, of the utter vanity of writing histories of complicated things, until I begin to hope that no one will write the history of this school and me. . . . I can see how the moment truth is told, all the old evil will rise in self-defence and repeat the old lies ; and the white-washers, who do not want anything to be very good or very bad, will be busy to reduce the fresco and the mouldiness on the wall to the same colour, and not least, any contortions or mistakes done by the man on the rack will be set down as his blemishes, whilst those who racked him escape. It is easy to be calm when you twist your neighbour to death, and men being twisted to death do not act with exactly the same power that belongs to them when at ease. The power may be very great, but it is all used up in simply bearing the pain at all, but little is left to work with. Then, again, who can tell all that process of growth in life and casting off delusions which result from the crucifixion of the lower self?

October 16*th.*—A beautiful day. Finished my course of sermons to the school to-day. They mark a new era. I know not how, but hitherto I have felt to a great degree, " How can I sing the Lord's song in a strange land?" so cruel and hard did the tyranny and lying-in-wait press on my spirit. This term God has given me a new power, and to-day in giving the school a cause and a standard I quite felt before I went into chapel that as I did so God's angel would fling out the folds of the banner all unseen in the chapel, and at the appeal to the truth of the stupid and backward, the standard would be planted and the great flag stream out. I think I shall never see or think of the chapel again without in spirit seeing the angel's standard floating there.

October 28*th.*—A satisfactory day. Moreover, a revelation of Scripture truth about God the Holy Ghost has shaped itself, and been borne in my mind to-day, a truth which has been flitting near me for some years, but to-day has become a living presence with me. I thank God.

November 3*rd.*—" The ambition of being the most trustworthy school on English ground."

November 8*th.*— Came back from Cuddesdon yesterday, after a pleasant day as far as Cuddesdon was concerned, but I never feel quite at ease when away during term time even on duty. Got into Oxford at 1.35 on Saturday. Called on Boyd, Harper, whom I saw for half a minute, Miss Wordsworth, and as they were all out, I had time to spend an hour at Dr. Acland's before driving over to Cuddesdon. A beautiful day on Sunday; had a chat with Canon Furse, whom I had not seen for forty years, and a very pleasant walk with Charles Mackarness, and Bertie and King and Sarah and Daisy Mackarness. Then in the evening was driven into Oxford for the sermon. I was extremely struck with the congregation; the great church was full of men, whereas I had thought that if the ground floor was filled it would be a good congregation.

I know I had something to say to them, so whether my sermon was a popular one or not I felt the message would reach some.   Next morning came in with the Bishop and Mrs. Mackarness by 2 P.M., and had a long talk with Miss Wordsworth, and went over Lady Margaret Hall, and started home at 4.35.

November 26*th.*—Mahaffy has done me the honour of mentioning me as a great authority on education in his last book, which has just been sent me.   This pleases me.

November 29*th.*—My birthday, a happy day; yesterday my blind lecturer, Mr. Marston, came in the middle of the day, and was a most interesting guest, and gave us a most telling lecture.   The school was quite taken, and when the iron was hot I struck, and suggested as he had before spoken to me of a scholarship of £30 per annum from the school to the Blind College.   This morning I got a very nice birthday letter from Mr. Birley, reminding me how seven years ago at this time the hymn book came into existence on my birthday.   I wrote back and told him of this gracious new birth of the scholarship, the first of the kind, as our mission in 1869 was the first of its kind.

November 30*th.*—Very much delighted with a letter from my dear mother in great praise of my Oxford sermon, which she is greatly struck with.   This pleases me exceedingly.   I was much gratified, too, to hear that Charles Mackarness too was much struck, so now I am sure that the message I felt I had to deliver touched the right people.

December 5*th.*—Had a grateful letter from the Blind College.   I am very thankful for that episode.   Have for some time been thinking over making an appeal to the school to have a definite foreign mission, when I got a letter from Mrs. Christian, asking if I could not do anything to help her father, the Bishop of Brisbane.   So I have been conferring with her, and hope to start something.

December 17*th.*—On Sunday night I had a serious talk on life and principles of heart and intellect with Miss Heutschy and Sarah and Margaret, which comforted me.

December 25*th.*—Back from Wellington yesterday, a successful Conference.   They have got into the habit of doing the only thing that can make the Conference do good work, referring matters to the committee with large powers. In this way the committee collect information, and as true results of what the men really think is arrived at as is possible. . . . Wellington itself ought to be razed to the ground. I never saw such a perversion of structure.

CHAPTER IV

METHODS AND IDEALS

THE merit which Thring would have most distinctly claimed for his work at Uppingham was its pains-taking adaptation of structure to training purposes. To this he attached supreme importance. The "almighty wall" was, as has been said, the phrase into which, after his manner, he condensed his view of the vital nature of this question of school structure.

Whatever men may say or think, the almighty wall is, after all, the supreme and final arbiter of schools.

I mean, no living power in the world can overcome the dead, unfeeling, everlasting pressure of the permanent structure, of the permanent conditions under which work has to be done. Every now and then a man can be found to say honestly—

> Stone walls do not a prison make,
> Nor iron bars a cage,

but men are not trained to freedom inside a prison. The prison will have its due. Slowly but surely the immovable, unless demolished, determines the shape of all inside it.

. . . Never rest till you have got the almighty wall on your side, and not against you. Never rest till you have got all the fixed machinery for work, the best possible. The waste in a teacher's workshop is the lives of men.[1]

[1] Address to the Teachers of Minnesota.

The individual study for each lad; the individual cubicle in the dormitory; the house, limited to thirty boys, with its separate grounds and domestic arrangements; the chapel and large schoolroom for a common school life; adequate appliances for manual employment, for amusement or recreation in leisure hours; all these entered into his idea of the "almighty wall"; his belief that nothing should be left to be done by masters which could be accomplished by the ordinary structure of school buildings and appliances.

Out of this central idea, as he often said, Uppingham had grown by a natural process of evolution.

There is a large percentage of temptation, criminality, and idleness in the great schools—a moral miasma—generated by known causes, and as certainly to be got rid of even by mere mechanical improvements—a little moral drainage—as the average sickness of a squalid district. . . .

Bullying is fostered by harshness in the masters, and by forcing boys to herd together in promiscuous masses.

Lying is fostered by general class rules which take no cognisance of the ability of the individual to keep them; and they cannot do so when each boy is not sufficiently well known for his master to understand, sympathise with, and feel for him.

Idleness is fostered, when there are so many boys to each master, that it becomes a chance when it will be detected and a certainty that no special intelligent teaching and help will be given, or indeed can be given, to the individual when in difficulty.

Rebellion and insubordination are fostered, when from the same causes many boys who are either backward or want ability, find no care bestowed on them, are obnoxious to arbitrary punishments, have nothing to interest them or give them self-respect, and learn in consequence to look upon their masters as natural enemies.

Sensuality is fostered, when these and like boys, from the same causes, are launched into an ungoverned society without any healthy interest, anything higher than the body to care for (the mental part being unmixed bitterness), thrown on their own resources, or want of resources, often exposed to scorn in school, whilst the numbers and confusion give every hope of escaping detection.

The atmosphere of schools is, in consequence, in all their out-of-the-way regions thick with falsehood and wrong; no more necessary, however, than a fog on an undrained field when the country round is clear, but considered necessary by the old-fashioned farmer because it has always been so.[1]

The contrast between school life as he had known it as a colleger at Eton before any work of reform had begun there, and what he lived to make it at Uppingham, best illustrates what he here says of the efficiency of structural appliances to forward intellectual and moral purposes. Throughout England in Thring's time schools had, no doubt, been gradually perceiving the truth of these ideas, and had been reforming themselves on many points of structure. How far this was due to his outspoken discussion and his example, and how far to other causes, it is not easy to say. The singularity of his relation to the question was that from the first he fixed upon final principles, framed a complete plan based on these principles, and then resolutely carried that plan into execution.

He certainly challenged attention distinctly enough to this constructive work. In a letter to the Hon. W. E. Gladstone in 1861 he says :—

. . . I believe I am correct in saying that no great school in England has any system or machinery established for dealing with each individual according to his powers excepting that which exists here.

[1] School Statement.

"Truth in schools" was what he significantly called his first manifesto on the question of school structure. To the main principles of that manifesto he adhered to the last. "Talking of truth, and honour, and trust is one thing, and having the structure true, and honourable, and trust-deserving another."

From the elements of true educational structure of which we have spoken he went on to other things.

"Honour to lessons" was a text from which he constantly preached, and it represented what he tried to carry out in practice. He believed that as far as possible the surroundings of school life should be noble and beautiful.

"Another grave cause of evil in schools," he says, "is the dishonour shown to the place in which the work is done. Things are allowed to be left about, and not put away when finished with, great roughness is permitted in the treatment of the room and its furniture. Yet there is no law more absolutely certain than that mean treatment produces mean ideas; and whatever men honour they give honour to outwardly. It is a grievous wrong not to show honour to lessons and the place where lessons are given."

"Honour the work and the work will honour you," was the epigrammatic form into which he condensed his thought. A noble schoolroom in which to meet or study seemed to him as useful in training the minds of boys as a noble chapel in which to worship. In his earlier days at Uppingham he employed photographs; at a later period he spent a considerable sum on autotypes to beautify the walls of the class-rooms.

In a letter he says :—

I have just got a new forward move. You may remember perhaps the photographs in my class-room and the idea of culture through them. Well, I have got twenty-six magnificent autotypes of ancient art in upper school now, and I mean to turn out by degrees all the mean furniture of the room, and I hope that this will make the low views and meannesses connected with lessons and learning drop off by the mere force of fine surroundings, just as good surroundings have made the whole domestic life of the school higher, and freed it from tricks and petty savagery. . . .

Some years after the great schoolroom was built he resolved, by the decoration of its walls, to illustrate more fully what he meant by giving honour to lessons. This decoration was carried out at a cost of some hundreds of pounds under the direction of Mr. Charles Rossiter. The room was formally opened for school purposes in 1882.

In his wish to stamp his idea upon the mind of others Thring made the inauguration of the room a high festival. Old boys and distinguished visitors gathered to show their sympathy, and Lord Carnarvon, who presided, was able with grace and truth to express his doubt whether, since the days of the painted porch in Athens, "training had ever been installed more lovingly or more truly, or in a worthier home." The occasion received a good deal of public notice, and speaking of it Thring says :—

"It was, I feel sure, a great birthday, and bringing into the light of day the grand principle of working with fit tools, and of having everything for the young as good as possible."

An old friend, after visiting Uppingham and seeing the decorations of the schoolroom, wrote to him :—

For my part I am a sad unbeliever (or at least a sceptic) in the effect of Pompeian red, as compared with cut names, and ink-stains ! I believe in the men, and the minds, and the courage, and the love, and the faith, and the blessing of God, which have made your school a great school and a good school. But you will forgive and overlook the scepticism and join cordially in the adhesion which I render.

The reply is characteristic :—

You don't mean what you say about the old meannesses. You only put out in a rough way the surface thought.

When St. Paul had God's express promise that he and the whole crew should be saved, he did not hesitate to say to the centurion, "Except these abide in the ship *ye cannot be saved*." God's blessing only rested on man's right use of means. God did not think it beneath His majesty to give special orders, during the time He was training and educating His people, as to the material and making of robes, the colours of ribands, the artistic disposition of a fringe. Everything was made according to the pattern shown by God. God filled with the spirit of wisdom the men who were to make Aaron's garments. And the workers in gold, silver, brass, stones, timber, embroidery, needlework, etc., are expressly said to have been specially inspired by God during the schoolmaster period of the Law.

Now I unhesitatingly assert that my own work has succeeded with the many just because God gave me a spirit of wisdom to attend to fringes, and blue, and purple, and scarlet ribands, and Pompeian red, and autotypes, and boys' studies, and the colour of curtains to their compartments, and a number of little things of this kind. And I lay claim to have been great as a schoolmaster on this, and on this only, in the main ; on having had the sense to work with tools, to follow God's guidance in teaching beginners by surrounding them, as He did, with noble and worthy surroundings, taking care that there was no meanness or neglect ; getting rid, as circumstances allowed, of name-cutting in school, which means "rebellious inattention, combined with mischief and vanity," or ink-splashing, which means "careless dirtiness, and contempt for the great thought-work" ; and all the little vilenesses which drag the boy-mind down. It is a slow process, but it is a true one ; it is not grand, but it is practical ; it needs patience, but it works by degrees higher life. May men think of me as one to whom God gave a spirit of wisdom to work all manner of work of the engraver, and of the cunning workman, and of the embroiderer, in blue, and in purple, and in scarlet, and in fine linen, and of the weaver, even of them that do any work, and of those that devise cunning work. I take my stand on detail.

The same lesson he enforced wherever the opportunity presented itself. In an address to the Teachers' Guild in 1887 he says :—

It is hard to escape something of the pig if lodged in a sty. The schoolboy has not escaped, and never will, till "Honour to Lessons" is the first article in the nation's secular creed. Everything that meets the eye ought to be perfect, according to the work and workers, as human skill can make it. Give honour, you will receive honour. I know that boys respond with honour when they and their life-work are honoured. . . . Honour to lessons is the first article in the teacher's creed.

Of the burning enthusiasm with which Thring began his teaching career he gave a vivid picture in an address to the Education Society in 1885. Speaking of his own teaching work while as yet he was only gathering experience in the national schools, he says :—

Many able men, Archbishop Whately amongst them, were at that time earnestly striving to put teaching into its most telling shape for the short-timed poor to get at. Indeed, a new epoch had come. For the first time in the history of the world, there was a demand that everybody should get some teaching of a regular kind. So not only the freedom of the work itself, and the fascinating novelty of untried ground, and the zeal of such fellow-workers, and the feeling of enterprise, discovery, and life was full of attraction, but a national crisis of the most momentous kind had come.

The air was full of hope, and bright with possibilities ; new opportunities under new conditions had arisen, and everything pointed to a great new birth of teaching power. Something efficient had to be done to make every child in the kingdom an intelligent worker in life, in spite of lack of time, or lack of brains. That was the problem. Some thought it could be solved. And if the elementary schools could be made to do it, a new era had set in.

There was a fair field. It was clear that with the short time that could be given, and the material to be dealt with, much knowledge was impossible; but mind might be roused; interest might be awakened; a sure path might be laid down; a path into a new world, which should tempt those who set foot on it to go on. There might be a feeling of gain produced, a feeling of things pleasant in the getting, and pleasant in the having. Mind was there. Why should not mind be dealt with? What was to prevent the exercise of new senses? of eyes taught to see and ears taught to hear? The rudder-strings of voyages through peopled worlds of mind-creations, the power to move, the hope to excite movement, pleasure, happiness, seemed within range. At least, it was not too much to hope, that the narrow walls of the dull prison, in which the omniscient ignorance of the village pot-house hero dwelt, might be broken down, and the vast beyond, with its mysterious humility of infinite delight, get a chance of being seen, or at least believed in. And if by degrees this living teaching prevailed in the schools below, and mind-power became mind-power indeed, what might not be credible in the future, when better methods and free, unfettered skill should begin their upward push, and simplify all the processes of learning? Enlightened growth by growing would displace worn-out systems; and thought and mind be moved on to their rightful throne; and intelligence, with memory as its day-labourer and servant, be lord of all in the schools.

Everything seemed possible in that dawn of liberty to work, that breaking up of the tyranny of knowledge, that wakening of love for working, and that new field for working love.

If there was no time for piling up knowledge, there were minds to be trained, and lives to be set free. And education might rise, a resurrection indeed, from the folio sepulchre in which it had been so long entombed.

From this quotation it may easily be inferred that Thring's teaching was not of the cut-and-dried type.

His whole teaching life was a protest against rule-mongering and its dry-as-dust methods. He dreamed of breaking through the monotony of the teacher's life, the treadmill round of mere preparation for the examiner, which is so apt to dry up and narrow mind and spirit in both teacher and taught.

In one of his school papers he is at pains to distinguish between the true and living teacher and the machine teacher, or, as he calls him, the hammerer.

The teacher deals with latent powers.—The hammerer hammers in a given task.

The teacher considers the worse the material, the greater the skill in working it.—The hammerer hammers at the nail, and charges the material with the result.

The teacher knows his subject to be infinite, and is always learning himself to put old things in a new form. — The hammerer thinks he knows his subject, and that the pupil ought to know it too.

The teacher loves his work, and every day finds fresh reason to love it.—The hammerer hammers at his work, and finds it more irksome every day.

The teacher thinks nothing done till the food he gives his pupils is digested and craved for.—The hammerer thinks everything done when he has hammered at the nail a given time.

The teacher encourages.—The hammerer punishes.

The teacher has faith in great principles.—The hammerer is the slave of little vexations.

The teacher is a boy amongst boys, in heart; in judgment, a man.—The hammerer has the hardness of a man, with the want of thought of a boy.

The teacher meets the young on their own ground, and from their own point of view.—The hammerer stands above them and makes laws.

The teacher in punishing considers what is best, not what is deserved.—The hammerer applies a fixed penalty.

The teacher deals in exhortation and hope.—The hammerer in truisms and lamentation.

The teacher is animated by a high and true ideal, towards which he is ever working, to which he is ever finding some response, even in apparent failures.—The hammerer's ideal is a shallow dream of selfish success, the non-realisation of which leaves him apathetic and querulous in his work, sceptical of goodness, hardened in his own opinions, and closed against improvement.

The teacher, as he believes in his principles and rules, earnestly strives to be the best example of them himself.

Unpunctuality makes authority grating.

Little changes make authority contemptible.

Little interferences make it hateful.

Pouring out knowledge is not teaching.

Hearing lessons is not teaching.

Hammering a task in is not teaching.

Lecturing clearly is not teaching.

No mere applying of knowledge is teaching.

Teaching is getting at the heart and mind, so that the learner begins to value learning, and to believe learning possible in his own case.

It was with this ideal before him that Thring pursued his vocation as a teacher. This was the spirit he tried to impress upon the younger masters who came under his influence, the spirit which he eagerly hoped would one day prevail in schools.

It was when masters failed to understand what he meant that he despaired most about his work at Uppingham ; when government threw its weight on the side of the mechanical teaching which produces the measurable quantity of knowledge that he despaired about educational progress in England.

Of his own actual class teaching, its power and its limitations, we have an interesting sketch in a short article, contributed to the *Athenæum* at the time of his death by Lewis Nettleship. After mentioning that in the school games which he shared with his boys, he "always played to win," Nettleship adds :—

Into his work with the sixth form he carried the same spirit (the "racer's spirit," he used to call it), and he did not conceal his indignation at their frequent slowness to follow him. His own independence and ardour led him to expect the same in his pupils, and he sometimes rode rough-shod over those who required their intellectual food to be carefully prepared for them, or needed special tending or stimulus. But to those who came to understand him the ideas which he scattered broadcast were an education in themselves, and in talking over a copy of composition or an essay he would say things the effect of which lasted through life. In choosing pieces of English or subjects for Greek or Latin verse he aimed at making the boys use their common sense and their imagination; "prose" and "nonsense" were the epithets with which many a copy was ruthlessly condemned and (sometimes literally) pulled to pieces. His interest in language was part of his general interest in what he called "living power"; it appealed to him as a vital instrument of marvellous power and subtlety, and he handled and explored it as affectionately as if it were alive.

When among his boys he did meet with response to his teaching; it touched him deeply. I find this note :—

U—— gave me great pleasure to-night. After I had looked over his Greek prose, and showed him how to do it, his face glowed, and he said I opened a new world to him, and made common things look quite different. One such speech as that from a boy makes up for a great deal of criticism, and being held cheap because I don't hack along in a hack way. He really felt it.

Thring's pupils agree that his power as a teacher, marked at all times, was most impressive when applied

to the exposition of Scripture in his morning Bible
lessons.

"Perhaps," Lewis Nettleship writes in the article
already quoted, "the most original of his lessons were
those on the Old Testament. He treated the early
history of the Jews as a kind of spiritual allegory.
Moses, Abraham, and Jacob were types of life and
character, in the minutest details of which he found
illustrations of God's dealings with man. However
unhistorical the method might be, it enabled him to
bring his own experience to bear upon his pupils, and
it taught them religion without theology."

Doubtless it was only the stronger and finer spirits
who felt all the power and caught fully the spirit of
these Bible lessons. Still the general impression made
at the time was very great. An old boy has put into
my hands a large volume of notes, carefully copied out,
paragraphed and laboriously indexed, which he had
made as a pupil of the Upper Sixth. The remarkable
care taken by a boy to preserve all that was said is a
striking tribute to the power of the master.

Thring's teaching, as shown by these notes, was
certainly not food for babes. It consisted of concentrated maxims drawn from the experience of life,
vivid illustrations taken from passing events, a bold
application of Bible examples to the facts and conditions of daily modern life. There is in it no talking
down to the level of boys, but a steady lifting of their
minds into the clearer air of lofty thought and noble
purpose.

Fragments of correspondence, which might be
multiplied indefinitely, show how permanent was the
impression thus made ; how living was the seed thus
sown.

"I think," one writes, "that what most strikes those of your old pupils who still cherish a love and regard for your teaching is the far-reaching foresight which it contained. I mean that though we could not see it then, we learn more and more every month that, properly understood, your divinity lectures, for instance, form a kind of practical handbook for our lives. There is hardly a question in our philosophy on which some one of the great truths which you pointed out do not bear. And I believe them to be a guide and help to the highest and truest way of living. It is the greatest comfort in these difficult days of doubt, and scepticism, and speculation to have these anchors to rely upon."

And again :—

. . . I want to write you a few lines just now to tell you of a feeling of gratitude to you which has been springing up in my mind in these later days more strongly than before—gratitude for the "doors" you threw open to us, and for the quest of the loving eye to which you encouraged us. This germ of loving observation has been growing, I believe, feebly, no doubt, but still so as to already be making its power felt, and suffusing life with happiness through enjoyment of the beauties in the avenues beyond the "doors." It is now when I have begun to experience the value of the teaching for myself, and try to unlock the doors for other eyes and feel sometimes the hopelessness of the undertaking, that I think perhaps it would be a pleasure to you, who must have felt the same many a time in a keener fashion, to learn that even after many days fruit is appearing and blossom of gratitude to the sower.

After the opening of the decorated schoolroom a clergyman writes :—

I thoroughly appreciate what the Earl of Carnarvon said, and it stirred me up just to write and add the humble testimony of a curate to the value of the training which you gave us.

Believe me, sir, that we never forget the immense privileges which we had in our Uppingham life, and we are now, as clergy, able to put before others some of the high aims in life which you used to put before us. As far as concerns my own life, your name is always associated with any good that I have learnt to be able to do.

"You taught me at Uppingham, in your morning instructions to us, to burrow beneath the surface of Holy Scripture," writes to him one who has now become a man of mark in the English Church.

Another says :—

I have often wished, and have heard other O.U.'s wish also, that you would give to the world some of your morning lessons to the Sixth Form. I can never forget your lessons on "The grain of mustard seed" from the New, and "Privilege" from the Old Testament; but unfortunately I mislaid my note-book when I left, and have now no tangible record of them. Perhaps many of us during our school life could not appreciate them as highly as we do the recollection of them now; but I can assure you that in occasional encounters with Free-thought, etc., I have found a few of your lessons of the greatest service and power.

"I do so wish," writes yet another, "that you would publish by subscription, for private circulation among your old pupils, what you told us on Instinct, Enthusiasm, Reaction, Punishment, and many other subjects. You could not do them a greater service."

And again :—

I really do value all I was taught by you more than I can say; and as I recall some of those lessons I feel most thankful that the words in which they were clothed were so strong and so striking that even such a "thick" as myself could not forget them, and thus was led to think out what they meant.

An old pupil selected for an important Church preferment and wide field of work writes :—

I write to tell you about it not from any feeling of elation, for really it is most humbling to realise one's own unfitness, but because I always feel that whatever power of work and influence for good I may have, I owe it first and chiefly to the early training I received in those dear old days from you and Uppingham. I can assure you that your teaching, and the high motives you ever set before us as the only thing worth living for, have never been forgotten. Many a saying of yours haunts me still, and has helped, and, please God, will help me still, and it is with much gratitude that I look back to all you did for me and others. Feeling this as I do, it seems only natural to tell you about all that interests and concerns one in the work of life.

It will be readily understood that one who held Thring's views about the living power of the teacher's work would find stumbling - blocks in anything like mechanical methods of dealing with that work, or judging it.

If education and training are the true aim of mankind, and power in a man's self the prize of life, then no superstition ever ate into a healthy national organism more fatal than the cult of the examiner.

Such was Thring's judgment on one great feature of modern educational systems. It is a judgment which he reiterates in a thousand forms—one about which his conviction grew more intense as his educational experience increased.

A system of examination and inspection, in proportion to its power, is death to all original teaching, to all progress arising from new methods, and even to all improvement which is at all out of the routine track. . . .

There is no dead hand so dead as living power thrust in on work from the outside. It is the doctor putting his fingers on the heart when he ought to feel the pulse.

Where examinations reign, every novelty in training, every original advance, every new method of dealing with mind,

becomes at once simply impossible. It is outside the pre-
scribed area, and does not pay.

To "smash up the idolatry of knowledge" was to
him the first step in true educational progress. To pile
up facts and accumulate knowledge is within certain
limits necessary, but it is not education. The primary
object of education is to call out thought, not to load
the memory,—to strengthen mind and give it versatile
power—not crush it under an accumulation of un-
digested facts.

Do the universities, the government, and the parents want
memory, or mind?
Do they want knowledge, or strength?

With such strong affirmation and vehement question-
ing did Thring challenge the tendencies of a generation
which he saw steadily drifting on towards "payment
by results," and other equally flagrant deflections from
educational truth and honesty. "The dead hand" was
the scornful phrase in which he summed up his idea of
government or other control dominating the teacher's
living power; his contempt for amateur external
authority undertaking to test the living influence of
mind on mind.

No one can understand fully Thring's abhorrence
of the "dead hand" of external power till he has
entered into his conception of what true education
meant. Life passing on to other lives—the entering
of mind into mind—the handing on of the torch of
thought and feeling from brother to brother—from
teacher to taught,—all this to him was no metaphor,
but a reality.

A teacher is a combination of heart, head, artistic training, and favouring circumstances. Like all other high arts, life must have free play or there can be no teaching. . . .

Teaching is not possible if an inspector is coming to count the number of bricks made to order. . . .

The inspector destroys teaching, because he is bound by law and necessity to examine according to a given pattern; and the perfection of teaching is, that it does not work by a given pattern.

Minds cannot be inspected. The minds of the class cannot be produced as specimens on a board, with a pin stuck through them, like beetles. Shoving in the regulation quantity is one thing, clearing the stuff out of the bewildered brain and strengthening the mind is another; and the two are foes.

The "transmission of life from the living, through the living, to the living, is the highest definition of education," he says in one place.

And this was what people proposed to measure and gauge and ticket and pay for at a valuation, like so many yards of cotton or bushels of corn!

Yet he had himself been an examiner at Eton, at Rugby, at Cambridge, and knew well the value of examination work. What was the place he assigned to it? A letter written to his fellow-worker, the Headmaster of Sherborne, at the time when the Government was proposing to reorganise the old foundations, explains some of his views.

To Rev. H. D. Harper.

1869.

I now come to the matter of examinations, which I think simply in a series of years contains the life or death of schools and education. First, I will say that I will join you in trying any scheme in our schools that may be practicable which you think advisable after having heard what I have to say.

I start with the assertion that the curse of English education has been and is the fact that a few honour men being produced, which any clever man must produce under fair circumstances, can and does hide the fact that no great school (as the public counts greatness) is a school at all to many, yea, to the majority of its boys.

And that no teaching, I mean the applying knowledge according to the specialities of different minds, is possible for any of the boys. The masters have not time to learn how to teach, and if they knew how, have no time to use such knowledge. Facts and rules must form the stock-in-trade of such places.

Is this course to be legalised as the sovereign remedy? Is the disease to be made health by law?

I start by laying down that Government has no business whatever to contemplate any honour examination, honour standard, or honour judgment on schools.

The sole business of Government is to pass a school. First, as having efficient machinery for the work it professes to do; secondly, as doing that work on the average respectably.

These points and others raised I will now deal with more in detail. Who is to be examiner?

Are we who have been working for years to have some clever young man with a bias sent down to test our work, not, mind you, simply as our work, but comparatively with that of five or six other schools? Now let me show some of the working of this.

In the first place, the style of examination must be adapted to the five schools, say, which are to be examined. As this is impossible, it will represent the most powerful of them—that is to say, the weaker must adapt themselves to a close external standard, or perish. Or if it represents a prevailing theory, the opposite will take place; the weaker schools will eagerly seize the idea, mould their work on it, and gather laurels at the expense of their greater and more self-reliant neighbours. In either case Procrustes is the model.

Take another view: a teaching school, call it Uppingham, is matched against sundry others of the cut-and-dried rule class. Is the teaching which is new and living, and therefore, if for no other reason, singular, to be exposed to an examination on different principles and condemned because it does not suit it? This is nothing less than saying that all originality is to be fatal by the Government plan.

Again, a school depends so much on the kind of material it gets. This is a fact. Our reputation in early days rested entirely on the care we took with individuals. Now the result was this. I know in many instances the stupid boys of a family were sent here, the clever elsewhere. Thus our real excellence stood in the way of our false excellence. How terribly would this have been aggravated had we had a Government examiner handicapping us against sundry other schools; what a temptation to drop honest work would have arisen in addition to the many already only too powerful. Then, if the exhibitions are to be open to this kind of scramble, I should never have dreamt for a moment of facing the deadly risk of making this school do true work. The guarantee of permanence would be gone, and no man would work such a work—merely to enter into a knowledge scramble with un-weighted competitors. It will end in the cram private rafts carrying off the credit by cram. . . . So far of the theory, though it might be greatly enlarged.

The following extracts, taken from a correspondence which touched upon the university examinations of the school, furnish further illustration of his point of view :—

. . . Many years ago I was examining at Eton, and set a paper in Greek translation. The boys had to read their work when done to the assembled examiners; I also looked over it all in private. When the first paper of these translations was read out, the then Headmaster of Eton, Dr. Hawtrey, a man of great reputation, said, as soon as the boy had left the room, "How beautiful!" and gave the highest praise to it. I had observed that there was not a single point in scholarship given of those on account of which the paper was set, and I accordingly had marked the paper low. Dr. Hawtrey might fairly have held me up as an incompetent examiner from his point of view, and might justly have objected in his own school to my system of marking. We were, in fact, looking at two entirely different things. I thought, as I was examining in Greek, that I was sent down to see whether the boys knew Greek, and till they showed they did, they got little or no credit for their English style. He was of opinion that a certain undefined literary power was the thing to prize, and so gave high marks for what, in his judgment, showed this. Now, what is a good translation has never been decided, and to this hour examiners are divided into two camps on the question. I belong to one camp, your examiner belonged to another. I do not blame him. I do not desire to contest his verdict. My object was, and is, to draw attention to the very elementary state in which these teaching questions are and prevent crude legislation; to suggest that inspectors are mortal; to ask for thoughtful treatment, and for some admission in practice, at least, of the very shifting and delicate character of the experiment now in progress.

The want of a fixed standard makes much that goes on absurd, and therefore is an important fact; but it does not affect the great question that rash judgments confidently laid down and handed in to amateur tribunals can easily destroy all progress in teaching in England. I very much doubt if twenty years ago I could have carried on my best teaching in the face of the strictures and suggestions of the last five years. I would particularly draw attention to the latter fact of suggestions being made to trustees. It has taken me the last fourteen years to go through the gospel of St. Matthew with my class. One of my best pupils the other day told me that I should live in memory more by that work than by anything else. But examiners come down and not only blame the work done, which they have a right to do if they do it courteously, but offer suggestions to the trustees as to how I ought to teach the Greek Testament. . . . It appears to me that it is a very serious question—this snuffing out of all new methods by the *ipse dixit* of examiners. It appears to me that if a school like Uppingham is constantly exposed to remarks expressed with undue confidence, and suggestions which ought not to be made at all, the small schools and beginners must be very badly off. Grave complaints reach me of what has to be endured sometimes in the lower strata. I look on the yoke of examination now in process of formation as absolute destruction and death to all progress unless a wise caution is exercised before the system gets rigid. I am sure the university has no intention of paralysing school life. I venture humbly to adhere to my statement at the Conference as not too strong and unjust; or, I would add, based on a single example; and I would plead on the one hand for the weak and defenceless that consideration should be shown to those engaged in the difficult work of schools; and the other I would solemnly warn, as far as any words of mine can do so, those in whose hands the examining power lies, of the graver danger there is lest they kill all progress.

To W. T. Jacob.

October 24th, 1876.

I have read the Report, and am vexed and amused at it. It is just what I expected. The calm assumption of infallibility which underlies a courteous document is very amusing if it were not also very noxious. The quiet supposition that their ways of work must be right; I quite see how deadly such a dead hand will be on English education. I both can afford to disregard it, and shall disregard it, and as long as the school is in the front rank of honour-winning, the Trust cannot be troubled or trouble because of it. But it is ruinous to progress and new and improved ways of work to have such judgments passed everywhere. I will give one example. A stricture is passed on the boys for not knowing various renderings and readings. Now I judge in the most positive way that it is bad teaching to confuse their minds with various renderings. This is one instance.

I will also observe on some other features of the examination which show the absurdity of such offhand judgments. The examiners do not know what subjects we put in the first rank, and what we subordinate. Some things they rate high, we simply do nothing in; some things we are very strong in, they are ignorant of and omit. Our grammar is not taught on their lines.

We regard etymology and philology as no fit subjects for

school education, and devote much thought and work to comparing English and the Classics which they know nothing of.

I do not consider the history of the English language a good school subject; I do consider its analysis and real grammar which they know nothing of. My divinity lessons sometimes take a term doing half a chapter of New Testament. I have been since the 4th of May engaged on Exodus xx., and finished it last Saturday. I have been engaged since 8th June in doing seven verses of St. Matthew.

These lessons have over and over again been spoken of to me as the very most valuable of all I give. I need scarcely observe how useless they are in a Divinity examination by an outsider. Then, again, both in my class and in the Lower V. the tail end has been but a short time in the class, and have not read much of the subjects that are given in as having been read. All these and many more things tend to make their examinations most deadly blights on teaching unless they are taken at their real value, viz. a rough general opinion given by outsiders on work which they have very imperfect means of forming a judgment about.

But such extracts as those given can only indicate the general tendency of his thought. "Freedom for the skilled workman" was his final word upon the question. If the skilled teacher does not know best how to do his work—how best to deal with the infinitely delicate problems of mind and life which confront him from day to day—then no external direction or examination can cure the defect.

Examination may be an admirable means of detecting inefficiency; as a supreme arbiter of school life, as a method of assigning the palm of mind over a whole kingdom, it is deadly.

He believed that the meshes of the examiner were steadily closing around the mind of England, and he stoutly resisted the threatened tyranny.

Thring had been brought up under a severe system, and one of the great objects of his educational plans was to alleviate the miseries and do away with the meannesses of school life as he had known them.   But he could be severe too.   Not Dr. Keate himself could be more stern and unrelenting than he when deliberate and premeditated evil had to be crushed.

He objected strongly, for instance, to the method of getting rid of school failures by expulsion.   On the other hand, when once a capital code had been fixed and clearly explained he had slight mercy on wilful offenders.

To a Parent.

. . . I am indeed exceedingly grieved at having been obliged to pass such a sentence.   But in a public school, apart from any other knowledge, I deem the getting out at night a crime never to be pardoned. . . . But in any case it is known to be expulsion.   I have again and again declared it to be, as an utter defiance of all order, authority, and trust. . . . I am indeed exceedingly sorry for the affliction it must cause you, . . . but in a great school there is no possibility of relaxing any of the capital penalties. . . .

Though perhaps no master ever took more pains to provide that flogging should not be employed indiscriminately, or without full trial and judicial condemnation of the offender, he yet believed firmly in the use of the rod.

He mentions that in his earlier experience in national schools he had once made the experiment for six months of never employing corporal punishment, but that he found it necessary to return to it.

This judgment his mature experience confirmed,

and it was one which he was always ready to justify.

He writes to a parent :—

With respect to corporal punishment, I think I can easily put you in possession of our main principles. The better the school the less corporal punishment there will be, but I hold it from experience to be idle to think that a large school can be properly managed without. First of all, I conceive corporal punishment to be the proper retribution for breaking main discipline rules, *e.g.* not coming back at the proper time, being out of a partition in a sleeping-room at bedtime, making a disturbance ; and secondly, in the case of little boys, for deliberate idleness. Learning is *pain*, and unless the unwillingness to face the one pain is met by another pain there is no remedy. Setting additional tasks in a good school soon clogs work. What can be more absurd than to increase a boy's work because he has failed to do the ordinary portion ? This is making bricks without straw with a vengeance. Keeping boys in, again, is detrimental to health ; any food punishment is the same. I hold, therefore, that whilst all fair excuses should be weighed and judged, and no isolated act is to be punished with flogging, excepting in rare cases, the machinery of a school will soon get clogged if there is not this quick and effectual way of cleaning scores in bad cases. Contrary to most opinions I do not inflict floggings for lies or sin against God, unless they violate school order too. I hold it to be very injurious encouraging the notion that a punishment at school can cancel in any way grave moral faults, and if it can be done I keep such cases quite apart from school punishment, preferring to speak to boys and try to bring them to a due sense of their guilt. . . .[1]

[1] The following passage touches upon this question and also illustrates the influence of Thring's thought upon one of the most vigorous educational thinkers of modern France :—

"In truth, I find two total and absolute contradictions in the teacher as imagined by the well-known Bishop of Orleans, and the as well-known Mr. Thring. 'Respect and authority' are the watchwords I meet with everywhere on the one side ; 'Freedom and independent development'

To a Parent.

Though it is not possible in a letter to enter fully into the question raised by your note of this morning, yet it requires some notice from me. First with respect to punishments. One of the main distinctions of a great public school is that in punishment passion and caprice should be eliminated. At Uppingham there is but one time for flogging—twelve o'clock each day; any offence, whenever committed, is reserved till then, and I myself always inflict it. . . .

No man is more alive than myself to the fact how easily punishment is made by a bad master the substitute for efficiency; everybody here is aware of this. The masters are not inefficient, and take special care with their pupils. I have yet to learn that a society of boys or men gathered from all quarters is to be managed without punishment, or ever has been. The question is reduced to a choice of punishments, and in spite of modern cant, I think flogging is the very best remedy for some breaches of discipline particularly. Our dormitories are not large; your boy would not have been found out had they been uncared for. I demur to the wisdom of perpetual surveillance, and do not mean to allow it here. Boys should be trusted, and if they break trust punished.

are those of the other. For centuries in France education is an authoritative, an arbitrary, and oppressive process. This is so self-evident that it requires no proof. Whatever the specific form, the principle is for ever the same; the autocracy has always subsisted, and the Jesuits have simply bequeathed their modes of teaching to the university; the master is a surgeon who operates on the child he has to educate. The object is to give the habit of submission. Mgr. Dupanloup's system produced discipline. The headmaster of Uppingham has left a host of admirers and fellow-workers. . . . In every sense the methods are divergent; nor do the students of one country as yet at all comprehend the results achieved by the other; the French, for example, unreflectingly decry the custom of flogging in English public schools, and never realise the fact that in France we flog the spirit, not the flesh—we flog the spirit till it is put down!"

The original expression is :—

"En France nous ne fouettons pas la chair, mais l'esprit; et l'esprit nous le fouettons jusqu'à ce qu'il soit dompté. Il saigne à l'intérieur."— M. Pierre de Coubertin, Address at Brussels Conference.

I demur also to the assumption that if a boy is not known to have bad faults at home, *ergo*, he learns them at school. Our experience directly contradicts this, and is to the effect that if a boy has a good home we never need be afraid of not succeeding with him here. We have no other fault against your son, excepting that having required great care and forbearance when he came, and received it, he has lately grown very unruly, as might, I think, be expected from the instructions he had received. I do feel deeply aggrieved that in utter ignorance of our system of punishments you should have sent your boy here under direct instructions to mutiny against our authority without giving me any hint of such a thing.

How could a government stand if this was often done? It reflects upon us as professional men, it reflects on the school, it sets up our pupils, however young, to be the judges and thwarters of earnest and experienced men. How can good come of it? as you express a hope in your first note it may. But however that may be, we had a right to expect the choice of refusing to deal with a boy at all under direct instructions to mutiny when sent here. I had a right not to be exposed to the ignorant and impertinent refusal of your little boy to be flogged for a grave discipline offence, and the open contempt of my lawful, thoughtful, and experienced authority involved in this. Your boy, too, has much reason to be grateful to M. —— for his care and consideration during his stay here. Masters do not deserve such a return for their life work. They feel as men. I am prepared in the face of the world to uphold any and every part of our system under a wise criticism and scrutiny, but not to submit it to the caprice of rebellious little boys.

While thus sturdily defending the right of the master to inflict corporal punishment he took the greatest precautions that no boy should be thus punished except under strictly defined conditions.

Foremost among these conditions was one which strictly limited, in his opinion, the numbers to which a public school should be allowed to grow. He says :—

A headmaster is only the headmaster of the boys he knows. If he does not know the boys the master who does is their headmaster and his also. The graduation of classes, and above all, the headmaster knowing each boy, and the assistant masters having to make *viva voce* complaints to him, knowing that he knows each boy, these ensure care and justice, and keep all the masters attentive to the discipline, preventing all arbitrary work.

His method at Uppingham was to himself inflict all corporal punishments.

"No master," he says in a note, "can in the slightest degree deviate from the plan of punishment laid down for the school by the headmaster. No assistant master is allowed to inflict corporal punishment. This the headmaster does with a cane on the back, at a fixed time and place, after a *viva voce* complaint from the master who wishes the boy to be punished."

The following note occurs in his diary :—

February 2nd.— . . . Had in D—— and B—— after chapel to-day and convicted them, and told them that I should require their withdrawal at the end of the term, and I flogged them severely. I was deeply touched after their caning by their coming up to me, and D—— said, "But won't you forgive us yourself, sir? Do forgive us yourself!" I assured them I would, and that I never would recollect it against them if they went on well, and that I thought they had slipped into their evil without being aware of what it really meant. Indeed, I could have cried myself, so much did I feel the trust and honour that these two poor fellows showed for me. It did cheer my heart wonderfully to feel what a true sense of the loving justice with which even heavy, very heavy punishment was inflicted had got into the school, when convicts in the midst of their punishment recognised it and felt it so. It is a glorious reward for much sorrow to have made such an impression on the bad boys of the school.

"A little judicious blindness and deafness," he

remarks in one place, " is a great virtue in a wise teacher."

A master came to him and said, " A—— must be caned ; he has been very insolent." Thring agreed, and A—— was caned.   A week later the master came and said, " A—— must be crushed ; he has repeated his insolent conduct."   Thring turned and said, " A——· shan't be crushed ; he is a very good boy, but just at present he is standing at bay like a rat in a corner. Punish him slightly for this, and for the next month shut your eyes resolutely to everything you are not obliged to see."   This plan answered, and the boy was rescued from rebellion, and the master and school saved from a great scandal which it was afterwards found might have been the outcome of the case.

To a House Master.

Your letter about W—— causes me great concern and perplexity.   I quite admit the difficulty of such a case, but I do not see how to deal with it.

Two things are apparent at once as general axioms : That much evil of a certain kind has to be put up in God's world, and any attempt to escape from this fact into a special circle has always ended in worse.   The whole question of the existence of evil in a society seems to me to be opened up the moment anything short of facts within the clutch of the law is brought forward.   And secondly, the failure in the training power if a boy has to be got rid of.

I do not say that such failure is necessarily any fault.   It is clear that a system will not stand above a certain amount of strain ; but, nevertheless, in all cases where it breaks down there is need of anxious examination whether it was inevitable or not.

I have already once before this term been responsible for the extremest measures against a boy for this same sort of impalpable rebellion.   I have only once before, and that was in very early days, proceeded to such lengths, excepting in the case of proved offences and grave breaches of law. If W——— breaks law he must answer for it. But even then much can be done in seeing the right thing at the right time, and not seeing too much. I do not think we are concerned with his influence on others unless he comes within the law a bit more than with T———'s influence, for instance, which is infinitely worse, but quite out of reach. I cannot but think you are too sensitive on this point. In the long run patient endurance and management does much more than summary measures which boys do not appreciate. They are very ready to make martyrs even of real criminals. Have you facts and evidence of any magnitude? a false step might be very serious.

Criticising certain steps which a master had taken to have a boy dismissed from the school, he writes :—

How little you did it with my knowledge or consent will appear from the fact that the central principle on which all my work has gone here is the *wickedness* of turning boys out of a school on any opinion of masters, head or other, and the duty of training each boy and teaching him, however intractable he may be. It is the one thing I have lived for. P——— thinks himself to have been treated with gross injustice. May not this have a good deal to do with his present bad character? . . .

I have requested ——— to leave him here another term. You will kindly be conveniently blind to anything that does not force itself on your notice, and gentle with what does. I have promised that the boy shall meet with friendly treatment and consideration.

A parent, writing on the mistaken supposition that his son had been punished for not giving up the name of a schoolfellow who had committed a grave offence, had said : " I rather think that shows the stuff of which our soldiers and sailors are made, and which is supposed to be the good result of public school training. What say you ? " Thring replied :—

He was not punished in the slightest degree for refusing to give up his companions. I was not even aware that he had refused to do so. Though in our code at Uppingham we hold "thieves' honour" to be only fit for thieves, and that no sneaking is worse than betraying the good and screening the bad; nothing baser than to live under a free trustful system and use its freedom to do evil or protect the doers of evil. The school does to a considerable extent act on this principle of upholding its own liberties.

Irregular and capricious punishment he held in strict restraint.

To a Modern Master.

I have settled this matter with your class. But I have been informed that you are not free from the charge of striking boys. If this is true, let me direct your attention to the accompanying printed rules, which, however, you are not ignorant of. And let me also state that a master who violates that rule does it at the risk of instant dismissal. So strongly do I feel on the point that even if it was proved that a boy had been struck some time ago, I should view such a breach of law as most serious. I do not know whether that charge is true or not, but it is right that you should know it has been made.

To the Same.

I will not mix up any other matter with this important question of striking boys. Before I came here I taught a rougher set than you have ever had, and under worse circumstances; I never struck a boy and I never will permit a boy to be struck. Any master who is convicted of breaking this law does not remain a master in the school. And if it ever comes to my knowledge privately, and not as an open accusation, I shall consider it quite sufficient reason for immediate notice. It shall not be done. You have mistaken a permission given in a special instance for disregard of the law.

I beg you will bear in mind that no merit, no attention to

work, no time of service will weigh in my mind against a breach of this law.

To a Master.

I observe with much concern both the number of boys you report for punishment, and still more the reasons you give for their punishment. I know the boys, and I have no hesitation in saying that nothing but grave incapacity for management on your part can account for some of them having conducted themselves as you report them to have done.

CHAPTER V

LAST YEARS—TERCENTENARY OF UPPINGHAM SCHOOL
—SCHOOL MORALITY—EXTRACTS FROM DIARY
(1883-1886)

In the last few years of his life Thring's whole
educational horizon was greatly enlarged. What he
had done for the cause of education, what he had said
and written about it, began to command wide attention.
In 1883 his *Theory and Practice of Teaching* appeared.
A second English edition which was almost immediately
called for proved that his seed thoughts had fallen on
more gracious soil than when he first expressed them
in *Education and School;* the demand for an American
edition indicated that he had got a hearing abroad.

Thenceforward to the end of his life he had no lack
of platforms from which to speak. He was chosen
President of the Education Society, and made his
Presidential Address the occasion for reiterating many
of the truths which had at first inspired his work, and
were now set forth anew with the backing of thirty
years of teaching experience. He was asked to visit
America, and failing that, to write addresses for various
important teaching bodies there. His work and
theories were discussed on both sides of the Atlantic.

The Church Congress, the Teachers' Guild, the meeting of Headmistresses, the Education Society of the University of Cambridge, the Teachers of Minnesota, are a few of the bodies before whom he was asked to unfold his ideas on education.

This widening of his field of influence filled him with happiness.

"The feeling of opening life," he says, "not of closing, is on me. Some observations in a Life of Moltke that I have been reading have seemed prophecies of my just beginning the most fruitful work of my life, though I am sixty-two, and within all is the buoyant sense of just having learnt to work and learnt to live a little, and of the life yet to be lived in this power. I know not, God knows what He has in store, but a more expansive feeling of the life work, freer, nobler, higher than the past, is in my heart. Perchance it means beyond the grave. Yet it does not feel so. God knows. I glory in the work He has allowed me to do, and the pains by which He crucified my foolish delusions of success. It is all being brought to a fruitful end, be it a new beginning or be it not."

And again :—

I feel somehow or other as if in Tennyson's words I "had rolled into a younger day," and the prison doors were opening in which one has been shut up so many years. I do not know why quite, but I feel it, and I thank God for it.

An interesting school commemoration which occurred in 1884, brought out with prominence some of his guiding principles. Archdeacon Johnson had founded the school in 1584, and so the tercentenary anniversary fell in 1884, thirty-one years from the time when Thring entered upon his work of refounding it.

It was felt by the old boys and friends of the school

that the time was a peculiarly fitting one for doing honour to the original founder, and at the same time strengthening the position of the new foundation. Thring had always delighted to connect his new work with the old. In 1878 he had presented a scheme to the Trust for such an increase of fees as would put the school on what he considered a firm basis. By this plan he mentions that £3500 per annum would be reserved for the Trust when the school was full, from money earned by the masters, to meet current expenses and provide for improvements, exclusive of the income of the old foundation.

He closes his statement thus :—

Then at the coming tercentenary of the foundation the three hundred years that have passed will give promise of a better three hundred years to come; and we may have good hope that this old school, when the cycle is full again, may still be found standing fast in the front ranks, still upholding in honour the time-honoured name of Archdeacon Johnson's school at Uppingham.

Still as the time of the anniversary drew near, he was not altogether in sympathy with what was proposed.

He dreaded the breath of false praise ; he doubted whether a celebration such as that suggested was in keeping with the practical, everyday principles which formed the foundation of his work.

I feel utterly out of heart for this tercentenary. When I think of all the inner failure, how little has been done, and how much the outward buildings and work seem, when I think even that little will probably all be swept away in a few years and the usual sham flourish here, I have no heart in me any more for tercentenaries. How I should have exulted in it fifteen years ago. I am wiser now.

The enthusiasm of old boys and other supporters, however, gradually overcame his hesitation, and finally he threw himself heartily into the arrangements for the gathering.

The appeal issued on the occasion shows the light in which he regarded the anniversary. . . .

The celebration of a birthday is an appeal to affection and honour.

The school does appeal to feelings of affection and honour on this, its great birthday, its tercentenary of life.

It appeals as one of the few original endowments of the reign of Queen Elizabeth. It was founded by Archdeacon Johnson in 1584, "By God's grace," as the first words of the old statutes declare, and endowed with lands purchased by him from the Queen : an honest gift made in the lifetime of the founder. All honour to him for this.

The Queen, at all events, honoured him and his work ; for when she granted the Charter in 1587 A.D., she caused it to be recorded that she herself was witness to the deed.

Such was the original birthday—the birthday of a good man's hope and gift, liberally given, "By God's grace," in his lifetime.

After this the school fared with varied fortunes, but no great change, until thirty years ago it began to be remodelled.

A simple principle, but an effective one, was, "By God's grace," once more the basis of the new departure.

That principle was, that each boy should have justice done to him, with its corollary, that no work can be done without tools.

Many different lives come from home into a great school to find a better training than home can give ; and they require many different means to shape them, or they do not get it.

In the last thirty years a sum of £91,000 has been expended, almost entirely by the masters, in order to carry out this conception of what a school ought to be. This expenditure constitutes practically a new foundation of the old school. . . .

Our tercentenary, therefore, appeals to all who love the old, and feel the power of being heirs of a good man's purpose.

It appeals to all who love the new, and are fired by hope, and a wish to take part in a living work. . . .

There was a large gathering of people to honour the occasion, and naturally the school received much notice in the public press.

Thring was anxious above all else that the celebration should not be a mere glorification of the increase in numbers and prestige which had made Uppingham take rank among the great public schools. On the whole, his wish was gratified. The speeches made upon the occasion by Bishop Harvey Goodwin of Carlisle, Bishop Fraser of Manchester, and others of the distinguished men who came to show their sympathy with what had been done at Uppingham, made it clear that they recognised and gave the first importance to the principles upon which the system of the school was based, and the religious spirit which inspired the work.

One feature of the celebration gave him infinite pleasure, both in the addition which it made to the school literature, and in the striking illustration which it furnished of the success that had crowned his efforts to make music a real part of school education. This was the performance by the school choir of an elaborate cantata, " Under Two Queens," the words by the Rev. J. H. Skrine, the music by Herr Paul David, two of his most devoted and trusted colleagues. The loyalty of the old boys and friends found expression in the collection of a considerable fund to be applied to school purposes.

His diary says after the celebration :—

July 4th.—Two things stand out distinct in the midst of it all. First, the great gain to honest work in England. Wherever any man is doing his best to be true, there the universal declaration of the need to do justice to each boy, and the respect paid to the dictum must have brought comfort and strength. . . .

July 5th.—Another comforting tact has come into my mind concerning the tercentenary, that the founder's expression, " By the grace of God," and my own has been brought out both in the papers and in the bishop's sermon, so that great motive, in the midst of this secular age, has come out well. This is a great comfort.

To Rev. Godfrey Thring.

July 12th, 1884.

I had not heard of dear mother's joy at the notice of the work here. It gives me infinite pleasure. Tell her that next to the work itself I always wished that she should know that I had tried to do a true thing. And I rejoice exceedingly that she has seen the truth of it acknowledged. I am so thankful it is all over. Thankful more than I can tell that we have escaped the poisonous breath of false praise, of numbers and intellect worship, and all I have striven against all my life long, and that the plain independent basis of doing right by each boy has been brought out so clearly. At all events, now the voice has been heard which for so many years has been smothered. And *that* is everything. Come weal, come woe, *that* is real success.

A letter written at this time illustrates the warmth of feeling with which Thring's work was regarded among the old boys of the school :—

How beautiful the little university town appeared in this the finest season of the year ! How charming the weather !

How happy every one looked, young and old ! How splendid as a mere spectacle the beautiful schoolroom looked, with its host of loyal boys, and old boys ! And as the little man who created and saved the present Uppingham sat in state, surrounded by bishops and noblemen who paid homage to his marvellous work, memory was busy within me, with varying emotion, as it recalled the small beginnings, the early struggles, the never-failing strong faith, the manly persistent effort, the fiery trial, the final great triumph.

The history of Thring's Uppingham is to me one of the most interesting, the most marvellous and advantageous to this country that I have personal experience of.

After the anniversary the Bishop of Manchester writes to him :—

LONDON, *June 30th*, 1884.

If our presence at your most successful tercentenary festival was any strengthening of *your* hands, *we* came away on our part with intense feelings of satisfaction at having been allowed to see and realise the great work which your many years of self-denying labour have achieved for Uppingham, and through Uppingham, for that great class of English society who so much need a rightly directed education for their sons. The only element of regret which mixed itself with that satisfaction was that people told me, on all hands, that in carrying out this work you had thought of everything but yourself; and when a man has "given hostages to fortune," I confess I think he ought not to leave that consideration wholly out of sight. Still, in the almost universal race for self, such a life as yours has been has a special richness of example, and it has been a privilege to me to witness it. . . .

It was not long after the tercentenary celebration that he was called upon to discuss publicly a school subject of the first importance which may be fitly referred to here. There was a prevalent belief among those best acquainted with English public school life that the question of school morals had been faced at Uppingham more fully and fearlessly than in any other of the great schools.   The knowledge of what Thring had done led to his being asked in 1884 by his old friend, Harvey Goodwin, Bishop of Carlisle, to address the Church Congress, which that year met at Carlisle, on " The Best Means of Raising the Standard of Public Morality." His address attracted much attention for the bold and yet delicate touch with which he treated the question in its relation to school life.   And certainly of all the problems which the training of boys presents to parents or masters, that of dealing with impurity in thought, word, and deed is the most difficult, and at times the most perplexing.   To detect and check the subtle beginnings of impure thought ; to create a healthy disgust for impure conversation ; to set up all possible guards against the temptation to impure act ; to arm boys for the inevitable struggle with their own lower nature or against the influence of evil associates, are tasks that call for insight, tact, judgment, moral courage, and every other quality which goes to make up training skill.   Many a master or parent, strong to deal with everything else, finds himself paralysed by the subtlety of the problem he meets with here.   While he knows that reticence is often dangerous, and that many a boy drifts to physical and moral shipwreck simply through the ignorance to which a false delicacy or sensitiveness leaves him, he knows also that an untimely or thoughtless freedom of discussion has perils almost as great.   He must decide in individual cases upon that stage in a boy's life, varying with different temperaments, where ignorance is the best protection, and that further stage where acquaintance with his own constitution and the functions of life, combined with knowledge of the fatal consequences of sins of impurity, can alone be trusted as a safeguard. On no subject of school life did Thring think more deeply or strive more diligently to discover the true principles and method of treatment.

He felt that the advantage or disadvantage of public school life often turned largely upon this moral issue. He knew that in the struggle between purity and impurity of thought lies for many boys, perhaps for most boys, one of the first decisive turning-points of life.

A great public school, in bringing large numbers of boys together, undoubtedly concentrates evil, and creates the chance for evil to be infectious. But it concentrates good too ; it gives wise management its best opportunity, and makes possible the perfecting of appliance for combating evil. The regular hours, steady discipline, abundant occupation, mental and physical, the oversight, more direct and constant than can usually be given at home, are all under judicious management favourable for carrying a boy safely through that most critical period of life when his mind first becomes a battle-ground between what is pure and what is impure.

Even granting a tendency to the concentration of boyish evil in public schools, Thring none the less firmly believed that, on the whole, it is less dangerous to find out that evil exists—easier to gain the power of resisting evil, as a boy among boys, than to confront the sins and temptations of youth for the first time as a young man among men.

His method was one of frank and open treatment.

"One point I would remind you of," he writes to a friend. "The Bible is God's great Police Court, as well as His

Temple, and till life ceases to be coarse, lessons on coarseness will be needed; also much of modern reticence is not purity, but lust."

"At nine," his diary in one place says, "I had all the communicants in the Upper School to speak to on the subject of lust. . . . I do thank God unfeignedly for the opportunity of putting these great truths before the school, so that none shall fall into that pit of hell unwarned."

In his address at Carlisle he enters into the question more fully :—

Curiosity, ignorance, and lies form a very hotbed of impurity. We pay heavily for our civilised habits in false shame, and the mystery in which sex . . . is wrapped. I confess that for curiosity I have no remedy to propose. Ignorance and lies are on a different footing. I suppose every one is acquainted with some of the current lies about the impossibility of being pure. The only answer to this is a flat denial from experience. I know it is possible, and, when once attained, easy. The means, under God, in my own case were a letter from my father. A quiet, simple statement of the sinfulness of the sin and a few of the plain texts from St. Paul saved me. . . . A film fell from my eyes at my father's letter. My first statement is that all fathers ought to write such a letter to their sons. It is not difficult if done in a common-sense way. Following out this plan at Uppingham in the morning Bible lessons, I have always spoken as occasion arose with perfect plainness on lust, and its devil-worship, particularly noting its deadly effect on human life, and its early and dishonoured graves. . . . Ignorance is deadly, because perfect ignorance in a boy is impossible. I consider the half-ignorance so deadly, that once a year, at the time of confirmation, I speak openly to the whole school, divided into three different sets. First, I take the confirmees, then the communicants and older boys, then the younger boys, on three following nights after evening prayers. The two first sets I speak very plainly to; the last I only warn against all indecency in thought, word, or deed, whether alone or with companions. Thus no boy who has been at school a whole year can sin in ignorance. And a boy who despises this warning is justly turned out of the school on conviction.

And again :—

Boys at school, also, should be protected by all their surroundings being framed — so as to shut off temptation. The whole structure and system should act as an unseen friend. There is much virtue, or vice, in a wall. Witness the one room. No words, no personal influence, no religion even, can do instead of the holy help of the wall, or overcome its evil, if evil. These words involve serious results in practice. They involve the teaching and training of every boy, with adequate machinery for doing it.

The young cannot be dealt with in herds.

The house accommodation should make every boy feel himself cared for. But this is a matter of infinite skill and much expense.

The class working should thoroughly handle each boy, and leave no unswept corners.

Many objects of interest should be there. One boy is caught in one net, another in another.

The whole atmosphere should be an atmosphere of work and life, with time fully occupied, and an involuntary, quiet throwing of light on all the boy life.

If this was the atmosphere of England, much impurity would vanish from schools. Neglect and faulty structure breed impurity as in a hotbed. Talk cannot get over this. Alter the conditions, or be silent.

It is enough for me merely to point out this difficulty. The good wall, within a certain range, is omnipotent.

Finally, he dwelt upon the necessity of school life having joined to it a home life. The purifying influence of good women, and a fuller recognition of woman's work and place in the world he looked upon as that which promised most for lifting mankind into a higher atmosphere of pure life.

After the Congress his diary says :—

October 7th.—Back from Carlisle on Saturday, and at last have a few minutes more or less at my own disposal. My paper was very well received. I myself never felt I had been given a message to deliver more than on that occasion. I do not think God's plan of creation by which woman was created as a help in life work has ever been fairly tried, and I have a boundless belief in womanhood and the power of good women for purifying the world. The Vicar of Leeds, Dr. Gott, has asked me to come and deliver it at Leeds next term.

October 17th.—Mr. Jacob tells me that many men thought my paper the best paper at the Congress. This pleases me greatly. I thank God for having given me power to honour women and their work, and to do something to raise them to their proper position of purifiers and raisers of the world.

In a letter written at an earlier period to his friend, Dr. Lionel Beale, who had consulted him as to the best ways of combating the spread of impurity in schools, he speaks of his own experience and methods. This letter Dr. Beale published in a leading medical journal, from which the following passages are taken :—

I was three years at a small private school which, I should have said from later experience, was eminently calculated in its arrangements to foster this evil ; I am bound to say I never became aware of anything of the kind. I was nine years at Eton ; during those nine years I was well aware from beginning to end of the luxurious unchaste class, but I never knew of the existence of Dr. Pusey's " besetting sin " in the school ; what there was of it never came to light, as far as I recollect, and most certainly would have been visited both with punishment and shame amongst the boys themselves— as actually took place in a near approach to it which I do remember. In other words, no boy at Eton in my time was of necessity exposed to temptation and betrayed in this way, at least without full means of escape. I speak thus cautiously from the known difficulty of proving a negative.

Friends of mine since then have told me this was not the case in private schools where they had been, but that the whole set was corrupt in them. This is not unnatural under circumstances of prison discipline, few amusements, small numbers, and the consequent impossibility of escape if one or two bad fellows have power. I have now been upwards of thirteen years headmaster here, perfectly alive to the possible existence of such an evil, and have never seen any reason to suspect its presence. I do not mean that I deny the possibility, nay, the certainty, of individuals occasionally being caught by it. One boy did consult me on the subject, but I deny that it has ever formed a definite temptation here. I have spoken to my medical man, and he unhesitatingly confirms this.

I will now touch on the second part of the subject, viz. what means should, in my opinion, be taken to prevent or cure. First of all, I most unhesitatingly condemn any precautions implying suspicion, and all approaches to individual treatment, unless an individual entirely voluntarily asks for advice.

Next, every father ought at an early period solemnly to warn his children against foul language and thoughts as the most accursed poison, and, when they arrive at the age of puberty, to write a short plain statement to the same effect, putting the deadly sin clearly before them in a few pointed sentences from Scripture, and also the utter destruction that lust too often brings, and the certain loss of happiness. This, I believe, to be a most important step.

Thirdly, as opportunity arises, which the Scripture lessons always give within a certain time, I always speak in the most decided and plain manner to my class. No boy in the upper classes here can sin from ignorance. I have heard that this plainness has had an excellent effect.

Fourthly, it is idle to suppose that there is any cure for animalism of all kinds unless higher tastes, objects, and occupations engross the mind. Good teaching for each boy, be he clever or stupid, something to interest all, whatever their tastes may be — carpentry, music, languages, athletics, gymnasium, games of all kinds, and a school garden is soon to be added ; these are the weapons with which we anticipate sensual evils, and ward off their attacks, and reduce them to a minimum. Nothing has been said of religion, for this simple reason—that religion, if true and able to act, acts through proper means, and moulds all external life in the best way. True religion does not act like a charm on sewage, but forces you to take a spade and drain it. Under proper circumstances, purity and chastity are as natural to young men as to young women, equally possible and happy. Proper circumstances mean plenty of occupation, higher objects, a knowledge of sin, without dwelling on details, no false exaggeration, but love of good, and exercise of mind and body. . . . I earnestly deprecate a perpetual pulling up by the roots to see how the plant is growing. Soul-growth, to be true, must be unconscious to a great extent, must be satisfied with honest efforts towards good and honest efforts to hate evil, and not be subjected to prying and dissection. My own conviction is very strong that even when the evil under discussion exists, it is better subdued by these general remedies than by more special applications. Above all, the legislature ought to stop with a strong hand the indecent pseudo-medical publications which deluge the country. The thoughts ought never to be allowed for a moment to rest on foul subjects under any pretext whatever.

The confidence with which Thring speaks of Uppingham's freedom during the earlier years of his headmastership from serious moral evil was no doubt well founded ; at a later period he had to grapple with the difficulty hand to hand. He did so with a strong hand, in some cases of proved guilt punishing with unrelenting severity, yet still depending chiefly upon the openness and frankness of treatment, to which reference has been made. Writing to a parent in 1880 he says :—

The evil of impurity is in English schools, and the numbers and want of discipline and increasing luxury make many unable to cope with it at all.   Twice before I have had to battle with it, probing each time to the very end every bit of evidence I got, and following every clue.   The second time was less than the first—this less than the second.

For the two last years I have taken to speaking solemn warning to the whole school at confirmation time—having the confirmees in one set, the communicants in another, and the rest of the school in a third.   And I plainly put before them the devil work of impurity, and warn them that I will pitilessly turn out any one who after such warning is found guilty.   So I am sure that no one who is not a new boy can be ignorant either of the sin or its consequences.   Well, I found out four boys, and required their withdrawal.   The sixth form petitioned to have the punishment remitted.   I told them I would not stand up before the school to repeat my warning which had not been carried out, unless they would satisfy me and the school that I was justified in doing so.   The consequence is, that the whole school to the end virtually have pledged themselves as a body to put down all indecency as a school offence.   This is the first time in the history of schools that such a result has been obtained.   Put it at its weakest and worst, it enables me to deal with the sin far more securely should it again be detected, and it puts the school in an entirely different position.   I am unspeakably grateful for this. It could only occur as the crowning-point of years of self-government and progress amongst the boys.

He attached the utmost importance in moral training to the opportunities furnished by preparation for confirmation.

Wrote to four or five parents about confirmation.   There, again, how fatal has been the injury to religion inflicted by the bishops (mainly through their pressure of work and want of time) having promulgated the theory of late confirmations. If a boy of fourteen will not be confirmed, or is not allowed to be, how seldom is there anything to catch hold of, or power of dealing with him.

One more note may be quoted to show the confidence his teaching inspired, even when the seed sown
did not take root.

A letter from an old boy asking me in a most despairing
way advice and counsel. . . . I have, thank God, certainly
been able to speak in a way to bring some health to his mind,
and I hope to his body also.   But it has been a very great
spiritual comfort to me to find my pupils turn to me for help
in their dire need, and that this is the impression made on
them, little as I am able in this incessant whirl and hunt to
see them in ordinary life.   Thank God for this sign of His
truth-working.

EXTRACTS FROM DIARY (1883-1886).

June 30*th.*—After dinner there was a meeting in the hall
of the Old Boys' Society.   At night I spoke of the society,
and my hope that as our starting school missions had been
copied by all the schools, so the Old Boys' Society had a
vitality still greater if once fairly worked, and if it got into all
the schools it would alter all English school life.

July 18*th.* — Exceedingly vexed and annoyed by cool
telegrams and letters from parents demanding that their boys
should go home.   We only have three fever cases, and a
dropping fire of measles.   It is so unmanly and mean to train
the young to be cowardly, and ruinous to school discipline.
The worst of it is, we owe it largely to the masters themselves,
sundry of these having been going about with faces as low as
their boots.   I have had the satisfaction of telling one parent
who sent a peremptory order for her son to come home from
a house which has had no fever, that if he goes he does not
return.   I mean to stoutly resist the assumption that individual
parents are at liberty to break up the educational discipline of
a great school.

The reader will have observed what great importance
Thring attached to the school confirmation.   A few
years before this time he had had a rather sharp

passage-at-arms with Bishop Magee, in reference to the times and conditions under which the confirmation for the school should be held. It was a case of two equally strong-willed and determined men differing upon a question of detail, which one of them at least was ready to magnify into a principle. The following paragraph has reference to this matter. Thring had the greatest admiration for the bishop's remarkable abilities, and refers to the address given at the time of their dispute as one of the most powerful to which he had ever listened :—

July 21*st.*—This afternoon I received a most touching message from the bishop who is lying in great danger at Stoke, to say that he thought there had been some coldness on my part since the matter of the confirmation, and if I thought he had in any way wronged me he asked forgiveness. I am so thankful for this. The impression has more and more grown on me that he was a good man with great difficulties to struggle with. Dean Macdonnell who wrote hoped I would answer without delay. . . . I at once drove over, as the only way of giving an early answer. The dean was not there, but I saw ——, and said how entirely free I was from any feeling against the bishop, and how much we had reason to thank him for the noble words in Christ's name that he had spoken in his Confirmation Addresses. It has touched me greatly, and I am so thankful that I can think of the bishop as having no cause of division between us. If God spares his life, as I hope He will, he will be a great man in the Church for good.

March 29*th*, 1884.—Received to-day from Felméri a translation of his account of Uppingham in the Hungarian Blue Book. It is exceedingly good ; several of the great principles, moreover, are put very clearly.

April 4*th.*—This evening took leave of ——, and on my charging him with disregarding my teaching and wasting his life, was much humiliated by his saying I frightened him so much he got into an utter muddle, and that he had tried his best. I told him I was very very sorry, but that he must learn to face the facts he had to deal with; that he always looked trifling, and was caught trifling too, and that a single word to me at any time would have had effect. But after all, I fear I have mismanaged the boy and it humbles me.

May 10th.—This day has brought solemn thoughts. My old tutor and friend, Goodford, Provost of Eton, is dead; the honestest man in work and character that modern Eton has produced, whose work, example, and life have done more to keep sound whatever soundness there is in Eton than anything else amongst all the shams I have known there. I honour him.

May 11th.—Have been reading General Gordon's reflections. Surely God has raised him up to be a great sign to this generation. Colonel Burnaby's application of the text, " It is expedient that one man die for the people," is no forced interpretation of the betrayal of him. . . .

June 7th.—I find it hard to feel sure that this disregard of money is quite right. But it is second nature when I get a man in earnest to back him and not to spare. God only knows the truth, and how far such spending is right.

June 8th.—This afternoon I have been looking over the old diary to recover the date of the chapel plans. I find the schoolroom plans came to me on Monday, 16th September 1861. I have been much comforted by reading it again. The way in which God has brought His work to pass, and that it is His work, and how one's heart was in it, and how it has grown, has come out so strongly as I read. I marvel how Marie and I ever lived through it. We should not have done so had not He upheld us in those fearful years. And yet as I read how dim and dull and commonplace the record seemed which, when written, was thrilling in my heart-strings quivering with pain, dropped in my life-blood on the page, and now it seemed all turned to common ink, excepting indeed the deep feeling of the great deliverance and a great work done.

July 12th.—The most astonishing thing has happened to-day. There has been a fellow named —— at the school these eight years, an excellent good fellow, but so inaccurate through bad teaching, and apparent inability to fix his mind, that I have simply again and again given up his exercises in despair, doing nothing because I knew what a good fellow he was. Lately I have been able to give him some credit for trying in the right way. Well, that fellow has shown up the winning poem—full of tender, true feeling, and graceful diction. It is a marvellous triumph of goodness wakening into delicate power in him, and a marvellous reward to me for working at each boy hopefully. Thank God.

July 18*th*.—Nothing is more strange to me than the curious similarity of mind and body. Here am I, just like a fellow with a raw wound that cannot bear to be touched. I knew my bank book must show an improvement, and yet till I saw it the very thought of the account coming in made me ill. Things are better. It makes me laugh when the tercentenary accounts talk of my indomitable will. I should like to know where my indomitable will would have been had not some little faith and God's Spirit upheld me. When I think what a coward I am, a self-contradictory coward, and how often I should have been done for, it does seem ridiculous. I suppose man must still talk in this way of man, but it is very little true.

September 24*th*.—Witts died the first week of the holiday. I feel it much, but I am exceedingly thankful that his last connection with Uppingham and my last memory of him should be the tercentenary meeting, when he met with a hearty welcome and public acknowledgment of what he had done on every side, and looked delighted and full of genial, happy feeling.

During the summer holidays of this year he had come to the conclusion that it might be his duty to resign the headmastership of the school. The purpose had been floating in his mind for one or two years, and he now seems to have seriously entertained the idea for several months, and only gave it up on the earnest remonstrance of trusted friends.

September 29*th*.—Altogether I feel glad to be at work again, but with the solemn sense of the unsettled state of the future for me. But I have absolute faith in God bringing all things right, however foolish my immediate feelings may be, however cowardly.

October 19*th*.—Truly, what a peace-making all round this closing scene is: peace with all those who have only been mistaken, not malicious—peace with the trustees, peace with the masters, peace with the bishop, peace with the town. Lord, Thou wilt let Thy servant depart *in peace*, according to Thy word. It is very striking; day by day some new sign comes in and gives me grounds of faith.

November 14*th*.—To-day I have told Marie my intention of leaving this place in the summer. I am sure I am doing right in not hanging on, and that God has led me to the right time. . . . I had a little boy named —— in to speak to who had been lying, and I spoke to him very seriously. When I had finished I held out my hand to him and he took it, and on my shaking hands and drawing him forward he fell on my neck weeping and kissed me, and I him. Now it is a glorious thing that wielding the power I do as the head of this great school, and being such a potentate, the hearts of the little boys in the school should some of them feel towards me so lovingly as to do this. I thank God for this sign that my work and life touch their hearts.

November 17*th*.—I feel keenly what a trial my resignation must be. I have settled to abide absolutely by Sir G. Couper's, Jacob's, and Birley's decision in the matter, and I have written to all of them. This is a great relief to me. The only thing that I have felt strongly in this matter has been, that whilst God in many ways, and in a thousand little particulars, has seemed to direct me to this point, I cannot persuade myself that without receiving as direct a dismissal or call as put me here I am right in leaving my post. I cannot quite persuade myself that I should not be leaving it without orders. Whether the thing seems to turn out well or ill, if I have orders, I am content. I cannot either feel any fear. Something upholds me and makes me think and feel that all will be well, however blind the future seems to be.

The opinion of those whom he consulted was entirely against his taking the step which he proposed. As he had no adequate means on which to retire, and as no preferment had even been offered him, I find it difficult to explain how he could at this period seriously entertain, as he certainly did, the idea of resignation. He seems to have been full of a simple faith that he would not be left without the means of support, if at the call of duty he resigned his post. More than one letter received about this time from friends of influence points out how overwhelming was the claim which he had established by his work upon those who had the bestowal of church preferment, and it is probable that he may have thought it likely that this claim would be considered. It is impossible to avoid the conclusion that if his long service had then received the public recognition which it deserved, there did not exist the slightest reason why he might not have been spared for many years of happy and successful work. But the yoke of toil could not be thrown off. For the moment this brought him only happiness.

November 19*th.*—A great feeling of peace came over me at having settled not to resign. I had a letter from Sir George Couper that quite decided me. . . . I have all along had a strong misgiving whether I was doing right in leaving my post without positive orders, and this doubt being set at rest is a great relief. The peace I feel is quite the peace of doing right.

November 28*th.*—It is many years since I have felt so happy : never so happy—so free from care—I mean. God is bringing His work to a happy end for me and mine, I believe.

November 29*th.*—My birthday. A happy day. Particularly delighted with Skrine and David having presented me with two hymns for the beginning and end of term, instead of the mawkish things we now sing. Delighted too to see our school literature grow, and broaden its base. I trust very much to our literature in days to come keeping the school true to high principles and giving them *esprit de corps.*

December 14*th*.—It is astonishing how this term I have felt lifted up into a new world of power and feeling. It seems to me as if my prayer was directly and wonderfully answered, and a spirit breathed into me that gives me power to speak and new things to say, and the feeling of being a προφήτης, uncaring for the blame or praise of men. I believe God has given it. It is quite a new feeling to me.

December 17*th*.—Indeed, this term has lifted me into a new world of feeling and power in all ways. Never since my working life began have I felt so untroubled in money matters. Never have I felt so above my work, so full of higher power. God has surely touched my heart and lips.

December 27*th*.—A happy week over, with a happy Christmas Day. . . . I have been working quietly all the morning at my London Address, and feel happy about it. God has given me a message to deliver, and I feel it to be from Him.

December 28*th*.—It is wonderfully strange and interesting to me to watch the life unravelling like a drama written and acted before one. How one thing of life leads to another, and at the right moment all comes out in order. I marvel, and watch, and wait, and pray, and praise. How are the years that the "canker-worm" has spoilt being given back.

December 31*st*.—The last hour of the old year. It has been an eventful year to me, and it closes for the first time since I have been at Uppingham with a feeling of peace. Thank God for this. Strange to say, the impression on my mind is, that I am about to begin a new life instead of being at the close of life. There is much of new interest and new work which I feel I can do unravelling out of the former life and work. I am re-writing *Theory and Practice* with great interest.

March 18*th*, 1885.—What a glorious gift to the English race Gordon's life is! For me I feel raised and cheered infinitely. It is such an incarnation of the Holy Spirit as He wished it to be, and coming in this age of cant and science it is like a revelation in our land. Sent off *Theory and Practice* to-day. I am so thankful. God has given me to speak truth, and though in England it is a lost cause, yet who knows, and it helps and cheers workers, and betters such work as can be done. I thank God for His speech given to me.

March 25th.—The concert over; the best I suppose ever given by an English school, or at an English school. Joachim here, Ludwig, and Herr Korleck, the finest trumpeter in the world, who was brought over to play in the Albert Hall, and has only played here besides. Joachim told the boys that they did not know what pleasure and delight they had given him by their singing, and their feeling for such music as that of Bach and Handel. The whole thing was splendid. . . . I was delighted in talking with Joachim to find that he really and thoroughly likes coming here. He said, "I do so like to hear those children sing," and that he is astonished at David's success with them.

May 14th.—I have invited the Conference of Headmistresses to meet at Uppingham in 1887 if I am alive and here. If the world is to get better education the women must do it. My heart is still full of my queen; the strangest mixture of joy and sorrow. One thing is of infinite power with me. I have touched the highest pinnacle of honour. Never shall I have such a glory of life as her life answering to and acknowledging me on her deathbed. And I prize it above all things as a call to care for nothing less holy, less pure—as half-opening the doors beyond the grave.

June 15th.—Miss M——, head of the —— High School, came in the afternoon, and I don't think we ever did a better bit of work than cheering and breathing life into that hard-worked, lonely-hearted woman. I rejoice in what we have been able to do. I think my queen would rejoice in it and deem our kindness to weary hard-worked women a noble thing. I feel that to help women is specially to be loyal to her. . . . I have been so much struck lately with the contrast of my early years and now in prophecy. Then the prophet eye was Cassandra-like, seeing evil and no remedy. Now the prophet eye is of Christ seeing the great life-healing moving through the world, and being part of it.

June 16th.—Jones-Bateman gave the school an interesting talk to-night. It is very refreshing getting these old boys back. In this last year we have had Swinny, Cameron, and Jones-Bateman. What a power for good this is!

June 17th.—Wrote to-day a formal invitation for the Con-

ference of Headmistresses in 1887 if I am alive and here.
. . . For me I more and more see that the legacy my queen
has left me and the message of Christ through the events of
last year is to help women, education, and purity. θεῷ δόξα.
I am *Lætus sorte mea*, however heavy-hearted at times or
surface-sad.

June 20th.—Very weary to-night. All the travelling and
the crowd of things sweeping through one's life combine with
the heavy daily work. The widening interest in the outside
educational world, . . . and the great questions of life make
life very interesting, but very weary too sometimes. I do,
however, rejoice in having taken into my heart *Lætus sorte mea.*
I trust, by God's help, never more to have strong desire for
anything but the working in the best way. My heart is
wonderfully at rest about my stay here now, and Paradise has
become a great reality in this world of daily mysterious life
and darkness.

June 22nd. — Educational correspondence increasing.
Nothing is more strange to me than the way in which an inner
world goes on regulating all the work and feelings, whilst the
influences and messages which make that inner world and
which it obeys never find outward expression of any kind to
any one, and yet are supreme.

June 24th.—My book came to-day. It is very nicely
turned out, and I am very pleased at getting it. There are
some very penetrating truths in it which will slide in and
break up in time many popular lies, and if accepted will
inaugurate a new departure in mental treatment, and the
estimate formed of mind. . . .

June 25th.—We have settled the tercentenary matters, and
I have given my £200 for the decoration of the old schoolroom. So that is off my mind. . . . Gordon's memoir is out
most opportunely at this moment. The extracts are the most
stupendous indictment of the late government, utterly without
virulence, but so calmly sarcastic and sad. ·

June 27th.—Yesterday morning we had our Old Boys'
Society meeting. I took occasion to note in returning thanks
for my chairmanship that the school mission was due to Mr.
Foy. Lewis came up after and said that ought to be known.

Haslam proposed putting in the south window of the school-room to commemorate the mission—the first in England—and Mr. Foy. I took up the notion and set it going at once. . . . I then went across to Rossiter and had a talk with him. He said it would cost £50. I gave him the order up to that sum and must take my chance of getting it. But I reckon it of vital importance to the school to have the school mission commemorated, and I like to give Mr. Foy his due. Walter Earle also deserves credit for having worked the matter. . . . The Borth songs were exceedingly appreciated on Thursday night. The school songs are an inheritance to the school.

July 3rd.—To-day I took a bold step. Remembering Lord ——'s talk and the letter I had from him a day or two ago, I wrote and told him that thousands were disgusted at the radical tyranny and bribery and its aimless murders, and saw nothing but the radical bribers of criminals on one side, and on the other constitutionalists, and did not know at present what to do, with no party able to work. That the fate of liberty rested with the old Whigs; if they would split with the Radicals and raise the cry of "Liberty" it would out-conjure "Liberal," with its now discredited cant, and I entreated him to think whether it could not be done. . . . What I have said is too true not to stick, and if it please God, it may prove a lighted match.

July 5th.—A hot day. School-keeping in July is a mistake, but we English somehow seem to be settling down into doing the wrong thing. . . .

July 7th.—Yesterday nearly all our ladies and myself—three waggonettes full—made a pilgrimage to North Luffenham, where we met Mrs. and Miss Johnson and two friends, to the Founder's tomb, which we brought crosses and wreaths to do honour to. The rector received us, gave us tea, and showed us the old registers and other documents, and the communion plate of the Founder. It was a most interesting and memorable afternoon; after three hundred years the meeting of the representatives of his family and of his foundation refounded gathering around his grave to acknowledge our obligation. I think it likely to be an annual visit. It was Marie's idea. I have been very much struck with the spirit blessing that my queen has brought me by *Lætus sorte mea*.   Day by day it is in my mind and on my lips when alone, and it has given me a peace such as I have never known ; and taken all the thorns of wish for change, and weariness and desire to escape from the pettinesses .here out of my heart.   It is a blessing of blessings, and I thank God for it. . . . This morning I had a very long letter from Lord ——.   My writing has done good and has been well received.   I mean to-morrow to send another letter and see if something cannot be done to prevent the fearful dishonesty of all moderate Liberals, throwing in their lot with the Radicals and aimless murder and bribery of the mob, and betraying our liberty to a tyrant majority.

July 10*th.*—A very hot day.   I have been much struck to-night in walking on the grass terrace walk, which we so often paced in fear and anguish in early years, with the change in these last years, the two last especially, and now this evening I silently rejoice in the main current and results of life. *Lætus sorte mea ; Lætus* in having been counted worthy to suffer, *Lætus* in the deliverance which suffering has wrought. Surely I would not wish to live my life over again, but more surely still do I rejoice, being what I was, that Christ's great hand has fashioned me and through necessary pain made me a prophet of truth for Him.   Well do I remember how, when I read Cassandra in my young-man days, I sadly thought Apollo still gave the fatal gift of seeing *was ich doch nicht wenden kann*, but now as a prophet of Christ I rejoice in the prophetic eye and the sight of the Kingdom of Life, in seeing "the fig-tree put forth her leaves and knowing that summer is nigh," where ruin only is the sight that meets the intellect.   I am glad when I know Henry has heard good of me, for my early days of danger must have been a great trial for him, as he understood nothing and only saw ruin possible.

July 22*nd.*—To-day for the first time in my life my bank-book, after a minute or two of habit of fear, has brought me no terror.   It is now only £1240 to the bad.   £1000 has to be paid in for the old school, leaving £240.   £100 from salary and another payment, leaving £140.   I have £60 on my private account, leaving £80.   Thank God, the next payments will see me out of debt. *Lætus sorte mea.* Gentle and true may I be, and not ask God for departure, or anything but spirit life for me and mine. *Theory and Practice,* combined with the educational address, have made a stir, and I am being quoted now constantly.

July 24th.—A kind of happy awe comes over me when I think, as is the fact, that the touch of a few minutes of highest life can be felt to be a full requital for years of pain, as God has shown me by letting me come near my queen on her deathbed, nay, her birthday to life. What abysses of divine felicity must be in heaven where life reigns !

July 30th.—The quiet last evening come at last. To-morrow we start for Scotland. The most eventful term of my life come to an end—eventful, that is, in the strange and wonderful world of thought and feeling into which I have been launched ; the great mystery of life which I have been lifted and moved into. . . . The clear and yet most startling language of life by which many little bits of life combine into a spiritual message full of happy awe, unmistakable, though but half-read, is a revelation. One thing at once I have gained unmistakably : the content that leaves dreams of change alone, and now— leaves me without a wish and scarcely a thought about being moved from here. . . . Then the addresses and the book and the call to take part in the world work of education is most strange. The way, too, I have been brought in contact with the high schools for girls is another message chiming in with the inward feeling that God, through my queen, and my loyalty to her, means me to be a champion of women. All this moves in my being always with a strange new power, and has altered, raised, transfigured my whole life. Then the being set free from debt lifts off me the life-long pain and heavy weight that crushed me all too much. . . . Altogether it has been most full of life. . . . To-morrow we go.

November 15th.—Been thinking much how dream-like life is, and how utterly ignorant we are of what is really going on. But I had rather be an unknown part of the inner life of Christ's world than sway empires. The Empire ruler puts in motion for good or evil external machinery which the inner life has to deal with, but the inner life is the only truth even then.

I believe it has been given me to make many lives happier and better. That is indeed a gift of God.

November 23rd. — Miss Buss was here. It was very interesting. She is an able woman, and well up in the whole educational movement. I was immensely pleased at her saying that I was the first man who had acknowledged them as fellow-workers, and that when my invitation to the mistresses to hold their conference at Uppingham came before the committee, they were silent and speechless, so much were they struck by the public recognition.

January 17th, 1886.—Another very interesting letter from Mrs. Kingsley; also from Miss Lohse, my New Zealand schoolmistress. It is most curious how many little "liftings of the veil," cheering bits of life and spirit power have been given me in the past month. . . . To-day I heard a thing which struck me much. My girls have been over the India-rubber Factory at Manchester; they saw there a respectable old man whose life-work for thirty years had been dipping balls in some liquid to vulcanise them. For thirty years ! and then to think of my repining over my life. God help me. May I ever be *Lætus sorte mea*, gentle and true. My sermons are now ready for the press. I hope to get them off to Cambridge on Wednesday. . . . I am happy to say Henry's contribution to the *Nineteenth Century* is not so against my convictions as I expected. In fact, his main point does not affect them.

January 18th.—It is very strange and comforting to me, the numerous messages of spirit life and of the "goodly fellowship of the prophets" that have reached me lately. Not least my correspondence with Mrs. Kingsley, and knowing that he and she had a strong feeling for Uppingham and the work here. It sweetens life wonderfully.

February 5th.—A most interesting letter to me from St. Cloud to-day asking me to write a special address to the teachers of Minnesota, and giving me a sketch of what is going on and what they want. How wonderful this communion of life is ! I pray God to put in my mouth what to say. I shall do it with great delight if it is given me.

March 2nd.—My trustee payment in to-day. They have

positively put me back again to the lowest legal rate allowed them. I marvel; even after all the past, I marvel. They seem incapable of waking.

March 10th.—I spent the whole evening drawing cheques. I still feel something like having to deal with snakes in doing it. But bank-book fever is no longer on me, though I am far from faithful even yet. I cannot but wonder at the trustees putting me down to the lowest payment permitted by law. It is curious.

May 25th.—It is strangely wonderful what a change for the better has come over me in this last year—how full of contentment and peace I have become. God has given a blessing. I was unsettled and longing for a change with a kind of resigned discontent and hungry acquiescence, and now my whole heart is quiet, and though not free from care, free from chafing, and willing.

May 27th.—I gave a short Socratic explanation to the Upper V. of what their body and life and mind were, and how they were nothing but a structure of inherited life-power, daily built up by the inherited wealth of life of all the great men who had ever lived, and how they had the glory of all the noblest life of the world given them to use. I hope and think I put them in a new world. Some of them certainly felt it much.

June 28th.—Went to see old Mrs. S—— to-day, who is able to come downstairs after her long illness—carried downstairs. It is beautiful to see such simple goodness. I feel greatly cheered that she should long for me to visit her. (I never spoke to her before.) Of all things in the world, to be a comfort to the holy and the weak is the greatest blessing God can give. How little the old lady can know how much her approval and wish is to me. But what greater thing can be given on earth to man than the testimony of the pure and holy weakness of those whose only claim is holiness and weakness.

July 24th.—I am very much touched by the quiet devotion with which Skrine strives to lighten my work and brighten my life. I am very grateful.

In the diary during the years with which we are now dealing, the thread of private and personal reference is often so closely interwoven with matters of more general interest that it is not always easy to separate them.   His letters, however, during this period illustrate even more fully than usual many currents of his thought and interest.

The selections from his correspondence in the chapters which follow belong for the most part to the last five years of his life, though for various reasons a few of earlier date have been inserted.

CHAPTER VI

CORRESPONDENCE WITH MRS. EWING

1883–1885

A TOUCHING episode in Thring's later years was his friendship with the gifted writer of children's stories, Mrs. Ewing. It was curiously illustrative of his character and his views of life that he attached far more importance, as living and efficient forces in the world, to writings such as hers, with their beautiful and tender simplicity of spiritual teaching, than to the rougher and more forceful products of great intellectual power. He had for years admired the work done by Mrs. Ewing and her mother, Mrs. Gatty. "I marvel," he remarks, "at the state of English literary feeling that has not made her exquisite stories famous and her with them." Writing after her death to an American correspondent he says: "Mrs. Ewing was the daughter of Mrs. Gatty, author of *Parables of Nature*, the most beautiful book in its way in the English language. The mother and daughter have opened a new world of higher life and thought and feeling for mankind."

For several years, although they had never met, he kept up a correspondence with Mrs. Ewing. Before her work had achieved the great popularity which it finally gained he had perceived her power, had become her devoted literary admirer, and in moments of doubt and hesitation had given her encouragement which she valued greatly. He was wont to refer to her as the Queen of Story-tellers, and in the family circle at Uppingham she came to be familiarly spoken of as the "Queen." He was in the habit of sending her his writings on educational questions, while she consulted him in regard to her literary work. The mutually helpful relations which existed between them are shown in their letters.

MRS. EWING TO REV. EDWARD THRING.

TAUNTON, *October 7th,* 1883.

I have had several reasons for purposing to write to you, and I hope you will forgive my delay in so doing. First and foremost is the kind gift of your book and the too kind in-scription, which I will not deny pleases me—such is human vanity! Both I and Major Ewing have been reading it—the book, not the pretty speech—with great interest, and I am now looking forward to lending it to a very clever and pleasant neighbour of ours, who is national school inspector here. He is genuinely interested in education, but I fancy is pretty representative of modern ideas, and I shall be curious to hear how your views hit him. . . . My sister tells me that you spoke of Somerset as your old country. I do hope that if in holiday times you drift back to your native soil you will give us the pleasure of a visit on your way. I can put up you and Mrs. Thring with fair comfort, and it would be a great pleasure to thank you both in person for the long-standing kindness and sympathy you have shown to me in my work. It is very helpful to be encouraged, and encouragement from you has value to stand against the fits of despondency in which I fear that, either from weakness of body or from a very much feebler order of intellect than I sometimes hoped had been committed to my use, I shall never be of any good to my generation. I have been partly hindered in writing to you from the pressure of vexatious business connected with a little story of mine, *Jackanapes,* which I have just brought out in separate form with seventeen illustrations by Caldecott —for 1s.—and of which I hope you have received a copy which I ordered to go to you more than a week ago. It is a favourite bit of work of mine, and I have been urged again and again to publish it cheap for boys. It has taken me three years to secure Mr. Caldecott (whose genius in his own line *I* reckon unique in his generation!). He is so busy and so fragile. But I did get him; and he has done nearly three times the number of designs the S.P.C.K. asked for, in his thoroughness and his kind wish to please me. I got Col. Deedes to admit him to the War Office to study uniforms of the periods; I have employed his own special engraver—the paper was made on purpose; I polished the text to my utmost, and now the S.P.C.K. says that "the Trade" says it is not worth a shilling! The secretary informs me that the booksellers refuse it *en masse*, and I must have it bound in coloured boards at once. The expense of this would just prevent my getting any profits from the sale, if it did not prove a standing loss on every thousand sold !!!

Now do you think I feel like a "Queen of Story-tellers"? I wonder what you think of the cost of it. I had a paper cover on purpose and put all the expense on fine paper, print, and pictures within, in the ambitious hope that if I could coax R. C. to illustrate some other tales for me (and he is very kind to me), these one-shilling volumes might be bound by those who cared for them into a form fit for the only place where one would care to be shelved—the library. . . .

TO MRS. EWING.

October 10th, 1883.

I love *Jackanapes;* it is perfect, and I cordially agree with you that Caldecott is unique; his women make one draw one's breath from the charm of their pure and exquisite loveliness, and his horsemen ride as never men have ridden in picture or marble before. I know him slightly. He married the sister of one of my boys, and has been here. The blackbird in the school aviary here sat to him for his immortal pie book, unconscious of his glory. . . . It may console you to know . . . that I have never got a penny by my writings.

But you ought to. . . . Never mind, you *are* the queen of story-tellers, and you have given to numbers, myself included, holy and pure refreshment from a living fountain. . . . Be of good cheer—your generation would miss you sorely with your tender feeling and delicate simplicity of touch. I am convinced that everything truly original *must* in every instance feel that it is perishing in the lost battle; but for all that, the lost battle of one generation in the kingdom of life is the victory of the next, and the cross in all things is the step to the throne.

I am glad to hear your nephew is happy here. I staked my life on the endeavour to make boy life better, higher, and happier, and I rejoice at every evidence that the leaven works. But I too feel to my heart's core the truths I would fain cheer you with. I am called successful, and in a sense I am, but I absolutely despair of English higher education; all I care for, all I believe in, all I have poured out my life to save, has during the last thirty years been in process of destruction by authority; the future looks hopeless, and whatever man can suffer of shame and pain and ruin I may say I have suffered and feared in this place.

But truth lives—life cannot be destroyed, and I catch glimpses from time to time of far-off openings into light, as I doubt not, with all your fits of despondency, you do at times. It was precisely because I felt you belonged to the living who get but scant measure from their generation, and feel keenly that it is so, that has drawn me on to do what I could to make you strong in conscious success. Believe me, resolute as I am thought to be, and have indeed borne myself in this fierce battle, a more miserable coward in inward fear and sensitiveness does not exist. I have sometimes in my emptiness almost wished some one would march me out, send a volley into me, and shy me into the nearest ditch, rather than go on in my weakness. . . .

MRS. EWING TO REV. E. THRING.

Epiphany, 1883.

I've been a good deal " driven " lately. Some most desperate struggles over the business part of *Jackanapes*, which

I hope now is fairly settled.   It's not easy to me, constitu-
tionally, so to speak, to put my foot down, but I have done it
on one or two points, and they have been yielded with magic
rapidity.   Perhaps the latest news from S.P.C.K. has something to do with this, viz. that they were selling it "at the rate
of 500 a day."   Nineteen thousand have been ordered already, ·
and the printers can't get them out fast enough.   This, of
course, is not likely to go on after Christmas, but it may fairly
be called a success, and as "after the event" no one is likely to
say kinder things of that favourite child of my brain than you
said before it, there is no one to whom I am more glad to say
that it is doing well.

But I never was more harassed about anything! and now
—when for a few hours printers, publishers, and binders have
paused in their attacks—an elderly clergyman from the neighbourhood of Barnsley writes to ask S.P.C.K. if it is aware that
in a publication called *Jackanapes* occurs language inconsistent
with the third commandment, and S.P.C.K. forwards to me,
and "pause for a reply."

If you can conceive what it is to explain matters satisfactorily to an excellent gentleman who thinks "what the
deuce" is taking the Lord's name in vain, who draws and
perçeives no distinction between what I speak *in propria
persona* and that I put into the mouth of an old soldier of
1815, and who, to crown all, is obviously of so entirely an
unliterary type that he would probably willingly exclude Scott
and Shakespeare from a boy's library, from any Christian's
library, if he could retain the tracts of Dublin Repository,
you will know what is before me!   By last night's post I got
a Union Jack from Portsmouth from a fervid admirer who
says Caldecott has done it wrong and wants it corrected in
future editions.   I believe it wouldn't be a bad plan to send
an essay on profane swearing to the flag people, and one on
the history of the flag that braved one thousand years to
the punctilious parson, and refuse to recognise the error.   It
might widen both points of view!

I'm very tired, and I must go to bed.   I do wish you and
yours every blessing and joy for 1884, and I renew sincerely
my thanks for your unfailing cheer to my onward way.

To Mrs. Ewing.

(No date.)

I have got *Jackanapes*. I wish if you are ever good enough to send me another of your works you would write my name in it yourself. Mrs. Thring (whose eyes do not allow her to read much) could not get any of the family to undertake to read it to her unless quite alone, from their feelings. A slight compromise was effected at last by changing the reader and partial privacy, and we got through it at intervals. I took the liberty as I was giving a lecture to the school last week to give you your queenly honour, and inform them that if I had the power I would make every man jack of them buy *Jackanapes*, and I have followed it up by making our bookseller get down fifty copies at once and dispose them all over the shop window. I like the paper cover with its design far better than boards. O Queen, live for ever! Long enough at least, I hope, to trample on the publishers.

Though thus corresponding on terms of intimate friendship, it happened by a singular series of chances that the meeting with each other which they had long wished for and several times arranged never took place until Mrs. Ewing was suffering from the illness which soon after ended her life.

The circumstances under which they then at last met made a profound impression upon Thring. Mrs. Ewing was then staying at Bath, and Thring, going to Somersetshire for the Easter holiday of 1885, stayed over to see her.

Next day I went to see Mrs. Ewing. She was very ill, but I was admitted, and I shall never forget her. I held it the honour of my life to have been received by her as a very dear friend, though she had never seen me before. She lay so wasted and so pale, more than pale; but as soon as she looked up the great eyes filled with light, and the whole face became a presence of light, not a face, and we had a few minutes (to me) of happy talk, and she asked me to say the Lord's Prayer, which I did, with her wasted hands in mine, and then I left her. I thank God for having allowed me the dear privilege of seeing her and comforting her. I went back on Monday and saw her again. She had had a very bad night, and her seeing me at all was a sign of the most perfect affection.[1]

May 7th.—I pray daily that she may be raised up again to prophesy the tender things of God's life which He has taught her to speak. She is better, I am thankful to say, and I begin to have a real hope that she will be given back to us.

On his return to Uppingham he writes to Miss Gatty :—

May 11th, 1885.—I hope you have got over the removal successfully, and that your sister, though she may miss her little birds and nest, has a more cheery view and can enjoy it. I pray for her daily many times.

I had no idea of my Address being read to her even, much less of her reading it ; but I sent it as a token of fealty to " my Queen," as a faithful subject should, and also the sermon which comes now. The whole family, who are most loyal to the Queen of Story-land, myself included, are busy to-day gathering their best flowers for our queen. Mrs. Thring specially sends the lilies of the valley, which are her own pet possession. I hope my queen is winning her Victoria Cross, and gathering in all manner of tender, delicate experience of life and God and the Holy Spirit which, I pray, may, in years to come, be a light in her heart. Give her my love, if she will accept it.

May 12th. — Yesterday we gathered a nice lot of

---

[1] " Of what may be termed external spiritual privileges she did not have many, but she derived much comfort from an unexpected visitor. During nine years previously she had known the Rev. Edward Thring as a correspondent, but they had not met face to face, though they had tried on several occasions to do so. Now, when their chances of meeting were nearly gone, he came and gave great consolation by his unravelling of the mystery of suffering, and its sanctifying power, as also by his interpretation that the life which we are meant to lead under the dispensation of the Spirit who has been given for our guidance into truth, is one which does not take us out of the world but keeps us from its evil, enabling us to lead a heavenly existence on earth, and so to span over the chasm which divides us from heaven."—*Memoir of Mrs. Ewing,* by her Sister.

flowers and sent them down to Mrs. Ewing. The whole family are her most loyal subjects, and I hope my queen will be pleased. How I trust and pray she may be restored to health and strength to prophesy her sweet tender messages of delicate life, of which God has made her His prophetess. I feel greatly honoured by her affection, and consecrated by it to a higher and purer life. When I look back it astonishes me to find how many years she has been an ideal in my mind, and her mother before her. And now I can give pleasure and help to my Queen of Story-land.

May 13*th.*—Alas! our flowers will not be seen by my queen. Very anxious news came this morning, that she has had to undergo a most painful operation, and is, I fear, hovering between life and death ; at all events, beyond the reach of our flowers, or anything but our prayers. I have felt to-day like one moving in a dream. I can but pray, but my heart is very low.

May 14*th.*—Ascension Day. Yes, my queen is dead. Yesterday morning about eight o'clock her gentle spirit passed away peacefully, and the sweet voice is stilled on earth for ever. Yet it speaks on for ever too. What a light has gone out, and how few comparatively heed it ! Though many will think of her loss, few will feel that her powers of tender inspiration were matchless, never seen before, and never to be surpassed in delicate life, in that breathing of the Holy Spirit which is living by its life, and by nothing but life. O my queen ! my queen ! A strange mystery to me hangs over our intercourse. The power I was able to be to her at a trying time, the not being allowed to see her two years following, and then admitted to her dying bed, for such it was. I feel as if I was con-secrated to some work to be done through her affection. At all events, it is a strange mysterious feeling of expectancy on me, and a call to a higher life and more spiritual devotion.

Monday, 18*th.*—How strange this modern life is ! Since I last wrote, besides much else I have travelled 540 miles. On Friday morning when I came out of first school, I found a letter from Mrs. Smith, her sister, saying, that if I would come, there was no one her family would more wish to take part in the last offices than myself. . . . Soldiers bore her to her grave in the quiet country churchyard. It was a most beautiful morning.   The grave was lined with moss and lovely flowers, and the coffin buried in crosses and wreaths of most beautiful blossoms.[1]   I read the service by their wish from the lesson inclusive to the end, and the last sight was this glorious heap of flowers, fit type of a life crowned.   Never shall I have such honour as the being associated with her last hours and her   .   last earthly life, our flowers gathered in gladness for her life crowned her as she lay on her last bed, and were even in her hands, fit type once more of the gladness that should be of the living life departed to Christ.   *Lætus sorte mea*[2] came in just before the last operation.   It had been looked on as an omen ; rather I look on it as a message from the world of truth sent us for blessings. . . .   Altogether I feel consecrated and raised into a higher world by this wondrous union at the last with her, the pure and inspired prophetess of God's life to men.

Returning from the funeral he travelled with a dear friend of Mrs. Ewing whom he had met at her home.

TO MRS. JELF.

May 20th, 1885.

I venture to send you the writings I spoke of on our most interesting journey.   The sermons and the fragment of print, and part of the *Charter of Life* deal with *value*.   The *Charter of Life* itself, though addressed to men originally, is eminently one for women to read, and I personally feel intensely strongly that woman's mission is there laid down, and the grand revelation of the Bride are *the truths on which the practice of the world hinges.*   The President's address I send to please myself, because I wish you to read it, as I am amused and interested in having officially delivered myself of such un-

[1] "On the 16th of May she was buried in her parish churchyard of Trull, near Taunton, in a grave literally lined with moss and flowers ; and so many floral wreaths and crosses were sent from all parts of England that when the grave was filled up they entirely covered it, not a speck of soil could be seen ; her first sleep in mother earth was beneath a coverlet of fragrant white blossoms."—*Memoir of Mrs. Ewing,* by her Sister.
[2] Mrs. Ewing's last book, *The Story of a Short Life.*

fashionable doctrines. Indeed, I please myself exceedingly in sending them all—first, because it is a pleasure to me, a great pleasure, to offer you anything; and secondly, because it is a great pleasure to me to be admitted to your intimacy and to exchange thoughts. I feel a kind of sacred bond in our having met where, and how, we did; even as I feel that the strange manner in which I was brought near my queen at the last remains for ever with me as a kind of consecration of my life. I did not know till now how large a space she filled in my thoughts, and has done for years.

To the Same.

May 25th, 1885.

The world does feel very empty to me just now. I did not know till quite lately for how many many years first her mother, and then herself, had been the central ideal in my heart of gracious womanhood. A great prophetess of God's tenderest inspired life has gone from us. O my queen! my queen! But what right have we to mourn on Ascension Day, with *lætus sorte mea* as the last message from her? But I cannot joy yet. I will strive to be holier and better, and above all, to reverence and uphold womanhood as a true vassal of "the Bride," from having been allowed to know her, and love her, and see her.

The diary says:—

May 23rd.—A hard week over. A week since I laid my queen amidst the flowers in her last earthly home. . . . My whole life rises at the thought of being associated with her last earthly hours. . . . Altogether my lower heart is heavy, whilst my higher heart is full of new faith and peace, and nobler life and happier patience.

May 24th.—A week over that I shall long remember. I have not gathered my senses yet in the great rush of feeling and the mystery of life, with the hard, fixed, daily work crushing in on it with such merciless sternness, seemingly so common-place or coarse, but really God's law of life to be obeyed. I began reading *Lætus sorte mea* again to-night, and at first could scarcely get on through the mist of tears, but I was strangely comforted as I read.   It was indeed a message from the other world to us. . . .

May 29*th.*—I have been reading *Lætus*.   My whole world has altered, and I am in a newer, higher, purer, and more unselfish world.   There is a strange mixture of pain and happiness, of death and Paradise in it; and strange purity too of motives and thoughts not of earth. . . . But above all things I am striving to be *Lætus sorte mea*, and to have no more repinings or unsettled wishes, and plans or fear or disappointment.   Airs of Paradise are nearer than ever before.   I am *Lætus*.

June 2*nd.*—I am in a new world and a higher world.   The utter ignorance and abasement I feel about all life and its mysteries is to me a most blessed result, when I consider how I once prayed against positiveness.   And then, on the other hand, comes the strange practical fact that all the lines of the practical life are as positive as ever, and the hard task is done with the hard firm hand as if there was no uncertainty in the world.   Such is the Christian solution of life; absolute weakness and humility and tenderness coexistent with a resolute acting power of unflinching clearness.   All day long *Lætus sorte mea* is in my thoughts.   I have not been as faithful as I ought to have been to that glorious gift of Christ.

To H. P. Chandler.

July 23*rd*, 1885.

Yes.   I knew Mrs. Ewing, whom I regard in my sober judgment as an experienced judge of literature, to be absolutely supreme in the art of story-telling; the queen, like whom there never has been any writer, and never will be, so pure, so translucent, such exquisite perfection of pellucid life flowing from heart to heart; such a breath of Paradise, divine, because it comes with life from a holy home, not because it speaks of holiness.   I will see that you have the best portrait sent you. A touching little biography of her is coming out now in *Aunt Judy's Magazine*, written by her sister.   I do not know anything else you could get.   I know Randolph Caldecott also slightly. But I do not think there is any account of him anywhere. . . .

To the Same.

My friendship with Mrs. Ewing and the close ties which on her deathbed became mine are one of the happinesses of my life. I rejoice at every opportunity of making her work known. Wherever her writings and those of her mother, Mrs. Gatty, *Parables of Nature*, etc., penetrate, there is a stream of purifying life to refresh mankind. Her life was the most perfect loveliness of life as life I ever knew or dreamt of. I send you in case I have not done so before a sermon of which she was the involuntary theme. I dislike funeral sermons. I did not intend to preach one, but it came. . . .

To a Friend.

September 10th, 1885.

Your letter chimed in marvellously with my present state of mind. I have always felt intensely how little our life turns on knowledge, but Mrs. Ewing's departure, and the strange association with her in death which was given me, has entirely lifted me into a higher world, and been a sort of consecration of my feelings and life. The circumstances were so strange that they impressed me more than I can tell, and the concurrent influences all converging to one point of pre-eminent nearness to her in her last hours, and her grave, though we did not, and could not, so it seemed, meet before, opened the coming world to me in a more living way than ever before; and I feel with you in your thoughts of a glory cut short here. May it not be because some special work is required to be done there?

CHAPTER VII

CORRESPONDENCE ON EDUCATIONAL QUESTIONS

1872

IN 1872 the Secretary to the Public Schools Commissioners wrote to ask Thring his opinion upon the following points :—

1. What is, or ought to be, the cost of instruction at the public schools?
2. What is, or ought to be, the prime "cost" as distinguished from "profit" of boarding at the public schools?
3. Assuming that each school must be looked at separately, on its own system, and that parents unavoidably insist on paying high rates at fashionable schools, would it not be possible to have better instruction for the more money?
4. Assuming the English system of instruction to be a training of the mind, as opposed to the continental system of storing it with useful and professional knowledge, what alterations or improvements would you suggest in the ordinary English curriculum?

Thring's reply to these questions was as follows :—

School payments are not arbitrary. If a school is a true school, it steadily sets before itself the teaching and training of *every* boy who comes to school. A school which only teaches and trains some boys out of a larger number is obviously receiving money it does not earn, if the payment is adequate ; or making the majority pay for the minority who are taught and trained, if the payment is inadequate.

The school unit of calculation is the number of boys that can be taught in a class by one master as his sole work.

We have found an average of twenty-five boys to each master throughout the school for the main work of classics, mathematics, history, geography, English, and divinity, the maximum possible.

A boy can learn in a supplementary way one modern language and singing, or drawing, or a minor subject.

The modern language masters can take eighty boys in classes averaging eight each, for three hours' actual work in their presence, per week, if there can be time found for this.

The singing and music masters cannot manage above sixty boys. The cost then of each boy for tuition will be represented by the sum requisite to keep three good masters.

Each of these masters ought to get at least £500 a year if he has to depend on tuition alone.

There must therefore be a sum of £20 per boy paid to the ordinary classical or mathematical master, and an addition of £12 : 10s. per boy for the other two. This calculation supposes the school full, and makes no allowance for working difficulties.

Boarding schools, however, undertake much more than tuition, and demand far severer work, and quite a different and higher average work than day schools.

A boarding school must command the permanent services and whole life and powers of a man of character and administrative ability. Schools which calculate on keeping young men only for a short time as masters are obviously inferior, lower the standard of education, and cannot be largely multiplied, as only a few can provide temporary tuition in this way.

A boarding-house to be first-rate ought not to pass the limit of thirty boarders.

A boarder in a first-rate school will cost from £30 to £40 per annum ; more if the management is not good, and if the system is wasteful or luxurious. This sum includes the whole cost of board, lodging, and servants. The difference in the margin allowed is not so much a difference in food as in house rent, servants, and general style. You are now in a position to judge what the rate of payment ought to be. In my opinion an average of £1000 per annum clear to each assistant master is a moderate payment for the kind of man required, and the very laborious, responsible, and high class work demanded.

If you think the payment I have assigned to the language masters, etc., high, I would observe that you cannot get a good foreign master for a less sum than a gentleman can live and marry on; and nothing, in my opinion, has injured English character and English education more than the employment of inferior foreigners.

I will now put the subject from another point of view.

At Uppingham we now employ for 300 boys—

14 classical and mathematical masters, myself included.
1 mathematical, exclusively.
1 German.
2 French.
2 music.
1 gymnastic and music.

——

Total 21

at a cost of about £23,535 per annum. We ought to have a regular science master at an additional cost of £500 per annum or thereabouts. Other school expenses amount to about £800 per annum, exclusive of funds for repairs, and for one or two minor pursuits, etc. This keeps about £80 per annum as the average cost of each boy in the gross. I consider this, at present prices, too low, even when the school is prosperous. A school struggling upwards, or inclined to fall, or classes too large for one man and not large enough to support two, or if masters are taken on for comparatively few pupils in any subject—any or all of these raise prices. Many other practical difficulties complicate the question—in applying a standard to special cases. Every large school has now to be required to have a considerable number of subjects going. Every large school ought to be compelled to have a great variety of supplementary employments, e.g. fives-courts, gardens, cricket fields, carpentry, museum, etc.

I consider assistant-masters here ought to get £70 per annum, however provided, as the gross sum paid on every boy in their houses to them, and that the school terms, if they are to include the "by" subjects now demanded, provide an adequate payment for the headmaster, and cover working expenses, ought not to be under £90 per boy.

I will now answer your questions categorically :—

1. In my opinion, where a school is nearly self-supporting, the cost of tuition at a first-rate school ought to be not less than £35 per boy; and, for boarding, such a sum over this as would raise the house-master's income to an average of at least £1000 per year. I think it a very good thing, a necessary thing, that the fashionable schools should be paid infinitely higher. In a wealthy country a profession takes rank by the payment received for work by the leaders of the profession. All will be lowered if they are lowered.

2. I consider the prime cost for boarding at a first-rate school cannot well be lower than £30, or higher than £50 per boy. I mean this to clear every payment which is necessary.

3. Clearly the great schools ought to teach and train *every* boy, and they do not even profess to try and do so.

4. Assuming the English curriculum to be a training of the mind, no boy doing full school work can with advantage learn more than two subjects in quite a supplementary way, though many boys will throw really much of their life into the supplementary subjects; and provision must be made in every school to allow some relaxation of main work to those who must do this, though, for myself, I am strongly against the modern side, and wish to see modern schools instead.

We allow a certain amount of Latin verse competition to be dropped in some cases, but I had rather, if I had the power, lessen the quantity than drop it altogether.

We do not think, on the whole, that the boys make up in their modern subjects, with rare exceptions, for any remission on the main school work.

The division of payments into payments for tuition and payments for board, though convenient, is in principle deceptive. The really valuable article paid for in the boarding school is the time of the master. His whole life is absorbed in the ceaseless work and weight of this responsibility. We are not lodging-house keepers. Yet, when tuition has been put down at from £30 to £35, and boarding at from £30 to £50, allowing no profit on it, where is the margin in terms not higher than £80 or £90 per annum—first for profit (or, at least, not loss) on the board, and then for this great demand of the whole life of an able man.   But if the ordinary British parent does not pay for this in his bill he will not recognise it, and takes a low, wrong view of the position and work.

I quite agree on the convenience of the separation of boarding and tuition fees as an arbitrary but useful basis, only I fear that to embody this through the kingdom as law, as the Endowed School Commissioners are doing, will work great evil in the public mind, the more so because the public are not yet alive even to the necessary standard of true tuition fees.

He had been consulted by those who were engaged in founding Wellington College, originally intended chiefly for the sons of army officers, and writes to the Adjutant-General :—

To General Sir Charles Ellice.

(No date.)

. . . Another point is the market in which you buy your teachers.   If it is the University market, then you cannot have the command of the leading young men of the day, or even attract them for any reasonable time as a class, unless the prospect of an early competency be held out   Schools cannot compete with the world outside either in fame or wealth to the successful man if he succeeds.   Many therefore will run the chance of success.   Schools can only offer a moderate certainty ; if they cannot do that, they are on a false basis, and must either cheat or starve.

. . . An honest school can only be cheap by diminishing the number of subjects taught at the public expense, and by a very bare sufficiency of servants and accommodation.   The actual cost of food only is not great.   In considering the latter point it is well to bear in mind how much can be lost if the boys are wasteful, which they always will be if they think the treatment niggardly ; and how much can be lost if the managers have no personal interest in the management, which will always be the case if only paid officials be employed.

Most of all, if boys are brought together out of their homes, something better than their homes, intelligently better, ought to be given to them.   If our officers are to go out from school with a galling sense of hardship and niggardly treatment, and with narrow views and embittered feelings, the training which tends to produce this impression, however just it may be, or liberal in theory, if not just and liberal to the foolish boy-mind, will cost the country very dear indeed.

To T. H. BIRLEY.

September 26th, 1873.

I don't know whether you sent me the *Manchester Courier* with the account of the laying the first stone of Knutsford College in it, and the proceedings of the day, but I most naturally turn to you to express my deep regret that one more gigantic and costly mistake is going to be perpetrated, and also to say how sorry I am that a speech full of such injurious fallacies as that of Mr. Hatch should have been the main feature of the solemnity.   There is no analogy as regards the working life of the two between the life of a parochial clergy-man and a schoolmaster.   I have tried both.   The parochial clergyman is brought in contact daily with every form of life and death that can stir a religious man's heart and keep his faith alive, and is then left to do his work or not as he pleases.

The schoolmaster is brought in contact daily with every species of petty vexation and wearing responsibility and is compelled to do a hard day's work spread over a number of hours, and day by day at a given moment, well or ill, to be at his post, whether he pleases or not.   What analogy is there between the two excepting in the one fact that if well done they are both important and holy works.   Still less analogy is there between a schoolmaster and a college tutor.   A college tutor lives in a place where his whole life is as shielded from care, and as glorified, as it possibly can be ; he has very little compulsory work, and vacations long enough to sweeten even slavery, and yet—it is notorious that the colleges cannot keep the majority of their best men even with the hope behind all this present gain, of college patronage, headships, and government to boot. I boldly assert that man is a fool who, in establishing anything which is to last many years, disregards the ordinary motives of ordinary men and average workers. I freely admit no man can buy martyrs, or go into the market and purchase the heart blood of men, but the argument cuts both ways, if money will not ensure excellence of the highest kind it does not shut it out, and money properly applied does ensure average excellence and makes the best easier to be got. . . . I protest in the name of English education and common sense against paying good work starvation prices, because you may get bad work for higher payments. The only legislation worth the name will proceed to fix a trade basis fitted to get the best work from average men taking a series of years, and will not fit its plans on exceptional men and exceptional times.

There are only three conditions under which good work may be looked for permanently. The first is when the work can offer such emolument at once as to make an early retirement easy and certain. The second is when there is no immediate gain, but the door is open to great ultimate wealth and rank if a man is successful, as is the case in the law. The third is when sufficient to enable a man to marry and settle is given early. The high class work market cannot be commanded on any other terms than these. The two first are closed to schools and schoolmasters, the last remains. If that is not conceded, then I assert without the slightest fear of contradiction that permanent good work is impossible. All the schools on the barrack system have raised their terms greatly, and if they are multiplied, the impossibility of finding many competent men who will work for starvation pay will become more and more apparent. As long as there are only a few such schools which serve as stepping-stones to other things, and which have not had time to get to their level, the truth is less apparent. I send some other papers to illustrate my statement.

To G. R. Parkin.

(No date.)

There is no point on which my convictions are stronger than on the power of boarding schools in forming national character. . . . There is a very strong feeling growing up among the merchant class in England in favour of the public schools; and hundreds go to schools now who thirty years ago would not have thought of doing so. The learning to be responsible, and independent, to bear pain, to play games, to drop rank, and wealth, and home luxury, is a priceless boon. I think myself that it is this which has made the English such an adventurous race; and that with all their faults, and you know how decided my views are on this side, the public schools are the cause of this manliness. I think you may add to your classification "and the merchants"; and that it is the fixed idea with every Englishman, in the lump, that it is the thing to send a boy to a public school, and the ordinary English gentleman would think he lost caste by not doing so. Then the boy world becomes a definite world by itself, and school life and its doings an important factor in the social world. The first germ of the boarding school I believe to have been the sending lads into the families of the great nobles to be educated in all knightly proficiency with the children of the house.

Then the first endowments took their rise from the monasteries which always had schools for the education of the clergy. Thus the public school is a cross between these two.

As regards class feeling, the thing wisely managed settles itself. As soon as it is possible to make a good boarding school work over a wide area, only those who have time to stay five, six, seven years or more at it have a chance. This at once silently decides that none but the monied classes can form the bulk of the school, this soon makes an educated class, and then endowments in England are used to help forward the poorer and less powerful but intelligent workers.

To the Same.

July 9th, 1875.

I do not of course know what to say to your troubles, as I am not acquainted with the circumstances. I can, however, state most positively two things: First, that a school such as Uppingham cannot exist unless there is a very strong religious feeling in the ruler, and power to concentrate it without the friction of controversy. And secondly, that if no religious teaching was given in the school work at all, the religious character of the school would be equally important, as it is the spirit of the teachers and rulers that signifies; the principles they are animated with in their work rather than any actual tuition that is put out by them. I do not know how this can be carried out in Canada. If it cannot be carried out, then Canada must be content with a lower type of educational life. The recent legislation with us puts practically all the schools in England under separate bodies of trustees and requires an examination and inspection—one or both—once a year. This would have come under a government board, the worst form under which anything can be done in England, had we not staved it off by getting the universities to undertake it.

What ought to be done is this: Trustees ought simply to be police with management of property, supervising and reporting power, but no authority whatever to interfere with the internal work of a school. Then there ought to be a council or councils composed of schoolmasters, lawyers, and men of authority in about equal proportions, before which all cases should be tried that required trial, and who should have power to issue new regulations, subject to Parliament. Then the headmaster ought to be supreme in all matters of work as being a skilled workman, and no amateur in authority ought to have any power to meddle with him. This last point I have secured for Uppingham. My trustees can dismiss me or my successor with six months' notice, without assigning cause, and without appeal, but they cannot tell us how to work, or interfere with our working.

To Rev. Edward White.

November 28th.

As regards education in England I am simply in despair, as far as mere human foresight goes.

In the higher school world there have been seven or eight years of commissions, talk and legislation, without as yet the point "what is necessary to make a school work well at all" having been raised by any one. And the whole of England is to be reconstructed by these blind, clever, ignorant men. Then below there is a simple scramble, with a great ignoring of what has been already done. I and many others doubtless have no fortress; all we believe is that if England throws up religious education it is the worse for England. But England is not the world nor the exclusive home of that truth against which "the gates of hell shall not prevail." I and mine will follow that, please God, *here* if we can, *elsewhere* if we cannot. Certainly at present the choice is a fearful one. The Caliban that our untaught fellow-countryman is *must be* got rid of, but it is a dreadful exchange if he is to be made a blind Samson ready to pull the world on himself, friend, and foe in his unguided intellectual efforts. However, I admit better that than Caliban, as there is some stuff in the taught man. I am quite prepared to take my chance. But I admit, when I see the lower orders evading honest work everywhere, and their rulers governing by a series of scrambling compromises, and the press glorifying our omniscience, and the wise liberty of universal jaw and noise! I cannot be very hopeful for England. My ideas of life are *work.* Of government, the plan of the men who *have worked*, chosen and supervised of wisdom; quiet experience rated high, and noise rated low. The exact opposite to my belief is taking place through the length and breadth of this land. But I hope as long as the *liberty to work in our own way* is left. That seems likely to go too, and a sort of Trades Union to become England; I shall have little hope then if alive and shall recommend my children to try another land if events take that turn.

To G. R. Parkin.

December 30th, 1875.

Holidays once more and a rest, so you get a letter from me to wish you and yours a most Happy New Year, and many of them. . . . I hope you will be able to get forward something in Canada by which every school will either be compelled to teach *each boy*, or be known not to do so, instead of the swindling fog of ignorance and false glitter which passes for school in England now, and is more and more increasing every day. The government during the past twenty years has practically been legislating against the schools, demanding everywhere either fresh subjects or a different kind of them, or both, thus calling into existence an army of crammers, and pulling down the schools in the direction of more branches of superficial knowledge. Then besides this, they have been reconstituting schools without having brought out a single principle by which to judge whether a school can do its work or not for *each boy*, and have put out schemes which won't work honestly themselves, and put the government stamp of approval on rotten systems. And this is all done with supreme self-satisfaction and an omniscience that quenches all hope. God protect Canada from such a mess! Every day makes me more and more despair of any truth coming out of the mud and mixture; add to all this, a tightening yoke of examinations daily threatening to get into central hands, and it is not a nice look-out, considering that the first axiom of all education is, or ought to be, that a rigid external examination power is death to original work, and all true progress. Only one thing is wanting, and that is in sight as a possibility, the demanding that religion shall be excluded from the schools. Confiscation has set in so fast in England, and the right over endowment as public property, without reverencing in any way the intention of the founders, got ahead so much, that anything may happen. . . . I don't value the religious question in schools half so much for what is actually taught the boys, as for the sake of the teachers. Woe to a land which prevents teachers from thinking and feeling that they are doing a work for Christ. My own prospects this new year are brighter and more full of hope than they have ever been. For the first time in my working life there is peace within and without and liberty in consequence to turn one's hand to work alone, and to get good work from the masters without hindrance. . . .

To C. W. G. HYDE.

(No date.)

We have got so far in England that the very word "teaching" only means putting out knowledge so that clever boys and girls learn, and the true meaning "that teaching is the dealing with the minds of pupils, and drawing out and strengthening their powers," is absolutely to most unintelligible, and it is useless to talk of teaching when the hearers understand an entirely different thing from the speaker. I am intensely interested in this question. It seems to me a positive curse to set up lumps of knowledge, other people's thoughts, as an idol, and by this idolatry to destroy for generations the true progress of thought and mind. Above all, it is a curse to enthrone strength, and to consign the ordinary good working mind and heart of the world to neglect and contempt. A good teacher, with fair play and time, *ought to rejoice in a stupid boy*, as an interesting problem, and when good and willing, a delight and a reward. . . .

If I can do anything to help your work it will give me great pleasure to lend my hand. If your teachers have the chance of really teaching, I mean, if they have the time allowed them, and if they have classes small enough, and if they have a feeling for mind and not for books only, a feeling for the weak and struggling, and not merely for the clever and strong, then you are far better off than we are in England at present, and may do great things. For my part I had rather have a hand in training the solid working power of the world than be glorified for any amount of successful stars. I simply think that the one great hindrance to the welfare of the world is the fact that power almost always is in the hands of men who have no bodies and are all head, and who in consequence know nothing of our common humanity. We schoolmasters have this mission, if we are true—a mission to give every one, be he clever or be he stupid, a fair chance in life ; and not to be, as has been too much the case, murderers —for it is nothing less—of the higher life of the great majority of mankind. Power-worship and contempt for ordinary minds, and putting knowledge above thought, is the modern Moloch.

In reply to certain questions asked him about the Uppingham system, he writes :—

UPPINGHAM SCHOOL, RUTLAND, *April* 1880.

As far as possible we do not take into consideration professional life and special training for special callings. We consider that a literary education, as it contains the best thoughts of the best thinkers in the best shape, is the most perfect training for man the thinker, whatever he may be obliged to do later in life.

If I wanted to train a soldier, I should not take a child and drill him every day and put him through the regimental movements; I should teach him to race, to climb, to swim, to be a gymnast, to play games, to make his body as strong, as active, as enduring as possible. It will be quite time enough to narrow this, and teach him the goose step, when he enlists. So also with the mind. If our literary and classical education is true, as I think it is, then it makes the mind strong and ready, and does not dwarf or shrivel it up, as narrower ranges do the unused limbs, if I may use the expression.

All have to learn classics.

All have to learn mathematics.

All have to learn either one modern language or drawing or science.

All have to learn some history or geography.

About 25 out of 320 learn science, the rest French and German, with the exception of the three lowest classes, about 50 boys, who have to learn drawing.

All have to learn singing who can. About 200 are engaged in singing, exclusive of those whose voices are broken.

There are about 120 pupils learning instrumental music at an additional charge.

We also make private arrangements at a small additional charge for bringing on pupils who require it in special subjects, classics excepted, which, as being the main subject of the school, receives no extra teaching.

I frame the annual plan of studies as far as power goes *alone*. But, as a matter of fact, I have just been working with a committee of masters whom I selected to revise and draw up the schedules which accompany this.

I do not present the plan to the Governing Body. They

have no authority whatever over the internal working of the school. I could not hold office if they had. They can dismiss the headmaster, but they cannot interfere with his work in the school.

The Governing Body are bound by law to hold meetings twice a year, and in ordinary years this is sufficient. The principal work at these meetings is the auditing the accounts, seeing to the money matters of the Trust, voting the money which is under their control, and assigning scholarships according to examinations which have been conducted at the school by university examiners.

The money questions with us are of the following kinds :—

Each boy pays £70 per annum to the house-master.

This sum does not pass through the hands of the Governing Body.

Each boy pays £40 per annum as tuition fee.

This sum does pass through the hands of the Governing Body, and is now distributed as follows :—

One-sixth } to the headmaster, fixed by law as the lowest
£6 : 15s. }   proportion.

£24 : 18s. per boy is assigned for the payment of masters up to the number of 320 boys.

£100 per annum is assigned for lectures, readings, concerts, etc.

£100 per annum for prizes in the school.

£1 : 10s. per boy for current expenses.

£6 : 15s. per boy for reserve fund.

There is also a sum of £1100 per annum from the original foundation, which is mainly expended in providing exhibitions from the school to any university or place of higher education, of the value of £60, £50, and £40, three every year, tenure for three years, and in a small salary of £200 a year to the headmaster.

The headmaster has no vote on the governing board. I should strongly object to having one. It is a great mistake to put the living, working power into the false position of being outvoted by a set of amateurs. As long as the Governing Body have the sole responsibility of their actions, however bad they are, the headmaster is not dragged in to any share of it, but if he has a vote he is, without having any real power.

The Governing Body are bound by law to consult the headmaster.

This clause works well if the Governing Body is intelligent and friendly, but if unintelligent and mean, the clause is no use, they do not obey it, and will not do so unless there is easy appeal to a higher court against their illegal decision. This is the real remedy. No governing body ought to be left without such an appeal. It is no use binding them by law, if they are the sole interpreters of the law.

No governing body ought to have any power to control or change the school.

They should be watchful authorities appointed to see that the school work is well done and all things carried on in order, and to protect the school in case of need.

The moment any interference is needed, both the governing body and the masters, if they differ, should at once carry every question to a higher tribunal, which alone should have any initiatory power.

This is common sense. If the living workers do not know how to work, how shall amateurs of no higher ability, frequently of lower ability and attainments, and ignorant of the work also, instruct them wisely in the manner of working?

In fact, the system of governing bodies in England has in my judgment worked very badly for these two reasons: they are men without knowledge of their subject, and always must be; and they are to a great degree irresponsible.

An easy appeal to a higher tribunal is wanted. This alone gives the professional men who do the work a chance of being heard.

The masters meet in my study once a week to discuss school questions. The headmaster is not bound by their opinions, though obviously they are important.

When I appoint a new master I endeavour to get him to be my helper in some degree by walking and talking with him. But if he shows himself self-satisfied, and without sense to take in my experience and views, I leave him to himself, and am satisfied with getting a sufficiency of average work from him.

Education and School had been written in 1867, just when success had crowned his long struggle at Uppingham, and when his unprecedented feat of having in a few years forced a small grammar school into the front rank of public schools might have been expected to secure for him a hearing on school methods. As has been said, the book, influential with the few, found at first no popular audience. He records with a feeling of deep disappointment, and as a sharp blow to his vanity, the small number of copies sold in the first year. To this failure to arrest public attention succeeded a long silence of sixteen years. That silence was only broken at the urgent request of a fellow-worker no less devoted than himself to educational truth and progress. The following letters explain the genesis of the *Theory and Practice of Teaching*, which appeared in 1883 :—

To Rev. R. H. Quick.

May 1882.

Your letter is somewhat like the bow drawn at a venture, and I doubt whether the arrow has hit Ahab. Without joking, though, it opens a wide question, and one which has been the subject of anxious thought with me for many years. I would willingly do what I can to help on the subject of my heart, true education—the subject on which life and fortune have been staked by me. Of course, publication and writing is one way of doing it. But—when I was young I naturally rushed into print, and as you know, *Education and School*, the only book on the real subject, neither sells, nor is even quoted in school discussions, though I have private reasons for knowing that it has not failed as a seed power. To take first the public question : a long experience compels me to accept the mournful axiom *populus vult decipi*. I cannot do the *decipiatur*, and they will not have the truth. If there had been no stir you would move me more. I began when there was as yet no stir, I was early in the field; I brought into the field knowledge trained by daily practice in national schools on the one hand, and a wide acquaintance with public schools on the other, and the rank of first man of my year in classics at Cambridge. If ever man's heart was in his work, mine was, and is. I know also that it has not been in vain. Apart from practical success here against odds which God only knows, I have from time to time had casual information such as you yourself have given me now, that the real leaders in education did get something from me ; but when I turn to the external facts I see an immense rush, legislative and popular, has taken place during these thirty years, and the net result has been that up to the present moment every principle I believe in has been either buried under a mass of rubbish or deliberately rejected. The practical government of education is in the hands of amateurs who have never taught. The intellectual throne of education is assigned with much pomp to intellectual Goliaths, who have never taught. Education is the only subject in which total ignorance of the real subject-matter, total ignorance of the trade knowledge gains absolute pre-eminence. The hour has not come.

Then take the publishers. . . . They are wise in their generation, but they shut the door against new truths, and the lending libraries put the final burke on, as they only want entertaining works, or the last scare. So you see I feel but little encouragement to put my thoughts on paper, or indeed possibility ; for I am poor and getting too old to trust to future success against loss. Moreover, as you rightly say my headmaster work is almost crushing, and unless I felt the most intense conviction that it was right and good to try and make an educational book, I could not find heart to match myself against time in this way. Meanwhile, the work goes on here, and I shall be very glad to show you that we are not idle, and have much variety of new power moving if ever you are inclined to pay me a visit here.

P.S.—I will bear the notes in mind in case the spirit moves me. If I had but time it might be different.

Rev. R. H. Quick to Rev. E. Thring.

Your letter makes me all the more unwilling to give up the hope of another educational book from you.   As you say, education is almost the only subject in which the doers never get a hearing, and all the talking is done by people who see everything merely from the outside.   But there are very few indeed who have practical acquaintance with school work, and at the same time literary skill enough to make themselves intelligible to the ordinary reader.   And these few, alas ! are apt to get disgusted and make excuses for not writing.   As they find plenty to do without writing or talking, they feel inclined to leave the writing and talking to those who have nothing else to do.   So the public has scarcely a fair chance. The public is certainly no seeker for truth, and reads as a gourmand eats—for pleasure, not health—so it cares far more for the cooking than for the wholesomeness of the diet.   But after all, there is a permanence about truth that there is not about nonsense, however well cooked, and those who bring home truth to even a few people on such a subject have, perhaps, an ever-spreading influence which would seem to them ample recompense if they knew of it.

This second appeal prevailed, and the book was written during the winter of 1882-83.   It appeared with a dedication to his friend as " the sole cause that it has been written."

To Rev. R. H. Quick.

September 3rd, 1883.

I am very glad that the dedication has pleased you.   You richly deserve any pleasure it may give you, for two good reasons.   You are the only man I have met with who has not been a mere partisan in education, who has not looked at it through professional spectacles of more or less self-interest, and been a modernist, because that was his line, or a classicist, because that was his line ; but has quietly looked and thought about what is *best*.   I had real pleasure in giving you such honour as I can give.   And secondly, if you knew how repugnant your request was to me, how for years I had made up my mind to mix no more in the hopeless struggle which the popular voice glorifies, and law has ratified as the right thing ; how repugnant it was to me to take the cherished gains of my life of work and go down with them into the lost battle, you would appreciate how completely true that dedication is, and that for good or evil you are responsible for the appearance of the book. I fear you will find much difficulty with your national schools. That accursed system of constant inspection is killing true work there also, and preventing men from sound progress.

The little volume at once attracted public attention ; a second edition was soon called for ; an American edition followed. His horizon had a sudden expansion. Workers in all parts of the world recognised in the writer a powerful and sympathetic spirit, and turned to him for counsel and assistance. He was flooded with invitations to address educational bodies ; he was asked to visit the United States ; he wrote an address for the teachers of Minnesota, and a school song for their annual gathering ; he went to lecture at his old university. The sense of new life working far and wide threw a halo of brightness and happiness over years otherwise much clouded with anxious cares. His letters are full of the inspiration of widening life.

To Rev. R. H. Quick.

July 24th, 1885.

Please look at the second edition. I have added much and some very important germinating ideas.

A curious change has come over the educational world, as regards Uppingham at all events, in the last two years. Up to that time a religious silence, deep and unbroken, was kept about Uppingham and myself whenever any discussion on education, written or *viva voce*, went on. Since then, I am quoted everywhere (government talk alone excepted), and if width of space is anything, the cause has made way. I have correspondence with the United States, Canada, New Zealand, Hungary, Germany, and know that the seed is being sown there. Your "echo" from Boston, U.S., is no solitary instance. Certainly, if modern life is the most barred and straitwaistcoated, it is also the freest the world has seen. "Stone walls do not a prison make, nor iron bars a cage" for it. Let a land imprison it how it may, if truly living it has the range of all the earth, and can drop and root itself somewhere or other.

To G. R. Parkin.

August 23rd, 1884.

I know very well what external disadvantages you labour under. Have I not gone through all of them? Do I not now even remember with a shudder, amongst many like evils, the Sunday services in a poky corner of a stuffy, stinking gallery of one of the worst conducted churches in England, which was my lot to begin with; and that, too, when keenly sensitive to externals and their influence, and basing all the school work to be done on religion? This was a specimen. I almost marvel now how I lived through the humiliation, the starvation of right means, the opposition, the debt, the evil speaking, and all the grit and hindrances to true work. It was touch and go at one time. But there is one virtue in a great true principle however smothered or strangled, as far as it has breath it makes life more worth living, and work higher. Like Job's prayer on the dunghill, one would not select a dunghill or match it with a cathedral; but if it is one's fate to be there, a right good prayer can be prayed in spite of—yea— because of it.

To Miss F. Lohse (Christchurch, New Zealand).

March 9th, 1885.

I agree with almost everything you say, excepting your respect for educational laws. We are being throttled by laws. A democracy is worse than a despotism for killing by law. Above all, two systems must never be mixed. A benevolent despotism does its best to make a perfect system; but half despotism and half liberty only means liberty to go wrong, and despotism to choke right. . . .

The great hope of our day appears to me to be the marvellous way in which work passes electrically through the world, and communion of purpose cheers workers in the most distant lands. . . .

For goodness sake, do not call in government; we shall all be in iron masks before long if we go on in England as we are doing. The face divine of high and thoughtful education will be seen no more.

To the Same.

July 6th, 1885.

I quite agree with your wish to prevent incompetent persons teaching, but a scalded dog dreads *cold* water, and I have seen such evil here from government interference, and have found so many difficulties while studying that very question here, as to make me willing rather "to bear those ills we have, than fly to others that we know not of." Besides, is not an incompetent master or mistress — incompetent because the wrong article altogether—a government machine with the government prize medal—much worse than any ignorance? A government machine, when life is wanted in a kingdom of life! and do not schemes which won't work honestly, turn out the dishonest minds, which, having been dealt with without care, see nothing dishonest in dealing with others without care? For my part, I believe in life and in liberty, but the tyranny of a mob is worse than that of a despot, and I dread above all things setting up mean authorities over the skilled workman. I should like to set going a confederation of skilled workmen all around the world to resist interference from amateur authority in matters of working detail. . . .

I quite understand how anxious you must be to get a little more order and discipline into your new and unformed world. But we in the last twenty years have had a powerful and self-satisfied hand grasping our heartstrings tighter and tighter, until I begin to hate the very sound of anything pertaining to government. . . .

To H. Courthope Bowen.

October 31st, 1885.

I have been thinking carefully and sadly over your letter, and am tempted to ask the question : Can nothing be done ?   If, as I see many signs abroad, the professional body are beginning to chafe under the terrible slavery, and resent it, can no anti-slavery league, however small, be formed?   I believe in small beginnings, and in a "solid core of heat," working outwards.   Is such a core impossible ?   Of course I see clearly enough that the present exponents of education in London won't do.   As far as I know them, they are the strangest mixture of red tape, crude dissatisfaction, narrow sciolism, revolutionary fumes, unworkable old, and unworkable new, kneaded up into an infallible pudding, that can be imagined ; but there is evidently much life in the general mass.   I don't say anything can be done ; I merely throw out the suggestion.   To me the course of events during the past thirty years is simply appalling.   Slowly, but surely, chaos, which nevertheless was *possible creation,* has been taken possession of by the iron room of the story, which every day contracted one panel till at last the living inmate found himself in his coffin.   The coffin is now very close.   If free education, with its locust band of inspection and examination, is to come up over the land, farewell teaching, farewell liberty, farewell life—and movement.   England's field of mind will be as dreary a waste as Egypt of old, when nothing that was not beneath the earth remained alive of its vegetation and life-sustaining crops. At all events, I hope you will not be dumb.   From time to time a working man finds his work passing into his life, and opening out a path, and bidding him move.   You, I think, have such a path opening, and feel the command coming, or come.   I don't know ; but if so, obey.   Follow where work leads. Speak where work knocks against the lips for utterance.

Sometimes his ideals found vehement expression even in the daily press.

An earnest attempt had been made by the founding of the Finsbury Training College for Teachers, to establish a means by which the teachers of public and

middle schools could get some professional preparation
for their work.

Writing to the *Times* (2nd Feb. 1886) in support
of the new effort, he says :—

Mind is not so absolutely uniform or so plain a surface as
to present no variety in dealing with it ; and the progress of
the world depends on how mind is dealt with ; and intelligent
exercise of mind is the crown of human excellence ; and teaching means the skill necessary to produce such excellence.
Infinite variety, all true progress, the highest work, and the
skill necessary to produce the highest work combine in the
ideal of teaching.

Therefore (he continues) any one can do it. Therefore, it
is unnecessary to train a teacher. But no one can unlock a
door without a key. The world is full of locked doors. Every
child is a locked door. But where are the keys? Where is
there any distinct conviction even that any key is wanted ?—
Nay, that such an article as a key to mind exists? The sloppy
idea of education which prevails, reduced to shape and practice,
means a set of trucks all in a row, memory trucks, with navvies
pitching ballast into them against time, or not doing so, as the
case may be. But loading up other people's facts is not training minds. . . .

One more point demands notice. There are not only no
keys, but the present system prevents keys being made.

A key is adapted to fit intricacies, and to wind in and out
of queer passages. The successful scholar is the man who has
run through his work most smoothly and found the fewest obstacles. And these are the men who are selected to deal with
the greatest number of obstacles and difficulties. I know by
personal experience that it is possible to turn out very successful work, winning work, without the slightest knowledge of the
real structure of the work which wins. I did it myself.
But in teaching, the structure of the work is everything,
and the power of turning out the perfect result nothing.
If for one year all rules and lesson books could be swept
clean out of the world, and the performers be brought
face to face with mind, the little boy mind, and compelled
to trade on their own resources, and forced to meet the

real problem of mind dealing with mind, and no possibility of truck work, why, then, there would be much tearing of the hair and, if the oriental fashion was followed, a great rending of the clothes, many backs left bare ; but a new creation would have begun, thousands of minds would come out of prison, and it would be no longer necessary to advocate the training of teachers.

To C. W. G. Hyde.

Free Schools—Tax-paid Schools.

The question of free schools has been raised, and the United States of America appear to be convinced that they are right in establishing what are called free schools.   As regards any lesson to be learned from the practice of the United States by European communities, it is sufficient to observe that, until density of population and want of unoccupied land make the conditions of life approximately the same in the United States as in Europe, there is no common ground to stand on in considering the wisdom or unwisdom of any political movement if practice only is looked to.   Success in the United States does not imply successful principles any more than the living at ease on a hundred acres, and wasting a good deal of corn, implies the living at ease and wasting corn in a crowded street.

Nevertheless, the shrewd experience of a shrewd landholder may be very valuable to a pinched and hard-pressed landless man ; and still more, I submit, will the shrewd experience of the hard-pressed man be valuable to the wide-elbowed owner of large estates.

I am one of the much hard-pressed, squeezed, landless Europeans.

Heavy pressure, and toes trodden on, tend to make the uncomfortable examine into the principles of crowds, and toes trodden on, and the elbow of your neighbour in your ribs.

The principles are the same whether two stand in a broad plain, or two thousand jostle in a narrow street.

And perhaps the question of the Government providing teaching for all the poor out of the taxes paid by those who can pay, which is miscalled free education, puts the problem of how far law can rightly interfere with private duty, and the solemn responsibility of manhood and life, in its most attractive form in favour of interference.   My assertion is that it is *dishonest*, that it *is a mistake*, that it is *deadly* for law to interfere.

Has every man a right to live ?

That is the first question.

That question is at the bottom of all discussions on property, work, wealth, and tax-paid schooling.

All civilised mankind thunders forth an emphatic " NO ! every man has not a right to live."

Then who has a right to live, and under what conditions has a man a right to live ?   That is the practical question for working men.   Every community, especially in its first beginnings, disposes of the question of the right to live by promptly lynching—denying, that is, the right to live to all persons who proceed to put this right in practice by living on the stolen work—the stolen product, that is, of the life of others.

That is the first, the universal answer.

The right to live is limited at once by the all-important limitation, that it shall not be exercised by preying on the life of others.   Where society only exists in the simple form of working in order to live, death is at once made the penalty of taking part of the life work—the property, that is, of another.

The man who does not work in order to live is put out of life.

And property or, in plain words, the right to live unrobbed on the work of life, is established as the first step above the savage state.

It is obvious that it makes no difference whether the work a man lives on is his own work or the inherited store of the work of his father or his father's fathers.

It is equally obvious that having been born without means of support confers no more right on the child to prey on society and live on plunder than his father, the beggar, had before him.

The next step in the social scale is when either the strong leader, or the society, undertakes to defend the life and property of the individual in return for a tax paid, either in personal service, goods, or money.

This is the first tax, the principle is simple.   The law in effect says, if you will pay me, I, who am stronger, will undertake to defend your property and life.

Every tax in principle is the same.   Every tax is a payment made by the individual to buy in return a given service.

Law cannot give a man's money to another man as a gift without perpetrating an act of dishonesty, any more than an individual can walk into a shop and empty the till, and give it to the starving orphan outside and be honest.

The shopkeeper may even be a cheat, but it is as much robbery to rob a cheat by force as to rob an honest person, even if you do give the money to the starving orphan.

And thousands of years of experience prove that no man, no society, can go on robbing, and being robbed, without falling to pieces.   There is no salvation in robbery by law.

Let me here interpose that law, compulsory will that is, is entirely different from Christianity, and freedom of action, and love, voluntarily working in special ways.   The muddling up these opposite principles has done untold harm to the world.

We are dealing with law.

Law then emphatically asserts that no man has a right to live who does not conform to the conditions of life, that a man must not prey on others, but maintain himself.   Christianity, however, asserts this with equal emphasis.

At what point does property cease to be sacred on the one hand, and at what point does the poor man get the right of taking it on the other, whether by law or by pistol?

That is the whole question at issue in the present day.

To take an example.   Has the lawyer, whose skilled work as a lawyer has taken him thirty years, expensive years, of unproductive labour to acquire, whose skilled work demands strength above the average, and who, after his thirty years of unproductive and laborious expenditure, runs the risk of failure and getting nothing; has he, if he succeeds, and gets for all this outlay over so many years of life £100 a week, rendered himself a fair object of plunder for the poor artisan, who began earning wages as a lad, and required no special skill or strength to earn them?

But if not, when does it become honest to rob a man earning higher wages for skilled labour and extraordinary power, and give them to men of less skill and working power, for worse work and less of it too?

If, again, it is not honest for one man to rob his fellow in this way, is it honest for ten to do it, or a hundred?

Are a thousand, even if they meet in the town hall, or twenty hundred thousand, if they send members to Congress and pass a law, to take the money and give it to some one else, honest?

Whether it is done by law or by brute force, alters the guilt of the doers perhaps, but it does not alter the guilt of the act.

A gift of money taken from other men who get nothing in return is robbery, whether pistol, sword, or law is the force that robs ; whether one or a million are concerned in the deed.

Again, the excellence of the object makes no difference in the honesty or dishonesty of the gift. Between two and three thousand years ago King Astyages decided rightly that Cyrus had no business to give the little boy's big jacket, which was his jacket, to the big boy whom it fitted, and to make them change. The fit had nothing to do with the honesty of taking what was not his and giving it away. The modern readjusters of jackets that don't fit are not troubled, however, by scruples ; like Robin Hood, with them to be rich is enough, they don't trouble about fit. Rob the rich ; give to the poor. A simple process, but it soon exhausts itself; and—it is not honest. But if we are agreed that a man has no right to live unless he supports himself, and that a man is relieved of his right to live in a simple state of society by being lynched if he lives by preying on the lives of others—their property, that is— we must equally be agreed that he has no right to bring children into the world, and they have no right to be in it, if they must prey on others, and rob in order to live.

No law has any right when a man has been industrious, thrifty, restrained his passions, and married late, to take his money in order to pay for the support of the children of his idle, thriftless, dissolute neighbour, who seduced, or married some unhappy woman because of his lust, and now demands that his self-denying neighbour should pay, by maintaining the children, for his gratifying his passions.

No law can make it honest to take a good man's earnings and give them to a bad man's sins, or improvidences.

But this is done by every law which taxes those who have to pay for the children of those who have not.

The moment the consequences of a man's idleness or evil deeds are taken off him, his power of idling and doing evil deeds is increased in proportion to the relief given.

If the drunkard's children are brought up by the State, the State is paying for the drunkenness of the father, and practically is buying his beer for him.

A tax which gives a working man's money to feed the idle man's child is simply beer money, nothing less. It matters not whether the food is bodily or mental. It increases the working man's hours of labour, or lowers the wages for them, in order that the idle man may idle and drink more securely.

It matters not whether the working community are willing to pay the tax or not; in principle, the shilling which the working man gives to the beggar does its dishonest and ruinous work of breeding beggars all the same. It is true that a tax, a beggar's beer tax, adds robbery of the working man to the injury done to the community, but the effect of the shilling is the same.

Again, it makes no difference at what point the shilling is given; if water is poured down a pipe it comes to the bottom of the pipe with certainty.

Let us construct a class thermometer to illustrate this. If zero be fixed at inability to pay, then, by Fahrenheit, freezing point will be the balance between paying and non-paying power, just where non-paying power begins. Our thermometer will read in this way :—

```
                    — —⎞
                    — —⎟
                    — —⎬Degrees of wealth and thrift.
                    — —⎟
                    — —⎠
Freezing point      — — Improvidence.
                    — — Unthrift.
                    — — Self-Indulgence.
                    — — Misfortune.
                    — — Bad work.
                    — — Laziness.
Zero                — — Idleness.
                    — — Vice.
                    — — Drunkenness.
```

The classes as classes, however slowly the change in persons may take place, are permanent, constructed by laws of nature on this thermometer basis.

As long as there is plenty of room the pressure does not exist ; but a wise State provides for a time when there will not be plenty of room, and an old State has to deal with a time when there is not plenty of room.

All above freezing point have the funds for paying for their own schooling.

All below freezing point in different degrees have not.

The tax for supplying schooling accordingly does not do anything for those above freezing point which they would not do for themselves.   They pay it in any case either to the State, or direct to their schoolmasters.

Below freezing point the tax is not paid, but the children are sent to school.   Those above freezing point pay for themselves and for those below freezing point as well.   That is all.

And when the tax reaches those at zero, those above freezing point pay for the idle, the vicious, and the drunken, and "free education" is nothing more nor less than "free beer" for the vicious, paid for by a payment of the good citizens, which is not free.   If the tax is taken without unanimous consent, then it is sheer robbery, and dishonest in principle, if only one is robbed.

If it is given by unanimous consent, it is simply the old fallacy over again of the rich man preferring to breed beggars by giving shillings to beggars rather than bear the inconvenience of listening to their whining, meeting their violence, or investigating and correcting the cause of the evil.

Giving other people's money to any one excepting for service done is merely a form of setting up a beggar factory. What is wise to do is outside the scope of the present question, which is merely concerned with the dishonesty and proved unwisdom of tax-paid schooling, and the fact that it resolves itself into tax-paid beer.

The writer in putting the case briefly is quite aware that he has left many unguarded points.   He is prepared to guard and fight them one by one.   It is not ignorance, but a discerning choice that has left them to the reader's good sense to dispose of for himself.

To resume, no man has a right to take another man's life-work and live on it, or give it away, be he rich or poor, use sword or law, or taxation.

History supplies examples and warnings. The heathen empires for thousands of years went on one unvarying plan, whatever names they called themselves. They fought, they conquered, they made slaves, they lived on the work of their slaves. They were all narrow oligarchies living on slave work. The only difference between them was, whether the plunder was divided amongst a few, who called themselves an empire, or kingdom, or whether the plunder was divided amongst a greater number, who called themselves a republic. But few or many, empire or republic, they equally lived on plunder. And they all perished through the natural laws which, in a fair time, lynch a nation which robs and idles, as surely as honest settlers lynch a thief.

Modern democracy in its cruder forms of Socialism, Communism, and Trades' Unionism, is doing the same as the ancient empires did. The ancients wanted the strong to take the work of the weak, and they took it. The moderns want the strong to take the life-wage of the weak also. It makes no difference whether the strong is the poor robbing the rich, or the rich robbing the poor, or a general scramble by law or force. The takers of other people's goods get lynched in the end. There is, however, yet another example much more valuable than the two above-mentioned, which are so elementary that the babies of the world are always trying them. But a grand experiment has been made and has failed, which endeavoured to remedy the misery of the world by getting rid as far as possible of the consequences of evil, and the training of pain. The 1400 years during which Christianity in various ways, but more especially through the monasteries, mistook Christ's commands to love and give, and translated them not unnaturally into being kind without considering whether kindness was love, and into giving without considering whether giving increased or diminished evil, have furnished everlasting proof that no man can do for another what that man ought to do for himself; and that no man can save another from the consequences of not doing it himself, when he ought to do it himself.

Modern governments and modern enthusiasts are now trying to do without religion by the strong right of majorities and taxation, what the mediæval world and the monk tried to do with a liberal heart and hand ; this, it is true, soon degenerated into preying on the workers, which the modern panaceas begin by doing. These great examples deserve careful study, and practically exhaust the question.

If the whole community agrees to give in order to eliminate misery from the world, they are treading in the footsteps of the monasteries and mediæval failure, and breaking the great law, that suffering educates mankind.

If only a majority agree, and impose a tax, they are robbing the minority, as the heathen empires did, and taking other people's money to supply tax-paid beer. In either case it is a failure, a failure that experience has given proof of over and over again.

In the second case it is a dishonest failure.

So much on the elementary principles of honesty and dishonesty in dealing with poverty in a community by establishing tax-paid schools. This closes one side of the question. If time allows me, I hope later on to show, as an experienced schoolmaster, the deadly injury to schools and teaching that tax-paid rule inflicts.

The moment external law grasps schools and teaching, death becomes a mere question of time. The life goes out of them day by day, as a pitiless, omniscient, indiscriminating power lays down the lines to be followed, and executes every one who dares to diverge from omniscience.

To C. W. G. HYDE.

February 1st, 1887.

I have endeavoured to put out clearly why I am utterly against free education by LAW. That is my contention, and the position I take up.

Law is deadly and immoral when it compels payment to those who give no return, and ultimately are undeserving. I am afraid I shall shock you very much by what I have sent, but we have bitter experience of law and compulsory support. It would take a book to treat of the question ; I have only dealt briefly with one single head.   If I find time to go on I will send you the results.   It is exactly because I believe that I am "my brother's keeper" that I abhor law dealing with my brother's moral life.   It kills the national feeling of brotherhood.   Those who thrive give their tax and wash their hands of brotherhood.   Those who receive claim it as a right because it is law, hate it because it soon becomes a pittance, and are at war with those above them for not giving more.   Brotherhood vanishes.

Remember I, personally, staked my all, my very life, in the endeavour to raise the standard of school.   I speak with confidence, as my conscience is clear.

I would help in every way.

I would have endowments.

I would encourage the brotherly feeling, and demand of it to be liberal and wise.

I would do everything to make education easy, and put teaching in the reach of all, except—kill brotherhood, by taking by force from my brother, and destroy liberality by robbing the possessor of his own, and quench love by saying, pay up your £1 and I give you a receipt in full for duty done.

Your arguments to me I heartily concur in.   But then, they are arguments on my side for love against law.   Be sure law slays love in a community.

To the Same.

February 25th, 1887.

I have looked at your papers carefully, and I can only say that if you take the practical experience of England, and the facts of our world, you are advancing upon a most dangerous road.

I do not at all deny that your plan may at the beginning be good, even necessary, for a time.   So were the monasteries, but I do say that unless changed, our experience cries "ruin," even more emphatically than the principles do.   I will, however, clear myself from the charge of being a "destroyer," and not a "builder-up," by stating first what I think ought to be done, and afterwards pointing out the objections to what is done.

Endowments ought to be given, and encouraged in every possible way, for first-rate education is so expensive that much help is needed. But in all instances, with two exceptions, which shall be mentioned presently, the main expense should be borne by the parents who use the schools. It is as much a parent's duty to provide mental as bodily food, and it would be as absurd for a parent to be content with what a tax-paying community thinks good education, if he can afford better, as to be content with the workhouse rations of a tax-paying community.

These endowments ought for all working purposes to be in the hands of the persons who work them, the skilled workmen, the teachers. Their expenditure and work should be subject to supervision either of trustees or other kinds of control, to see that the expenditure is not fraudulent or unduly wasteful, and that the work is up to a fair average. Anything in the way of interference beyond this is fatal.

The main lines on which the schools are to be carried on are fit subjects for legislation in the first instance.

The two exceptions to payment which are wise are, first, from the lowest school to the highest scholarships should be endowed in each school to enable their promising boys or girls to continue their education either in the school itself, or in a school of higher grade, or at a university, so that a promising pupil might go right up from the bottom to the top of the scale by his own exertions. I find four or five such scholarships quite as many as this school of 300 needs annually. Besides these, which are won by competition, every school ought to have privately the power of easing off the expenses of a small percentage of meritorious and needy boys whose brains do not make them prize-winners, but whose merits make them deserving. Then I agree also that the very poor should have just the elementary teaching of reading and writing provided for them gratis in a humble way, so as not to compete with any paying school.

That is the very briefest sketch of an educational system which will continue to work.

Now for the tax-paid school system from the school point of view :—

1. You lodge in the hands of the community the judgment

on education.   But how can the ignorant be fit judges of higher mind ?

2. You put the teachers, the skilled workmen, under the lash of amateurs and very incompetent amateurs too.

3. You let authority decide the methods of teaching as well as what is to be taught. No original or new improvement which does not fall in with those methods is possible. But unless we are perfect in all we do, and the manner of doing it, this is fatal. Remember, I am not theorising; I am speaking of the slavery we in England, with all our closely packed multitudes, and formalised traditions, are suffering. Your whip will be scorpions in time compared with ours, as we have had for centuries a better system going.

4. You prevent by all these chains the energy of individuals from starting different kinds of schools. Unless you are perfect this is fatal.

5. You dry up all the sources of life. We have in our poor law 300 years' experience to prove that as soon as the community is taxed to provide what the individual ought to do as a Christian duty, the individual pays his tax, and washes his hands and his conscience henceforth of the whole concern, and settles down to his selfishness in total and sublime forgetfulness of love and life and neighbourly duty; all is dried up. The average middle-class Englishman simply wipes the poor clean out of his table of duties. "Why! he has paid the poor-rate. There is the workhouse. What more pray do you expect?" Then where are you to stop? If mental food is supplied gratis, why not bodily food? Some day that argument will be pushed home. Law destroys living individual effort. The despotism of republican laws can be far more despotic and omnipresent than the laws of a despot. The worst fetters are the dead hand on the heart, and when once external power controls the teaching it is the dead hand on the heart, for from the teaching the nation draws its life.

The tyranny is death. The moment examinations from without are powerful enough to shape the work no real teaching progress is possible.

Religion must be treated as a by-subject of intellectual knowledge, as the differences in religious belief render state-paid religion in schools impossible. But religion is education.

The man who pays for tax-fed schools will not, and often cannot, pay also for a school of his religious cast; he has been crushed by law. So by degrees religion ceases to be thought of great importance. The nation is educated into thinking it by-play.

.   .   .   .

I quite agree with you that as a Christian I should rescue a child whatever his parents might be. I go so far as to tolerate a wise and guarded state law to do it. But Christian love working is not law. Law with us, as mentioned above, destroys the action of Christian love. The average man pays his tax and washes his hands of the concern when he has done so.

Also rescuing the pauper child from moral death is an utterly different thing from pauperising the poor and rich by maintaining children whose parents can and ought to do it.

The two propositions belong to two different worlds.

I am my brother's keeper.

But a law which forces me to keep the vices of my brother destroys the willingness to do it. And a law which even requires me to do what I would willingly do from love extinguishes love in ordinary cases.

You cannot whip a man into love and enthusiasm.

Believe me, we have bitter experience in England of what comes of substituting law for liberty, and we are going to have worse still in the matter of education. The slavery and triumphant praise of wrong methods is getting worse daily. I have no time to say more.

To the Same.

March 16th, 1887.

As for agreeing, I don't think it signifies. We mean the same, and only differ as to how to carry out our meaning.

I just wish, though, I could put you for a little time into the government vice here and give you a good squeeze. Our English experience of squeeze and meddle and muddle might save you over there much future trial. . . .

TO THE SAME.

March 22nd, 1887.

You are welcome to publish my statement.   Remember I think as strongly as any man living that it is the bounden duty of every Christian to endeavour to rescue the fallen, help all who need help, and be his brother's keeper.   What I deny is, that this can be done by law.   What I assert is, that law kills the Christian doing of it. . . .   I entirely agree with everything you say about preventive methods, and the power of true education.   Ignorance has been tried long enough. But the whole question is the question of law.   Law compelling and, alas! griping and managing.   We in Europe have deadly experience of what law means.

The moment law enters into the domain of life it kills, just as in a family there could be no love if law was called in, and the magistrate.   Law is not Christian.   It is a lower level. National life lasts so long that a few centuries give but little illustration of principles, which are also met by a thousand checks and counterchecks.   But I see the attempt to do for others what they ought to do for themselves running in a line of ruin under different forms through all history.   I see it blasting English life at the present moment, school life particularly. . . .

TO THE SAME.

August 6th, 1887.

I had the great pleasure of being at home, and able to go about with Mr. West during his short visit.   He did us injustice in not making arrangements to stay with us more than a day.   It was a bright day for me, and we all liked him very much.   I feel now as if Minnesota, and St. Louis, and your schools were more in the flesh for me now that we have a living link between us, and a visible ambassador in Mr. West.   We did all we could for him in so short a time, and showed him all there was to be seen.

P.S.—I am much cheered in time of trial here at Uppingham by feeling that the life is not shut in by Uppingham, but has wings and flies over to you.

CHAPTER VIII

GENERAL CORRESPONDENCE

1877-1887

To Rev. Edward White.

I HAVE read your paper pretty carefully, and the only thing I object to in it is the phrase "sacerdotal *hypocrisy*," for which I should substitute the word "*unreality*," for two reasons: The one, because I think the men you principally have in view sin from a fierce identification of their own self-will with the cause of God, and are fanatics rather than hypocrites. The other, that my experience of life leads me to think that the hypocrite, in the modern sense of the word, as conscious deceiver, is very rare, and that most ὑπόκειται, actors of parts, are either self-deceived, or perverse men, not intentional deceivers. "Unreality" would quite express the sham of the thing, and would equally satisfy me who believe in apostolical succession, but hold that its true fruit is humility, and you who would denounce it, as we both agree in putting *life* first, and whether the vessel be of gold or of clay do not want to drink poison out of it, or think poison not to be poison because of the cup that holds it? There is no Venetian glass in God's kingdom.

I fully think you have hit a great blot in our religious practice. I have long intended, if God ever gives me parish work again, to have Scripture readings after the fashion of my morning lessons in school, where sometimes I take a term in getting through half a chapter of the New Testament, and in some instances of the Old also. I will see that you get the two or three sermons of mine that I spoke of; our bookseller is wonderfully slow.

This year has been to me a year of wonderful danger and trial, and wonderful deliverances, and most of all of the greatest freedom and breaking up of chains within my heart. All the year long I have carried my working life and its visible fruits "in my hand" in the expressive Scriptural phrase, and have had to face ruin and overthrow all day long, oftentimes faint and weary, and, in all except the living life, cast down. The New Scheme and the Typhoid came together — the New Scheme just confiscated my life and cast me and the school to a great degree under the heel of local amateur alien power, and grim and hard has the struggle been. We were within our last week of school existence when we made the dash that saved us, and three times has the local power tried to ruin the school by recalling it, and three times at the last moment has deliverance come. I assure you, I understand the book of Exodus in a way I never did before. Some men learn nothing, and forget nothing, excepting their own mistakes, and it is incredible how the hope of one more onion in the flesh-pots, or the want of it, will not only shut men's eyes and hearts to the freshness and glory of freedom, but make them ready to face any old habitual familiar form of things, though it may be almost certain destruction. I simply stand hard and try to be true, come what will, and some good men and true stand fast with me. But on the other hand, perilous as it has all been, it has been blessed above measure. The school has stood by us beyond belief, and the boys have not given us an hour's care. Only think of our being able to carry on in this new place without any external restraints and yet no lawlessness. One example, I have some hundred and seventy boys out in the cottages here in studies, and we have not had a single case of complaint on either side, very creditable to the people as well as to them. You please me much by your confidence in thinking of putting your boy under me, if all's well, but I assure you I have been very much supported by Nonconformists in spite of my strong opinions. One thing, I believe our blessed Lord meant "all Proselytising" when He denounced the Pharisees. I mean all trying to win disciples by attacking others, or doing anything excepting build up truth. . . .

To the Same.

May 18th, 1878.

I should much · like a good talk with you, but I fear there is little chance, I am so seldom in town, never for any time, excepting indeed that fatal typhoid period, when I was harassed out of all fitness for human society.

Things are very bad now, but I have had that wonderful Borth miracle, that passing of the Red Sea, and am strengthened. Yet I fear stripes don't make an apostle, and St. Paul would have looked at my bank-book with calmer eyes, and better digestion than I can bring up to it by a deal, I am sure. But I do feel, however I may break, that it is all right, and good will come, as it always has come, from the crushing. And I do know that, humanly speaking, if I had been dishonest to my convictions, I should now be rich and powerful, and none of this would have come on me.

I am glad to hear what you say about communion, but it is what you always have said. I abhor that platform of a common non-belief; I want us to believe more strongly, more deeply, to be, if you will call it so, more sectarian than ever, more full of fire in putting out our convictions, but *never to attack others*, and to give the most complete personal liberty of communion to every one who is a disciple of Christ, throwing the responsibility of communion on the Christian individual, not on the Christian body. Every one who loves Christ ought to welcome every one who is willing to come on those terms. Honest men will never get rid of strong differences of belief, but godly men and honest can and will get rid of offensive ways of showing it, and can and will unite heartily in many good works, and when they cannot do that, in sympathy with one another's efforts, sympathy shown by giving elbow-room, and free play and not opposing. There is room for all workers. There is no room for fighters. A few acres maintain the husbandman, a wilderness is needed by the hunter, and a world by the fighters, and is too small after all.

To G. R. Parkin.

September 23rd, 1878.

. . . But I feel sure that no school can do continued good work unless the religious element is strong. It is not what the school teaches that signifies so much in this. I should say the same if no religious teaching went on at all. It is the teachers themselves that are affected. If the teachers are not animated by a strong religious spirit their work must be low. Take care in creating your new world that you see clearly on what principle you are laying down its lines. Do not set up discordant elements. There are two grand distinctions in system, and they will not coalesce. There is, first and best, the trust: the training in inward trustworthiness, the making each boy a responsible missionary of trusted liberty. But then all the surroundings must be sound and trustworthy. There must be no mob, no boy democracy of partially neglected numbers, but the house must be a home with a home feeling about it, and home arrangements. If this is so, the boys may be out of sight, have studies, have bed compartments, and only be under a general supervision. The moment, however, the home feeling and arrangements are exchanged for the barrack idea all the appliances must be changed also. As trust is not your main principle no concealment ought to be possible. Everything must be open and visible so as to allow direct authority to act. In a dangerous town you must have broad boulevards which can be swept by cannon. Law and discipline are the idea in this case, worked by force if necessary. Honour and truth are the backbone of the other and as little mistrust as possible, whether in arrangements or in working, should be seen. . . .

To the Same.

January 23rd-24th, 1879.

I think public opinion in England is very cordial towards Canada, *very*, at present. Altogether a greater feeling has grown up. Lord Beaconsfield, whatever his faults may be, has brought in a reaction against the sordid retail shop notions of our Empire; and Englishmen are beginning to feel generally that they are leaders in the world, with an Empire to lead in which the truest economy is to recognise noble duties. This especially touches the English feeling for Canada, not least on account of the Dominion's volunteering for the army in case of a Russian war. That came home to us very much.

I think you would be intensely interested by *A Legacy, Memoir of John Martin, Schoolmaster and Poet*, edited by the authoress of *John Halifax, Gentleman*. It is very sad but wonderfully hopeful for the future to see the beginnings of a living life of a high order from amongst the people. Fanny Kemble's *Records of a Girlhood* are very interesting, and well worth reading.

You can't think how much it cheers me to hear you are getting on in your work and making ground in sound education for your country. There is no greater work to be done on this earth. I find as I go on that without being less sensitive to the stings one's constitution becomes better able to bear them, and that eels do "get used to being skinned" somewhat. . . .

"Better fifty years of living than a cycle passed in books." *Doctissimus ille* or *eruditissimus ille* is but a bad epitaph when all is over for the man who had human beings to deal with, and as a choice preferred intellect.

To the Same.

September 9th, 1879.

You are seemingly having the experience of all pioneers. Never mind, pioneering is noble work, though the bystanders, on beaten paths, do scoff at the dirt and torn breeches of the pathfinder. Cheer up. Fifteen years of imperfect health or more did not prevent me from regaining health at last. But I agree with you in your determination to husband your resources. It is right to make the most of life, and to get people to do what they ought to do. Much evil has been done by pauperising morality. No man can do for another what that other ought to do for himself; and beyond a certain stimulating example of self-sacrifice it is not good to go.

Hang results. What have we to do with results? All we want is a good cause and such a conviction of right means at work which some results are necessary to give. I am considered a very successful man; from a certain point of view justly considered so; I declare most solemnly and seriously, that during my working life I have steadily seen the battle go against me year after year until I now utterly despair about English education and my own best hopes. . . .

To Rev. Godfrey Thring.

March 13th, 1880.

I got back from Cambridge on Monday, where I had been special preacher. It is well over ; I do not feel in harmony with the very heterogeneous audience one has to address. I was lodged in my own old rooms. I had not slept in the bed for thirty years. It was very ghostly. I was much struck though with no change of *feeling* having come on me ; as I lay there I could easily have thought all those years a dream, and that I was to get up and begin at the point of life I had left in that room.

.   .   .   .   .   .

You would be immensely pleased with our aviary in the school gardens, a bank enclosed for thirty feet by twenty in fine wire, and sheltered to the north and east by thatched hurdles, so it is quite natural with plants and grass and bushes, and a large aquarium in it. The birds are so tame and interesting ; the siskins run up and down Mr. Haslam's beard, and curious to relate, I believe we are the only people in the world who know the habits of the common blackbird, and one of its notes. We have linnets, redpoles, greenfinches, a robin, sparrows, hedge-sparrows, bullfinch, goldfinch, two Australian paroquets, blackbirds, thrushes, siskins, and a plover, and it is very interesting watching them, especially now they are beginning to sing. My other novelty is a thing I began in my class-room long ago, and have never had funds to go on with ; now I have a little public money to deal with, and I have a series of magnificent autotypes of ancient art hung up in the great schoolroom. I hope by degrees to get all the mean furniture out, and I am sure that by making the surroundings of lessons beautiful and noble we shall destroy the low schoolboy notion of learning, just as we have destroyed by the same kind of change their low domestic life. The town work is all going on well, so I have much to be thankful for.

To E. F. BENNETT.

August 17th, 1880.

I congratulate you on the birth of your son and your wife's safety. That is my first answer to the big question you ask me. For it is a big question, though in its main lines clear enough. The answer turns on two things : First, what is meant by poor? Secondly, whether you want to live in God's world or man's world?

I mean by poor in the bad sense, a resourceless, selfish coward. The tramp is one end, the noble idler, however much money he may have, the other end of the word.

The poor man has no business to beget children. "Cut it down, why cumbereth it the ground?" is the sentence that has gone forth against all such, and their like, and in man's artificial world of cowardly wants, man condemns every one who troubles the routine theory of comfort. A man or woman is not poor who has a stout heart, faith in truth, and working power ; as far as they fail in this they are poor. I mean, if a man is broken-hearted because he cannot continue on the same level of human fortune on which he started, or cannot bring up his children on the same level, although able to do Christian work, and to train them to do Christian work, so far he is poor, and ought not to risk a lot which he has not the courage to face ; but sometimes these reverses come on man and woman after marriage. Well, it is God's message to them to arm for battle, to throw away worldly standards, and come weal come woe to quit themselves as good soldiers of Christ. I can assure you, though you may not think it, and perhaps may not believe it, I have drunk this cup to the very dregs, and drunk it during many years, and faced in heart all the shame, and all the bitterness, and very bad it tasted ; but I would not give up the liberty and blessing and strength it gave for worlds. It is a long story, I cannot tell it you, but you may guess what a penniless man had to face, run heavily into debt by the first master he appointed, his family strong-willed, and not believing in his work, or his power, his masters much like dogs in couples with a rabbit started, his school authorities dead against him, etc. etc., forced to go on for years on the edge of ruin, single-handed, with no help. Well, don't

get bitter.   In God's world men are intended to get their daily
bread from Him, to be dependent on Him every hour, to look
up to Him for orders, and for wages evening by evening to the
end.   Man can die but once, and "how can men die better
than facing fearful odds, for their wives and for their children,
for their country, and their God."   This belongs to civilians
just as much as soldiers, and it belongs to every man who does
honest work in God's world. . . .

To the Same.

August 24th, 1880.

There is no greater blessing than to have a true sympathy
with toiling suffering humanity, to be able to feel *with* it, not
for it.   A world is split asunder in these two little words.   But
don't be embittered.   Money is *not* power.   Money can do
nothing in the spirit world.   If money was power our churches
and hospitals and grand establishments would long ago have
made the English world an earthly paradise, but a great cry
of sorrow and crime below, and a great iciness of self-satisfaction
and fault-finding above, protest against money being power.
Feeling, spirit, heart sacrifice is power, *life* is power, and the
beggary cannot be cured by money; it can only be cured by
life.   The landlord can move obstacles out of the way of life,
as a man can break down a dam in a river, or take stones out
of its bed, but he cannot do anything to make the stream flow,
if it is not there, excepting by pouring his own life in amongst
the dry half-exhausted pools.   It is one of God's great prison
laws by which He coerces the world, when it won't be governed,
that selfishness shall breed beggary.   It is one of God's great
remedial blessings, that this trial shall reach many who are
able to see and feel it to be a blessing as well as a punishment,
and who therefore are fitted to remove it.

I quite agree with what you say about the pothouse, but as
long as the poor man *will* have the pothouse, the rich man
cannot help him.   Slaves make tyrants as much as tyrants
make slaves.   And it is a very difficult problem when the
slave has been made, how to unmake him again.   But one
thing is certain, the slave heart must be got rid of; nothing
else is of use.

My theory is, that the most religious thing that can be done now is to provide good amusements for the poor and educate them to use them.   But unless you can make them support themselves, pay for them and by degrees start them themselves, little or nothing in my judgment has been done ; you can no more do another man's life for him than you can eat another man's dinner for him.

This truth is the foundation of all true work.

This truth is Christ working in the world on earth, instead of God giving men instruction from heaven.

Believe me, your new experience and opened eyes are a great blessing, though they smart perhaps furiously at present. I think Mr. —— is wrong in not removing unostentatiously every possible temptation from the boys.   " Lead us not into temptation."   Good government secretly has no belief whatever in honour and truth, is suspicious to the last degree in its precautions, and knows that the constant force of the stream (the constructional system) in time overcomes all the sinews of living effort, and that if the stream is a favouring of evil, a certain percentage of evil will come, which need not come. On the other hand, good government acts and behaves as if there was no such thing as dishonour and falsehood when it comes to deal with its human beings.

I do not understand great opportunities of evil without evil unless there is a wonderful perfection of life elsewhere, both in treatment, and structure and plant.

Neither do I understand how this is possible unless out of school is apparently perfect freedom.

It is exactly out of school where my system of making the society responsible for the individual has worked best and been most needed.   The school understands that it has no business to stab, when it is only the friendly hand held out and the weapon put by the friendly power into the boy world that enables the boy to do it.   Again, that boys should be punished as a society for what they have not done, is quite intelligible if boys, as a society, are rewarded for what they have not won.   As to carpentry, etc., every fresh interest in a school is a fresh barrier against evil, and every fresh subject is a net which catches some one and educates those who are usually neglected and left to rot.   But how far such things are practicable depends on the funds at disposal ; and in these days there is so much sham and scamped work and cheating in schools, that a school which tries to be true has a hard time of it, and must be prepared for great disappointment, and much calumny. But whatever versatile power is at the disposal of the school should be tried. In your case for one thing, I should try practical engineering and outdoor surveying work with the boys. I would make sculptors if I had the chance, anything that called forth high power if I had the chance. Yet remember, the wise man does not work his theories, but his facts. The wise man takes into consideration the material he has to deal with, the instruments he has to use, and the temper that is in the air of our generation, and he will not attempt watch-making with sledge-hammers, though he himself may be a watchmaker such as the world has not yet seen.

To his Mother.

November 18th, 1880.

We are in the midst of building here, making a small transept to the chapel on the north side for the organ, and the trustees are going to have a swimming-bath built, and indeed, if things go well, every year will see some improvement in brick and mortar going on. It is very strange, how after so many years of a kind of prison life here, suddenly the barriers seem gone and a fresh power of new life in the place. I see clearly how necessary the difficulties and pain and disappointments were, but at the same time it is a great refreshment to have even a trembling hope of happier work, and more peaceful days.

To Rev. Edward White.

February 5th, 1881.

I think if you are to do away with all subscriptions and tests, the power of rejecting false teachers must be increased in proportion. I tolerate any boy in my school, till we are absolutely unable to keep him, but I should not tolerate for an hour a master who set himself against the teaching and aim of the school.

There is no doubt that any man who tries to live the New

Testament, and reads it for that purpose, will find it plain enough, whilst those who take it for a code to be known will find it tangled enough. Yet the life experience of experienced lives will always form a large part of the teaching and authority of the world. The thing is, men seek the web-spinning of the clever brain instead, and will insist on gathering apples of knowledge even from the branches of the tree of life. It is very curious, did not one see the reason in the too common personal bitterness felt, how utterly strong words and feelings are tabooed. There is no personal hate in true strength of feeling. Again, it is so convenient when you want to get rid of a difficulty to imprison it. People nowadays put every living thought that burns into prison. In old days they caught a few thinkers and put them in ; the last stage is more deadly than the first.

I believe it to be a law of God's world that the living truth of any movement may be exactly measured by the amount of resistance, and dull obstruction, and bitter antagonism it has to encounter during its growth, and that debility in life is marked by easiness of progress in the first instance.

One reason that I should like to see you here is that we have many seed plants going both in town and school, new movements of life-power which are partly visible, and require to be seen, partly matters of principle which require to be talked and not written about.

To G. R. Parkin.

May 7th, 1881.

I feel I ought to write again, as I was so downcast in my immediate feelings when I wrote my last letter that it might mislead you. Especially, it is not true that in case of my giving up Uppingham or Uppingham giving up me, "I know not where to lay my head." I have a small patrimony of my own, and though I should be very poor, I should not be homeless.

Moreover, I have the fullest belief, and what is more, a *real feeling* that neither I nor my family will ever greatly suffer because I have given up money and fortune for the truth's sake.   I wish to make this παλινωδία to you, now that my better self has returned, and the immediate bitterness of the news has had time to settle.   On consideration, I feel confident we shall not have a great reverse, but shall be protected in this our Sion, which with all its sins I more and more see daily, from what I find elsewhere, to be a solitary fortress in the land, a stronghold of true effort, which is found but faintly and doubtfully in other places.

Your success cheers me immensely.   I see in it some touch of common life with us here—a giving and receiving of strength from one another, which makes me ashamed of looking on this narrow ditch in which I am digging as the world, and its clay banks as the horizon, and its muddy bottom as the end of all things.   I congratulate you heartily. . . . But stick to your early principles.   Don't sell your success.   The temptation will come to grasp the crown by ever so little betrayal of the good old beginning.   "Get thee behind me, Satan," be on your tongue, ready when the time comes. Remember, no compromise is possible with a principle, in details it is different.   Stop short as much as you please ; but never compromise.   A fine piece of work must be perfect or it is nothing.

To Rev. Godfrey Thring.

June 6th, 1881.

I was both amused and delighted with your wrath.   I like a fellow who can get into an unselfish rage ; it does me good to hear a little strong language in these days of one-sided evil-speaking, lying and slandering ; when no one is allowed to call "a spade a spade" unless he is a *Liberal!* and your Liberal has no spades to call, only dung-forks, which those they hurl filth on must accept as agricultural amenities.   For my part I like a good unselfish burst of wrath, and I believe it to be as wicked to bear false witness *for* your neighbours by soft words, as against him by hard.   And I am not at all sure that we have not lost more by the false charity which will not call wickedness wicked, than by the old bigotry which gave the name so freely to good.

To the Same.

September 16th, 1881.

The Bishop of Oxford and his party left Borth on Tuesday, all his family having been here on and off. It has been very pleasant renewing the old friendship, and our holidays have been very much the better for their being here. He begged to be particularly remembered to you. He is infinitely better in health for his stay, but I fear he is very far from strong, and I dread his return to work; he is not fit for it, I am sure; but we are paying the penalty in these grinding days for the shirking and self-indulgence of our forefathers in office, and, like old hunters, nothing is left us but to be shot when screwed, unless we have private fortunes, and can afford to turn ourselves out to grass at our own cost. Who do you think has been here, and sends hearty greetings also to you? —the Dean of Windsor. I called on him afterwards, but unluckily did not find him at home. He looks well in face, but walks with two sticks and is quite the old man, but very cheery and bright.

To the Same.

October 21st, 1881.

I think very likely if you had had what you call a good education you would never have written a hymn. The grind of the school-days had much in it that was exceedingly *repressive*, and whilst I give unabated thanks for the power of working against odds that my early training gave me, I make very large deductions indeed for the waste of time, and the deadening and cramping effect of much of it. I lost a freshness and spring of imagination that has never come back.

.   .   .   .

In my comments on the past, I was rather thinking of the wonderful jobbery and pension scandals that took place, which have now thrown us back on the honourable position of this great nation having nothing to give their great men but £50 per annum, unless a special Act of Parliament is passed. A *reductio ad absurdum* with a vengeance. I have a great respect for our fathers in many ways, but the pendulum swung very far in the upper circle of politics.

To G. R. PARKIN.

January 6th, 1882.

As regards yourself, follow your circumstances. True work grows. A man need not be afraid of anything that grows by a natural growth. One man has one path opened to him, another another, but every man who bides his time, and is developed by his work, has his own. . . . I must tell you (I may have told you before) of the new plan of decorating rooms which has struck me as so wonderfully capable of extension. Mr. Rossiter, our master in painting and drawing, just got my girls to paint a number of water-colours on ordinary paper in their room, of flowers, etc. Then he mounted them on linen or canvas, and fastened them as a frieze along under the ceiling, and for all the world they look like wall-paintings, and in our climate will be far more durable and less exposed to harm from damp. But the great point is that any lady sitting in her own room thus becomes a wall-painter. Just think what an extension of decorative power this is. We are getting on capitally with the townspeople. We have lawn tennis, and football, and cricket going for them, and classes open, and we are decidedly making way in improvement and a good spirit. My school aviary is a great success. It is simply a large wire enclosure of a sloping bank with grass and plants quite natural, and water turned on at any moment with small open sheds for shelter, double-roofed, the inner roof thatched, the outer, wood working on hinges, so that we can lift it up at any time in case they nest inside. This answers admirably. I have twenty-two or twenty-three kinds of British birds in it, so that really a fair knowledge can be gained already. I have invented, too, an excellent bird-trap which I put on the aviary. It is made of the same wire netting as the aviary, and does admirably. I give a ground plan, the lines represent wire netting a foot high, and its length is six feet by four broad, and there is a long mirror at the end, which attracts the birds, two net-pockets at each corner for taking the birds out, and a movable door to apply when necessary. There is no click or spring, the birds simply walk in and out again through the open space, if no one is there, but they are inextricably entangled in the wire maze, as soon as we want to catch them. There is no bottom to it. It is a wire frame resting on the ground. I think this aviary a great addition to the school resources; we have given also an additional compartment to a small club of the boys.

To G. Herbert Thring.

October 30th, 1882.

With regard to Texas; I am exceedingly anxious that you should not emigrate to America—the United States, that is. I cannot bear the thought that child of mine should abjure the name of Englishman. But this is sentiment. My real reasons are : I have the most absolute certainty that fearful troubles and misery are in store for the United States before they take final shape as a great country, in the true sense of great, if they ever do. They started into national existence on a political plea for rebellion, which will justify rebellion, and *produce* it, whenever there is a screw loose, till the end of their history.

They have based their national fabric on the stupendous lie that all men are equal, not only in the eye of the law, but as men. They have added to that lie the equally stupendous hypocrisy of despising the negro more than any other nation has done. Then, whereas it is the wisdom of every intelligent policy to separate, as much as possible, the glitter of power and the greed of money from power itself, they put up the whole power, glitter, and wealth of their country for sale every four years, and turn the nation into a set of swindling adventurers. Then history reads us no more certain lesson than the impossibility of vast regions under conditions of climate and soil which make different races of men, ever being united in one rule, on terms of equality. Now the north, the south, and the west are so different, and with such different interests, that there must be disruption.

Then, beguiled by having plenty of room and none of the real problems of civilisation as yet pressing hard upon them, they are not gathering experience, but are giants in strength and conceit, and babies in political eyesight, wilful and fractious nursery squallers. All these things make a great convulsion, nay, many great convulsions certain. They may begin at any moment; they must begin at no very distant period. Therefore, I cannot look with pleasure, or security, on my son throwing in his lot with a race which has so bitter a future before it. I do not say that the United States may not have a grand ultimate destiny, but I do say that by all the laws of the universe they will arrive at it, if they do arrive at it, through very great trial and suffering. This is not prejudice; it is a quiet judgment formed quietly after years of thought on the progress of the world, the rise and fall of empires, and the principles which determine the fate of nations. A race which runs its head against any one of the great secret laws of God's world breaks it sooner or later. The worse for it the longer the consequences are put off. And I do not think it wise to cast in one's lot in a kingdom unless with the intention, if necessary, of sticking to it for good and all. I propose these ideas for your consideration. There is no such immediate hurry, though immediate thought is good and necessary.

To Rev. Godfrey Thring.

November 16th, 1882.

I quite agree with you. A fellow in earnest wants all the help he can get, and a little good praise is a real boon, and a bit of solid ground to stand and work on an antidote to vanity; only fools are vain, even without a cause. . . . Be sure that no painting, no art work you could have done, by any possibility could have been so powerful for good, or given you the niche you now occupy. As long as the English language lasts, sundry of your hymns will be read and sung, yea, even to the last day, and many a soul of God's best creatures thrill with your words. What more can a man want? Very likely if you had had all that old heathendom rammed into you, as I had, and all the literary artist slicing and pruning, and been scissored like me, you would just have lost the freshness and simple touch which make you what you are. No, my boy, I make a tidy schoolmaster and pass into the lives of many a pupil, and you live on the lips of the Church. So be satisfied. And what does it matter, if we do the Master's work?

To G. R. PARKIN.

BORTH, *August 11th*, 1883.

I have sent you off my new book on teaching. The University has turned it out very prettily, and I think you will like the inside. When once I was fairly in for it, it was a great refreshment to me writing it. The pent-up feelings and experiences of forty years came with a sense of relief to the point of the pen. I feel it is real and has life in it. I feel too that it is the only thing of the kind, and that some few will prize it as they did *Education and School*, but whether like *Education and School* it has not been born before its time or after cannot be known yet.

There is great dissatisfaction in England at present about education, but then there is a dense ignorance also, of the omniscient kind, and the ground is occupied thickly by expensive shams and false glory. I guess there is no room for my unwelcome truths, and that they will be crowded out like the seed that fell among the thorns. However, come good come ill, the deed is done, and the seed will not perish.

I have a great trouble coming which would once have been a great excitement, if not pleasure; our Tercentenary takes place next year, and there is to be a great gathering, and fuss, and subscriptions, and glorifications, and where poor truth is to find shelter in the midst of it, I don't know. I think abuse is easier to manage than praise. If they understood at all what the work has been, and why it has been, there would be more hope; but they don't; and there is much idea of mere success, accompanied by all manner of petty interests and rivalries, in the air. I don't know what will come of it all. But it has to be gone through. I daresay like many, many other things it will come off the reel naturally enough, and be far better than it looks now. Here at all events, at Borth, who am I to doubt and be faithless? The very stones on the beach would rise up against me. Nevertheless, one does not understand till one grows old, and cannot look indefinitely forward how large a part hope played in the earlier days of trial.

To Rev. Godfrey Thring.

April 9th, 1884.

My dear fellow, we must take life in a free, loving way, as sons in a father's home. Goodness knows what poor creatures we all are, but when we come to the loving heart, and when we see ourselves allowed to help on the life and love of Christ's kingdom, then however little our feelings may sometimes go with our convictions, we are sure that Christ is giving us His blessing, and making us His men, and accepting our lives.

To E. F. Bennett.

June 6th, 1884.

But beware how you start what will pull you in two pieces, away from your real work, and prove too heavy, or too seductive.

I have a most decided opinion, conviction rather, on the subject of "risking everything." For God's sake, don't do anything of the kind; begin nothing which you cannot stand defeat in. I always count the cost of absolute failure on beginning a new thing. I grant there are circumstances which demand our all. A soldier is bound to go into battle; but it is wicked for an amateur to do so. I know by an awful experience the protracted agony of a cause where ruin stares you in the face if unsuccessful. I did not mean to run such risk, but I had to do it. The temptation to give way and cheat just a little is dreadful, and the pain so appalling, that nothing but the certainty that it is the cause of God can bring any power to endure it. I entreat you not to embark in anything which you have not capital enough to uphold in case things go wrong.

To G. R. Parkin.

March 5th, 1885.

The one bright spot is the colonial feeling and the federation question, which has really got hold of the nation in a good way, with good leaders. *It must come;* the only question is who will reap the benefit. Exactly the same causes which turned the heptarchy into Britain, viz. the increased communication, now magnified into electricity and steam, will make the governments of the future federations—*by a law of nature.* Few pause to consider how Europe even now, with all its bitter hostilities, is nevertheless to a vast extent a Federal Government and conducting three-fourths of its business by federation. . . . The English-speaking race is by nature master of the world, especially when combined with the only other colonising power, Germany, its kinsfolk. Whether we like it or not, that is our position. *England* can ruin itself, and throw away its honour and its work, but the English-speaking race cannot do so. . . .

Your programme is the right one. More than that, in one form or another it must come to pass.

We ought at once to put ourselves at the head of a great empire. We ought to fly our flag on every unoccupied land essential to our great colonies. . . . Egypt and the Soudan frontier to Khartoum and connected by rail with Suakim as a matter of course. Free trade with all our colonies; differential duties with other nations. Each colony to undertake to provide according to its strength for its own defence, and if not threatened, a small contingent for the imperial army, and a common Parliament for such purposes, or Bills for such purposes to be passed in a majority of the Parliaments.

These I hold to be the main features of such a scheme and feasible. And things look well for that in England. The enthusiasm excited here by the offers of the colonies is great and solid. . . . I think the solid English courage and sense is as strong as ever if it only gets a chance of showing fight. My own belief is strong in a great future; but with a fearful judgment coming on us first through the love of lies developed under this Government. . . .

To Miss Miller.

June 23rd, 1885.

As I owe to Mr. Ruskin's *Modern Painters* more of thought and fruitful power than to any other book, or any other living man, I am not likely to speak or think of him with anything but feelings of gratitude and admiration.

Nevertheless, in the grim battle of life I see oftentimes that strange discouragement follows on experiments where some brilliant truth is sent into the field with just a little falsity of an unpractical kind mixed up with it. Truth is strong; nothing living ever dies; but there is nothing weaker on earth than a truth out of due proportions; disease, I have been told, is only localised life. One rule, too, I have fixed in my heart's core, "never to attack." Leave it to the scavengers of the world to cart away rubbish and glorify themselves in dust and destruction. But Ruskin is no scavenger. He has put forth more suggestive thought than any other man. I only know his *Fors Clavigera* by extracts.

You are quite welcome to abuse the clergy to me as much as you please. I marvel at the purblind, asinine way in which they tyrannise and crouch both at the wrong time and with the wrong persons; but then public abuse of the clergy means abuse of their cause to the multitude, and then I simply draw my sword and should be hard to beat. In like manner "rich and poor," and "clergy and radicals, etc." What are rich and poor clergy, etc.? I too look on men with a different eye. I worship "the Holy Spirit of Truth," and when I see the holy truthful effort, however imperfect, and by whatever name called, there I see God. Though I am as strong as ever, I was on the fact that the highest truth takes the highest body finally, and that the highest body is destined to enshrine the highest truth and tends to produce it. So rich and poor, and clergy and radicals, and dissenters are fellow-men, struggling under difficult and varied conditions to better the world, and the lower moral and spiritual stratum of each section is vile, selfish, and blind. Consider what a vast amount of self-government is involved in the life of the rich. Self-control in food and drink, and desires of all sorts. The sharp-eyed Greek noted this, as he did most worldly facts, and said, "Right gracious is a home of ancient wealth; upstarts who never thought to reap fair crop are cruel wasters ever, and hard-eyed." If the rich did their duty thoroughly, there would be no misery. If the clergy did their duty thoroughly, there would be no misery. If every earnest worker worked, and never fought or attacked, the world would be much better. At least we should get rid of the idolatry of force, and not fall down on our knees before the fuddled giants who in their vanity-mad strength knock about their country as a drunken navvy does his wife.

Pray let me suggest to you two tests of the truth of work. One, Truth may be measured by the antagonism it excites in the world of respectability. Two, Highest Truth may be measured by the accusations against it of being opposite to what it is. Christ was condemned by the religious as a blasphemer; by the turbulent world as a rebel; the early Christians as murderers and sensualists. Be comforted; trials both make truth true, and prove it to the sufferers to be true.

I have read your *Training and Teaching*, and I need hardly say agree with it. That you know already. But I am less sanguine than you about getting a hearing, or doing any good here if one does, and perhaps a greater believer in life working through life slowly to more perfect life. I have seen in my thirty or forty years of work all I cared for and believed in in *Training and Teaching* killed by the dead hand—the dead hand of amateur authority. On the other hand, I have seen many lives touched by life and new openings into all the world, windows out of which the dove flies and returns the sacred branch that tells of a new world of growth. Believe in work, in life. I believe in nothing else. So though I despair, I yet do not despair. I know there are seeds sown, and who can tell the future of a seed?

To the Same.

PITLOCHRY, *August 10th*, 1885.

I do not agree with your and Mr. Ruskin's estimate of *Modern Painters*, and I gave him my grateful thanks for it the only time I met him. It is a noble book, and did noble work at the time, and will continue to do so. It did what I should have thought impossible; it smashed up for ever the narrow technicalities of artists, and altered the point of view not only for them, but for the whole world, and gave the seeing eye, and thought, and feeling a practical reality which they will never lose, but never had before. I do not, however, disparage his later work, of which I know comparatively little, not having read more than three or four volumes. But the fierce practical complexity of struggling humanity and its problems suffer more from any ignorance, or disregard of what is possible in human nature, than intellectual subjects outside the area of sin and suffering do. There is, however, sure to be much worth pondering and much to arouse a reflection in everything he writes. I, however, am grateful to him for having put me into a new world of observation, beauty, power, and progressive thought, which amounted to what I have called it—a new world ; and every day adds to this obligation. . . .

TO MRS. CHARLES KINGSLEY.

January 18th, 1886.

The books have come, and I am very grateful to you for sending them, and for writing to me. I prize your autograph in the *Brave Words* very much. It cheers me much to find myself, as life goes on, associated, however far off, with those who have worked for righteousness and striven for the good cause, as *he* did, a real pioneer. Your praise of my address is sweet to me. I felt a grim pleasure in uttering the pent-up feelings of my heart before an audience of modern educationalists after having seen all the principles I believe in, and staked my life to uphold, squeezed out of existence by the champions of progress. I am bound to say my words met with a good reception from my hearers. But I feel so out of the educational and school world that I have little heart to do anything but work ; that, even, is done under great restraint. The prison closes in daily. I must be insolent enough to venture to approach you with unfeigned praise for the idea of "Daily Thoughts," and the carrying out of the idea. It is admirable. Your thinking me worthy of your personal confidence, and telling me about your sons and yourself, is very delightful to me ; the more so because it is yet another instance of that spiritual telegraph which is for ever sending messages through the world from heart to heart, which the birds of the air stand on with senseless feet, and no one knows but those who receive the messages. I am astonished

at the secret movements of the communion of the " Goodly
Fellowship of the Prophets " in this strange world and all to
whom the prophet voice is sweet. . . .

To E. F. Bennett.

February 17th, 1886.

I myself have one law in life which may be put in the
shape of this axiom, never to go into battle without having
made up my mind what to do in case of utter defeat.   If
you or any one else has a pittance secure, however small, to
cover your retreat if your venture fails, venture.   But—I
speak feelingly—never venture your all, or venture at all, if
you cannot play a waiting game a little, or accept a partial
reverse.   Many a private school has been smashed up by an
outbreak of scarlet fever ; and no mortal man can guard
against it in these days.   With all its advantages our lower
school would have smashed up if Bagshawe had not been a
man of some substance.   As it was, scarlet fever, which he
could not prevent, brought about by the culpable neglect of a
parent, cost him between one and two thousand pounds.
Health again, your own and your wife's, believe me, in the
protracted agony of daily possible ruin must suffer severely,
may easily meet the worst.   I know it.   I have been through
it.   I have faced death very close indeed in this way.   It is
simply terrible.   I lay before you facts of personal knowledge
and experience, you must judge how far they apply ; but facts
they are.   I wish I could be less of a Job's comforter ; but I
wish to serve you and help you to a right judgment. . . .

To J. Churton Collins.

June 7th, 1886.

I sent off by the early post a letter which you can make
any use of you please, if it is not too late.   You misunder-
stood me a little.   I have no objection to fighting in the lost
battle.   It makes no difference to me whether the battle's
lost or won when I go into battle.   I believe in life.   I
believe in life in the end always winning, and if I fight I fight

from belief in life, and am quite unconcerned at being a seed "which is not quickened unless it die."

But you will see when you have time to read my addresses that I am fighting on a different field, where I find less deadness ; and, moreover, I do not think my name and experience worth much in the university world, and am disinclined to mix myself up with their follies.   As to science, is it not true, that with fine observation and skilful research, there never has been a time when the baby has been so pronounced in reasoning power ?   Science is, theoretically, established knowledge ; but the modern men have beat the augurs in guessing, the astrologers in hunting hares in the sea, the gnostics in inventing worlds, and jumble up chains without links, and every conceivable form of illogical sequence, to say nothing of the amount of their own words they browse on.   The collection of facts, as with the alchemists and astrologers, is wonderfully good, quite unrivalled, but their wielding of facts. . . .

It cheers me to think that I gave you help.   All I can say is, for me life has unwound and disentangled itself day by day, light brightens on past pain, and as old age comes on, all things become more living, more real, and lead up to a perfect end.

To the Same.

June 16th, 1886.

My dear son, as I would fain call you if you call me "master," yet without any idea of uttering a word, or breathing a breath, save only what you yourself invite.   I have one negative creed.   I loathe and abhor and renounce all *force ;* physical or intellectual, it has no place in my world ; it is the detested idolatry which my whole existence is set to undermine, therefore nothing can be further from my belief and practice than the thought of thrusting myself on you even by one poor word.

But your letter was very interesting to me, both from what you said of the high priests of force, and also from your acknowledgment of having received help from me, which came home to my inmost heart, and has induced me to write to you now.   I write because you have been cheered by a few words of mine.

I write because, as life moved on, the most absolute certainty has come to me by living. If I were annihilated this moment, I should bless God for having been allowed to live. Far more, if I were to have to toil and suffer in this sorrowful but glorious earth-life through unnumbered ages, and the sorrow and suffering continued to bring the living life with it that it has brought, I would gladly accept sorrow and suffering here on earth. How much more then, when I expect, and am sure, that a very few years more will place me with these precious life-powers in a world fitted for highest life, with life intensified, and all the pure great life of ages gathered there, besides those whom I have dearly loved and who have lived lovable lives. Yet now hear what, I think, gives me the right to speak as I am speaking, what at all events makes what I say something very different from a dreamer's dreams. There is such a fierce reality in it, though language can very little express the manifold and complex life which makes it so real, that I feel that, if body and soul were torn asunder bit by bit, each bit would still be a perfect conviction of the great feeling of immortal life and happy progress. I can fairly say that I started life after Cambridge in the front ranks of successful working-men, and felt no fear of anything —man, work, or danger. I can fairly say since then I have honestly faced every mental problem that has come before me —sceptical, agnostic, scientific, moral—and have successively dealt with each, mastered them, and assigned them their proper places. I believe, nay I am sure, that the world in which my spirit lives is constructed with a complete knowledge of all possible doubts and difficulties.

I have spoken of happy life. Well, I do not believe there lives on God's earth a man who has lived through more sorrow, shame, toil, danger, drags, and insult than I have. This I know, whatever tries other men, everything that had deadly power to try me came. For fifteen years, from thirty-three to forty-eight or fifty, I never knew real health, and had to work on in pain and weakness day by day. For thirty years the only thing I ever really longed for was *bed*. It sounds mean, I daresay it is mean, but it is true, and I wish to tell you the truth. Whatever joy or sorrow came, and there was much of both, the overwhelming sense of weariness and endless pain made bed, forgetfulness, the only human solace that satisfied. It is only in the last three years that I have begun to joy again in my waking life. Yet, strange contradiction to all this, one of those great contradictions which life and living harmonises—*solvuntur vivendo*—I count myself blessed to have been allowed to live such a life. I cannot even now bear to think of living it over again, yet year by year, aye, day by day, I felt the warrior joy of life and the conqueror's joy of getting the mastery. In my worst agony I could not pray to have it taken away, so utterly by degrees did I feel the power and light that came. And now all creation has opened out to me by living, and everything that I count happy I know to have come out of the self-mastery and training and truth which those years of anguish brought. My positive creed is an absolute, unfaltering certainty of life triumphant.

I believe and know a Lord and Giver of Life. I feel Him working in and with me. I see Him in His world. I under-stand the world plan. I read the past and see the happy progress, whatever backwaters or eddies there may be in Life's great river. I see the future, and know what our own times mean, and in the rough what is coming, and whatever back-waters or eddies there may be whirling individuals or nations backward for a time in life's great river, I see the great river sweeping all on equally to a happy end. New revelations come as new facts rise, and daily awakenings into new existence, which the light already lighted casts light on and interprets.

My creed is life. Blessed is Life the King. Blessed is the life I have lived, yea, with all its depth of agony, blessed it was and blessed it is. Even on this earth blessed has been and is the gift of life, if there was nothing more to come. But blessed above all blessedness is the absolute certainty that *life cannot die*. No, not a living tear, nor a sigh of life perishes. It is all seed power ; it still lives somewhere, and, whilst I have my human follies and human feelings and can indeed rejoice and sorrow over the merest trifle, for it is of the nature of the keenest power to be most sensitive, nevertheless, whilst gaining happy enjoyment of trifles, every hour deepens and strengthens the sober conviction of being born at death into a nobler world and an immediate happy power of unhindered life. How I should like to talk over the plan of the world with you and its working.

In August and half September I shall be at Pitlochry, Perthshire, and shall be happy to put you up for a week. Then we should have leisure. If this is impossible, I would give you such time as I could get here before we break up in July.

To the Same.

January 26th, 1887.

I have been down in the deep waters too much myself not to feel greatly touched by your letter. I have quite forgotten my words. I only recollect my unwillingness, and that I did finally write rather a severe letter. I congratulate you upon having got a hearing. . . . I hail the proposal at Oxford as a stirring of the waters, but I dread a fresh deluge of cram. You will probably have seen by my letter in the *Pall Mall,* which, indeed, I wrote as a statement to the editor that I could not write, when he asked me. I did not mean it to be published, but it did not signify; it correctly represented my views. I fear you would have liked more backing up. But I do so dread new forms of cram. You will be glad to hear that my books and addresses are getting very widely read in America. I send you the last I have perpetrated. I am, however, due at Cambridge on Saturday, 5th March, to lecture on the invitation of the Teachers' Syndicate. I am going to give them a taste of working experience, such as no one but a working man could have written.

I really must thank you very much for your letter, very much. I am not used to getting acknowledgment. . . . It is new—it is pleasant—it cheers me very much.

CHAPTER IX

CORRESPONDENCE—CHIEFLY WITH OLD BOYS

NOTHING moved Thring more than seeing any one of his old pupils giving himself up to strenuous and unselfish work. And certainly he had something of the Napoleonic eye for recognising soldierly effort, the Napoleonic art of saying the word which rendered courage higher and devotion more complete, which made each man feel that on him depended in no small degree the fortune of the day. Short, crisp letters, almost like the bulletins of a general upon a campaign, were going out constantly from his study to cheer men engaged in trying work. Sometimes it was to a missionary abroad, sometimes to one at home. Wherever an Uppingham boy went to a post of difficulty the headmaster's eye followed him.

A series of letters written to a clergyman who had taken work in a neglected colliery district will illustrate the spirit in which this kind of connection was kept up with his pupils.

To Rev. Harry Mitchell.

November 16th, 1881.

I lose no time in sending you working drawings of a Fives-court. Wishing you heartily success, and fully believing that the most religious work of our day is the finding good amusements for the people, believe me, etc.

To the Same.

March 16th, 1882.

I have been too busy to write to you before in answer to your very interesting letter; because it was so interesting to me, that the sort of brutal telegram note in return would not in any way have satisfied me. You cannot tell how much I value your confidence, and how it goes to my heart, and cheers and nerves me for work to think that your feelings for me allow you to write "as to your mother." I never valued a sentence more than I do that one of yours. You are indeed a big headmaster. Do you know that I learnt my most valued lessons in teaching as a teacher in National Schools when I was a curate? So you see I am only returning to the fountain-head that which I drew from it when work of mine, as you tell me, helps you. I send some notes on teaching, as you touch on the subject, which may be of some service to you. I drew them up for myself and the masters. They are, however, being published in the *Educational Journal.* I did not intend that sort of thing. But I got into a kind of explanation affair with the Journal, and they behaved well, and on their asking leave to print it, I consented. . . .

I am so glad you do something special for the children. What a frightful mistake the Church Services have generally been for them, and the way they have been treated in Church.

I often think of the Bristol cutler, Plum. My brother was in his shop talking to him, and a boy came in to buy a knife. Plum left my brother (who was rather a swell) and paid extraordinary attention to suiting the boy with a knife to his mind. When he had finished, my brother remarked on the pains he had taken. "Why, you see, sir," he said, "that knife's a great matter to a boy; if I give him *a good one,* he'll remember it as long as he lives, and always come to me again." A fine and true philosophy—*always give the children a good one.* Alas! how often, how universally forgotten.

I have something to show you on these lines when you come here again—our schoolroom beautifully painted under

Mr. Rossiter. This will kill the mean idea of lessons. Surround lessons with noble surroundings and the whole boy world will alter. So I am following Plum.

Our Aviary is getting on capitally, and is a great pleasure to me, and again to the school. The school has just acquired Mr. Bell's house and property, and will shortly have Pateman's. Then the whole hill from the schoolhouse to the end of the lower school will be in school hands. This will make the position very complete. I little thought to see so much come to pass externally.

To the Same.

(On his objecting to address the school about his work.)

March 18th, 1882.

Never mind lack of speech. Don't worship talk, worship life. Remember the greatest leader the world ever had, God's chosen leader of His people, Moses, was no speaker. Talk is destroying England.

The next letter requires a word of explanation. For the second edition of his *Theory and Practice of Teaching*, Thring received fifty pounds. He at once forwarded the money to his old pupil in the collieries, to be made use of in his parish work. In reply to a letter deprecating so large a gift of hardly earned money, he writes :—

May 13th, 1884.

I look on myself as a kind of big baby. Are we not all big babies, if we are anything—babies in our Father's care, just doing baby work ; doing it well, if we do it as babies, humbly, trustfully, without self-will ; doing it ill, if we are thinking it our own, or going our own ways ?

I just feel that every word of that book was a gift. The experience was a revelation given me in work ; the writing it was just a forth-speaking of God's gift of speech. I never felt anything more utterly not myself ; myself only, as having a heart empty enough to be filled, cleansed enough not to foul the inpoured treasure. Believe me, the effort to work with the Holy Spirit is all. The powers we have are nothing—talents, which God gives or takes away, without altering the real man, the man, whose heart decides the use made of them, whose love determines the value of his work. So, dear fellow-worker in the vineyard, take the money, and be cheered ; not we, but what we are made by the Lord becomes a power. Any cloud is the same till the glory fills it with light. I cannot see that a giant, who does half work or grudging work, is better than the child who does all he can. Still more, I do see that the child who sows God's seed is nobler and greater in the working world than the incarnate cannon who is a world-famous destroyer.

You want the money to help your people to the light. Use it as you please.

To the Same.

September 26th, 1884.

What a fellow you are !—like Harry Percy who came in to breakfast daily, and met his wife's good morning and question, "How many hast thou killed to-day?" with "Some fourteen or so—a trifle, a trifle," an hour after, you stick up schools in the most casual manner. I quite begin to expect to see the Wigan examiner on my breakfast table with the bread and butter.

But I do rejoice in your vigour and success. And I rejoice heartily in your onslaught in word as well as deed on Mr. Mundella and State frauds *re* the nation, and sneaking communism. I cannot understand why I and you and other hard-working men and women should be made to pay to support our neighbours' illegitimate children, illegitimate beer, or any other illegitimates, which is what the School Board underselling the Voluntaries, or starting better schools, comes to.

This is scarcely the worst ; the tyranny which, as if we had got to perfection, is going to force all the minds of the country, all the teachers and all the taught, into the same cursed Chinese shoe, and kill all progress, is more fatal still, and worst of all, the practice which separates brain work from religion and morality, and calls it education, is simply the devil let loose.   Altogether a more iniquitous fraud on the national conscience and purse cannot be imagined.   It is heart-breaking. But I am delighted to see one of my men making head successfully against such abomination.   I have never been so downhearted in my life about England as now.   The nation seems given over to a lying spirit.   "The prophets prophesy falsely (modern science to wit), the priests bear rule by their means (our Radical Government), and my people love to have it so, alas ! "

To think that we should betray all who trusted us in Africa, in Afghanistan, in Egypt, shed blood in torrents when a firm word at first would have been enough, bribe crime in Ireland, and that all the betrayal, bloodshed, and bribery should only lead to ruin.   Best remembrances to you and Mrs. Mitchell. I am proud of you.

To the Same.

October 29th, 1885.

Your packet this morning gave unmitigated satisfaction ; the family appreciate a joke, and your "free education" will irradiate the day.   I have not stopped laughing over it yet. It puts my dictum of "a devil's parody" into visible shape. Cannot you send it to a Conservative management to be published and distributed far and wide under the title of "Free Education Box"?

No, I shall never ask for anything.   God put me here, and He will take me away.   If I was Bishop I should have to wait till I got a parish big enough and nasty enough for you. . . .

My dear fellow, I don't overrate you.   I have lived and worked long enough to know that he who does what God gives him to do with the most complete emptying of self is God's man.   And when I see a man doing what God sets him to do well, I know the first half of the problem of life, and a bit of the second.   I owned to being greatly cheered by my American success.   The good cause will live ; it wants a hearing, and now I know it will get it.

I send you two copies of "The Charter of Life."   I feel very strongly about the views given me to put in it ; you can have more if you want them. . . .

To the Same.

March 25th, 1886.

I am delighted with your *début* as an agitator. Seriously, I heartily sympathise with and congratulate you. Of all the evils that the wicked men and liars who at the present moment bear rule over us are bringing on England, the worst is *slavery.* This appalling curse, all the worse when it takes the garb of an angel of light, which is daily more and more thrusting its dead, unfeeling hand of external power into the heart fibre of living work, I dread above all other modern devils, and their name is legion. I hold that the evils and miseries of wrong-doing are God's ministers by which men are brought to cure *themselves,* and that the man who meddles with them *by law* (unless in the case of crime) is first a fool, and secondly a fighter against God. If men would but recognise that misery comes from vice and cannot be removed by law, they would not be such fools. The Israelites, no doubt, could have been brought out of Egypt by a great battle, but *Cui bono?* They would only have changed from sensual slaves to sensual tyrants. God passed a good many coercion bills, and executed a pretty stiff number of rebels in the wilderness. I loathe the meddling. We shall be destroyed as a nation if it goes on. So you see I am fully in accord with your action. We must work with all our souls and strength to make people a law to themselves, and if they won't be, let them suffer the consequences till they will. This is God's way of working. For 1400 years Christianity thought it could interfere with the laws of labour and capital, and a pretty mess they made of it with their alms and gifts. And now a kind of Antichrist is trying the same dodge, and a pretty mess, as was likely, *liberté, égalité,* and *fraternité*—that is, living on your neighbour—has made in France, and will make in England. God forbid that we should be fed with Government pap when we squall, *à la* Gladstone.

N.B.—Squall loud.

To the Same.

December 2nd, 1886.

I congratulate you heartily, though it must be very hard for you to leave Pemberton. I am going now to blow the other trumpet in opposition to my last blast.

I am sure that the best work requires to be tested by absence and new direction. Death does it in time if promotion doesn't.

I am sure that clergymen make a great mistake for their people's sake if they do not, if possible, take a sufficient holiday every year to let their people feel how far the better life has become their own. And from this point of view I can well believe that your removal from Pemberton may be a benefit not only to you but to Pemberton, as throwing them on their own resources after a good foundation laid for them to go on with. I am an intense believer in life and the living power of true life; if a plant does not live of its own vitality, depend upon it the soil is in fault, not the plant, if the plant is hardy. Oats grow, but they grow slowly. . . .

To the Same.

June 15th, 1887.

I congratulate you on the success of your operations on behalf of the Pit Brow women. I have been going in lately for women's work, and had the annual conference of the leading headmistresses at Uppingham last week. It was intensely interesting. They were so different from the popular idea of the learned, or the woman's right, type of thing; such lady-like, nice, quiet, superior people, we all felt it a pleasure and honour to entertain them, and to them it was an official recognition of much importance. I gave them an address at their request, and we had a conversazione and some school songs in the great schoolroom on the Friday evening.

The following letters were written to an old pupil who had consulted him on certain social questions of the day.

In such questions Thring's interest was profound. But though a reformer by instinct and in practice, he yet deeply distrusted many popular methods of social reform, because he believed that they violated fundamental principles of human conduct which could not be neglected with impunity.

To T. E. Powell.

December 6th, 1883.

I am exceedingly interested in all these sanitary movements and fervent hopes of improving the lower strata of society, and exceedingly alarmed at the later phase of legislation, which may be curtly summarised as " bread and treacle to the babies that squall loudest."

In my opinion we have no *Government*, we only have an executive, tools of the *popularis aura*, waves that are strong only through the movement behind them of tumultuous weakness in bulky motion.

I have one strong political principle : an intense belief in liberty, the other side of which is, an intense dread of mean authority, and an intense contempt for all people, cries, and creeds which, in whatever shape, restrain and enslave true work, impose conditions on the skilled and thrifty workman, and demand that people should do for others what they ought to do for themselves. Help as much as you like, but never give all. Help as much as you like, but never turn a free man's free agency into a tax he is forced to pay, and the non-workers can claim by law. I cannot see why I should be forced by law to support by law my neighbour's illegitimate children, or Government encourage him theoretically to cut my throat if I don't. This is really at the root of the whole matter ; and I agree with Miss Octavia Hill in looking on Government confiscation of the property of the workers to support the non-workers, by whatever name you like to call it, as the greatest curse that can befall this or any nation. However complicated the problem becomes, and God knows how complicated it has become, the original start is plain enough, and nothing will ever be cured by running your head against the laws of nature.

It is a law of nature that man should work, and be sober, and temperate, or else starve, he and his.

It is against a law of nature to tax the sober worker to pay his drunken neighbour's bill, or maintain him in lust.

His drunken and dissolute neighbour runs up a long bill against laws of nature, and then, encouraged by *no governments*, proceeds to cut his neighbour's throat because he has a credit at the bank of nature and nature's God. I do not mean for a moment to say that the rich are good and the poor bad, but I do mean to say that as a class the men who maintain themselves by work are good, and as a class the men who cannot maintain themselves by work are bad. In both cases I take into account their immediate ancestors.

Law can and ought to remove impediments. Christian men and women can and ought to help the poor to set things going which they are too weak to set going, but they can no more rightly take away from the poor the necessity of keeping going the thing when started than they can eat his dinner for him. It makes me laugh to hear men talk gravely of doing away with landlords, etc. Some one must be owner, and if he is not a slave, must have the power of getting work done for him.

Farewell liberty, if we are to have much more of the doing for people what they ought to do for themselves. The modern cry of *panem et circenses* has been raised. Our-top-of-the-wave men are listening to it. It means down with the workers, make them slaves ; up with the non-working rabble, make them masters ; and cruel masters they have always been, unbelievers in anything higher than themselves, devout worshippers of the lash for others, as it is the only thing they understand.

There, I have given you some morning lessons under the great disadvantage, however, of not being able to qualify and explain as I go along.

I am a Radical Conservative—that is, I want quietly to change everything that is, but to change them slowly and on the old principles, reforming everything. I must shut up. The bell has sounded.

To the Same.

December 29th, 1883.

As regards your letter, the whole question is summed up by what you state at the beginning, "a fair chance for all *who will work*," with the addition, "as far as external power can give it." But a fair chance only means that hindrances should be removed, not that one penny of other people's work should be given. Not one penny given to relieve man, woman, or child from doing what they can do ; or from the responsibility of proper forethought, proper self-denial, proper work. The true socialist starts from the broad fact that all I can gain by my work is mine, as against any other single man or clique. The advantages which gave me the power to work successfully were given me by workers directly or indirectly. They are mine as against any other individual men. The State has a right to take taxes from me in order to protect, or work the State. Every such tax, every tax that is not robbery, is either an insurance payment for security and against loss, or it is a commercial payment to the great national partnership for facilities to carry on business. But the moment the State takes my money, that is, my work, to give it to you, under any pretext whatever, it is a robber, and that State sooner or later will pay the robber's penalty. The State has no more right to take one man's property and give it to another than the pickpocket has.

One thing is certain, like the case of the poachers. Whatever difference of opinion there may be about *ferae naturae* and their rightful owner, one thing is certain, *ferae naturae* live on land or water, and a man who has neither land nor water cannot be the owner. So in property, however complicated the problem gets to be, property means stored-up work, and stored-up work means the brain-power and life-power as represented by intelligent management and hand work put into it. Those who have put neither into it cannot have any right to property.

I am quite aware of the logical statement that the community has a right to determine on what terms the individual shall live in it.

It is logical enough, but logical insanity, as is often the case in words applied to life. In the first place, there is no such entity as the community; for all practical purposes you might as well say the Abracadabra has the right, etc. Secondly, if by this is meant that whether we like it or not, all we earn is to be put in a common stock and divided out, who is to divide it? And who is going to work? You cannot break laws of nature which have made the work and powers of men vary in value.

That is what I mean when I ask why should I maintain my neighbour's illegitimate child. I mean by illegitimate every child brought into the world who demands more than his parents can give him, or to whom Government makes a present of my money.   The School Boards are promising to be an excellent example of public robbery.   But no community of robbers can exist long.   I quite admit that, morality and the Christian duty to help apart, the illegitimate children may be very dangerous.   Jack Cade taken up by a popular government is a very important person, but for all that the quart pot will not hold a gallon, let him or Gladstone affirm it ever so much, and I for my part do not see if one drunken bully is not fit to govern me, why ten thousand drunkards are more fit, or ten thousand uneducated fools.   The great problem always is, how to let the wiser minority govern and at the same time satisfy the foolish majority; or how to let the practical difficulties of the foolish majority influence sufficiently the selfish, self-satisfied want of experience of the educated minority. But who is aiming at this?   Not our rulers.

The upshot of the practical question is simple, very simple. First, many people are in the world who have no right to be in the world—the fruit of the sin, self-indulgence, and improvidence of their parents, who have broken the laws of nature.

Second, a fair chance does not mean robbing people by law to support these people, but guarding against their helpless condition being made a prey by the stronger.

This is all that Government can do.   Government does not mend the original breaking of nature's laws by breaking others.   God meant misery to follow on indulgence without self-restraint in high and low.   Is the peer dying at seven-and-twenty, used up, less punished by natural laws than the poor man in the slums?   On the other hand, the rich and the educated sin grievously in not personally seeing their poorer brethren, working amongst them, helping them to make a start, or get over a difficulty; but never doing for them what they ought to do themselves. . . . You can no more do the work of raising a man *for him* than you can eat his dinner for him. He must do all he can, and he has a fair chance given him if he is on the lowest step, if he is given a fair chance of living a decent life.   If he lives a decent life, then his children will have a fair chance of rising another step, and men do rise and fall incessantly on this principle.   Meantime, don't meddle with the question of large families.   The question is the right of marrying. . . .

My school was an embodiment of the principle that there is no true life without true body; or, in other words, that true externals must be provided for life—by others, if the life is too weak to effect it all itself—by the life itself, if it is strong. But I did not rob other people to do this. I poured out my own heart blood and my own earnings like water. I think the Christian man is bound to do his own work in the most living way, and if his own work is mechanical, to have some living work to supplement it, however slightly.

There, I think, the infinite love of Christ comes in to make the individual say in a wise way all mine is thine, instead of pandering to the robber cry all thine is mine. I have given fortune and life, but I was not robbed of it. There is the distinction. Government spends other people's money, and has no right to spend it excepting for their good. An individual spends his own and has a right to spend it, even if he is a fool in the way he does spend it.

To the Same.

February 2nd, 1884.

Your problem about bygone wrongs theoretically presents no difficulty for two reasons. The first is that every generation, according to its lights, rewards the work that is valuable in that generation. You cannot separate the generation into two sections of right-doers and wrong-doers, still less can you subdivide those two sections into the right-doing or oppressed poor on the one side and the wrong-doing oppressors on the other. Grant, for argument sake, the class oppressor. What is it made up of? What does it represent? It represents the dominant belief of the time, and is made up of the great majority of the people. Take the *bête noir* of modern wisdom, feudalism. Feudalism represents the fact that in a time of great violence and personal insecurity fighting was the most valuable work, and mutual aid in fighting the main business in life. In its better form it took the shape of fighting for law, order, and self-protection. The methods of law, order, and self-protection were rude and rough enough, but the intent and principle was this. In its worst form it took the form of combinations of robbers for the sake of booty. In either case, fine fighting qualities were exceedingly valuable, and the work of best fighters was rewarded accordingly, and the poor and lower orders—the majority—were as heartily *ex animo* devoted to this work as the nobles who led them. In fact, in the rougher form of it, nothing in the world has ever been more democratic. There never has been a time when personal merit (bravery) had better scope for winning a way to fortune than in the feudal times. But at all events, the nobles were nobles because they were supported heartily either as protectors or robber chiefs by the people, who shared in and supported their work. In modern times, the acquisition of wealth by trade, or other arts of peace, is the road to distinction, and the most valuable work is rewarded by wealth. Whether that wealth arises from an Arkwright inventing a new machine which brings prosperity to millions, or from a manufacturer cornering the market at Birmingham, makes no difference. The fact remains the same, that the people work willingly to support the main objects of modern life, and if the people did not work, either from the profit it brings them, as most do, or because of their dire needs as the victims of unthrift do, there would be no rewards of work. It is all humbug talking of "they toil not, neither do they spin," or lies. It is all humbug or lies talking of the few preying on the many. There are endless complications, no doubt, and much that is wrong, but the laws of work and property are laws of nature, and violent readjustments of conditions of society are wicked and silly, and violent denunciations of past conditions are wicked, silly, and ignorant to boot. You cannot confiscate either past or present labour with impunity. Make the labourers better men, and the misery ceases. Laws cannot mend sins. Private men can strive in their sphere to do it. Secondly, it is astonishing how short a time and in how few instances individual anomalies last in a country like this. There is a Lancashire proverb which puts in a graphic way the shifting character of wealth apart from merit : "There are only three generations between clod and clod." There is an incessant dropping out of the unworthy from their place of vantage, and an incessant rising of the worthy into their place. In a couple of hundred years this is very demonstrable. As to marriage, if a marriage is entered upon sensibly, I still think with the Psalmist, "Blessed are those that have their quiver full." The evil there too is in the unthrift and self-indulgence before marriage, and in rushing into certain misery, as many do.

There is plenty for good men to do in bettering the world, but only one way of doing it, making people better, helping, living with them ; not being liberal with other people's money, and turning the weak, self-indulgent, and idle into beggars. This applies at once to the question of education. The principle of supporting your neighbour's illegitimate child corporeally or mentally is the same. I never would break through a law of nature to give relief temporarily. If it is dangerous, try and put it in the way of getting itself out of danger. But non-religious schools bear witness to the problem not being met in a right way. I am clear on the functions of Government. Government ought to take in hand strongly every question which affects the community as a community, and compel public works to be carried out or carry them out. But Government has no business to take my money and give it to a cause which does not bring me any personal benefit, especially if I believe that cause to be wrong. All sanitary matters, all removal of hindrances to work, belong to Government. To see that the nation is educated also, I think, belongs to Government. But I cannot think it belongs to Government to prescribe *how*, or to destroy by public money private effort, and to impose the will of 2,000,000 people on 1,999,000 because of that small margin of majority.

To the Same.

March 25th (1884?)

. . . I do mean what you suppose me to mean. It is an entirely false view of facts at all times, and in all instances, if a broad period of time is taken, to imagine that in any homogeneous nation there is any divided interest, or that class means to tyrannise over class with the intent of wronging them, but universal μοχθηρία. I mean the inseparable evil of human nature makes large bodies of men difficult to deal with, and produces through evil great and real problems, which can only be reached by curing evil, not by moving the pieces on the chessboard. For example, at the present moment how the lower strata are clamouring against the self-indulgence of the wealthy. Well, be it so; but who thinks that for one man who openly destroys by self-indulgence his family or himself in the upper classes, a thousand do it in the lower, on fair average of the respective numbers? Will this evil be mended by putting a thousand drunken brutes in power where now we have one only? I trow not. Or to go back: What can be more silly in reviewing the past than the throwing aside the times and circumstances of which life was composed? The first need of man is protection, and the earlier stages of civilisation consist in combinations for protection, where the best fighter deservedly gets the best pay; this soon passes into the much more difficult problem of how to rule the conquered. Then Christianity by ennobling work has gradually thrust out war as the one road to success, but has introduced all the complex problems of wages, wealth acquired by stored-up work, *i.e.* capital, the different value of different kinds of work, and all the perplexity of intricate crowded modern competition knotted into tangles by our old friend $\mu o \chi \theta \eta \rho i a$. Apparently the newest modern lights darken a darkness that is incredible, only it is here. No one seems to have any more statesmanlike knowledge or remedy than our dear friend Aristophanes, a passage from whom, versifying Mr. George, Mr. Gladstone, and Mr. Mundella in different degrees, I send you as the best summary of the political wisdom which would tax the worker to support his neighbour's illegitimate child, and give by law to the sturdy beggar what he must by nature's law get for himself, or sooner or later perish. Billeting the strong pauper on the rich only makes him more of a pauper still. The heathen world spent its whole time on the theory that you must first conquer, and when you are conqueror, do nothing but live on your conquered neighbours. The advanced spirits of the modern world are endeavouring to do the same, only they wish to put the ignorant and idle pauper on the neck of the intelligent richer worker. But the pauper theory is the same in both cases. No shifting of the pieces will alter the great fact that there are no opposing classes anywhere, excepting so far as $\mu o \chi \theta \eta \rho i a$ prevails. Work and rewards of work from the beginning of the world to the end are the basis of kingdoms. A rich non-worker or a pauper are in the same box; they are funguses—funguses which, if neglected, destroy the tree. The French Revolution was an example of the rich fungus destroying the kingdom. Our state is in danger of the poor fungus doing it. Miss Octavia Hill put a great truth into a most simple axiom the other day when she said that "it was far easier to supply the poor with proper dwellings than to teach them to dwell properly in them." There is the whole difficulty. The bad rich want to rob the poor, the bad poor want to rob the rich, and proceed to legalise forms of robbery. The great law is: Help—*never give*. And be careful how you help. No help is help which does not help towards self-help. Every generation is in reality struggling with the same problem, viz. how to minimise $\mu o \chi \theta \eta \rho i a$, and develop unity of work. Or rather, that is the real problem which is being struggled with; but sometimes nations for hundreds of years do little but play at conquerors and conquered, a very bloody and disastrous game, whether played by Mr. George and his paupers, or by a French Emperor and his paupers; poor or rich, the $\mu o \chi \theta \eta \rho i a$ of self-indulgence is not cured by indulging it; and in life problems no man can do for the life of another what that other's life ought to do for itself. God's eternal law has made each man's life a unity capable of being *linked on* to another's, but not capable of ceasing to be a link, with all its own weight to bear. In a living growing people every part is living growth, and the moment you take any man's duty off him you turn him into a fungus. There are many problems, many adjustments which each generation has to settle, but no antagonism, no oppressor and oppressed, till you confiscate by *law* the earnings of one set of men and give them to another. All difficulties arising from the free play of work competition, freedom of contract, etc., are difficulties which mostly arise from $\mu o \chi \theta \eta \rho i a$, which law cannot alter unless law has made them, as is sometimes the case.

A few letters written to a son will serve to show his views on life questions where his most intimate private feelings were deeply concerned.

To G. HERBERT THRING.

November 28th, 1879.

I write on your birthday, and you will get it on mine. Many happy returns of it to you. May you work and live so that every year as it brings your birthday round may bring round with it the feeling of life richer, better, purer, and more unselfish.

You may believe how much I feel Alington's death, but I feel far more his living power. If you want to be a soldier, be Christ's soldier; gather the hardy—far more hardy— laurels of manly, quiet, ceaseless work, and your birthday shall be to you happy, and the day of your departure the truest birthday of all. Work hard, enjoy your working life, and as you work, what you are to do will become plain. Have a strong present life for good, and you will have a plain future life. God bless you, my boy.

To THE SAME.

February 20th, 1880.

I should wish you every day and night to read from ten to thirty verses of the Gospels carefully, and so go through them quietly and begin again. Life will interpret them as you go on living, and they will throw light on life.

To THE SAME.

November 27th, 1880.

My earnest prayers for you day and night are that you may bear yourself in God's world as one full of God's life— loving work, true and faithful ever. So shall every succeeding year be to you, as it has been to me, more full of blessing, and every care and sorrow turned into a greater power of life and hope.

To THE SAME.

April 17th, 1882.

Time moves on. Have you ever really, seriously, as is befitting the great question of life, considered whether you would take the best of services—under the great King, where whoever is true never fails—and take Holy Orders? I do not wish in any way to influence you, beyond putting before you my own belief, and my own experience of the truth of my belief, that rich or poor, married or unmarried, quiet or troubled life, in the long run that which is both best, and felt at last to be best, is given to the servant of Christ. No answer is needed for this. But the common world atmosphere of "How can I get on?" so pervades the whole world, and clouds the question, that the true issue, "How can I most truly put out my talents for my Lord?" is sometimes, nay, often never before the mind at all.

April 21st, 1883.

Let me put down a few things which I wish to stick by you in life. Read carefully a portion of the Gospels every day. Believe me, the one great feeling of my life has been, and is, the blessing that seeing and feeling the truth of Christ's life, and the way in which life works in the world, and in one's own heart, and the happiness of overcoming lower and baser nature, has brought.

Remember the one great maxim of working life, that though there are thousands able to do work, there are very few who can be depended upon to do it exactly as their employers wish. Men, in fact, whose employers feel that when they have put a thing into their hands, they can have it off their minds —it will be certainly done.

Look earnestly at the work how that can best be done, *not* how *you* can do it. Never despise work; complete mastery of little things makes a great man at last. Black shoes if a proper authority tells you to do so. Do all the work you can; volunteer for it if there is any such chance; willingness and capacity never fail to get on. Extra work willingly done is very gratifying to a superior. It is often possible in times to be so useful as to get nearly indispensable to superiors. Never expect gratitude, or make a claim for willing service, or grumble. The more work, the more experience. Many a man has succeeded because he has been really put on; many a man has failed because he thought he was being put on when he was not.

Never forget a kindness done to you in low estate. You cannot repay it if it was unselfishly done, but you can feel it, and have the greatness of heart to silently do your best. Love truth. Truth is doing your best. A man who does not do his best defrauds somebody of something ; he defrauds his employer, himself, and God. The two last always, the first very often.

All work is religious. Your religion will be shown by doing your work unselfishly and well for Christ's sake. May God bless you. This day with its two letters is a solemn day to me and to you.

The following letters were written to an old pupil who had just been asked by Dr. Bickersteth—then Bishop-elect of Japan—to accompany him to his distant mission, a call which was, after some hesitation, accepted :—

To Rev. L. B. Cholmondley.

March 1st, 1886.

Mrs. Christian has spoken to me of your possibilities and the anxious thought it naturally causes. I will willingly do what I can to help you, but as I cannot know all the circumstances, anything I say must be taken with the reservation that I only supply some data for you to form your judgment by. The first thing I will say is the emphatic statement, that *no one but yourself can decide.* This is a law. We take our main steps in life alone, as much as we die alone. There are responsibilities which no man ought to evade for himself, and no man can righteously take for another. This is one which you now have before you.

As regards the question itself. I think it is a call ; yet not so obviously, not so brought about by numerous little circumstances as far as I know, as to make it an absolute binding necessity. Again, this last statement of mine is one which your own heart alone can rightly have a real opinion about. You are in my opinion extremely well fitted for the sort of post you are asked to take. The country is very highly civilised, and requires a really educated man.

Your father and home have in my judgment a fair claim to your earnest consideration of their wishes. More than that they probably do not want. Putting them out of the question for a moment, for argument's sake, my own verdict would send you, and bid you God-speed. But I must repeat solemnly and emphatically that it would be wrong in me to judge, under the circumstances in which I am placed, of imperfect knowledge and no direct authority.

You will have my hearty approval if you decide on going. You will have my full concurrence in the goodness of your action if you do so.

With every prayer that you may do the best, believe me, your sincere friend.

To the Same.

November 2nd, 1886.

I shall not cloud the question by words or argument, which are not my concern. I feel exceedingly clear on the main principles, and have no difficulty in stating them. First of all, you must judge for yourself, no one can take the responsibility of your choice from you, or ought to try to do so to any great extent.

Secondly, no one can tell beforehand fitness or unfitness, excepting in very marked cases; relatives and friends least of all. It was His mother and His brethren who said He is beside Himself, and came to stop Him.

Thirdly, the ultimate question is, whether the summons is a call or not. This greatly turns on circumstances known only to yourself, and the Authority that gives the call.

Fourthly, if it is a call it may not amount to a call to that special thing, but be a message rather than a call.

Fifthly, the acceptance or refusal of a real call may, if the motives are good, be very evenly balanced, and either choice be good.

Sixthly, you, and you only, are any judge of the real voice to you, you only know how it fits in with your secret life, you only know how far you find yourself, the call, and the work in harmony.

You and you only have to weigh these things, as if there

was no other judgment in the world but your own. There is no other. All other things are data for your consideration, nothing more.

Lastly, whatever you decide on, leave the result to itself. You only have to decide to the best of your power rightly, after that what comes of it is no business of yours. God gives success, God gives failure, and both are right to him who gets either. And may God the Father, God the Son, and God the Holy Ghost, guide you aright.

To the Same.

November 24th, 1886.

As far as I have any materials for judgment I feel convinced that you have come to a right decision. May the blessing of God rest on you. But remember whether it seems to turn out well or ill has nothing whatever to do with your being right now, nothing whatever to do with the true blessing hereafter, so cheer up when hard days come, as they come to all who do true work. "Be strong and of a good courage," defeat does not mean overthrow in the kingdom of life; full often it is the travail pang of the happy new birth.

In my judgment you are pre-eminently fitted for the work. You are going amongst a people one of the most *civilised* in the world. Such people know a gentleman, know education, and appreciate them. I heard only yesterday that they have applied for ladies to go out and conduct a great girls' school, with full liberty to make the girls Christians if they make the girls educated women as well. So then "Be strong and of a good courage." The blessing is with you.

Thring's method of giving advice, not by dealing with the circumstances of the special case presented to him, but by reference to general principles of conduct, is well shown by the following letter. It was written to a friend who held an educational position of importance, but who had been asked to give it up and undertake an entirely different and difficult work, for which he was supposed to have special qualifications.

I write a hurried line, as time presses, on the call you have received. . . . I do not presume to advise, still less to use any persuasion, yet I think the thoughts of one who has thought much over such life questions may be of value as data to help your own judgment.

Such calls, though occasionally no doubt neutral, present themselves to my mind as either temptations or *calls*. If they are side winds coming in from outside and drawing a man off his life work from motives of vanity or *chance* of gain dangled as a bait, they require careful scrutiny, and probably are temptations, presenting glitter and possibilities in the place of solid, sober, everyday work.

On the other hand, if they are calls to powerful work, especially if a competent authority makes the call, and they grow out of the working life by a natural growth, and carry it on in a higher but not less real sphere, then they seem to me Providence opening the door and giving the command to move. I well understand your feeling. . . . But as far as I do apply my principles, it all the more makes me think the call a call from God. Since all great things are done out of the deeps of hearts that feel, and have had self-love and personal ambition killed. It may be that before you could do the great work in the true way, you had, like Moses, to be overthrown, and sent into the wilderness to commune with the shepherd thoughts of an humbled heart. At least I know all I care for has come out of the sorrows, and all such power as I have has been changed and transfigured by defeat and pain. In fact, your sorrow makes me think it is your call. Yet do not mistake me; I offer no judgment. "No man can deliver his brother" is true in these things also. I only throw out some thoughts for you to toss about, and sift, if perchance they may in any way be of service to you.

In another case he writes :—

As to your missionary feelings, there is no missionary like a schoolmaster, but I do not say it may not be your line to take more direct work of the kind, only remember, *injussu imperatoris de loco tuo non discedere.* You have your work already given you, and you are a deserter unless you have an equally clear command to leave it and go elsewhere. God's voice in these days is the circumstance, or concurrence of circumstances that hedges in a man's life without his direct agency, and to break through that hedge by one's own direct agency is wrong. I too would willingly leave Uppingham, the place is full of bitterness to me, full of trouble, care, and doubt; but I cannot go till I get the command; and the recovery of health looks to me very like the command to stay. At all events, I must stay till a call comes, and a path is opened.

And again—

I am quite unable to do more than just throw out an axiom or two on any question relating to your life and work. Follow circumstances by the light of your best convictions. That is all I have to say. Never make them. Do nothing ὑπὲρ μόρον. How strangely the acute practical Greek mind caught all the great practical truths, and stamped on them all some striking word-stamp for all time. . . .

To Rev. A. H. Boucher.

March 7th, 1879.

I congratulate you on your place, and on a very good education. It will not signify twopence ten years hence, or two, or one, whether you were a wrangler or first senior Op. I have no difficulty in delivering my judgment on the question you put before me. Your life work depends in a great degree in your getting a training in unfamiliar places before you begin in your old home. When you have done that you will be able to master your position there and take up your own ground. Without it you won't. You should go to a town parish, under a really good man for a few years. Your whole life work will be raised by it into a different world of power and interest. I could envy you your proposed travels. Some twenty-six years ago I was going over the same ground, and it still lingers in me with much freshness of life.

Begin your working life away from home. It is impossible to develop freely at home.

To the Rev. E. F. Miller.

[St. Thomas's College, Colombo.]

March 24th, 1881.

I am exceedingly glad to see from the newspaper duly received last week that you not only have won much praise, but appear to have somewhat weathered the great financial difficulty that threatened to overwhelm you. In these days a headmaster's office is one of incessant strain and trial. It belongs to our struggling selfish times that it should be. It is the fashion, in England at all events, to look upon all workers who hold any office as slaves of the mob, and to kick and cuff them accordingly. This makes work very gritty and difficult, and if I was a soldier I should find it hard to stand it. But in school work there is so much which the public can neither give nor take away, that in spite of all its trials it is full of life and blessing; and when by chance the public appears to be laudatory too, as seems to be your present case, an unexpected help comes.

You cannot think how much your telling me that my letter gave you courage reacted and gave me courage too. Sometimes I feel quite overwhelmed by work and worry, and the great issues and the small means and the obstructions. But somehow or other, time after time in the strangest way, the rocks open up and the paths go through, and *injussu imperatoris de loco meo non discedam* brightens up into fresher work out of a mere dogged resolution not to sink. As for trustees, when have trustees ever been otherwise than weights on life? So take —— as the necessary thorn in the flesh. The school here is going on very well, . . . I feel very hopeful of the inner growth, and have a sort of faint dream that the idea I began with towards setting a new teaching power on foot may yet be realised, so far as sowing a seed goes at all events.

To Rev. A. H. Boucher.

November 28th, 1885.

As regards politics, I think a clergyman's duty is clear not in any way to identify himself with a party in his parish.

I do not mean that he is not at full liberty to talk politics in private ; but, wherever he is present as a clergyman, and would not be present if he was not a clergyman, he ought to keep his tongue clear.   At the same time, the great principle of right and wrong, the facts of history, the true statement of what he believes, I quite think he both may and ought to put out, leaving it to his hearers to judge which party most truly comes up to that ideal.   I think you, for instance, quite at liberty to preach on Church Defence, if you attacked no one, and occupied yourself in building up truth. . . .

Thring's more casual judgments of men and things, scattered here and there through his letters or notes, as he hurriedly dashed off the thought of the moment, are often singularly epigrammatic and picturesque.   A few illustrations are added here as giving additional insight into his methods of thought and views of life.

. . . People who are squeezable when they ought to be firm, will, I fear, be firm when they ought to be squeezable. That is the law of incompetency.

. . . In many ways a most superior man and most zealous for good, and always at work, but an unhappy trick of somewhat hairsplitting, and considering a good sentence as powerful as a good fact will always somewhat impair his power.   A man who once loses the single eye, or does not get it, which pounces on the thing to be done in spite of irrelevant pros and cons, however specious, never gets rid of the flaw, I think.

. . . If I call myself anything I call myself a Radical Conservative, as all my heart is for change, and all my heart and head for a change that shall not pull down but gradually build up—for growth, that is.

. . . His weak points are fear and flattery. . . . Be sure of this, he is not going to face a public row in opposition to the school power, and I am not at all convinced that we might not win him over quietly. He *loves* the winning side, and *smells* it afar off.

Lord Iddesleigh, though I have not seen him, I believe, since Eton days, was familiar to me not only from his public life, but he and my cousin Lord Hobhouse married sisters, and I knew their brothers well also. "He was a very perfect gentle knight;" too gentle for these fierce days—not from his noble rejection of abuse, but from not stating hard truths hard enough in dealing with hard men.

. . . He is a specimen of that most perfect type of man, a first-rate English clergyman, and it was pleasant meeting him.

. . . Magistrates' justice is an ill-lookout unless you prosecute a poacher, and then you will get justice and the poacher more than justice.

The best way of resting is to work as hard as we can, because by working hard we get the strength to make hard work easy. The curse of the fall was weariness in work, for Adam had work before the shaping and keeping of the garden. The Sabbath was for rest from natural weariness.

Many an injustice is triumphant because the champion of justice has not fought well. Before you engage the navvy who is thrashing his wife, you must be sure he will not thrash you amidst the applause of the spectators, who love a fight and don't care for wives and justice.

He is like a wet cloak that will wrinkle in any direction it is flung.

Once turn your back on light, and ever after, wherever you go, you move in a moving shadow of self. . . .

A little leak sinks a ship, a raft that is all leaks floats; in proportion to excellence compromise is impossible. Never compromise, stop short, leave alone, but don't spoil. . . .

Greatness is great, you cannot make yourself great. . . .

Argument is like an air-cushion; the clever manipulator has only to give a little more or less pressure to the windbag, and it takes what shape he pleases. . . .

Moderns learn as taskwork and keep drawers in their mind for knowledge instead of drinking it all into themselves, making it part of their lives, thinking of it, being it. . . .

Many men, like dead thorns, have no life in them, but much scratching. . . .

When culture is enthroned in the throne of life and takes the place of life that made it, the Vandal and the Goth must be let in with their axes and hammers; it is too beautiful ever to be cast out; it must perish to give life free play again. . . .

Christianity is an incarnation of a new truth always, thus the life of Christianity depends on the life of Christians.

The stream makes music as it ripples over its hindrances; the pebbles bring out its music.

. . . But few men are aware in early life, if ever, how scarce an article a man who will quietly do what he is wanted to do is, and how common an article a man is, who can do a great deal that he is not wanted to do, and who does not do anything satisfactorily.

Truth is giving your best always, never cheating God or man or yourself of time or work due. That is truth. . . .

CHAPTER X

"WORK TILL THE END OF LIFE, AND LIFE TILL THE END OF WORK"

1887

THE year 1887, the last year of his life, opened with much private care and anxiety pressing upon him, in addition to his public work. The spring of that iron will which had carried him through so much was beginning to relax. He was not a very old man; as the traditions of his family went he was comparatively young. But he had done work to fill a much longer life, and the pace was beginning to tell.

"This term," he says in January, "opens with fear and pain. I know nothing. Life is too powerful for me. I only see Thee, O God, working in the midst of the storm. Have mercy on us all, I beseech Thee. . . . One thing I see clearly, as I have often seen before, that if one does work with a single eye every conceivable disparaging or evil motive will be imputed, starting from the calumny of the idle, that the labour you have trained yourself through years of self-denial to perform without flinching is what you like, forsooth! God help us."

And again :—

Altogether I am in a boat on a stormy sea. But I have

two strong trusts. Sure I am that we have striven with a single heart to do God's work here; sure I am that He has accepted it, and that my children will never suffer for what we have done for God.

Herein lay the chief secret of his trouble. What he had faced for himself with courage and faith was not so easy to face as his strength grew less for those who leaned upon him. Very human is the thought which he mentions as passing through his mind when he heard of the great material success which had crowned the labours of an old acquaintance.

January 25th, 1887.—I could not help for a moment contrasting the treatment my public work has received, and what his private work has gained. It is all very well, but a verse in the Psalms is one thing, and that verse translated into —— rich and prosperous, in the face of my torture and many cares, is another. But an hour or so set all right again. I am well content. *Lætus sorte mea,* Come weal, come woe. I have learnt to see how much whipping one wants. " It is good for me that I have been in trouble," and we often forget that trouble would not be trouble if it only attacked one's strong points. Trouble means the blow on a sore place. God's will be done with me and mine.

It was at this time that he decided, under the pressure of anxiety, and more or less, I think, unnerved by it, to ask his trustees for an increase of salary, to which he believed he was in law and equity entitled. The scheme by which the school was governed provided for a minimum and maximum proportion of the fees which might be assigned to the headmaster. For two years only, after the Borth period, the maximum proportion was granted him ; now he asked that it might be given him for the remainder of his headmastership. He believed that his long service entitled him to make this request. Few will be disposed to doubt the strength of such a claim.   After some months of consideration it was refused.

To set off against the cares which weighed upon him, and the work which was exhausting him, were many cheering messages from distant lands. "My lecture as President of the Education Society has been translated into German, and published in one of their educational magazines." He hears that some of his addresses have been republished in Canada ; an article on Uppingham and his work had been accepted by the *Century Magazine* in New York ; an Australian teacher writes to make inquiries about his school music ; visitors from America come to study his work at Uppingham, and they tell him that he would be surprised to know how much his views are discussed among transatlantic teachers.

February 24th.—I have undertaken to write an address for the High School teachers next term ; also next week to speak to an assembly—a club, I believe, of the Newnham girls.   It is curious how Mrs. Ewing's life and memory have set me going on all this woman's work, which I believe to be the most important step in practical life.

March 2nd.—Vivian Skrine and Mr. Hartley here from Poplar to-night.   They gave the school an excellent, simple, strong account of the life there and its difficulties.   I feel it a great boon to have such a breath of true life sent into the school.

March 16th.—The confirmation over, and everything most good.   The service was very impressive, and the bishop gave us an excellent address.   This morning a cheering letter from Mr. Hyde of St. Cloud in America asking me to write a song for his Normal School class, and in other ways giving me glimpses of the power God has given into my hands for true life.   It is very wonderful the way life vibrates through the world in these days.   To-night I give my last address, and then every boy in the school will once more have been spoken to as a soldier of Christ.   Amen.

March 21st.—A great communion yesterday, solemn and blessed. Yet it is curious to know how weak the sense of Christian brotherhood is, and how little the community, the loyalty to one body, is felt. At least thirty of our communicants were absent in spite of the address, and the strong way in which I laid down the need of communion. Nothing moved them; they did not come.

March 22nd.—For the first time for weeks I am not hunted by work. Hope to do my education guild lecture leisurely to-morrow. I thank God with all my heart for the peace He gives my spirit in spite of many troubles, and for the inspiration He gives me, and freshness of work and inward power. It is very strange the feeling of the gift, and very comforting.

April 11th.—Easter Sunday over; a great epoch always. We had such a communion, I am thankful to say, as I have scarcely ever had before. I think 180 boys must have actually been there.

May 22nd.—A most strange experience. My soldier friend of the Welsh Fusiliers, writing to me yesterday, said he knew about me long ago, as in Australia —— (naming one of the greatest reprobates we have ever turned out) had taught many to love and revere my name. It is marvellous. Truly, life is better than writing, as I have always thought, and if God has made my life live in this way, then the thoughts ready to be written, but for the press of work, may well perish unwritten. Also, they have been born out of the work. Heard this morning that we shall have seventy headmistresses here on the 10th and 11th.

. . . A long extract from the diary of dear old Swinny from Lake Nyassa—an account of the first journey through the country he described that has reached England, I take it. This is very full of life. How rich life is becoming in messages of life! I move about in a kind of dream sometimes, so strangely does the reality of this spirit world contrast with the lower reality of this bodily world.

May 24th.—It is more dream-like than ever. Yesterday at ten o'clock I spoke to the school with pride of dear old Swinny's journal, and I meant to have written a cheery letter to him that very day, when on coming out of school I was met by the news that he was dead. Alas! my brother. How I shall miss in my daily prayers the thought of your affectionate, true heart and simple manliness. A finer specimen of an English nobleman it would be hard to find. Now he has joined Alington.

. . . How mysteriously things work, and with what mysterious coincidences of good and evil the events move on side to side—a divine harmony of blessings set over against the troubles.

May 29th.—Yesterday I had a letter from the chairman of my teachers' guild meeting enclosing one from Max Müller, expressing unqualified praise of my lecture; also telling me that Pritchard, the astronomer and writer, had written equally warmly about it. This is cheering. . . . I have practically finished my address to the headmistresses. A wonderful relief to have it off my mind. The pace this term has been severe. . . .

The work was never so severe, however, as to lessen his interest in the smallest boy with whom he had to do.

Such a nice essay from a little boy in P——'s form, full of misspellings and sentences which are not sentences, but full also of life, having thoroughly grasped in a boyish way the life-problems discussed.

June 8th.—The most honourable, touching, and prettiest thing, I believe, that ever happened to me happened to-day. The two little B——s, whose father is in India, who came this term, rang the bell this morning, and were shown into the study where I was, and then they brought out their father's letter, and said they could not read it, and asked if I would read it to them, which I did. To think that these boys would come to me (they are not in my house yet, though I told them I would do my best for them when they came) to read their father's letter for them, after they had been here a month, quite long enough to get over the new boy, is something glorious. How it shows what a kindly feeling there must be in the school as a whole to make it possible. It is a great honour to have been allowed to inspire such a trustful feeling. How it sweetens this hard life. I will set it down against the trustees. . . .

It was characteristic of the man that almost as much space is devoted in his diary to the incident just recorded as to the important public event which took place on the two following days, and of which something must now be said.

We have seen that the conference of headmasters was summoned to meet at Uppingham in 1869 with many anxious questionings about the response that would be made to the invitation. In the years that followed, the wisdom of that venture had been proved. The conference had given rise to much sympathetic and useful interchange of thought, and had broken down the ancient isolation of the greater schools. But in these same years new and powerful educational forces had come into play. Among the most interesting were those directed to the higher education of girls. Under the leadership of women like Miss Buss at Highgate and Miss Beale at Cheltenham much progress had been made; the high schools and colleges for girls were becoming a power in the land, and the impulse was extending to the universities. The leaders of the movement had much indifference and prejudice to combat, but they had no ancient traditions to hinder them from recognising the value of intercourse and co-operation. The tardy example of the headmasters had been promptly followed, and a headmistresses' conference had been organised to give unity and greater efficiency to the new movement.

It was therefore singularly appropriate that now in 1887 Thring should invite the headmistresses to hold their annual meeting at Uppingham. He had hailed with the greatest satisfaction this fresh growth of genuine teaching life. To woman's education on womanly lines he attached supreme importance. That the first ten years of the child-life of all mankind age after age passes continuously through the hands of women seemed to him one of the most significant facts in the whole range of human affairs. Character power and the perfection of trained skill were alike the need of those whose work was to mould character when most ready to receive impressions.

No training could be too complete for those marked out by nature as the guides and teachers of all childhood, if only the training were true and working towards true ends.

It was chiefly with the desire to give such public recognition as was in his power to earnest workers in a good but still struggling cause that he asked the headmistresses to Uppingham. He felt that the old education should extend a hand of hearty and helpful welcome to the new, and he wished to give to his co-labourers the best that he had to give. Of true work and working machinery he could show them much at Uppingham. Of the spirit in which his work had been done they might catch something ; he could outline for them the lofty ideal he had conceived of their work. So the invitation was given and gladly accepted. It was a delicate touch of sympathy, slight and simple enough in itself, but one that no headmaster had thought of before, nor, I believe, has it found imitation since.

Of his thought about the meeting he writes to his friend, Professor Felméri, in Hungary :—

Jan. 3rd, 1887.—I am very much interested in the education of women, the queens of life, sent to teach us how much more powerful, lovable, and lovely weakness is than brute force either of hand or head, and I shall do all I can to put it in a right channel. This summer, if all's well, the Conference of the London Society of Schoolmistresses will, by my invitation, meet at Uppingham,—some eighty ladies—mistresses of high schools from various parts of England.   They were greatly pleased at being invited; it will be very interesting, and I think much good will come of it. . . .

After the meeting he says :—

I have delayed answering until I could send you a copy of my address to the headmistresses—the lady teachers of England—who held their annual conference at Uppingham this year by my invitation.   It was a grand day.   Fifty-nine actually came, and we did all in our power to honour them. We put them all up, fêted them, gave them a concert, and in all ways entertained them as royally as we could.   It was the first official recognition they had had, which made it the more important, and a greater pleasure to all parties.   They were a delightful company, entirely free from all nonsense; not a trace of "woman's rights" about them, but most sensible, sober-minded workers and thinkers. . . . Everything went off with the most splendid success; and a very remarkable set of able and interesting women they were. . . . They have all now gone, but I feel the great importance of the meeting more and more as I gather my thoughts after it. . . .

In his address to the conference he referred to the headmasters' meeting held in the same place eighteen years earlier :—

I hold it to be a most happy omen that this same room should have the honour of being the first schoolroom of our public schools for boys to welcome you and your conference to-day.   A most happy omen, when I look back and consider what a little seed was sown in December 1869, and then reflect how different in power and place, how important your assembly is as compared with our weak little life-germ; and I may add, in the highest sense truer and better than anything we masters could set on foot.   Both because the rough, instrumental work of the world is done by men, whilst the fine and delicate life-power, with its influence on life, is done by the women; and also because you are fresh, and enthusiastic, and comparatively untrammelled, whilst we are weighed down by tradition, cast, like iron, in the rigid moulds of the past, with still heavier chains of modern improvement imposed by present law on our life. The hope of teaching lies in you.

One other passage may be quoted, as illustrating the views which he held of woman's true relation to men in carrying on the work of the world.

There is another eternal fact equally unforgetable when once seen—the eternal fact of helpfulness, which is yours. The divine privilege of being helpers. Woman was created to help—to make good, that is, the deficiencies of the world of man; to come in in times of strain and trial to relieve and cheer; to take, as it were, on themselves the part of angels on earth, ministering spirits, good Samaritans to succour the wounded, standing somewhat apart from the fray, to bring hope, and kindly, gentle support; in a word, " helps meet for man." And here, again, we meet the double truth which has attended us all along, of a higher and more sovereign influence, committed to your hands, and of true working power—the truth, which this conference embodies, of trained working skill. For how can they help who know not how to work? We meet again the truth, which has accompanied us from the beginning, that man in no mean spirit is intended to do the rough work of the world, while it is the divine mission of women to follow on his work, to put the finishing touches, to help, and bind up, and soothe, and cheer, and throw a halo of gentler life round this hard, warring, daily contest of good and evil struggling and toiling in their pain. Work-power is wanted. You are busy in giving it; but it is helpful work-power, not destroying; gentle work-power, not forceful.

After the conference the diary says :—

June 11th.—These two most important days come and gone. Everything went off most beautifully. The ladies were exceedingly gratified by their entertainment, and our masters and the school ladies, I believe, quite as much so. . . .

The conversazione and music were perfect. It seems strange that there should be so little to say of what I believe it to be —one of the most important things we have ever done. . . . Thank God for His goodness.

June 12th.—The more I gather my thoughts after the great meeting of last week the more important does it all appear to me. It is a great epoch to them and to us. I do believe life has been breathed into the body of masters, and that they are conscious of a new atmosphere. . . .

It is all like a dream the work of last week, and its life-power, but a dream that supports wonderfully. . . .

Many letters remain to show how much their reception, the school itself, and its headmaster, impressed the visitors. In sending a beautiful edition of Ruskin's works as a memento of the visit, Miss Buss, the President of the Conference, writes :—

June 13th, 1887.—It gives me great pleasure to be requested by the Association of Headmistresses to ask you to accept for your library a few books, in remembrance of our visit to Uppingham, on the 10th and 11th inst., a visit which has been a source of great interest and enjoyment to us. It ought not to pass without leaving a token in your possession, for it is an event in educational history of no small significance.

We, who have worked so long and aspired so constantly to raise girls' education to a higher level, have often felt the need of more direct encouragement and a fuller faith in our endeavour, on the part of men engaged in similar work.

We may therefore very fitly mark as a red-letter day in the educational calendar the day on which one of the leading headmasters of the country entertained the headmistresses at their conference in his school.

Miss Beale, writing from Cheltenham, says :—

June 1887.—I felt at the last quite incapable of saying anything—the early service—the address—church, which made one feel all that suffering had wrought out—and then that very beautiful concluding address wrought up one's feelings, so that I could not trust myself to try to say how grateful we felt—how glad to feel that there is such an influence, such a spirit at work in Uppingham; it is one thing to read and hear about it, and another to see and feel it. . . .

Others felt no less warmly.

July 6th.—My visit to Uppingham will always be one of my happiest memories. It was most helpful and encouraging to see your beautiful school, and to feel that you sympathised with us in our work amongst the girls, and so cordially held out the right hand of fellowship towards us. No school has ever impressed me like Uppingham. Other schools may be bodies corporate, but Uppingham has a soul.

July 11th.—You will let me tell you what a great pleasure it has been to me to be allowed to know a little of you and your work. Your thrilling words will linger in the memory of many of us, and will, I hope, stir us up to be true to what we must have felt in our hearts to be the only principles of education worth working for. Many thanks for all you have done for one at least of your audience.

July 12th.—May I take this opportunity of saying how often your books have reinspired me with fresh hope. And when I see a mistress flagging, through some disappointment in a pupil, of whom we had hoped much, my one thought is to lend her one of your books in order that she may take heart and seek for causes of rejoicing. Years ago I have felt tempted to write to you in order to express my gratitude for the help your words have been to me in my labours here.

I fully appreciate the importance of our conference being received by a headmaster, and not only do I rejoice on personal and educational grounds, but for the sake of our loving president, Miss Buss, who with other older members bore the burden of opposition in days that now, happily, belong to the past.

His answer to another letter which he received at this time may be appropriately inserted here.

Mrs. Charles Kingsley had long been deeply interested in his work at Uppingham, as he had been in the work of her distinguished husband. In 1886 he had visited Mrs. Kingsley at Leamington. At that time he writes :—

I was greatly touched and interested by my conversation with Mrs. Kingsley. It quite seemed to me a continuation of my talk with Mrs. Ewing on her deathbed, though Mrs. Kingsley is not dying. She is seventy-three and an invalid. The spirit power of such communion is very wonderful, and a most exceeding great reward it is to have the experience of one's life made helpful to holy and gifted women.

Mrs. Kingsley had now written to him very warmly of the meeting of the conference of headmistresses and of his address.

To Mrs. Charles Kingsley.

June 13th, 1887.

My dear and honoured Friend—The tears came into my eyes as I read your earnest, glowing words about the work it has been given me to do. I feel to my inmost soul that it is given ; that both the eye to see and the lips to speak have been given. The revelation has been quite as great a revelation to me as it can be to any other. And the writing power comes at the time—a gift. I feel also how through long years of trial, and waiting, and pain, long years accompanied by many strange interpositions of external circumstance, the heart and eye have been trained and cleansed for sight, not least by my curious intercourse with Mrs. Ewing, whom I was only permitted to see and actually speak to when dying, on her bed of death, as it proved within a fortnight. Her influence, the influence of a woman, and the purity and goodness of my own wife, have been great teachers. And God has given it to me to speak. I do feel very solemnly what a happy burden is laid upon me. "The Revelation of the Bride" once seen, even a glimpse caught of its pure glory, and practical meaning, can never be forgotten; but men are too low, too sensual, as yet, to receive it; but woman will listen and believe it. I feel sure that the fate of the world is in the hands of the women. Eve brought power worship and knowledge idolatry in; the Blessed Virgin, Mary, and her true daughters, the noble wives especially, are to cast it down from its throne again. The lady teachers have taken the MSS. to publish. I will write at once to have it done well, and order twenty copies to be sent to you immediately it is out. It is my intention to publish the seven addresses I have delivered now in one volume as soon as I can get a publisher. Pray accept my most grateful thanks for your letter, which is of more value to me than any I ever received. I myself believe that last week was a great epoch and landmark in the world history of spirit life. You make me believe it too.

A note from a Swiss friend in reference to the conference is thus referred to, and the quotation may fitly close the consideration of his relation to women's work.

June 28th.—A letter from Miss Heutschy saying how much she has been helped by my addresses. It is very cheering to find how many struggling workers get help from the pain I have suffered. I cannot help being struck too, especially in connection with my Queen, at how many women have been cheered and had their toil brightened by my help. Thank God for this! I do trust He has given me power to head a revolt against power worship and force, and to help the weak. May I ever be a protector of women and children and the weak. And do Thou, O God, protect me in my weakness.

But the spirit which could think so clearly and speak so strongly for the cheer of others was, in these days, being undermined and unnerved by petty material cares. At a meeting of the trustees of the school held in London, and which he attended, it was decided that his petition in regard to an increase of salary up to the limit allowed by law could not be admitted, apparently on the ground that money was required for new class-rooms.

His speech at the break-up was remarked as being of singular power.   It was the year of the Queen's Jubilee—the influence of the British Empire through-out the world was much in men's thoughts—the many threads of living interest with which he himself and his school had become linked with distant lands stirred his imagination.   So after the usual announcement of prizes and school honours he pointed out to his boys how the life of a great English public school goes forth year by year to all the many lands of the Empire ; and how essential it was that this life should be high and true and pure.   The glorious national inheritance which they enjoyed was every hour widen-ing ; they were like a city set on a hill.   Woe to them who touched this inheritance with the hand of evil, and woe to them who betrayed.   Woe to all meanness of thought or aim ; woe to all who forget the high duties which must ever be joined to the exercise of world-wide power and influence.

The few rough notes in which he had outlined what he wished to say, and which were all that he made use of in his school addresses, remain to indicate this current of his thought.

On the evening of the break-up day he writes :—

July 27th.—There is something almost awful in the sudden cessation of the fierce pulsation of life and work at the end of term.   It is hard to believe that it is all over.   Yesterday I worked for twelve consecutive hours, barring scraps of meal-times.   To-night all is over, and quiet and stillness reigns. It is very wonderful.   This morning I felt so ill that I feared that I should break down. But I got through. I am reported to have made the best speech I ever made, and indeed I think I did, for I had much to say, and God gave me the power to say it. . . .

July 28th.—Very shaky, but getting better. It is the severest term for the ceaseless roll of good and evil that I have ever been through in my life, and I am quite awestruck at the sudden stillness.

. . . . Altogether I feel greatly cheered in spite of trustees, etc. The living things seem to have so much life.

Shortly before the break-up he had preached his last sermon for the term. The text was, " And now cometh the end."

The summer holiday was spent in Scotland, where he had taken a house, "Ladyhill," near Birnam. Through the letters written during the first weeks of his rest there runs a vein of sadness and discouragement.

"It certainly is very strange," he says in a note, "but how true, that the moment a man steadily pursues any truth, especially a new truth, he must to the very last be met by opposition. There is a still stranger truth also, of which our blessed Lord was the great example when He was put to death by the Jews as destroying their religion, and by the Romans as a rebel, that, as events unwind, every consistent worker on principle finds himself put in the position of opposing what he has always worked for, and his opponents posing as the workers. It is a strange turn of the wheel which puts the trustees in the position of the liberal upholders of school interests, and me as an obstructive greedy for money."

The quiet holiday, however, did him good, and before it was over he seemed full of the old fire and energy.

But the long day's toil was drawing to a close. "Work till the end of life, and life till the end of work." Surely his prayer had been more than fulfilled.

His last term opened on the 22nd of September.
He was full of school interests.   The appointment of
a new master—the reception of new boys—visits from
old ones—messages from fellow-workers in many parts
of the world occupied his thought.

New demands for public work kept coming in on all
sides.   "Next Sunday," he says, "I am to preach at
Worcester Cathedral at Gott's[1] request, and to give
away the school prizes on Monday. . . . I have been
writing a bit in the holidays, and in consequence have
undertaken to prepare a paper for the Industrial Education Association of New York, which last term I
declined to do. . . ."

September 26th.—Hard at work again, yet how happy I
should be in the work if I could shake off —— and the
money nightmare.   But as it is, there are many glorious gains
and solaces.   My new class to-day for the first time ; the
nicest class by far that I have had for some years. . . .

September 29th.—Yesterday took early dinner at Glaston
to meet the Bishop of Salisbury and Mrs. Wordsworth.   A
pleasant time.   Walked back to Uppingham and showed
them the school.   Went to the Tucks, and talked to Mrs.
Tuck about the publication of the addresses and poems.
Her ideas are good, and will, I think, work. . . .

October 4th.—Went to Worcester with G—— on Saturday,
and came back to-day. . . . Preached in the cathedral on
Sunday night, the dean said to 2000 people.   Certainly the
congregations in the cathedral morning and evening were
wonderful.   The next day took part in the opening of their
schoolroom, and was appointed to make the speech of the
day.   The next morning went to the High School for Girls,
and Miss Ottley asked me to speak to them, which I did.
Nothing could have gone better.   I was wonderfully struck
by the contrast of that grand possibility of religious peace,

[1] The Dean of Worcester.

with the cathedral in its glory, the ancient associations, and the absence of fierce work, with the life here. It was a new world, partly known before, but never felt so much as in this visit in term time. . . .

October 8th.—Heard from Fisher Unwin that he will publish my Addresses, giving me a royalty. I wrote to D—— about the cricket song. To my great delight he has put it in print at once, and means to publish it in a small volume, with all the songs of a general character. I am greatly pleased with this.

October 10th.—Skrine told me to-day that he wanted me to publish the Agamemnon translation. I shall not, however, do so till I have thoroughly revised it. It does not come up to the standard of literature, I think, which would enable it to stand, apart from its being a translation, on its own merits.

October 11th.—Delighted at getting to-day a cheque of £35 school payment from Haslam on account of the auto-types I got for the school some ten years ago. I never expected to see the money except in driblets, and not much expectation of that. It has come like a present. If I could only have the money that has leaked away in setting the school going efficiently in this way, I shouldn't be badly off. But God knows, and it is no mean thing to be able to spend without its being known or thanked for, in an ungrudging spirit, and He has given me that power; money's worth, I am inclined to think.

October 12th.—I got a letter to-day from the New York Industrial Education Association, very much pleased that I will write them an article, and hoping that I will not make it less than 12,000 or 15,000 words. This is very cheering, and it gives me full space to do my best. I pray God to inspire me and bless it. I have much ready. Then my composition paper came back typed, and I am rejoiced to find that I have practically another lecture ready. . . . Then for the first time in my life my mind is quite at ease in money matters, partly because my expenses are now within control and within my income, partly from a much stronger faith, and a feeling of daily help, and messages from God. My health, too, is better. I took a really good walk to-day, and my strength is improving.

A master's wife remembers her last talk with him at about this time. She had been speaking of the greatness of the work which he had done at Uppingham. " I do not think much of the work I have done," was his answer ; " but I should be glad if, when I am gone, some one in the other world should touch me on the shoulder and say, ' Mr. Thring, I have been a better man for having known you.' "

On Friday, the 14th, he took tea with a dear friend, the wife of one of the masters. Some ladies were present, and he was full of life and spirit, joining heartily in the merry conversation of the party. When the other visitors had gone his talk took a graver turn, and his last words to his hostess, as he left her door, were : " Believe me, a life lived in earnest does not die ; it goes on for ever."

On Saturday he had much to do. It was the last working day of a working life. " My article for New York is getting into shape. I hope to finish the first draft of it next week." His Sunday sermon, too, was being written. Care was not wanting, for the refusal of his trustees to grant him at the close of his long life of toil the full salary allowed by law had wounded him deeply. But he was full of happiness too. " It is astonishing to me how God at this crisis has so filled me with peace and many cheering messages, and interests of life. . . . The money question, I feel sure, will be brought right in the end. A most cheering letter from an assistant schoolmistress about the address."

In the evening he read as usual the Psalms and Evening Prayers in the schoolhouse. Those who heard him recalled afterwards, with something akin to awe, the last sentence of his household reading in those Psalms which he loved so well, and which had ever been the channel of expression for his deepest feeling :

"So he fed them with a faithful and true heart, and ruled them prudently with all his power."

They knew it not, nor he, but assuredly it was his own epitaph that he read.

"And now to bed; sermon finished, and a blessed feeling of Sunday coming."

Such are the closing words of the last entry made on that last Saturday night in the diary to which he had confided his inmost thoughts for nearly thirty years.

The Sunday came, but it was to be his last on earth—the last on which he was to appear in the chapel which he had built, or in the school of which he had been for so long the central figure,—the moving and inspiring spirit.

He was not well when he got up, but went to the morning service in chapel. It was observed that he did not kneel during the Litany, and his chaplain, seeing this, watched him, but he rose as usual and went to the altar to read the Communion Service.

He had read the Lord's Prayer and the first Collect of the Service, when, laying his book down on the altar, he signed to the chaplain, Mr. Christian, to continue the service for him. He was evidently in great pain, but very calmly, refusing with a gesture the assistance of those who, seeing his sudden seizure, had stepped forward to offer it, he walked with a firm step down the aisle between the long rows of his kneeling boys, by whom he was never again to be seen alive.

From the very altar, and from "the very act of administering Christ's soldiers' oath to his schoolboy sons," the veteran warrior of Christ passed to his death-bed, resolute and unflinching to the last.

There followed a few days of wrestle for the life which was still strong in him. Danger was not at first anticipated; for a little it seemed as if his strong constitution might triumph over the inflammation which had been the result of a sudden chill; but a fevered and anxious mind added its weight to the fever of his body; on Friday it was known that his case was hopeless; on Saturday morning, 22nd October, he breathed his last.

Amid a great concourse of old boys and others who had come together to do honour to his memory, and to join in the mourning of the school, his body was, on the following Thursday, laid to rest in the ancient church-yard of the parish. The day before it had been trans-ferred from the schoolhouse to the school chapel. There, as it rested before the altar, surrounded by the hundreds of wreaths sent from all parts of the country, his boys and colleagues looked for the last time upon the face of him who had made their school great, and had for more than thirty years ruled it with a strong hand and loving heart.

A monument, fittingly simple and massive, marks the spot where the body of the tired worker lies.

A noble statue, by Brock, adorns the school chapel, and recalls to new generations of Uppingham boys the strong lineaments and masterful figure of their second founder—of one who was both a king of boys and a leader of men.

A brass tablet on the chapel walls has the following inscription :—

In grateful remembrance of Edward Thring, whose writings animated the art, and whose life enriched the work of teaching. A few English and American teachers erected this tablet.

'HONOUR THE WORK, AND THE WORK WILL HONOUR
YOU.'

CHAPTER XI

PERSONAL AND OTHER RECOLLECTIONS

I FIRST met Thring at the Headmasters' Conference at Winchester in 1873. I was introduced to him by Dr. Ridding, then Headmaster of Winchester, and Chairman of the Conference. As Thring came down the hall of the college, Dr. Ridding prefaced his introduction with the remark : " Here is the man who can tell you more about education than any one else in England." The observation was made, I believe, in all sincerity, and I think also in all truth. It illustrates the impression he had made on some of the most clear-minded men among his professional contemporaries. Those who had to govern large schools could perhaps best judge what it was to both found and govern one.

" The work at Uppingham is really unique in our generation. . . . I doubt if there was another man in England who could have done it." Thus wrote the late Dr. Scott, long Headmaster of Westminster School, and Thring's contemporary at Eton and Cambridge.[1]

[1] For personal recollections of Thring, and for a study of his work and character based on intimate acquaintance as a pupil and colleague, the reader may be referred to the interesting volume published soon after his death by the Warden of Glenalmond (*A Memory of Edward Thring*, by John Huntley Skrine. Macmillan & Co.). A slighter study is that by Rev. Canon H. D. Rawnsley (*Edward Thring, Teacher and Poet*. T. Fisher Unwin). Both of these volumes furnish striking illustration of the profound impression which Thring made upon those who worked under and with him.

Among the assembled headmasters at Winchester one noted a certain deference paid to Thring which could not be accounted for entirely by the fact that he was the founder of the conference. It seemed a homage paid to the intensity of his moral earnestness. In the gathering were men reckoned among the first in England in the power of fluent and graceful speech. His speech was not graceful ; only on rare occasions was he fluent ; yet what he said in angular phrase, and often awkward sentences, had in it a singleness of purpose and an originality of character which even among distinguished men gave his thought a stamp of special distinction and separateness. Something of this effect was perhaps due to the concentrated energy with which he threw himself into the subject before him, whether it were great or small. "Nothing seemed small to him " was a reminiscence of his early curate days which has already been quoted. The characteristic clung to him through life and became the subject of other reminiscences. One of these is worth reproducing from the accurate illustration which it gives of his character and mental habit.

An archbishop was asked, "What kind of man is Edward Thring?" The archbishop was about to poke the fire, he paused, and holding out the poker, said, "Why, he was this kind of a man ; if he were poking a fire, he would make you believe that the one thing worth living for was to know how to poke a fire properly."

The emphasis which he laid upon minor questions often gave his expressions in speech or writing the appearance of exaggeration. In the mouth of others this might be true ; in his they simply reflected the attitude of his mind. The thing immediately before him was all-important. The action of the moment meant everything. The most insignificant person was of the utmost consequence. In dealing with the simplest everyday questions his constant habit was to refer them back to great principles. This attitude of mind was perhaps his most distinguishing characteristic ; it was the keynote of the separateness of character which all who came in contact with him felt and acknowledged.

Preaching before the school on the first anniversary of his death, and while yet his memory was a vivid recollection in the minds of all, one of his fellow-workers could say :—

I do not believe he would have neglected a school lesson for the chance of becoming an archbishop. I do not believe he would have omitted one portion of the day's routine, if that omission had injured a single boy, for the position of the highest eminence his country could bestow. . . . He was one to whom the most insignificant unattractive boy was as precious as the most brilliant, who regarded the most troublesome characters as God's stray sheep to be brought back into the fold of God's grace.

" He ennobled the smallest detail of school life," was a remark made by one of his masters to others at the time of his death.

In a note written soon after Thring's death, Mr. Birley, who for so many years was trustee of the school, says :—

I do not think that there was another man in the world who joined in such a degree the iron will which makes a great headmaster with the tender sympathy which reached the heart of the smallest boy.

Such was the tribute of those who saw him close at hand, and had worked with him year after year. ‘

An old Uppingham boy has sent me the following extract from a letter written to him by his mother on hearing of Thring's death :—

I always felt in talking to him that he spoke with a sort of noble heavenly instinct, scorning all this world's axioms and accepted rules, seizing on the good and pure and true with a passionate love that kindled an answering glow even in the dullest and most apathetic soul. But I believe a nature like his suffers far more than others, and now that is over, and the joy begun.

A fellow-teacher writes of him :—

To talk to the man or to correspond with him was like breathing Alpine air. He was a splendid fellow. If a man had any little spark whatsoever in him, Thring could blow it into a blaze. I never had such genuine hearty sympathy from any man as I had from him.

A father who had seven boys with him at various periods writes :—

I think the essential character of Thring was that with all his firmness of opinion and principles in everything he undertook in connection with the school he still had a boy's heart within, and thus was admirably fitted to be a leader as well as master of schoolboys. And I think his great love of truth and manly conduct influenced the whole school, and that most Uppingham boys have turned out honourable, sensible, working men in this generation.

No doubt his own nature often made him chafe unnecessarily under the restraints and hindrances to which he was subjected.

" I think," he says, " Freeman's derivation of our name from the Dog-and-Hawk Vassal must be true, for I always feel something of the wild man in me—a passion for liberty, and a detestation of needless barriers. I have often thought it

curious that it should have pleased God to deny the two great
earthly longings of my heart, which were earthly—free space of
room, and a little plot of ground and home of my own.   But
I can easily see how good it is that it has been so."

But with all his vehement impatience under restriction
in any form, and his sensitiveness to indifference and
opposition, he was a man in whom the wells of happiness
were deep and full.   His diary and correspondence
scarcely do justice to the brighter side of his life.   He
notes this himself :—

I am often struck in writing this diary with its likeness to
common history, how one puts down all the vexations and
none of the good or but little.   How can one tell the quiet
hours of faith and hope, the encouragement that comes into
the heart, the feeling of work done, and the deep conviction
low down under all the storms that God blesses the life here
and will bless it; that He has done a great work, and will
make it go out into all lands—yes, is making it do so, even
though it perish here, or perish in England, or be quite
unknown as having come from hence?   All this cannot be put
down on paper; all the weariness and vexation can to some
extent.   Still less can that strange compound be expressed by
which one long continuous surface stream of care and disappointment and vexation coexists and goes on at the same
time with the strong undercurrent of determination and quiet
confidence and spirit consolation.

For nine of his hardest working years—from 1867
to 1876—Thring spent his summer holidays at Grasmere, where he leased a house known as Ben Place.
His enjoyment of the Lake country almost amounted
to a passion, and his love for it found expression in
a collection of verse published under the name of
Dreamland.
At Grasmere many of his happiest days were spent,

and much of his best work was done.   Here a succession
of friends and Old Boys came every summer to visit
him, and in the free intercourse of holiday life, when he
threw off his burden of cares and became a boy again,
they learned to understand better than in any other
way the happy and joyous side of his nature.

His diary was only kept during term time, and so
gave little record of these bright and happy interludes
in his life.

After the Borth period he went for several years to
the Welsh coast for his holiday, and found infinite
delight in renewing his association with the place and
its friendly people.

A letter written to me during one of these visits
shows how readily his spirits responded to holiday
influences.

To G. R. Parkin.

You must manage whenever you come to be able to spend
some of the holidays with us.   I should like to see you at
Uppingham again, but if we live, a bit of holiday life at Borth
is an absolute necessity.   We do not live elsewhere.   We toil
and moil and breathe and gather in, but here we live free life
and are full of pleasant schemes. . . .

I have just written another sonnet which I send you,
suggested by the merry party of young people and our joyance
here.

> And age is winter?   I am growing old,
> Grey hairs have long since straggled into place,
> And feet, once winged jests, that laughed to race,
> Plod slow and halting like a tale ill told.
> What though the frost upon the roof lay hold,
> 'Tis a poor house whose battered frame the wind
> Can whistle through at will and roomage find,
> Whose bankrupt tenant all his goods hath sold.
> But warm and bright old Christmas sits at home,

Keeps mirthful house with noise of dance and jest,
Or silence sweeter still, when feet that roam
Meet round his hearth and gather of his rest.
Let thriftless summer lightly come and go,
Old age hath steadier fires at his command that glow.

There, you see I may be cowardly, but I am not down-hearted. . . . I have been greatly interested and pleased at the success of the Australian cricketers. Mark me, cricket is the greatest bond of the English-speaking race, and is no mere game. This Australian visit has unconsciously done much in this way towards a feeling of brotherhood and common life. . . .

At a later period he spent summer holidays in Cornwall and Scotland, but they never quite took the place of the Lake district, for which he had an abiding affection, and over which he delighted to guide his friends. Very memorable to me is a week I spent with him at Grasmere in 1874. He had just been set free from his work ; under the influence of the mountain air and mountain scenery, the tangled and complicated problems of school life at Uppingham ceased to worry, and he lived for the time in his ideal world of educational truth. His interest in everything belonging to education seemed like a perennial stream. As we climbed the hills or drove around the valleys of that picturesque country, he was always ready to spend hours in eager conversation on every question touching upon school life. I doubt if any one ever saw Thring at his best who had not met him when thus free from the harassing routine of daily work, and when his thought and imagination were stimulated by contact with nature in its more noble and beautiful forms.

With living nature his sympathy was strangely intimate and inspiring. In the country walks which he shared with friends, and which made no small part of his happiness, the universal push of life in spring, the wealth and superfluity of vegetable and animal life in summer seemed to lift him out of himself, and quicken every power of thought. His conversation then became full of illustrations drawn from nature.

He was interested in every wayside flower, every bird's note, every striking bit of scenery, every shifting cloud which changed the appearance of the sky.

He had the habit of powerful iteration common to many men upon whom fundamental truth has made a profound impression. Those who listened much to his speeches, sermons, or conversation, became accustomed to look for well-worn phrases and forms of expression into which he had condensed his thought.

" Life " was the word that was most frequently on his lips, and always in his heart. To teach his boys to live a " true life " was his dream and the crown of his ambition. It was remarked that he never preached a sermon without bringing in some reference to " life " or " true life," and in most of his sermons there are many such references. But it was truly said by one who knew him intimately that in the man himself there was ten times as much life as in all his sermons put together. It flowed out on all around him. No visitor to Uppingham, or only a very shallow one, ever mistook for self-conceit or vanity the intense earnestness with which he threw himself into the elucidation of educational problems, illustrating his views from his own work and experience. One never thought of his being a master of his subject—his subject possessed him and carried him out of himself.

Some recollections furnished by his friend, Bishop Mitchison, may properly find a place here.

My first acquaintance with Edward Thring, and what came of it, is illustrative of the generous and loyal character of the

man.   It began many years ago, somewhere about the year
1860, or a little later.   I was then a very young headmaster,
with a miserable tumbledown set of domestic buildings belonging to my school.   I was just beginning to rouse my governors,
the Dean and Chapter of Canterbury, to a sense of their duty
in the matter of new buildings, and I was now anxious to
inform my own mind as to plans of buildings, class-room,
dormitories, and the like.   I had been invited over by Dean
Sanders to preach for him in the cathedral at Peterborough,
and to him I broached the question, adding that I had heard
much of Mr. Thring's success at Uppingham, and was disposed
to go over and ask to see his buildings and arrangements.
The dean encouraged me to do so, adding, "You will find
Thring the best of fellows, and most willing to help you to the
utmost of his power."   I went, and found it even as he had said.
I walked over from Manton, presented myself at the schoolhouse, and stated my errand.   I was at once welcomed, and
taken over one or two houses, and shown everything.   As we
went he expounded, prophet-wise, the principles he kept in
view, which, I confess, I only imperfectly comprehended in
the very abstract and somewhat paradoxical form in which he
stated them, and was disposed to say in my heart, "Doth he
not speak parables?"   But this did not interfere with my full
appreciation of the cordial, sympathetic manner in which he
welcomed me as a brother of the craft, and did his best to
send me away greatly helped in the object I had in view, and
encouraged to pursue it.   I was able to profit largely by what
I saw in Uppingham in the planning and arrangement of my
new buildings at Canterbury, and I prevailed on my friend to
come over to the opening festivities, at which, in a speech, I
expressed my great obligation to Mr. Thring for the hints I
had got from him as to construction and arrangement.   It was
the very least I could do, but Thring never forgot it, and often
reminded me that I had been one of the few honest men of
his acquaintance who had publicly and unreservedly acknowledged the extent to which I had picked his brains.   My
imitation was not a servile copy; I modified at my own
discretion; and when Thring's first edition of *Education and
School* came out, I being then an occasional contributor to the
Contemporary Review, undertook a review of his book.   While

I praised it generally, as it deserved, I did not scruple to criticise details freely. The article was anonymous, so I thought it right to confess authorship to my friend. Next time we met he affected indignation. "You praised me," he said, "at the expense of my system."

After this he came over to Canterbury one year to preach our anniversary sermon in the cathedral. The school was growing, thanks, among other things, to the new buildings which my dean and chapter had with great liberality erected and furnished according to my desires. At the end of that term our numbers stood at 120. Thring did not know this little detail; but, by a strange coincidence when he ascended the pulpit, he gave out for his text, Acts i. 15 : *"The number of names together were about an hundred and twenty."* His sermon turned on the inherent power of growth in Christianity, because it was an embodiment of truth, and he argued from analogy to the power of growth in a good school founded on true principles. Much of his discourse got lost among the bewildering echoes of Canterbury Cathedral, but at the end of each point sounded forth in tone and manner so familiar to those who often heard him speak, "And was not this, think you, a mighty power?"

I am indebted to H. Courthope Bowen, Esq., for the following sketch :—

I had known Mr. Thring by reputation and in his books for some time before the opening of the ill-fated Finsbury Training College in 1882 brought me first into correspondence, and then into personal contact with him. I have sent you all of his side of the correspondence that I can find. Even to one who knows nothing of the forlorn attempt these letters are even now striking enough. Guess what they were to me in the thick of the struggle, alternately hoping and hopeless. What a ready and ever-generous sympathy he had! How earnest and enthusiastic he was! He made me feel, as well as know, that even to fail in the endeavour to make a better education possible had a touch of worthiness, of true service in it; and education, as you remember, he ever held to be one of the noblest of services. Old Latimer, I think, must have been some such a man as he—intensely in earnest, because intensely convinced, and with the same picturesque metaphoric way of speaking and writing.   And no one was ever more intensely convinced than Thring that the honest educator was doing God's work—directly, not indirectly—work from which God's eyes were never moved away.   This was no form of speech with him, but a veritable fact.   Most of this one can perceive from his books or his letters.   One says at once, here is a spiritual brother of Carlyle and Ruskin.   But for one who felt somewhat as he felt about education to meet Thring, and to talk with him, was an experience never to be forgotten. Violent emotion, we know, is apt to become hysterical—is liable to result in weakness, intellectual as well as physical. Thring was pre-eminently an emotional man.   But his emotion was not violent—it was deep, it was intense, every fibre of his being seemed to vibrate with it; it moved in his eyes, it trembled in his voice, it set him pacing up and down.   Yet it did not result in weakness, but in activity or strong desire for activity.   It seemed rather a spur than a hindrance to his intellect, except that it made his mind work as it were by flashes, without sustained sequence, and utter itself in striking metaphors, which, though oftenest brilliant, were at times too hurriedly caught at, and rather hurt than helped the effect of his words.   But whether his fashion of speech was mainly happy or not, it made and left an impression on one unlike anything else.   Right or wrong, hasty, fantastic, or keen-sighted, he made one feel that he was veritably in earnest; that he was not speaking of a mere hobby or as a specialist, but was telling you of what to him were vital truths, and as the feeling grew one saw him to be a "mission'd spirit," not indeed of those "who stand and wait," but rather one of those "who at His bidding speed," who would rather try and fail than stand and wait.

All his life Thring was a poor man.   After thirty-three years of strenuous work, and what was considered a successful career at Uppingham, he left behind him only the patrimony, secured on the family estate, which he had inherited as a younger son, and the insurance with which in early days he had protected his life for the creditors who lent him money to carry out his plans. All his own earnings and the very considerable legacies which were from time to time left him were swallowed up in the making of Uppingham.

For some time his income from the school was small. After he had been headmaster for several years he writes to a brother that, as the result of the strictest economy, he has, exclusive of house expenses, £750 a year for the payment of debts. With the growth of the school his position gradually improved, and during the later years of his headmastership his income amounted to more than £3000 per annum. This may be considered as fairly large, though small when compared with the income of several other headmasters of great schools in England.

But Thring, as the son of a country gentleman, had been brought up in an affluent way. While himself most simple in his personal tastes, he never, I think, understood rigid economy in the use of money. Not merely the habits of his early life, but the necessities of his position as head of a great and growing school, made his expenses great. Besides, where he had an object to accomplish, when he had sympathy to express, when his enthusiasm had been aroused, the want of money and considerations about the future were seldom allowed to stand in his way. To encourage men to build in the early days of the school he was accustomed to make reductions from his capitation fees. He contributed largely from his own means to all the plans for the improvement of the school. He met the generosity of others with a spirit as large as theirs. It has been mentioned that Mr. Witts, on taking a mastership in the school, subscribed £1000 to the fund for the building of the chapel.   I have found the following note written to Mr. Witts immediately after the offer was made :—

I have thought since you left me that if you have any mis-givings about the £1000 for the chapel, and rather repent my having taken you at your word at once, which perhaps I ought not to have done, that if as you go on you find it press you, the matter might be smoothed by my remitting the taxa-tion of the last ten boys of your house till the last £500 was made up in this way ; I would gladly do so if you find it advisable.

When the migration to Borth was decided upon, the masters themselves had to provide the necessary funds. In an official report to the trustees, Thring stated that he advanced or assumed personal liability for more than £3000, and it was long before he was quite released from this burden.

His papers disclose numberless illustrations of the too liberal way in which he gave to every cause which appealed to his sympathy.   To missionary efforts in many parts of the world he was constantly contributing both from sympathy with the cause and to maintain the name and fame of Uppingham as a missionary school.   A series of letters written at intervals to a friend who was struggling with a difficult educational experiment is marked by a tone of lofty encouragement, but not less by the fact that nearly every letter con-tained a remittance for the support of what he thought good cause.

In writing to him I once casually mentioned that had I the means to do so I would like to work out a certain educational idea in Canada.   " Put me down for £50 to carry out that plan," was his prompt response, quite unasked for and unthought of.   A cheque for

£30 goes in a letter which apologises for the smallness of the contribution, and promises more, to a memorial to Mrs. Ewing.

But these are only isolated instances of what was the habit of his life. Imprudence it will be deemed by some ; by others a noble unworldliness.

Although overwhelmed by debt through the greater part of his life he yet steadily and unflinchingly resisted the temptation to make money at the sacrifice of his school principles. How great that temptation was, and what a strain was involved in resistance, the readers of his diary will have learned. When his father, long sceptical about his work, but struck at last by the success which was crowning his efforts, offered to ease his burden, he declines the aid unless given as to a work done for God, and not because of its worldly success. This was at a time, too, when the burden of debt lay most heavily upon him.

Amid the beautiful and noble school buildings erected at Uppingham, upon some of which he had spent so much of his thought and means, it was found when he died that the headmaster's house—the one in which his own comfort and convenience were most concerned—was the one building in the place about which the least thought had been taken.

Thring never received any public recognition such as has been over and over again given in England to men connected with public school life who have not accomplished a tithe of what he did for education.

In 1884 various journals had put his name forward as the man who could best fill the post of Provost of Eton, which had lately become vacant. The suggestion had for him no attraction. His diary says :—

May 18*th*.—There came by post from —— the paragraph from the *World* in which, after speaking of persons fitted for the Provostship of Eton, and mentioning my name amongst them, it says that my appointment "would be welcomed with acclamation as the too long deferred reward of a most distinguished career." I have sent it down for mother to hear. She will like it. . . . It is the last thing I should select. . . . In the meantime, I look on it as one of God's "stepping-stones" which takes one across a difficult stream. It shows me that I am not forgotten, and that whatever is good will be given me. I am so thankful for the help. Then I do so rejoice for the children's sake. . . . It will give them faith to find that good comes out of the sacrifice—good which they can understand.

To W. F. RAWNSLEY.

June 7th, 1884.

Thanks for the provost news. As my name has been discussed it is interesting to me; though strange to say (considering my temperament of old) it has not ruffled even the serene surface of my soul.

The fact is, the paragraph in the *World* is worth to me a great deal more than the reality of its diction would be. There is no place in the world for which, in my own judgment, I am more unfitted. My long practical experience of work is fatal in the kingdom of glamour. It would be an awful trial living in the midst of a splendour I cannot sympathise with, unable to touch it, yet supposed to be in power, and all the time with the keenest feelings on the subject. Moreover, I am poor, and the provostship is a white elephant; £2200 a year where £4000 say must be spent to do the thing according to custom, is not a bed of roses or a reward. I cannot help laughing grimly when people talk of Government rewards, and thinking sometimes of Miss Waghorn left to die in the workhouse. . . . Hornby is just the man for the place, and they get a new headmaster.

During this year, however, he had a distinct impression that his work at Uppingham was drawing to a close. The precedents of English public school life certainly made it probable that preferment of some kind would be given him. He learned that a friend of some influence who had lately died, had on three occasions written to Mr. Gladstone to urge him to give public recognition to the work done at Uppingham. On this he remarks :—

How all this shows me the guiding hand ready at the right moment and in the right way to give or not to give. It all makes me feel more patient, less fearful, less troubled by the bank book. . . .

But other considerations came to influence his view of the question.

In 1886 a friend, with wide connections and a high position in public school life, wrote to ask him if he would permit his name to be placed before the Government of the day for such Church preferment as would justify him in giving up his arduous post at Uppingham. He writes in reply :—

June 28th.—Your letter is like your generous self. But I am obliged to go dead against it. For many years I have had no party politics, but my whole soul was stirred to its depths by the Mid-Lothian campaign and the torrent of personal vituperation by which the present Government gained power. I felt degraded as an Englishman. I had rather starve (which I am not likely to do) than accept anything at the hands of Gladstone and his colleagues, much less ask it. . . . No, I never have felt the same utter contempt for English politicians that I do for the present Government. I do not wish to argue, but simply to state an elderly man's quiet, deliberate mind. Never fear for me. I am quite content. A man must stand and fall by his creed. And I am happy to stand or fall by mine. I counted the cost when I began my school career. I am quite satisfied. There is no harm in being poor. The right thing will come at the right time. I shall be able to square my accounts in a few years, and then I shall be master of the situation.   A thousand thanks for your wonted generosity and interest.   I do not forget it, though I do not accept it.

Only two or three months before his death the Bishop of Peterborough, Dr. Magee, wrote to offer him an honorary canonry in his cathedral, as "a public recognition of valuable services rendered to the cause of education—in the fullest and highest sense of that term—in this Diocese."   The emoluments of the office were *nil*—the only duty involved, that of preaching an annual sermon in the cathedral.   This was the solitary offer of Church preferment which Edward Thring ever received.

He very rightly declined the well-meant proposal, feeling, as he explained in a letter to a friend, that he owed this to the dignity of the great school which he had created.   In the early days of struggle and difficulty, recognition of this kind, he said, would have been useful and encouraging ; now it could do no good to himself and would injure rather than assist the school.

When we consider how often work done in English public schools has led to the highest positions in the gift of the Church, the offer thus made to the greatest educational worker of his time verges upon the ludicrous.

But there is no need to question the adequacy or fitness of the reward which fell to Edward Thring's lot. The man for whom his country and its rulers found no public recognition holds a place higher than either could give in the grateful memory of thousands to whom his teaching has been a help and his example an inspiration.

INDEX

THE END

Printed by R. & R. CLARK, LIMITED, Edinburgh

MACMILLAN & CO.'S STANDARD BIOGRAPHIES.

ALFRED, LORD TENNYSON: A Memoir. By his SON. With Photogravure Portraits of Lord Tennyson, Lady Tennyson, etc. Facsimiles of portions of Poems, and Illustrations after Pictures by G. F. WATTS, R.A., SAMUEL LAURENCE, Mrs. ALLINGHAM, RICHARD DOYLE, BISCOMBE GARDNER, etc. Two Vols. Medium 8vo. 36s. net.

FORTY-ONE YEARS IN INDIA. By Field-Marshal LORD ROBERTS, V.C. With 44 Illustrations. New and Cheaper Edition in One Vol. Extra Crown 8vo. 10s. net.

THE SOUL OF A PEOPLE: An Account of the Life and Belief of the Burmese. By H. FIELDING. Demy 8vo. 14s.

THE LIFE OF JOHN CHURCHILL, First Duke of Marlborough. Vols. I. and II. : To the Accession of Queen Anne. By Field-Marshal VISCOUNT WOLSELEY, K.P., K.C.B., G.C.M.G. Demy 8vo. With Portraits of the Duke and Duchess of Marlborough, James II., William III., the Duke of Monmouth, Duchess of Cleveland, and other Illustrations or Plans. Fourth Edition. 32s.

CYPRIAN: His Life, His Times, His Work. By EDWARD WHITE BENSON, D.D., D.C.L., sometime Archbishop of Canterbury. 8vo. 21s. net.

LIFE AND LETTERS OF WILLIAM JOHN BUTLER, late Dean of Lincoln, and sometime Vicar of Wantage. With Portraits. Demy 8vo. 12s. 6d. net.

MEMORIALS (Part I.) **FAMILY AND PERSONAL,** 1766-1865. ROUNDELL PALMER, Earl of Selborne. With Portraits and Illustrations. Two Vols. Demy 8vo. 25s. net.

LIFE AND LETTERS OF FENTON JOHN ANTHONY HORT, D.D., D.C.L., LL.D. By his Son, ARTHUR FENTON HORT, late Fellow of Trinity College, Cambridge. With Portraits. Extra Crown 8vo. 17s. net.

THE LIFE OF CARDINAL MANNING, Archbishop of Westminster. By EDMUND SHERIDAN PURCELL. With Portraits. Fourth Thousand. Two Vols. 8vo. 30s. net.

THE LETTERS OF MATTHEW ARNOLD, 1848-1888. Collected and Arranged by GEORGE W. E. RUSSELL. Two Vols. Crown 8vo. 15s. net.

FRANCIS BACON: An Account of His Life and Works. By EDWIN A. ABBOTT, D.D., Author of "Bacon and Essex," and Editor of "Bacon's Essays." 8vo. 14s.

THE LIFE AND LETTERS OF DEAN CHURCH. Edited by his Daughter, MARY C. CHURCH. With a Preface by the Dean of Christ Church. A New and Cheaper Edition. Globe 8vo. 5s.
[*Eversley Series.*

SAMUEL TAYLOR COLERIDGE: A Narrative of the Events of His Life. By JAMES DYKES CAMPBELL. With Portrait. With a Memoir of the Author by LESLIE STEPHEN. Demy 8vo. 10s. 6d.

JAMES FRASER, SECOND BISHOP OF MANCHESTER: A Memoir. By T. HUGHES, Q.C. Crown 8vo. 6s.

LIFE AND LETTERS OF E. A. FREEMAN. By W. R. W. STEPHENS. Two Vols. 8vo. 17s. net.

LETTERS AND MEMORIES OF THE LIFE OF CHARLES KINGSLEY. Edited by his Wife. Two Vols. Crown 8vo. 12s. Cheap Edition. One Vol. 6s.

BISHOP LIGHTFOOT. Reprinted from the "Quarterly Review." With a Prefatory Note by the BISHOP OF DURHAM. With Portrait. Crown 8vo. 3s. 6d.

LIFE OF FREDERICK DENISON MAURICE. By his Son, F. MAURICE. Two Vols. 8vo. 36s. Popular Edition. Two Vols. Crown 8vo. 16s.

LIFE OF ARCHIBALD CAMPBELL TAIT, Archbishop of Canterbury. By RANDALL THOMAS, Bishop of Rochester, and WILLIAM BENHAM, B.D., Hon. Canon of Canterbury. With Portraits. Third Edition. Two Vols. Crown 8vo. 10s. net.

CATHARINE AND CRAUFURD TAIT, Wife and Son of Archibald Campbell, Archbishop of Canterbury: A Memoir. Edited by Rev. W. BENHAM, B.D. Crown 8vo. 6s. Popular Edition, abridged. Crown 8vo. 2s. 6d.

LIVES OF THE ARCHBISHOPS OF CANTERBURY, FROM ST. AUGUSTINE TO JUXON. By the Very Rev. WALTER FARQUHAR HOOK, D.D., Dean of Chichester. Demy 8vo. The following Volumes sold separately as shown :—Vol. I. 15s. ; Vol. II. 15s. : Vol. V. 15s. ; Vols. VI. and VII. 30s. ; Vol. VIII. 15s. ; Vol. IX. 15s. ; Vol. X. 15s. ; Vol. XI. 15s. ; Vol. XII. 15s.

THE LETTERS OF HORACE WALPOLE. Edited by PETER CUNNINGHAM, F.S.A. Nine Vols. Demy 8vo. With 50 Illustrations on Steel. £5 : 5s. Hand-made Paper Edition, with 67 Illustrations on Steel. Cloth, £10 : 10s. Vellum, £12 : 12s.

RICHARD BRINSLEY SHERIDAN: A Memoir. By WILLIAM FRASER RAE. With an Introduction by Sheridan's Great-Grandson, the MARQUESS OF DUFFERIN AND AVA, K.P., G.C.B. With (5) portraits of Sheridan, and of Mrs. Sheridan (Elizabeth Linley), Mrs. Tickell (Mary Linley), Halbed, and Mrs. Sheridan (Esther Ogle), with her son Charles, besides numerous facsimiles of letters, and other Illustrations. Two Vols. Demy 8vo. 26s.

THE LIVES OF THE SHERIDANS. By PERCY FITZGERALD. Two Vols. Demy 8vo. With 6 Engravings on Steel by STODART and EVERY. 30s.

MACMILLAN AND CO., LTD., LONDON.